Edith Pargeter is a distinguished author of historical fiction. Her work includes the *Brothers of Gwynedd* quartet and *A Bloody Field by Shrewsbury* as well as the *Heaven Tree* trilogy. Under the pseudonym Ellis Peters she writes best-selling mediaeval whodunnits featuring Brother Cadfael as the sleuthing monk. She lives in Shropshire.

D0964019

Also available from Futura
THE HEAVEN TREE

EDITH PARGETER

The Green Branch

Futura

A Futura Book

First published in Great Britain in 1962
by William Heinemann Ltd

This edition published in 1987 by
Futura Publications, a Division of
Macdonald & Co (Publishers) Ltd
London & Sydney

ISBN 0 7088 3057 9

Reproduced, printed and bound in Great Britain by
Hazell Watson & Viney Limited,
Member of the BPCC Group,
Aylesbury, Bucks

Futura Publications
A Division of
Macdonald & Co (Publishers) Ltd
Greater London House
Hampstead Road
London NW1 7QX
A BPCC plc Company

CHAPTER ONE

The Commote of Kerry: *September* 1228
Aber: *October* 1228

The boy in the beech tree narrowed his eyes, staring due east into the rising sun.

The stabbing points of light scintillating out of the wooded cleft of the brook below him pricked at his vision; the steep knife-cut of the valley lay open to the long rays just piercing the mists, and the light had found the dancing water between the trees. He raised his sights steadily to stare over the glitter, intent upon the blunt promontory where the walls of the half-finished castle rose, and the vast coloured sprawl of the King's camp brocaded the sheepless hill-pastures.

Secure in their numbers, the English could show their bright devices there; but let them stray aside into the woods and a flicker of scarlet or the flash of a crest would cost them dear. More than forty had been pricked out of the reckoning within call of their own camp in the past week alone. Harry himself had put shafts into two of them, as they crept out in the dawn to their rabbit snares, too eager to be cautious. They were hungry men, the justiciar's army. If they had touched meat in the last three weeks it must have been the flesh of their own horses. The villages had been abandoned before them, the cattle and pigs and sheep driven off into the wilderness, even the game in the forests beaten methodically westwards out of reach.

The insistent daggers of reflected light jabbed at his eyes. Shaken by a sudden uneasiness he deflected his attention from the patchwork of tents and pavilions, blinked away the broad receding valley beyond, with its folded bordering hills shadow on shadow, blue on blue against the strengthening sunlight, and peered more sharply at the thread the broken lights were weaving among the trees beneath his perch.

His heart lurched in his breast. The refractions of water had left the water-course; they were winding uphill towards the saddle of the ridge, as though a silver serpent trailed its sinuous length through the woods on the flank of Gwernesgob. Not the play of the stream, but the incautious glitter of helms and arms. They had not even the sense to blacken their lance-heads before they went foraging.

He scrambled headlong down from his tree, barking his knees and palms in his haste, and began to run like a hare through the underbrush, turning his back on the broad valley through which the sunlight was gushing now like bright water, washing the lingering mist before it into the recesses of the hills of Kerry.

His two Welsh foster-brothers were coming side by side down the green ride between the oaks, David tall and slender and grave, like his mother, Owen square and brown and bright. They were wrangling, and as usual about him.

'I told you we should never have brought him,' Owen was fuming. 'Thirteen is too young, he'd have been better left at home. Why did you ever let him come? You should have known what a pest he'd be.'

'He begged so,' protested David mildly. 'And he's as good a bowman as many a grown man who serves me, that he's proved.'

'Ay, if we could but keep him at an archer's distance, but the brat will get to close quarters. The third time I've been put to it to fetch him away from their very lines, and what's his mother going to say to me if I go back without him? If you had to indulge him, why did you make me his keeper? I'd sooner play herd to a young wolf!'

David laughed. He had his mother's laughter, rare and warm and brief, even a little rueful, as though the weight of royalty always silenced the peal too soon. 'She'd never have trusted him to anyone but you, as well you know. And wisely! He has but to take one step astray, and you're after him like a

6

hen clucking after her chickens. If you were less anxious for him, you'd abuse him less. You're fretting yourself for nothing, Harry has his wits about him.'

'*I'm* fretting! Who was it began turning the camp hind-side-first for him the minute he was missed? Let me once get my hands on him,' promised Owen grimly, 'and I'll turn him hind-side-first, the imp.'

The boy burst out of the bushes on to the path below them at that moment, breathless with running, and flung himself willingly into the brown hands with which Owen had threatened him. They shook him hard, but did him no violence. It was always Owen who threatened, but usually David with his grave sense of duty who performed. They held him between them, both abusing him together.

'Where've you been these two hours, you rogue?'

'Didn't I forbid you to leave camp alone? One more offence and I send you home under escort, you hear me?'

He fended them off sturdily, heaving with breathlessness. 'No, but listen! I'll answer for it, I will, only later. The English – I was watching them from the hill, and –'

'Well I knew it!' said David, and cuffed him a time or two by ways of asserting his rights, only to be startled by the sudden passion with which Harry caught at his hand and held him off.

'Will you *listen* to me? There *are* English abroad. I saw them from the hill, a raiding party crossing the saddle yonder, heading for Dolfor.'

He had their attention now, they caught him one by either arm, at him with abrupt questions.

'How long since?'

'How strong a company?'

'In whose livery?'

They shook him in their eagerness, but there was no need, he flashed back at them, sparkling, the hasty answers that trod sharp on the heels of the questions.

'Not a quarter of an hour. I made them thirty men at least. I saw them coming up through the trees, and watched the way they took. They kept within cover, but where the sun falls you'll find them by their mail and their lances. They had all their wear bright,' he said, quivering with ardour and scorn. 'If we go down the river we could take them at the ford.'

They exchanged one glance as bright as steel over his head, and dropped him and plunged back by the way they had come. He had to run his hardest to keep up with them, but he held his place at their heels doggedly, clutching at David's arm as he ran, panting out his protests in advance at the prohibition he felt to be hanging over him.

'You'll take me with you?' he cried apprehensively. 'It was I saw them!'

'So it was,' said David, spreading an arm to slide the boughs away from his face. 'That's your part well done, now let us do ours.'

'That's unfair! Why did you bring me with you, then? And you wouldn't even have *known* – '

He was pouring out so much of his energy and his attention in indignation that he forgot to mind his step among the underbrush, and came down heavily over a twisted root; but he picked himself up hurriedly and rushed on, hopping and rubbing his scratched shin as he went.

'I'll stay out of sight, I swear I will, only let me come. Why not? What am I here for if I'm not to be allowed to fight?'

They broke out into the clearing three abreast. The boy was still clamouring aggrievedly as David called, and the clansmen came boiling out of the shadowy silences of the forest to their prince's voice, themselves dark and sylvan and silent as trees.

'Ah, let him come,' said Owen impatiently, 'or he'll deafen us. I'll see him placed well out of harm's way. And I'll see him paid his wages if he stirs a step from where I put him. You hear that?' He turned one formidable flash of his dark eyes on Harry. 'Run, then, get your bow.'

Harry fled on the instant, in terrible haste and with ears tight shut in case David should call him back and take away what Owen had given him. They had forborne from scolding him for leaving his arms behind when he slipped out of camp before dawn, so he must have been wise in deciding that he would be safer in the guise of a plain country boy in homespun should anyone detect him lingering in the woods near King Henry's camp. But this, his first experience of a real engagement, would be a very different matter. He was in desperate haste for fear they should go without him, but he tugged his way feverishly into the banded-mail hauberk the armourer had cut down for him from one of David's, for he knew he would be sent back to put it on if he appeared without it.

He almost skinned his fingers stringing his bow. John the Fletcher had made it for him and brought it down from the hills at Christmas; it was nicely matched to his weight and reach, and he loved it above all his possessions, except the sword the Prince had provided for him from the royal armoury. The splendour of Llewelyn himself was on the sword, for he had carried it in his first battle, when he was newly of age at fourteen, a dispossessed boy setting out to wrest his princedom from his uncles. Worn it and blooded it, too. Harry might have carried it in this campaign, but he was not yet the master of it as he was of the bow, and though it had cost him a struggle he had elected to stick to what he did best.

They were not in the field for his worship and advancement, after all, but to expel the justiciar from Welsh Kerry where he had no business uninvited, neither he nor that queer young king of his who made such large and sweeping gestures to so little purpose. The whole border raised, Clifford, de Breos, Pembroke, Gloucester and a dozen other lords marchers called together, not all of them too willingly, to bolster still more securely a wealth and power they themselves were already beginning to resent: and what was the result? Not ten miles advanced from the impregnable rock of Montgomery and their supply lines were cut to ribbons, and there they floundered and starved, building frenziedly at a fortress the winter would never let them finish, while a fifth their number of Welsh tribesmen made circles round them and picked them off at will.

He pulled his leather guard over his knuckles and ran from David's rough lean-to hut to overtake the company. They had melted eagerly into the trees along the ridge, leaving only a handful of shadows quiet and watchful about the silent and almost invisible camp. David had no more than twelve of his father's household army here under his command, and as many free tribesmen; the greater part of the host lay securely over the ridge of Kerry with Llewelyn, and from that base encircled and harried the rising castle.

At the edge of the forest they broke cover and plunged in the long, lunging strides of hill-runners down into the cleft of the river, here no more than a dancing stream only a mile old. There was no one to see them but the hawks circling over the rough pastures, and the woods soon began again, shrouding the thread of growing water.

'What if they've passed the ford ahead of us?' Harry asked anxiously, scurrying at David's elbow.

'Then we shall be between them and their camp, to halt them if they turn, and they'll meet their match somewhere along the track to Dolfor.'

'Does our father know of them?'

'I've sent him a runner. He'll take his horsemen by the road, and ride round to meet them. But unless they've taken alarm they'll walk their mounts down that slope, and we shall be in time. Hush, now, or we may miss Iorwerth's signal.'

An active boy could have leaped the Mule anywhere along this early stretch, but only in one spot did its steep banks level into an easy plane by which horses could be walked across. The track came down the sheer slope by long traverses, the trees crowding close over it almost down to the water. On the near bank there was a narrow level of meadow, and then the semi-circle of the woods. The steep hillside to eastward cut off the morning sun; here it was still dawn twilight, moist with September mist.

The archers and lancers parted the bushes and vanished into the ring of the forest, choosing their positions with deliberation. Somewhere high on the hill a green woodpecker, disturbed, launched its shrill, hard cry of laughter, twice repeated.

'In good time, they're on us,' said Owen on a breath of

exultation, and dragged Harry well back into the trees. 'Here, up with you into the crotch and stay there. You'll have a clear field, and never be seen yourself. No matter what happens below, you stay there. You hear me?'

'But if I'm needed?' argued Harry, hauling himself into the crotch of the oak-tree and glaring down challengingly between the boughs.

'Let me see you set foot to ground until it's over, and I'll take the shaft of a lance to you,' promised Owen fiercely, and leaped away to his own post of honour at David's shoulder.

That was no way to address a man who had been accepted into the ranks. If they let him fight at all they should allow him the same rights of judgement as his companions. Harry stood shaking with excitement and indignation in the bowl of the oak, which was broad and solid as one of the outcrops of rock that studded the upper pastures. He shifted his position fretfully, bracing his feet and flexing his drawing arm in an agony of certainty that he would fail of his aim through want of the firm earth under his soles, or find his drawing hampered by the branches. He fidgeted and scuffled, anxious and aggrieved, until the bird that was no bird called again, with a wilder disquiet in its hard laughter.

Then quite suddenly the excitement that had set him trembling with fever froze into a cool, happy competence, his breathing lengthened and quieted, and the head of the arrow he had fitted to his string dipped gently and nosed at the clear space between the branches, fixing its sights at the height of a horseman's breast above the landing of the ford. The line of the shaft drew taut and steady, like a hound pointing game.

Below him in the bushes Meurig from the villein tref at Aber, who was by rights only a packman with the army but could never be restrained from fighting, grinned up at him briefly and kissed the blade of his blackened lance, hefting it lovingly on the flat of his hand. It quivered, true-balanced, as though it would have taken flight of itself if he had not closed his grip and held it back.

Then the English came. Harry saw a flicker of colour

11

moving sidelong down the wooded slope, where a month ago the leaves would have hidden all. Above the first, another showed on a higher traverse. He heard the gentle clashing of harness, then the deliberate pacing and the occasional slither of hooves in the thick mould. They were very quiet and very cautious, threading their way slowly down to the water.

When they broke cover at the edge of the stream the boy saw with pleasure that they were leading their horses. That made things easier; there was a better chance of killing the man and taking the beast uninjured, and less probability that man and beast together, whole or hurt, might break through the ambush and escape. Harry coveted nothing the English had so much as their horses, tall, great-boned creatures double the size of his shaggy riding pony at Aber. By to-night, with God's blessing, he might well own one.

David withheld his signal until the first half-dozen men were over the stream, and a seventh in mid-crossing. This one rode, disdaining to lead his horse even down the steepest of the descent. A young man in a fine chain-mail hauberk and a buff surcoat, with the visor of his ornamented helm raised to uncover a bright, bold, arrogant face, everything about him a little elaborated and a little insolent, but undeniably handsome. When his chestnut horse trod astray and stumbled in the stones of the stream-bed the knight who had crossed before him darted back into the water to take the bridle and lead him ashore, with a gesture so obsequious that Harry, used to the sturdy independence of free Welshmen, almost laughed aloud. But the rider waved him off imperiously, swaying to the check, and drew in his rein with quick, reassuring gentleness.

One of King Henry's barons, surely, since knights ran to wait on him. A Poitevin, perhaps, one of those foreign lordlings who were exotics even to the English, and such a fruitful source of discontent among them, as he had heard the Prince say gratefully once on calculating the measure of the King's host as they moved in from Montgomery.

The chestnut horse was just heaving himself up the bank when David loosed his bowmen. Cynan's signal shot took the mounted man too high on the shoulder, and clashed and hissed from the rings of his hauberk to bury itself quivering in the bole of a tree beyond. It drove him back hard in the saddle and brought his horse up on its hind feet, pawing the air and bellowing. A rain of arrows followed the first on the instant. Harry loosed with the rest, but never knew whether it was his shaft that found its mark. The first man ashore loosed his bridle and span round clutching at his middle, to drop and lie kicking. The horse crashed away into the trees.

The mounted man recovered himself gallantly, hunched in the saddle over his bruised shoulder, and rode straight at the bushes. Two of his fellows mastered their plunging horses and flung themselves after him. Two more were down, dragging themselves frantically into cover and hauling feebly at their swords. Those who were still winding their way down to the water left the path and came crashing dangerously down the steep, to splash through the ford and ride to their leader's aid. Behind them the woodpecker laughed again, and was answered. A handful of David's regulars had crossed the river and worked their way round to cut off the retreat.

The Welsh archers circled invisibly in the thick undergrowth; only Cynan broke cover and ran for the edge of the water to draw off the mounted men from his prince, and when they whirled instinctively to pursue the only visible quarry they presented newly composed targets to the hidden hunters. Whimpering with excitement, Harry reached over his shoulder and fitted a third shaft, and for a few moments saw no clear mark at which he might aim it, the clearing boiled so frantically with a confusion of screaming horses and shouting men.

They were recovering their wits now after the first astonishment. Their commander, deflected for a moment by Cynan's flight, came back vigorously to his first cast, for the thicket from which the archer had broken cover must surely be the one point from which they had wished to distract attention. He set spurs to his horse and hurled himself at it again, driving the beast crashing through the bushes in a rain of leaves and twigs, with three or four knights hard at his heels.

David had drawn back, but no more than a few yards, and

the speed of the onslaught took him by surprise. He sprang back, warding off the sword that swung at his head, but went down in the tussocky grass against the bole of a thorn tree; and before Owen could leap to cover him the chestnut horse was reined in and wheeled about beneath Harry's oak-tree, to drive down again upon the fallen man.

Harry shortened his range and shot, too hastily and a little unsteadily, and the arrow thudded harmlessly into the ground. He said afterwards in his own excuse that he had thus betrayed his presence, and made his leap to forestall being pricked out of the branches with a lance; in fact the unfleshed shaft vibrated unnoticed, and the man on the horse never looked up, but Harry's prince and foster-brother was on one knee in the trampled grass, and his assailant with gripping knees and bloody spurs was urging his frenzied mount down upon him to stamp him into the ground, and Harry never stopped to think at all. He flung his bow aside with a yell of rage, and swinging outwards from the crotch of the tree hurled himself down upon the shoulders of the man beneath.

He fell with a shock that drove the breath and the wits out of him, and knocked the rider flat over the pommel of his saddle. The horse reared in terror, lashing out before and behind with frantic hooves, and man and boy together came down in the turf.

Harry lay gulping air in agony for one long moment of thunders and confusions. He heard Owen's voice raised in a cry of alarm, he heard close to him and seemingly all about him a stamping that shook the earth and filled his bones with jets of fear and pain. Then a great hand took him by the upper arm and hauled him clear of the threshing hooves with a jerk that almost started his shoulder out of joint, and a hand, the fellow to the first, swung him another yard out of danger with a box on the ear.

He rolled over and lay with his head in his arms until the earth ceased to rock and heave, and he had recovered a little of his breath, and sense enough to feel gratitude rather than resentment for the blow, which in its casual exasperation marked the continued existence of a world he understood,

14

and in which he could move and act with confidence. His elders, as often as they had been compelled to retrieve him from perilous places, had invariably avenged themselves for the fright by boxing his ears as soon as he was out of danger. He didn't hold it against them; it was another face of the indulgence they showed to him, and the value they set on him.

The ground steadied under him, and dimly he began to feel the shock of his bruises. He opened his ears first, very cautiously, and the clamour of fighting survived only distantly, where the woods threshed still to the pursuit of those who had broken through the cordon. There were voices calling across the wounded and the dead, arguing, cursing, groaning. There was in particular a near, known voice that said with brusque kindness:

'Come, get up, you're not hurt. Not a scratch on you!'

The hand that had been probing gently along his bones stroked its way down his back and slapped him lightly on the rump. He doubled his fists into the grass, hoisting himself up against a steadying knee, and opened his eyes upon his foster-father's bearded, weathered falcon's face, with the fierce salient bones of cheek and jaw glossy brown in the brightening light, and the deep lines and hollows dark and quivering with secret laughter.

'We came just in time to see you take wing,' said the Prince. 'I've seen many a clumsy nestling learning to fly, but never, I swear, so unlikely a bird as you. Were you out of arrows, that you had to fling yourself at him?'

Harry opened his mouth only to ask anxiously: 'David?'

'Untouched, never fear. Not a man lost, only a slash or two among us. And seven good horses taken, and one or two more we may pick up in the forest yet.'

The mention of horses brought Harry fully to life, sitting up bright-eyed in Llewelyn's arm. He looked eagerly round the clearing, now trampled and scored with hoof-marks and littered with debris from the bushes. There were dead men lying still in the grass, and some not yet dead who moaned and twitched. Cynan was back nursing a bloody arm, but grinning well-content, and Meurig was going round the wounded

15

retrieving bloodier lances, not roughly, not gently, as though he plucked them out of trees.

Harry's bruises suddenly burst into a frenzy of aching and throbbing, as though he had newly quickened to the reality of wounds and deaths. He swallowed nausea and held it down, sick with excitement and reaction. But David was there across the sward, slender and lively and whole as ever, kneeling over one of the wounded, and the sight of him was satisfaction enough. And Owen was there, too, gentling a frightened horse that still sweated and shook, and looking across at his young foster-brother with a frowning thought-fulness, between anger and approval; and it was good to be able to meet his eye brazenly and stare him out, secure in the Prince's blessing.

'There's a prize here waiting for you,' said Llewelyn, 'if you can ride him, saddle and harness and all, and fairly won. The man I can't spare you, but the horse is yours if you will. Come, look at him! He looks better eye to eye than from between his hooves. And he spared to trample you, like the good-natured beast he is.'

The chestnut horse shuddered with subsiding violence under Owen's stroking hands, his gleaming coat creamed with waves of foam like a beach on an ebbing tide. Harry withdrew his eyes from him with difficulty to look wonder-ingly at the man who lay stretched in the grass.

They had drawn off his helm, and uncovered to the light a thick tangle of black hair, limp and heavy with sweat, and a fine-featured, clean-shaven face now pale and pinched. Even so it had still its arrogance, but an arrogance innocent of offence. Helplessness became him. He lay gracefully, the long black lashes curled on his cheeks as appealingly as a girl's.

'Is he dead?' whispered Harry, for the first time trembling to the possibility of death. It did not seem to him that he was looking at an enemy.

'Not he! He'll live to a ripe old age. He's no more than stunned. And if you'd been in any case to hear the crash he made as he came down on the roots of that oak where you were nesting, you'd not wonder at that. A matter of a couple

16

of ribs broken and a badly bruised shoulder, that's the tale of his hurts. Look well at him, Harry. Do you know what you brought down with him?'

Harry shook his head, marvelling. The still blue eyelids had began to quiver, the black, straight brows to frown with returning pain.

'When you filled your hands with his person you took seizin of Hay, and Radnor, and Builth and Brecon and I know not what besides. This is he that came into half the baronies of the border only three months ago, when old Reginald died. William de Breos, none other!'

The sound of his own name penetrated the Lord of Brecon's dazed senses. He opened hollow dark eyes, staring blankly at the tall man and the sturdy boy who stood over him. Behind the drawn brows recollection worked slowly.

'William de Breos,' he affirmed in a rueful thread of a voice, 'none other!'

He remembered the child, though he had seen him only for one flashing instant as a bolt from heaven. The grave face, the large, concerned eyes touched off obstinate laughter in him, but he reigned it in to a courteous and considerate smile. One should be very careful with laughter, it so easily shifts to the other side of one's face.

'I salute you, sir,' he said solemnly, tremors of pain contorting his smile. 'You are the only champion who ever engaged me unarmed in single combat and brought me down, and by God, I think you're the only one who ever will. Will you not tell me the name of my conqueror?'

The flattery and the irony and the wilful, experienced charm tangled Harry's senses in a net of gossamer, and he was lost. 'Sir,' he said, stiff with shyness, 'my name is Harry Talvace.'

'Talvace!' A good Norman name on a wild, brown Welsh boy. He frowned over it faintly for a moment, but it was too hard for him. The heavy lids sank again, the flush of reviving colour ebbed as suddenly back to grey.

Harry broke away abruptly from Llewelyn's arm, snatched up the unlaced helm from the grass, and ran to fetch water

17

from the river. He kneeled beside his prisoner, burning with pride and admiration, tremulously bathing the broad forehead and moistening the bruised lips, even the horse forgotten.

When de Breos at length opened his eyes again and saw the boy's face bending over him, tense with solicitude and desperately serious, it was already a question with them which was the conquest and which the conqueror.

The escort emerged from the river valley and turned eastwards along the green coastal plain, between the salt flats and the mountains. Harry dismounted to walk beside the cart and talk to the sick man on his rough brychan. For him this was going home, and going home with glory. He had never tasted what it meant to be a prisoner. He talked eagerly, pointing out the long, silvery shimmer of water beyond Lavan Sands, and the soft coast of Ynys Mon beyond, tapering out to the small blue hog-back of Ynys Lanog of the saints. But it was October, and there was a grievous sadness on the sea, even at noon, and for all his raillery and his teasing and his brave laughter, de Breos was sad.

'Aber of the White Shells!' he said, biting into one of the sour late apples Harry had gathered for him at Nanhwynain, and shivering as its sharpness set his teeth on edge. 'What shall I do at this Aber of yours?' He frowned at the clean pattern his strong white teeth had left in the hard flesh. 'I tell you what, Harry, my friend, if I loved you but a little less I should wish you to the devil. What a plague were you doing in the first place, spying on our Babel of a camp from the hill there? What were you looking for? It wasn't glory, for you came unarmed, so much you told me. Then what was it?'

The moment of silence and hesitation surprised him, for the boy had been talkative on every other subject. He had but to touch him, and the confidences came pouring. This time it seemed he had put his finger on a tender spot, and for a moment the issue hung in doubt. He would have drawn back courteously and yielded the point if his curiosity and his vanity had not been pricked. He had had everything he had

18

chosen to ask of the child, and he would have this no less surely. He waited, stubbornly smiling, until the moment of constraint melted in a rush of impulsive words.

'I have an inherited quarrel,' said Harry, eyes glittering, 'with a certain Englishman. I hoped to catch a glimpse of him, and get to know my enemy.'

De Breos kept his countenance admirably straight; it was no great labour, he liked the boy too well to want to make light of the issues that were important to him.

'And have you never seen him, then, this enemy of yours?'

'Not yet,' said Harry, and shut his mouth with a snap.

'Who is he? It may be that I know him.'

'By name you surely will. Many a time I have been wanting to ask you about him. His name is Ralf Isambard of Parfois.'

De Breos stared wide-eyed, the apple gripped between his teeth. 'Isambard? Lad, but you're aiming high! What in the name of all the saints can you have against the Lord of Parfois? Why, the man could be grandfather to you! And trust me, he's no mettle to venture lightly, not even for princes.'

'It is a matter of *galanas* – a blood-debt,' said Harry sternly, suspecting that even the astonished respect he read in the alert face before him covered a shadow of mockery.

'But surely Welsh law will allow you to compound a blood-debt for a price,' suggested de Breos delicately. Ralf Isambard! he thought, and could have howled aloud at the incongruity. Life had a way of being out of balance, but to hear the blind puppy gravely declaring his enmity to the old wolf was out of all bounds. These Welshmen! But the boy was not even Welsh, he bore as uncompromising a Norman name as de Breos himself, and one fully as old.

'Not this,' said Harry grimly. 'Even if he so desired, I would not forgo it. But he knows nothing of me. The quarrel is my father's.'

The pale, hazy air over the sea thickened into heavier cloud on the mountains on their right hand, but already they could see the great shoulder of rock that crowded the fields into the surf beyond Aber. In less than an hour they would be home. Harry watched the unfolding outlines of the hills, and

19

was aware of the eyes that studied him frankly from the cart.

'What did old Ralf do to your father, that you keep so bitter a mind towards him?' The voice was warm and sympathetic and candidly curious. He could ask for things with a child's avid directness when he chose, and there was very little Harry could have denied him, not even the preoccupations that lay at the roots of his life and urged him towards maturity.

'He put my father to death. Long ago, just before I was born. My father was a master-mason in Isambard's service, and there was a matter of a Welsh boy who was taken during a raid and was in my father's care at Parfois. King John gave orders that the boy was to be hanged, and Isambard would have done it, but my father took the child safely away and delivered him back to the Prince of Gwynedd. You saw him by the Mule ford,' said Harry. 'He is my elder foster-brother, Owen ap Ivor ap Madoc.'

'Ay, well I remember him, the one that shepherds you so close every step you take. But if they got clear away into Wales, how did your father fall foul of the Lord of Parfois a second time?'

'He went back,' said Harry simply.

'In the devil's name, why? If he'd been in the old wolf's service surely he knew better than to confide in his mercy?'

'No help, he was bound. He was building the church there, and he'd sworn to remain at Parfois until his work was finished. When he'd despatched Owen safely on his way home he went back to keep his word. And there he was done to death. And my mother and I might have fared as ill if there had not been a certain lady there at Parfois who stood our friend to her own hurt, and brought us off safely into the care of the Prince of Gwynedd. And here we've been ever since. And that's why I'm foster-brother to Prince David and to Owen, and my mother is waiting-woman to the Princess Joan.'

'So that's how a Talvace came to grow up into as wild a fighting Welshman as the best of them. I own I've wondered. And this good gentlewoman who befriended you, what became of her?'

'She became a saint,' said Harry, as though that solved everything, and needed no amplification.

'Faith. I wish she would teach me the trick of it, if she found it so easy,' said de Breos, ruefully laughing. 'What must one do to become a saint? Alive, I trust? I have no ambition to be a dead saint. They so often come by uncommonly nasty deaths.'

Harry looked sidelong at him in flat incomprehension; the word was ordinary currency to him, and had no implications of canonisation about it.

'She went to live in a cell up there,' he explained, tossing his head towards the hills that closed in gently upon the forked cleft of Aber. 'Saint Clydog lives there, and they built her a second cell close to his. She lives in prayer, away from the world. She's been there thirteen years now. Sometimes we visit her, and sometimes she sends John the Fletcher down to us if she wants anything. But she never comes herself.'

'So they pass their days in prayer and meditation, do they, she and Saint Clydog? And nobody else for a dozen miles round to trouble their peace!'

'There's John the Fletcher,' said Harry punctiliously, the gentle irony escaping him, since it was not at his expense.

'Oh, by all means let us not forget John the Fletcher!'

'My mother says,' confided Harry impulsively, 'that she did it because she did not wish to marry. And yet she was so beautiful!'

'Better and better! I shall have a third cell built there. So she escaped marriage by embracing sainthood, did she? Not having your mother's more practical way of escape into the Princess's service.'

'But my mother did marry,' said Harry promptly. 'She married my father's good friend, the mason who always worked with him. It was he brought Owen away home, and after that he dared not venture back into England.'

'God's blood, Harry!' cried de Breos, rolling his head back among the rugs with the first full-hearted shout of laughter he had uttered in his captivity. 'I think you must be the most mothered and fathered of any fellow ever I met. Three mothers

21

and two fathers on the earth, and yet another sire under it! How is it they have not torn you in pieces among them?' And perhaps they would have, he thought, breaking off there sharply, if the boy had not been the bold, tough, self-willed creature he was, if he had not had that audacious Norman jaw to his immature face, and those levelled, challenging sea-green eyes.

Well, at least the dead one must let him alone, he thought, and then caught back even that thought, for perhaps he was taking it too easily for granted. No one can be more demanding than the dead, or the living on behalf of the dead. And no one can be worse traduced than the dead, when the living begin to make demands for him. What did the boy really think of that father of his who could no longer speak for himself?

De Breos stirred painfully, easing his swathed trunk on the rough brychan, and flinching from the stab of the broken ribs. He had been a fool to ride for so many hours earlier in the day, he was stiffening badly now. He looked at the coils of cloud drifting down the mountain, he looked at the darkening silver of the sea beyond Lavan Sands, turning to lead before his eyes, and he shivered. No wonder the English exiles shrank together for solidarity in this barbarous place. No wonder Talvace's widow clung to her own kind, and made haste to barricade herself in behind another man's name, and furnish her son with one more father of his own race.

'And which of your many parents do you mind, Harry? For they can't always speak with one voice.'

'I mind the Prince,' said Harry very practically, and grinned aside at him wickedly. 'Would not you?'

'I would! The stakes would have to be high before I risked displeasing that gentleman, were I in your shoes. And yet it seems to me you have very much your will with him, my friend.'

'He is very good to me,' acknowledged Harry blithely, 'and never angry with me but with reason. But terrible when he's angered.' He used the words of fear, but he did not know yet what fear was; there was laughter bright behind the awe in his eyes. 'Once I tied old Einion's beard to the strings of his harp

22

when he fell asleep over it in hall, and when he awoke and went to play he got in such a tangle he thought himself bewitched. I never saw the Prince so angry. I got the worst beating I ever had from him, to teach me where respect is due.'

But it had not been severe enough, de Breos saw, to stop him laughing for long, or make him approach either Prince or bard with timidity thereafter.

'I was sorry afterwards, I never thought how he would start awake like that and be frightened to find himself fast. But that was a long time ago,' he said hastily, recollecting his present dignity as escort to so notable a prisoner, 'nearly three years ago, when I was still a child.'

'I understood it so,' de Breos assured him gravely.

They were drawing near to the forked cleft of woodland that slashed steeply into the towering hills. He could see in one iron gleam of light the thread of the river pouring down across the track and lacing the flat fields to the salt marshes beyond; and higher, withdrawn into the mouth of the valley, the great wooden wall of Llewelyn's castle half-obscured by the clinging huts of the villein hamlet at its gate. Within the wall the timber keep towered on its high motte, and the squat roofs clustered under its shadow. There was a light haze of wood-smoke over the whole great maenol, withdrawing it from the ebbing day. This neighbour land of his which he had hardly seen in his almost thirty years had never seemed so alien.

'I confess I never tied a bard to his harp,' he was saying lightly while his heart chilled in him, 'but I once set fire to a chaplain. The old fool was so long-winded, and the devil left a burning candle so near to the skirt of his gown. A passable exploit in my father's son, but unwise in my uncle's nephew. Bishops in the family are a mixed blessing, Harry. But that was long ago, too, of course, when *I* was still a child.'

William, my friend, he was thinking, with the hot discontent and the cold languor fuming in him like the clouds over Moel Wnion, what are you going to do here, without pastime, without exercise, without women? Oh, for the freedom of that third cell in the hills, with the resolute (and beautiful!) lady who had no use for marriage. Can she really be content with Saint Clydog? And John the Fletcher, of course! It would never do to forget John the Fletcher.

The backs of the riders ahead had straightened as they sighted the walls of home, the horses raised their heads and distended their nostrils to snuff the familiar pastures. The looming barrier that threatened him beckoned to them; there were stables and fodder waiting for the horses and well-warmed beds for the men. And after all, need his own bed be utterly cold? There are women everywhere.

Welsh ladies of rank are virtuous, that's well known. But all? Llewelyn had a bastard son before he married, by a lady with a pedigree nearly as long as his own. The young man proved troublesome, I recall, and is now safe under lock and key at Degannwy to keep him from his brother's throat. As I shall soon be under lock and key here at Aber.

'I hope you lodge your captives above-ground, Harry,' he said, eyeing the dark walls. 'Light is the last thing a man should willingly surrender. Except breath,' he added with a sour smile.

He was instantly sorry for that tone. It was unfair to take out his spleen on the boy, who could so easily be made to pay for an innocent and helpless attachment. He had not missed the way Harry copied even the tricks of his speech, the turn of his head, his seat in the saddle. He had no boy of his own, only a covey of little daughters, and the flattery of being imitated was seductive, he had to watch his every move.

'There are no dungeons here, my lord, we live in daylight. The journey has been hard on you,' said Harry anxiously, 'but here you'll rest and mend. And the Princess my foster-mother will deal generously and lovingly with you, that I promise you.'

'Well, if I never saw her before, at least I have some obscure claims of kinship on her.'

The connection was tenuous enough, one of the knots of expediency in the complex net of alliances that made a spider's web of the border country. His father in late middle-age had contracted a second marriage with the darkest and prettiest of the flurry of little girls who had followed David into the world. Young Gladys was no doubt properly glad to be a coltish widow at sixteen – or was it seventeen? Presently they would marry her to someone else, if God was good to her someone nearer her own age.

'But be careful, Harry, how much you promise in someone else's name. If my entertainment is less than generous and loving I shall hold you accountable for what's wanting. I've no doubt I'm going to pay a princely price for it.'

Hardly two months set up in his honour, and he had to put it into pawn to ransom his body. But he was resolutely smiling again, and the mouth that was so pleasing even in its drooping weariness had regained its good humour. It was time to gather about him what powers he still had, for they were passing among the huts of the village, and the guard at the gate was already drawing aside to let them in.

Harry fell back for a moment outside the gate, and de Breos well knew why, and considerately refrained from looking round. What boy could resist riding ceremoniously into the maenol on his new horse, fair prize of war? And the plain truth was that he could not reach the stirrup without making use of the shaft of the cart or some convenient stone, and was too proud to get one of his men-at-arms to heft him into the saddle. Better not to see the mounting-block against the timber buttresses of the wall, and the boy's quick dash for it.

In a moment he was alongside again, upright and solemn on top of the tall chestnut horse; and though his men grinned broadly behind his back they kept their faces steady as stone in front of him, only their eyes laughing. He was well liked, none of them would have the heart to spoil his triumph.

The women of the village left their work and came running to catch at stirrup leathers and walk alongside their men into the courtyard. Rhys ap Griffith, who had been in practical command of both the escort and its commander, reined aside unobtrusively and let the boy ride forward alone.

The cart stopped. Out of Llewelyn's great hall came his seneschal, Ednyfed Fychan, with a knot of lesser officials at his heels, and from kitchen and armoury and kennels poured every man who could drop his work and come to welcome his returning fellows. Harry had a worthy audience for his grand entry. But it was not for the elders, not even for his ancient tutor Einion, that he put the nervous horse through a little performance of dancing and sidling before he brought him to a halt.

Two women had appeared from the retired royal apartments in the far corner of the maenol. Harry's two secular mothers, no doubt. But which of them provoked this touching tribute of pride and ambition, the flourish with which he dismounted, the vivid colour that mantled in his cheeks? Very surely not his own true mother! De Breos examined the two approaching figures with detached and yet gradually quickening interest.

One of them was small, with great dark eyes in a face like a blown rose; not so slender as once she had been, perhaps, and not so young, but her black and white and red was a lasting kind of bloom. The other was half a head taller and a hand-span slimmer, a grave woman with light brown hair dressed in coiled plaits on either side a long, fair-skinned face.

There was no doubt which of the two was Gilleis Boteler and which was the Princess of Gwynedd. This was where Llewelyn's heir had got his fairness and slenderness; and this, surprisingly, was the face that could inflame young Harry's unpractised heart without his knowledge, and make him flush and glow in her presence.

De Breos saw nothing there to start the spring gushing. She had a sombre authority, a too quiet and too indifferent grace in her movements, a certain pale good looks; but she could never have been beautiful, and forty years had worn her thin and weary, brought the bone too near the skin and the mind too close to the fretted surface of the flesh. A little while and she would be old. He took his eyes from her.

A groom had taken Harry's reins from him as he alighted, and the boy turned his shoulder on the seneschal and ran to meet the two women. He bent his knee to the Princess, and then lifted his face to her as he must have been lifting it at every meeting and every separating, all his life long, for the kiss of kinship. She took his head between her hands and kissed him with a simplicity that was old habit to her, and handed him on to his mother to be hugged and made much of. But for one moment, with Joan's hands pressing his cheeks and Joan's lips touching his forehead, he had started and quivered to a tension which was out of his experience and beyond his understanding. De Breos had seen it pass through the braced shoulders and the long, sturdy back like a shudder of bliss. There was no mistaking it, the boy was deep in love with her.

The woman with whom someone else is in love, even a wild green boy, is always worth a second glance.

De Breos raised himself gingerly, holding by the edge of the cart, for Harry was coming running back to him.

'Will you light down, my lord? Will you come to the Princess?'

Yes, he thought, I'll come, and with such arms as I have, too. There must, it seems, be something there worth the finding. The women had joined the group of men, and the Princess was talking to Ednyfed Fychan. She did not look across at the prisoner, perhaps not even to seem to be hastening his clearly difficult and painful descent from the cart.

But you shall look at me, madam, he thought, feeling the old quickening fluid of challenge sparkle through his blood like wine through the heart in drunkenness. You shall look at me, and see me, too, you who have seen almost everything there is to be seen in this realm, but never William de Breos, never until now.

'Lend me your shoulder to alight, Harry, I'm mortal stiff. No, don't leave me so. It was you broke my ribs for me, and you may prop me up until they knit. By rights you owe me a good shirt, too, I would I had one by me this minute. No matter, let me be seen at my worst, and there can be no disappointment after.'

She turned her head as they came, the man moving haltingly and wearily with a hand on the boy's shoulder. She had been aware of them all the time, and she turned her head at last because it seemed to her an unkindness to let the sick man come so lamely all the way to her. She was generous, even rashly so; Harry's first promise was fulfilled almost before it cooled on his lips. She left the seneschal, and came to meet them.

Harry walked carefully, matching his step and his breathing with those of his prized captive, proud of the weight on him. She did not miss that. She missed nothing. You see? There's a sign here for you as well as for me. Here's your little falcon, royal by adoption, tamed. Consider the implications and look at me, look well. Does he come to every man's lure?

'You are welcome to Aber, my lord de Breos,' she said, in a low-pitched voice which was the greatest beauty she had shown him. 'You are not well, and too tired for ceremony. If you are pleased to go to your lodging I will have linen and water brought to you there.'

'And if I refuse it?' he said with a rueful smile. 'Would you take the sign? And let me go on my way when you had fed and warmed me in your house?'

'I see you know the customs of Welsh hospitality,' said Joan, faintly smiling in return. The eyes she raised to his face were grey and clear and very deep. What they saw was not his handsome body and bold, fine features, but the convulsive clinging of his fingers on Harry's shoulder, the drawn lines and the sag of discouragement round his mouth, that so bore down the wilful smile, the crippled beauty of his movements, and above all his youth, so willing to be boisterous and insolent, and so confined and cramped now into helplessness. 'All the same,' she said dryly, the smile a thought warmer now, 'I think in your condition you should not ask to leave to-night.'

No,' he agreed, watching her face steadily. 'No, I will not ask to leave to-night.'

'No, even if you opened the gate to me now I would not go.' Generously and lovingly she'll deal with me, will she, Harry? I've seen the generosity, that can walk abroad in courtyards and show itself in front of all men. But the love, that's a different matter. It needs silence and retirement. And time.

Time of which, by favour of de Burgh's obstinacy, we may yet have enough.

'Ay, we know, child, we know,' said Gilleis good-humouredly, pausing on her way to the linen-press to rap her son lightly on the back of his shock-head with a thimbled finger. 'There never was such a paragon. The voice of an angel and the step of a deer-hound, and no bounds gallant and noble. These three days since you brought him home with you you've never stopped singing his praises, we should know the tune by now.'

Harry had talked himself out, kneeling on the rug at Joan's feet with his arms spread familiarly on her brocaded knees. He still behaved as one having his child's rights in her bed-chamber. Many a time he had played on Llewelyn's great bed, and many a time she had watched him, the lordly little stranger, and been charmed by his assurance almost into believing that his roots were there.

'But is he not everything I've claimed for him? Didn't I tell you he could hold his own at whatever he touched? Even with as great a bard as ours,' said Harry proudly.

Joan sat with her hand loosely clasped between both his, her eyes fixed on her own mirrored face in the polished silver over his shoulder. Her hair was already unbraided, and hung to her waist in heavy brown tresses. She was looking some-where beyond the mirror, beyond the walls of the room, and there was a sadness about her mouth that made his heart lurch with fondness.

'He's a man like other men,' she said. 'Voice and face and form, God made him well enough.'

'If you cry him up so,' warned Gilleis, teasing him, 'you'll have folks saying you are but crying up yourself for having the better of him.'

'No, truly, I never thought of it!' he protested indignantly. 'It's not the fighting well, though he bears as good a report as any man in England. No, it's the way he took it when the luck went against him. And even now – if you could know how sad I've seen him when there was no one by. And he

29

did not deserve it! Do *you* know, do *I* know what it is to be a prisoner? And yet you heard him at supper, how he talked, how he laughed –'

How he laughed! With all of him, the reared head and the broad, young, sinewy shoulders that rocked to the cadences of his mirth, and the unbelievably smooth round throat pulsing above the furred collar of David's cotte. How he talked, between the laughter, with a fiery flow and a heady sparkle, like pouring wine. The pale face in the mirror flushed a little, remembering. She saw herself mute and grave beside him, unable to laugh with him even when he gave her occasion. He had asked punctiliously after his stepmother, letting his civility carry an unmalicious edge of absurdity, too gentle for irony, but she had not smiled. She had been playing the game too long, perhaps, this intricate game of courts and kings and destinies. She had grown used to regarding her daughters as pieces on the board, movable within three generations. Her daughters, yes, but not her son. Never her son.

'And then to-night, when our lord's courier came, you saw how he took that, too, though it was bitter bad news to him. You heard him. How many men could have carried it so well?'

Bad news indeed for an Englishman, that the war in Kerry was over, and the English host retreating ignominiously into their own borders from the winter's early frosts and the threat of starvation. She heard again the seneschal's voice retailing the news over the trenchers, and de Breos swallowing it manfully. How many men could have carried it so well?

'The terms of peace are already agreed, but for some chaffering over details for form's sake. There'll be a matter of a few head of cattle to pay for the privilege of taking back Kerry intact, but that's a small matter.'

'Not to the empty fellows I left behind there! It will be a marvel if the King gets one beast back into England uneaten. And what of Hubert's fortress? I felt in my bones it would never be finished.'

'It's to come down. Down to the foundations, my lord.'

'God hears everything! His folly, he christened it, and folly

30

it turns out to be. Madam, I hope you never play with words? They have a way of coming full circle into the wind, and hitting in the face the fool who thinks he aimed them. There'll be an indemnity to pay for the work of levelling it, I make no doubt?'

'It's still a matter of argument, my lord, how much.'

'It need not exercise you. Whatever it may be, I shall surely be paying it.'

And all this while she had not said one word. Words are terrible weapons; even without his warning she would have been chary of using them here. When at last she ventured, the ground quaked under her; she had never known it to be shaken so.

'I am afraid, my lord, you can take no pleasure in this news.'

He had lifted to her face one brilliant flash of his dark eyes, for once nakedly unsmiling, and answered in a voice so low and rapid that she barely caught his meaning: 'Can you, my lady?'

'Come,' said Gilleis, closing the chest upon the gown she had just laid away, 'get off to bed, now, and let the lad rest. Do you think women can't see a handsome face for themselves, and value a good heart, too? Say good night to my lady, and be off to your solitary splendour, since you won't come and keep company with Adam and me.'

Harry slept with Owen, in the ante-chamber of the apartment David enjoyed as acknowledged heir to his father and though he could very well have gone to his mother's lodging while his brothers were out of Aber, he would not for the world have ceded his rights.

Harry kissed Joan's hand obediently, and offered her his cheek. He trembled when her lips touched him, and she felt the heat of his rising blood under the smooth skin; but all she saw when she held him off from her was a flushed child, a little fevered perhaps with sleepiness. If she could have heard, he thought, how eloquently he poured out to de Breos those praises of her that stopped short in his throat in her presence, she would have known better how to value him, and found him a man's work to do for her sake. When he brought her all the intoxication and excitement of his first sally in arms, a splendid prize of war to lay at her feet, she only smiled and caressed him with the same serenity as if he had run to show her a new toy. She was too much with his mother, whom he loved dearly, but who never took him quite seriously.

He looked back from the threshold to say earnestly: 'Madam, Father Philip says we should remember in our prayers all poor souls hard beset, and all prisoners. Will you pray for my lord de Breos?'

She did not look round, but her eyes in the soft metallic sheen of the mirror sought for his, and the reflected look was at once tender and grim, as though she smiled at him while she fended off another who stood behind him. After a long moment of silence she said in a low voice: 'Be content, I will pray for him.'

'Such a boy!' sighed Gilleis, kissing his cheek and putting him briskly out of the door. 'Did ever you know him so concerned for any of us? The times I've heard him gabble his prayers too fast for sense, if he did not forget them altogether, but for my lord of Brecon he'll have us all on our knees. But there, his geese were always swans. And the young man has a way with him, too,' she owned, smiling. 'It would be hard to deny him liking.'

Joan sat silent and motionless before the glass, watching the long tresses of her hair smoothed and floating from the comb. Fair still, but the honeyed brightness was growing faintly dulled, faintly dry, like grass just beginning to bleach in the height of the summer. Time tarnishes the colours of flesh and hair and eyes with a fine, corroding dust. The cords of this throat had grown a little slack, the delicate white flesh was grained and tired. Dust clouded even the eyes grey as glass, as though all her life had been Lent, and the spring was gone by with no Easter to give it meaning and her devotion respite. She saw that the last May blossom was already withering on the bough, and almost before she could reach her hand to it, it would be gone. Surely she had been a girl once; but the girl had died irrevocably at fifteen, when she had left her dolls behind her to take up the burden of state, and conceived the child for whom she had been busy ever since constructing a kingdom. She had been too much pre-occupied, even too well content, manipulating men and thrones and powers to have time to gather the May.

'Well, in a week or so now my lord will be safely home,' said Gilleis cheerfully.

'God be thanked!'

She had only to look deeply enough into her own face in the mirror and she saw him there, his darkness flashing through her pallor, his steely metal gleaming through her gentler authority, bone fused into bone and eye matched with eye, an eagle looking through her face from his nest within her mind. She had grown into him flesh to flesh and spirit to spirit long since. If he suffered a wound, she bled. Had there ever since such another burning of two into one? Had there ever been a marriage so absolute as this?

'Go now, Gilleis, I shall sleep directly. Good night!'

'Good night, my lady! I'll leave the lamp burning.'

The soft, light footsteps receded hollowly down the wooden stair, for the great bedchamber and its wardrobe were raised upon a tall undercroft so that the windows might look out over the curtain wall and enjoy the prospect of the straits and the distant silvery chain of the coast of Ynys Mon.

When she had heard the outer door below swing heavily into place, Joan rose from her stool and ran quickly down the stairway, and dropped the great wooden bolt into its socket. When had she ever done that before? Why should she do it now? Who would dare to lay a hand to her door? She was her own ramparts, her own armoury, an impregnable fortress. And images cannot be locked out. If the image of a man had ventured to walk through the invisible barrier, how could he be fended off by those meaner safeguards she had never needed? To bolt the door was to admit and acknow-ledge him. He would be within the room with her, penetrating her sleep with his wakefulness all night long.

Nevertheless she left the bar in place; and going back to her room she prayed passionately for all prisoners, and all poor creatures hard beset.

33

Harry started upright in his bed in the chilly darkness of after-midnight, torn out of a disturbed dream that uncoiled from him instantly and left no images behind, but only a sense of tension and fear. His heart was thudding heavily as though he had been running, but it seemed to him that he had been running towards the fear, not away from it, and had been on the point of embracing it when he was jerked awake. He put out a hand instinctively for Owen, but the bed was cold where Owen should have been, and he remembered that he was alone.

He sat hugging the fur coverlet about his nakedness and listening to the silence, and the unfinished dream, formless and furtive now, hung over him waiting in the dark. It was foolish to be afraid. He had only to lie down and pull the covers over his ears, and drift away again without haste into sleep. Broken dreams seldom came back.

But he did not lie down. He crept out of the big bed and felt for his hose, still straining his ears. The dogs had not given tongue. Yet there had been a sound, something soft and rustling and hardly audible, the braced fingers of a hand feeling its way all along the rough timber of the outside wall of his room, as though a blind man had passed by.

Now that he had given it a form he was less afraid, and infinitely more curious. He pulled on his hose hurriedly in the dark, and tugged his cotte over his head, emerging to freeze into quivering stillness again. If he had not been listening with such strained attention he would not have heard the second sound, though it was louder than the first; and when it came he had no idea how long the interval had been. It was a dull, muted fall, somewhere muffled between the buildings towards the corner of the curtain wall. Harry opened his door cautiously, waiting with held breath for the dogs to begin scolding, but the kennels were at the opposite extreme of the maenol, and there was no sudden flurry of baying. Nothing moved in the darkness of the moonless and cloudy night but the boy slipping with the ease of old knowledge between the buildings, running as inquisitively and rashly towards the thing that threatened him as he had run in his dream.

He rounded the corner of the tower and checked for a moment in alarm, for the door at the foot of the staircase was open, he knew it by the hollow sound the cavity gave back to his passing step and his loudly-beating heart. Why should the Princess's door be standing wide at this hour? He wavered, in doubt whether to run in to her and assure himself of her safety, or pursue the sound to its source, but it was no more than ten yards to the angle of the tower and the narrow walk that separated it from the curtain wall, and curiosity drew him on.

A shadow started erect among shadows, close under the wall where he could hardly distinguish one darkness from another. A low voice challenged in an urgent whisper: 'Who's there?' And on a quick gasp of recognition and recovery: 'Harry! Is that you?'

'Madam, is all well –,' he began breathlessly aloud.

She laid a hand over his mouth and hushed him sharply. He felt her palm cool and hard and steady against his lips, and was calmed. She was the mistress of all here, and not by courtesy but by right of will. If she took no alarm he need feel none. He reached his arms to hold her, and stumbled over something heavy and warm that lay at her feet. A man, his arms spread against the foot of the curtain wall, his hands two pallors in the dark just bracing themselves laboriously to thrust him up from the ground. The shock of his hair fallen forward over his face was the darkest centre in the many darks that were beginning to disentangle themselves before Harry's eyes. He was breathing in deep-drawn, laboured breaths, and the first thrust, as he levered himself up, fetched a flinching groan out of him.

'My Lord de Breos!' whispered Harry, and began to shake again with the certainty that filled him. Here in this narrow and private place, at the foot of the wall on the landward extreme of the maenol, the woods not far away, the night moonless –

'But he could not!' he breathed, outraged and incredulous. 'He *could* not! He gave his *word* –'

'Hush!' she said peremptorily, gripping him by the arm.

'Help me with him, quickly, and be quiet. We must get him back to his bed before anyone else hears.'

Bewildered but obedient, he lent his arm, and between them they hoisted the fallen man to his feet. Joan drew the long right arm about her neck, Harry on the other side clasped him about the body. They moved all three as one flesh, braced and shuddering, and at the first step de Breos straightened himself and lifted his weight from falling upon them. He did not speak, he did not raise his head, but with their aid he walked.

'But how could he?' Harry said in a bitter whisper through his clenched teeth, addressing Joan as though the man between them had been deaf or dead. 'He gave his parole!'

She heard the rage and shock in his voice, and smiled wryly in the dark. At thirteen he still lived in a simple world where all bonds were automatically honoured, and all words held good. He had a lot to learn about men, and even more about compassion, but life would teach him soon enough. Let him continue in his delusion, however it galled him; only she need ever know from which wall the climber had fallen.

'Be quiet,' she said, but very gently. 'Only let us get him home.'

Under his breath the boy fretted still at the smart, swallowing indignant tears. 'Had we to put leg-irons on him? If we cannot take *Brecon*'s word – '

Hurt and ashamed, he leaned an angry shoulder to prop open the door of the prisoner's lodging. Why was he even allowing himself to be drawn into this conspiracy of silence? The shame he felt was for himself, because this man had been a piece of his life, and he had been innocently proud of him, and to have him exposed to scorn was a humiliation Harry himself would have found hard to bear.

'Close the door,' said Joan, drawing a sharp breath of relief.

They lowered their burden between them and let him slip down on to the pillow and lie still. Even with the door closed they could distinguish shades of darkness here, their eyes being used to the night by now. They saw de Breos raise an arm with a slow, heavy movement, and lay it over his face.

They waited some moments, Harry did not know for what; perhaps for the silence to reassure them that no one else stirred, perhaps for the breath to steady and grow calm in them before they ventured to speak.

'Are you hurt?' Joan asked at last, very quietly. They knew by the tensions of his stretched body that he was conscious and aware.

'No,' said the man on the bed in a muffled and bitter voice. 'Not as I deserve.'

'It was folly to attempt such a climb,' she said in the same muted tone. 'You should have known you could not bear the strain, half-crippled as you are.'

'It was more than folly to attempt it,' the moving mouth said from under the sheltering sleeve, 'as well you know. It was villainy. And I repent me of it. Now deliver me over and have done.'

'My lord, even my prisoner is in some sort my guest, and his honour touches me closely.' She turned towards the boy: 'Harry,' she said with authority, 'you will say no word of this to anyone, ever. It is between us three alone.'

The man and the boy stiffened as if with the same impulse of recoil. 'He broke his bond,' burst out the boy, smouldering.

'So has many another, once, under sharp distress, and lived to do honour to his name none the less.' He was holding out against her for the sake of his sore heart rather than his sense of justice, and she knew it, though she chose to attribute to him the nobler motive. 'Don't be too hard on a single fault, or who will be fit for your acquaintance? Some day you may need a gentle judgement yourself, Harry. It's a long way through the world.'

It was easy enough to move him, the proud fondness that had made this betrayal so hard to bear was already fighting on the side of de Breos. 'I shall obey you, madam,' muttered the boy, grudging but abashed. 'I'll never speak of it.'

'Good! See you remember. Let God do the judging. Now we had best go back to our beds, and forget we ever left them. The matter is closed. My lord, I shall send to inquire after you in the morning, I trust you will have taken no harm. Are you indeed unhurt? Are you well enough to lie alone?'

The voice from the bed was harsh and right. 'I am as well as any man can be who has met himself face to face and is ashamed of what he sees.'

'Is there anything you need before we leave you?'

'Nothing,' said de Breos, 'since you are so merciful as to put this past hour clean out of mind. Nothing but a better heart in me, and that I think you may have given me already.' He lowered his arm suddenly from his face, and heaved himself up on one elbow. 'Harry! Come here to me!'

The boy drew near the bed with a dragging step, the old compulsion pulling at his senses. Even though the darkness hid the admired face, the voice when it pleased could be so intimate and so winning. And Joan, who was perfection, had warned him against judging too hardly the faults to which he had never yet been tempted.

'Harry, for what I attempted to-night I am heartily sorry. I never shall offend again. Whether you will still take my word I do not know, but for what it is worth to you I give it.'

He lay down again abruptly without waiting for an answer, flattening his shoulders into the brychan and turning his head away. Harry stood irresolute for a moment, wanting to find something generous to say, moved towards him and angry with himself for being moved. It was flattering to be asked to forgive, it filled him with the large delight of magnanimity, but his injury was too recent and grave to be so easily adjusted.

'Come,' said Joan, taking him by the arm, 'let him alone now.'

Harry allowed himself to be led mutely from the room. The night air was cold on his cheeks and eyelids. Sleep leaned on him out of the chilly zenith. She laid her arm about his shoulders and led him to his own door, thrusting him gently within.

'Go to bed, and leave fretting. To-morrow will mend all.'

'If you knew,' he whispered grievously, 'how well I thought of him –'

'So you will again, child. One slip doesn't make a man a

38

villain. Go to bed and sleep. This is not the end of the world. And think of him kindly,' she said, a sudden desperate appeal shaking the quiet thread of her voice. 'Think kindly of all poor sinners. If you think yourself wounded, what must their sufferings be?'

'I will try,' he said, almost in tears, and stumbled bemusedly back to his cold bed with the tremor of her distress still vibrating in his ears.

When the door had closed on him she turned and slipped like a silent shadow back to the room where de Breos lay, and let herself in to him without a sound.

He was lying coiled hard into himself on the bed, his face to the wall, his long arms wound round his body tightly as cords. He did not move when she came in, but he knew the moment of her coming by the slight shifting of the darkness and the drift of air that came in in her garments; and by something more that distilled from her presence and set every nerve in him quivering with tension, until his skin was a web of agony constricting him unbearably. She did not speak; it was not to be made so easy for him. In the end he would have to speak for her, but the effort was like a death. Had he not said enough already, and plainly enough?

'Why did you come back?' he said in a voice harsh with anguish. 'What more do you want from me? I repent, I shall not offend again. If I could undo what I've done I would but, God help me, that's out of my power. Is it confession you want? Well you know it was to your window I was climbing. What did I want with escape while you were within the wall?'

'I know,' she said, and did not move.

'If it had not been for the boy –'

'You need not fear the boy. You have him by the heart still. He'll hold his tongue.'

'That you may know the whole of it, I let myself drop of design. I've climbed in at too many chamber windows in my time to fall from one now. The thing was child's play. I could have broken in upon you if I had willed, but when it came to it that was not what I wanted. You must come out to me – of your own will, of your own charity –'

39

'Yes,' she said hopelessly, 'you knew how to fetch me forth to you. I am here. Of my own will.'

'You were to take me up and pity me – and, by God, you did!'

'Was that pity?' she said. The low, lovely voice was helpless and wondering. 'I know only that I had to come to you. And will you not even look at me now that I am here?'

'No!' he said in a great gasp of protest. But in a moment he gathered himself effortfully and turned to face her, and dragging himself erect swung his feet to the beaten earth of the floor. 'I played my game too well,' he said. 'It 'proved to be no game, or if it was it's I who pay the forfeit, as is only just. I'm taken in my own trap. As God sees me, I love you! I love you, and I cannot touch you!'

He sank his face between his hands and closed his eyes, waiting for the fluctuations of darkness and cold that would mark her going; but there was no lifting and no settling of the blackness within his aching eyelids, and when he looked up again she had drawn a step nearer, and stood within touch of his hands.

'Well?' she said. 'Am I to stay or go?'

'Go!' he implored her groaning. 'In the name of God! And quickly!'

But still she did not move, and in a moment his arms came out blindly and fastened on her as the dying fasten on the Host, dragging her down into his heart.

CHAPTER TWO

Aber: *January to September* 1229

'The price of your liberty,' said Llewelyn, spreading one great brown hand to the heat from the brazier, 'is two thousand pounds, my lord.'

'I have had it in my mind with curious insistence that it might be,' said de Breos with a face innocently grave, 'ever since it came to my ears that the indemnity for the razing of our good justiciar's new castle in Kerry was fixed at that amount. You will allow me a little time to ponder the odd chance, I hope – and to recover the breath I am going to need sorely before this parley is over.'

They had fought a few preliminary bouts already before the Christmas festival, measuring each other with passes and ripostes ever since Llewelyn had ridden back into Aber with his bodyguard in November, and the empty seats below the fire had filled again with the lean, wiry lancers and bowmen of his household army. They came home in high feather, and the bards paid them due tribute. Even to de Breos's English eyes the victory the Prince had won in Kerry showed as greater by far than could be measured by the small ground of the commote for which it had been fought. It was the first setback to de Burgh's steadily advancing personal power, and no doubt it had duly impressed King Henry, who was not altogether whole-hearted in his love for his justiciar. There were profound possibilities of mischief and disunity there.

Delays were always methodical with Llewelyn, whose native impulses were for passion and hate; if he had learned to control both, it was the interests of Wales that had schooled him, and his achievement of patience and subtlety

41

was a prodigy against his nature. Love can do the impossible, even tame barbaric princes to caution, cunning and humility; and Llewelyn, Prince of Aberffraw and Lord of Snowdon, contained within his great, lean, violent body enormous resources and reservoirs of love, for Gwynedd, for that larger vision of Wales which de Breos saw sometimes reflected in his expressive eyes, for his son who was to inherit Gwynedd and complete the creation of Wales, for every oak and whipcord clansman who followed him unquestioningly. And above all, for that grave, quiet woman who sat erect and still at the table, intent on her husband's counsels as other women on their embroidery frames.

Yes, for their sakes, Llewelyn could evade and postpone when he chose. If he had let November and December slip away without formulating his terms, it was only to secure the ground under his feet, to establish his position with the King and ensure that he should be able to press his demands with every prospect of success. Henry had already set up the Princess again in her manors of Condover and Rothley, those two favours he was for ever snatching away and giving back as his mood changed. The indications were hopeful for Llewelyn's plans, and ominous enough for his victim. Yet the King was his only appeal; and of a weapon as double-edged and pliable as Henry not even a master-swordsman could ever be quite sure.

'Two thousand pounds is a deal of money, my lord,' said de Breos carefully, playing with the half-empty cup he dangled in his fingers.

'So I said to the King's envoys, but they would not lower their price. And could I ask less for a de Breos than I was paying for a half-built castle?' The hawk-face was solemn, but the far-sighted eyes in their fine nets of wrinkles were laughing.

'But consider, my lord, that whatever terms we agree between us are still subject to the King's sanction. Might it not be better, if only for the form of things, to abate a little and avoid so exact a parallel?'

'Abate?' said Llewelyn, suddenly leaning forward in his

chair and flattening both hands with a loud, confident clap upon the table. 'When I dance a measure with the King's envoys I can speak their roundabout language as well as any man living, and to them, for the royal record, it may be expedient to use the forms laid down. But here between us two let us have plain truth. His Majesty may take comfort in recording the campaign in Kerry as ended by negotiation, but never doubt for all that he knows, as I know, that Kerry was a war lost and won, and I won it. If I pleased I could extort from you a profit above what I am paying out to him to save his face. If I don't do it you may take it it's because I never set out to make gain out of this issue. The war was none of my seeking, why should I pay for it?'

'By the same token I might complain too, for God knows I never sought it, either.'

'And have had nothing but ill-luck out of it, I grant you. But that's the fortune of war, and I did not cast the lots. I might as easily have been in your hold now at Brecon, parleying for my liberty as you for yours.'

'Should I ever have that happiness,' said de Breos, looking up from his play with a sudden glittering grin, 'I promise you I'll exert myself to entertain you as royally as I have been entertained.'

'You're very civil. And I should hope to bear my confinement with as good a heart as you have done. And that's no light compliment. I wish every man as high a spirit in captivity. While your father lived I hardly knew you, my lord, but now that we've been thrown together I tell you to your face, I like what I see.'

The dangling cup had stopped swinging between the long fingers, it hung still, only the liquor within it trembling. The smiling face froze for an instant, the colour ebbing beneath the fading gold of its summer tan. Joan made a sudden sharp movement of her arm upon the table, and set the quill rocking in the ink-horn. But Llewelyn had continued warmly, his voice riding heedlessly over the moment of constraint.

'I like you, and I'll deal with you honestly. If you have any

43

thought of making use of the King to hold up this agreement by refusing his approval, be wise and put it out of mind. If I extorted twice the sum from you, he would still sanction it. His Majesty received a reverse in Kerry that has made him value my quiescence dearly, and to have good relations with me – at least until he feels his chances of success stand higher – he'll sacrifice you without a qualm.'

'But you, I think,' said de Breos, recovering his assurance and his sparkle, 'are equally anxious to stand well with him for the time being. De Burgh is still to be reckoned with.'

'He is.' Llewelyn's voice was grim. 'Well I know it. And the best protection I have against him for me and mine is a master who cannot quite love him, if he could but find an alternative to him. I need King Henry and he needs me. He needs me contented, and I need him reassured, and on those terms why should we not do honest business together? But his need is the sharper, as you must know if you know this new design he has of sending one more expedition into France. He is buying my quietness, and he shall have it. No man of mine shall step over the border while his back is turned; I have enough to do here making safe my own borders. You will do well to go along with me and take what terms you can get, the King will not lift a finger for you.'

De Breos took that silently, frowning over his linked hands. The light from the candles glowed in the stones of his rings. His wife had sent him a train of pack-horses laden with clothes and comforts from Brecon as soon as she received word of his captivity, and loving letters with them. He had no need of borrowed clothes now, and his own finery left David's far in the shade. A mistake, perhaps, he thought acidly, to be too magnificent if you are a prisoner, it tends to put up your price. He cast one quick glance at the Princess, erect and regal against the rough dark panelling of the wall. Her hair was dressed in two great coiled plaits springing from above the narrow golden diadem, and ending in a loose, shining tress on either side her fair face. Jewels only made her pallor radiant, sharp and thin as a flame; but no flame ever burned so steadily.

'Well, it appears I have no choice but to pay,' said de Breos at last.

'Unless you purpose to remain a prisoner here, it seems your only course.'

'I hardly think captivity would agree with my lord de Breos for ever,' said Joan, turning her head to look at him with the shadow of a smile.

'Madam, in your house I swear I should never complain, but I doubt I should soon outwear my welcome. Very well, I agree. Let it be drawn so.'

'There's a matter of an instalment due from me this coming Easter,' said Llewelyn. 'A mere two hundred and fifty marks. It could very well be discharged without leaving England.'

'It shall be. And what more? I see there are more provisions in your draft.'

The hand that had drawn it was Joan's. He should have been prepared for that, yet it had confounded him. She was in all her husband's counsels, his right hand wherever he himself could not be, his best envoy and diplomat; he had brought this to her as he brought everything. Perhaps she had even advised; there was no telling from her expression: she sat neutral and withdrawn, only the deep, intelligent eyes moving intently from face to face as they fought out an encounter which was already as surely lost and won as the campaign in Kerry.

'Yes, there are more. I desire, my lord, an undertaking from you that you will never again appear in arms against me.'

'It seems to me,' said de Breos with a wry smile, 'that you are trying to rewrite history. In how many years out of the last fifty has there not been a de Breos in arms against Gwynedd? And what is my answer to be when King Henry summons the march of arms next time?'

'You must answer him as God gives you wit. My demand stands. Moreover, I do not think you are ill-disposed to it, if truth be told. There have been times when de Breos and

Gwynedd have been allies.'

'There have, for pure respite between the ages of fighting each other. Well, and what else? You have me interested now. What's still to come?'

'A closer alliance between us two. I want to secure my borders, I want you at least taken out of the tale of my enemies. My lord, I have a son, and you have four daughters. I desire that you will give your daughter Isabella to my son David in marriage –'

'My lord, this is unexpected!' cried de Breos, wide-eyed.

'– with the lordship and castle of Builth as her dowry.'

'Ah! Now we have it! Builth is the plum. A good, solid mid-Welsh rock, full in the path of the justiciar's advance northwards.'

'There are advantages,' said Llewelyn, 'for you as for me. And the child would be in good fosterage here. I mean earnestly to enjoy a closer association with you, if you will join me. And I am offering your girl a royal match, and a good, fair, gallant lad to husband. That's but to praise my own, but praise him I must, for he's all I've claimed for him, and so any man in north Wales will tell you.'

Any man but one, thought de Breos, glancing from Llewelyn's glowing, eloquent face to the shut countenance of the Princess, in whose deep eyes a sudden unclouded tenderness burned for a moment at mention of her son. That other prisoner, the turbulent young man kicking his angry heels in the castle of Degannwy, would have used very different words to describe his half-brother, though he would find no one else of his opinion, or none openly willing to affirm it. Griffith and David, each of them brought out the devil in the other, oil and water were not more irreconcilable. Between them they might yet destroy everything Llewelyn had built up.

But the builders never recognise the destroyers treading hard on their heels. If they did they would drop their tools and sit down in the sun.

'Well?' said Llewelyn. 'What do you say?'

'What can I say? I am as sensible as you of the advantages, and David is very well, I could ask no better for Isabella. But remember I have four of them to set up in marriage, and Builth is a great portion.'

'So is Gwynedd, my lord. I take it to be the greater of the two.'

'And both will be yours, my lord, if I agree to your terms.'

There was no denying that, and Llewelyn did not try. They measured each other eye to eye for a moment, and then they broke into delighted laughter. The woman sat forgotten, watching them with a small, hollow smile. She took up the pen, and delicately re-shaped its point with the little knife that lay beside the ink-horn. They would be needing it soon. No doubt Ednyfed Fychan was already waiting for the summons, and wondering what took them so long.

'God He knows, my lord, what trammels we're spreading for our children. Your daughter is my stepmother, and now your son's to become my son-in-law. What does that make us two to each other? But so be it, we'll venture it. She shall bring you Builth, and you shall have your pledge of me. Your terms are accepted, my lord,' said de Breos, and held out his hand to seal the bargain.

On a frosty February morning when the fringes of the sea along the salt flats by Aber were laced with snow along the tide-line, an escort of knights from Brecon rode in from the direction of Bangor to convoy their master home in state. They came with ceremony, and were received ceremoniously. Whatever the mean circumstances of de Breos's arrival in Aber, his departure was designed to wipe them out of mind.

The escort lay overnight at Llewelyn's court, and was entertained royally. Old Einion extemporised interminably on the valour, fame and prowess of the distinguished guest, and lamented his going.

'God's life!' said de Breos, listening to Harry's breathless translation, which was but a pale version of the florid original.

47

'One would think it was a great feat of arms to be knocked off a horse by a half-grown boy leaping out of a tree. I wish he had let his imagination soar the first evening I came here, I should have been in a better conceit of myself.'

'He's on the Prince now,' reported Harry, frantic to keep up with the chronicle. 'He's singing Cynddelw's song about the battle on the Alun, when our lord was a boy.'

'Ah, I thought we should not be long in reaching Prince Llewelyn. What does he say of him? Translate!'

'He says: "The Alun ran red with the blood of his foes that day. So perish all who injure or affront the bold darling of fortune, the great Lord Llewelyn." '

'To which all good Welshmen must cry: "Amen." But I am not Welsh, I may hold my peace.' And by God, I'd better, he thought, stiffening his throat against the too easily rising words. I've drunk more than enough, it would be folly to blurt out something fatal now, when I'm all but free. If this is freedom to which I go!

'You must be very happy to-night,' said Harry, leaning confidently on the arm of his friend's chair.

'Happy?' The note of surprise was so light that it did not strike him how strangely it came from a man just released from prison. 'To be going home? Ay, very happy!' And indeed he was laughing, and if there was irony in the laughter it passed the boy by.

And this must be the end of it, he thought, watching that formidable splendour glitter and glow at the centre of the royal table. I must go back to my wife and children and be content to be very happy. In any case, what more can there be now for a man who's known what I've known? It should be possible to live again without it somehow. I have a good reputation for keeping a high heart in deprivation and captivity. Let's see how well I deserve it. And what else I deserve, God spare me! So He may, if this be truly the end, but there is a point beyond which one should not tempt Him.

'And when you come to us again,' pursued Harry blithely, 'it will be as an honoured guest.'

'Ay, so it will. And there'll be no occasion then for you to

48

blush for me, even in secret.' It was the first time he had ever made reference to that incident, which seemed to have slipped out of the boy's recollection as lightly, and left as little mark, as the occasional blows he got from his brothers. He half wished the words back even now; one should never ask for forgiveness, but always charm it out of people unawares; very few have the hardihood to wrest it back, once taken. But he need not have troubled, for Harry had not even marked the allusion.

'And you'll be coming to celebrate a match that makes you closer kin to us.'

'True, Harry, a match very near to my heart.' He heard the double meaning in his own words and was aghast. Was this how he willed that necessary ending? William, my friend, draw in your horns, he warned himself sternly. It was over. But he felt how his own heart stood out against him, and would promise nothing.

'Don't you think my lord, that there was a purpose behind it when I was the cause of your coming here? For you see how well everything turns out. And later, perhaps in the autumn, the Prince intends to send David to court, and have the King recognise him as heir to Gwynedd. The Welsh lords have acknowledged him, and the Pope, and the King's government, too, but he has to make a state visit and do formal homage for all the lands that will be his —'

'I know it,' said de Breos, letting the mead pass him by on this round. 'I shall have the honour of being among his sponsors.'

'— and Owen will attend him on the visit. And I — I mean to come with them, if I can get my way.'

'You?' said de Breos, surprised. He looked sharply at the brown, intent face, caught the green glitter of the eyes, and understand. 'Still on that cast! And what would you gain, Harry, even if you found your ancient enemy at court? Under the King's eye you'd be safe from him as he from you, but what folly to parade your name and your face before him and alert him to the threat untimely!'

'Untimely?' said the boy, burning up like a goaded fire.

'I'm nearly of age, by then I shall be fully a man.'

'You will be fourteen years old, and Welsh law will say you are a man, and may no longer be beaten by any of your many parents, however well you may earn it – ay, I know! But there's more than that to manhood, and not least the learning of a sound and sensible humility. Judgement and wisdom are not come by magically on your fourteenth birthday, and you'll have grave need of both before you match swords or wits with Parfois. It is not brave or noble to provoke formidable men lightly, Harry, it is only rash and presumptuous.'

Words, he had once said over this same table, have a way of coming full circle into the wind and hitting in the face the fool who thinks he aimed them. These beat up into his face like spray, stinging his senses. Take them to heart, he warned himself urgently, while there's time. Rash and presumptuous you are, but draw back from this coil now, and leave the Prince of Gwynedd in peace.

'I purpose to do nothing lightly,' Harry was protesting, wild to have his encouragement and good-will. 'I want only to see the Lord of Parfois in his own place, to watch him and get to know his mind. How else can I ever hope to match him? Do you think I've waited so long and cannot wait a little while now to have my growth and my strength? He need not even know who I am, I shall be no more than one of David's pages, and my name he'll never hear.'

'He'll never need to hear it. Your face, they tell me, is close enough to your father's image to sign you his.'

Harry received the check with such dismay that it was plain he had not considered this possibility, but he rallied doggedly: 'In fourteen years he may have forgotten my father.'

'That, Harry, you do not believe. I've lived but distantly with your kin here, but I know this, not one of those who ever had to do with him seems to forget your father. For better or worse he was, it seems, a most memorable man. And his likeness is graven there, as you yourself told me, in the stones of his own church. No, be wise in time, Harry, let the past be.

50

The man is old, death will be reaching for him soon without you to nudge her.'

'His death belongs to me,' said Harry, suddenly so low and so passionately that the question of how he thought of that lost father of his seemed to be finally and irrevocably answered. 'I'll not give him up.'

'Harry, Harry, I see you are a Welshman by conviction, after all. You and your *galanas*! How many fine young men have wasted their lives pursuing these endless blood-feuds? You be wiser, and live to do more for the earth than manure it with your blood. Your father would praise you for it, if he was the man I take him to have been. Stand to your rights when you must, and against your fair match. But this man is perilous.'

His eyes came back, whether he would or no, to the raised chair at the centre of the royal table. The circlet of red gold in Llewelyn's still dark and lustrous hair burned like a ring of fire in the torchlight, and the face beneath the diadem was molten bronze, quick with movement and passion and energy. He had cast off his light cloak, and unlaced the cotte and shirt from a throat like the strong brown bole of a tree. The short necklace of polished amber stones throbbed and strained to his gigantic laughter.

'Have to do with men if you will, but spare to meddle with demons. Leave the lion and the leopard alone, Harry. They kill!'

In the morning the knights of Brecon rode out from Aber towards the Conway, with William de Breos at their head, and the train of his servants and pack-horses trampling off the hoar-frost for a quarter of a mile behind him.

The women watched them go from the narrow window of the Princess's apartment.

'A happy issue,' said Gilleis, glancing contentedly after them along the track between the rimy fields. 'Builth gained, and a powerful ally bound to David's cause. Harry fetched home a dear prize in his first battle.'

Joan said nothing at all, but she stood gazing until the

51

scarlet and gold of the flying cloak faded into a bright pin-prick against the hazy distance, and even the last infinitesimal point of light vanished in the glitter of the mist-wreathed sun.

The Prince's favourite Cistercian house of Aberconway complained of want of barn-space at its grange of Nanhwynain that autumn, and insufficient sheep-folds in its high pastures under Snowdon. Llewelyn sent his best mason, Adam Boteler, to estimate the need, and promised labour and materials for the work; and within a week Adam came home to report that there was a hard month's work on the barns alone if the brothers were to have all they wanted, and the prior, encouraged by his lord's complacency, had promptly indented for an extension to the living-quarters as well.

'I'll take a dozen or so of my own men down there this coming week,' he said, tramping into Llewelyn's presence, steamy from his ride, a fine tall man in his middle forties, flaxen-haired still but for the strands on his forehead that had bleached into white without ever being tarnished with grey. 'The rest of the labour I need I can raise there. God knows they'll need but little skill to heft rough-cut stones into place. I wish, my lord, you'd find me something to build with a thought more craft in it than sheep-folds. How's that lad going to learn his trade without practice? He's too easily wearied of work as it is, he'd liefer be off after hounds with Prince David, and small blame to him for that, but learn he must, if he's ever going to earn his way in the world. At Nanhwynain likely I'll be better able to keep my weather eye on him.'

'He's young yet,' said Llewelyn, stretching lazily with his feet spread out to the fire between the central columns of the hall. He had come in from hunting not an hour previously, well content after a brisk day, and the warmth of the room was on him like a soft, heavy cloud. 'Let him run wild a little longer.'

'He's young when it's work in the wind,' said Adam, grinning, 'but he's the first to lay claim to being a man if it's fighting or tilting, or any such play. He's game, that I will say, like his father before him, and better able to fend for himself in a fight. Harry was never any great man of his weapons. But game! I've seen him take such knocks, from lads double his size – and the little one's own son to him there. He got a fall the other day I thought would cool his ardour, but he sneezed it off as though his mother had cuffed him.'

He sat back with a sigh and a smile, the big, deft hands that had cut stone for thirty years slack between his thighs. The two Harries elbowed each other in and out of his re-membering eyes and dreaming voice. The one had fastened insistent hands on his life the minute the other had loosed it, dying.

'He'll not be best pleased if you take him with you to Nanhwynain,' said Llewelyn, yawning. 'He's set his heart on going with David to London.'

'My lord, you've not promised him anything?' asked Adam, alarmed. The Prince might now and then slide side-wise out of some obligation to the English of which he could not be more directly rid, when a new and urgent heat burned old agreements out of mind; but he would never break his word once given to the boy.

'No, faith, but he may have got round Owen. David was all for refusing him out of hand, but, as fast as David denies, Owen's prone to grant. He growls, but Harry has him round his finger. For my part I shall be glad if you take the child away with you. But it's for you and his mother to fend for him as you think best.'

'I think best he should settle to his craft in earnest,' said Adam grimly, 'and I'll take my oath his mother will think as I do. You know, my lord, why he's so set on going to court? He has that wild-goose mind of his fixed fast on the Lord of Parfois. He was prowling in ambush for him in Kerry – that we got out of him chance-come, one night when he dreamed – and you may wager he's after him now at court, having missed him there.'

'Then it shows a proper spirit in him,' said Llewelyn approvingly, 'though I grant you he's over-young for the venture yet. I never thought of it myself. I thought he was just mad curious to see the world, like all boys.'

'So with your leave I'll have him away with me into Nanhwynain, and let him sweat the valour out of him cutting stone.' Adam rose and hitched at his chausses, stamping off the dust of travel a little stiffly. 'Gilleis will sleep more easily, knowing he's with me, than thinking of him strutting in front of Isambard at Westminster with that bodkin of a sword of his.'

'And faith, so will I, for I had thought once to have put the old wolf out of his reach long before this, if Wales had not kept my hands full and over-full. But Talvace was his blood, not mine. And mark me, even if you take him with you now,' said Llewelyn, prophesying with certainty, 'it's but to put off the day, for in the end go he will, I've seen it in him more than a year now. There's not a one of you who knew his father, Adam, not one, loves him as does this child who never knew him. He's had him from our mouths so often and so long, he's lived by him like holy writ, and maybe hated him a little while he was loving him, too, for being so far beyond all matching – I wonder did we do right to make him so fixed and fond?'

'Ah, he's taken no harm. When he thinks it gnaws him hard, but how often does he leave himself energy to think? As healthy a young animal as ever tired himself out running for love of it. He'd rather climb rocks than cut them, that's certain. We shall have enough tantrums before he reconciles himself, but his mother'll sort him. I'll go and find her,' said Adam, his blue eyes gentle, and tramped away to his own lodging in search of his wife.

Gilleis heard him out with a flushed face and a hot, indignant stare. The large black eyes in her rose-and-white face dilated and glowed.

'The deceitful rogue! Not one word has he said to me about it. And I suppose he was going to confront me with it the day they mustered, armed with the Prince's promise, was he?

54

I was to have no say in the matter! But we'll have a surprise for Master Harry when he deigns to come home from his gallivantings.'

So Harry, bursting in cheerfully an hour later bruised and tumbled from wrestling with his fellows, half a swart early apple in his fist and half in his cheek, walked into a hotter welcome than he had bargained for, and was put to a hasty review of his recent undiscovered sins to account for his mother's irate face and challenging eye. Hopefully he selected the most venial, and advanced contrition like one proffering flowers.

'Is it the big pitcher? I know, Mother, I'm sorry I chipped the lip, it slipped out of my hand against the rim of the well. I meant to tell you, but I forgot.' That was no lie, and owning to it now, was no indiscretion, whatever the cause of her present frown, for she was bound to see the damage for herself the next time she went to draw water.

'Pitcher? Who's talking of pitchers? I've something else to say to you now, and you'll do well to listen. No, you'll not get round me like that. Let me go!'

He was already an inch or two taller than she, and strong enough to lift her in his arms. He had but to hug her tightly and she could not get free, but this time she warded off his embrace and held him at arm's-length, drawing back her hand to box his ears. He caught it by the wrist and shut a kiss into her palm. It was part of the game to parry her attacks, though they were about as formidable as the pouncings of a kitten earnestly at play.

'Harry, will you leave go of me! I'm not in fun, I tell you.' And indeed she was not, she fought him off fiercely and stood confronting him with flashing eyes. 'What's this I hear about your going as page to David on his visit to King Henry's court? Yes, you rogue, it's come to my ears, but not from you, dear, no! The last to hear of it from you would be your mother. It was all to be cut and dried before I knew word or hint of it, wasn't it?'

He took his hands from her, suddenly solemn, and stood looking from her to Adam and back again.

'I knew you wouldn't want to let me go,' he said honestly. 'I hoped I might persuade you, if the Prince gave his blessing. Where was the harm? David's my prince and my brother, why shouldn't I go with him? And think what a chance! David's great triumph, with all the English court to do him honour, and I'm not to be there? Oh, Mother, you wouldn't be so hard!'

'And the Lord of Parfois? He played no part in your plans, I suppose? Ah, you may well draw back, sir! I'm not so easily deceived.'

Harry did not argue with that, though he had often found her easy enough. She was very pretty in anger, and looked like a flushed young girl, but this was no time to tell her so. He cast an appealing look at Adam, who had often stood his ally when he had needed a man's support.

'No use, my friend,' said Adam, shaking his head. 'Even the Prince won't help you to your own way this time. You're coming with me to Nanhwynain to build the brothers their new barns, and that's your Michaelmas jaunt, Hal. Best come to terms with it.'

Harry dropped his hands and stood glaring. 'I won't go!' he flamed, backing a step to have them both in his eye and share his defiance between them.

'Will you not, sir? We shall see!' Gilleis drew a calming breath. 'Harry, it's time we had this out once for all. You've lived all your life with princes, and it's been small help to you in knowing what you are and which way you're to go, though God knows I've been grateful every day for their goodness to us all. But you're no prince, and no Welshman, and the sooner you own it the better for you. It's not for you to waste your time on blood feuds, it's no part of your duty to take vengeance on the Lord of Parfois. You forget these grand notions, and get to your real obligations. It's for you to learn your father's craft and grow up with your father's virtues, if you want to do him honour.'

'Honour! While the man who did him to death still lives and goes his gait in peace? There isn't a free man in Wales but would spit at me! And do you say this to me, Mother?

Haven't you spoken of vengeance often enough? Haven't you cursed Parfois many a time when you talked to me of my father?'

'God forgive me!' she said, paling. It was many years since she had let her bitterness break out to the child. How long was that memory of his that called her witness now for his own resolute hate? 'If I did, I was at fault. Vengeance is God's business, not yours.'

'And may it not be both? Doesn't God need instruments to His hand? Oh, Mother, don't keep me back, not you! He was twenty-nine years old, he had marvels still in him – you told me –'

'And so might you have in his stead,' urged Adam, 'if you would but apply yourself. You have a part of his gift. Use it for him, do his work.'

'But I'm not my father! I've work of my own to do, and the first thing I must turn my hand to is Ralf Isambard. If he dies in his bed, I'm no man and never can be. The debt's mine, not yours. Not even yours, Mother – mine! You can't ask me to leave it unpaid.'

'There are better ways of honouring your father's memory,' said Adam patiently. 'Master his art, and try to outdo him if you can, and he'll be prouder of you than of all the fighting men in arms. We're not nobles, lad, to meddle with life and death, we're craftsmen. It's only by long chance and royal charity you grew up in a prince's bed, and it's time you faced your own estate.'

'My father was born noble,' blazed Harry. 'Many a time you've told me so.'

'And the sequel, too. He left his nobility and chose to be a craftsman. That's your father himself pointing you your way.'

'But my choice need not be his. I'm his son, not his shadow. Do you think I don't remember all you told me of him? He judged and acted like a lord, even when he was denying his birth. He treated his craft as his barony. Yes, and died for it, for his rights and his pledged word, and what prince could do more?'

He was shouting furiously and straddling defiantly as if he stood over his father's body and warned them off from defacing it. They cast one startled glance at each other, acknowledging with honest fear the justice of his argument and the shrewdness of his understanding. It seemed they had reached the point where there was only one answer to make to him, and that satisfying to nobody.

'Be that as it may,' said Gilleis, reflecting back her son's glare, 'you'll do as you're told, and no more nonsense. You're not going to London, that's the end of it. You'll go with Adam, and you'll work faithfully at whatever he bids you do, or I hope he'll make you rue it.'

She melted then, quivering, and reached a hand to stroke away a bead of dried blood from one of the minor grazes he had got in his second fall. 'Oh, Harry,' she said, laughing through starting tears, 'you to go bearding a man like Isambard, and you can't even hold your own yet with Meurig!'

He flung off her hand furiously. 'I won't go! I won't!' he shouted, and lunged half-blindly at the door.

Adam moved with large, tolerant strides between, caught him by the arm, and with the other big, hard hand clouted his cheek lightly and turned him back into the room. It was no use struggling; Harry froze into stillness and kept his dignity. Adam could have held him one-handed and beaten him into submission without an effort, yet Harry could not remember a single occasion in his life when those capable hands had struck him anything harder than the lightest of token blows. Talvace's son, like his father before him, was everlastingly safe from any violence at Adam Boteler's hands, whatever the provocation he offered.

'Will you not?' said Adam good-humouredly, and stood him squarely before him and shook him sharply just once. 'You'll come, Hal, and you'll work, never doubt it. What more you'll do hereafter we'll wait and see, and I dare say there'll be many a surprise for all of us. But as yet you're not your own master, better make up your mind to that.'

Harry cast one brief, measuring look at him, and averted

his eyes, but the tensed muscles relaxed a little under Adam's palms.

'And now you'll submit yourself to your mother and kiss her hand, like a good son, and let's have no more shouting and no more: "I won't!" '

Harry went into her arms stiffly, but at the touch of her he hugged her passionately, and then tore himself loose and ran from the room, as angry with himself as with her.

She looked after him and her face was quick with anxiety and apprehension, but she said nothing more then. Only at night, lying still beside her husband in the September darkness and chill, and feeling him wakeful and aware, she stirred suddenly and said in a whisper: 'Adam, he'll go. He will go. Like Harry. He'll leave me and go off after a point of honour, and I shall have no way of stopping him.'

'Hush, now!' said Adam, laying his arm over her and drawing her to him. 'You know you wouldn't have had the one do any other than the thing he did, and there's a piece of you fighting on the boy's side even now. But at least we'll hold him fast till he's a grown man. And think, Isambard is fully five and sixty years old by this, and his span running out. Leave time alone to take care of him, and he'll be in his grave before the lad escapes us to go looking for him.'

'Yes,' she said eagerly, clinging to him, 'he's old, that's true, he's old. Oh, Adam, if I lost Harry!'

She used the name as he did, for a single image that was sometimes the father and sometimes the son, and always loved out of all measure.

'You shan't lose him,' he said into the cool cascade of her hair. 'Never fear! Go to sleep, love, and leave fretting.'

He held her until she slept in his arms, the slight weight cradled against his heart. The feel of her littleness moved him achingly, and the clinging of her hands was a painful sweetness, for he knew that what they embraced in him was still the frail image, the residue that Harry Talvace had left there, the print of years of love and brotherhood. Often in the early nights of their marriage she had stirred out of her sleep and reached out to him, calling him by Harry's name.

And what right had he to resent that or any other mark of his subservience, he who had taken her to himself to establish his lifelong claim to both the Harries, the living and the dead?

But fourteen years is a long, long time for two people to walk delicately together, trusting and sparing each other and living by the same secret light. And now, holding her gently on his breast and feeling the soft cadences of her breath in the hollow of his throat, he knew that they had something there between them that was more than tenderness and better than forbearance. He felt it to be love; he did not question for whom.

CHAPTER THREE

Aber: *Easter* 1230

Adam wrote from Nanhwynain at the beginning of April, in the clerkly hand he had learned long ago at Shrewsbury Abbey and never forgotten:

'All goes well here and the work well forward, by reason of the early end to the frosts. The walls unbedded of their furze and well set, and the brothers well content with their barns, so your Grace shall be sure of grateful prayers. With the boy I am well pleased since we came back here. He takes well enough to the craft here, where he has not so many sports to be enjoyed. He has not his father's skill in carving, but does moderate well, and has a fine eye for line and proportion, and a will to perfection, and all in all as good a lad as ever stepped when he puts his mind to it, and nothing grudging in him. With your Grace's leave I purpose to remain here through the Easter feast, the weather continuing so fair for building, and the brothers being so urgent for possession of the enlargement to their house. My prayers shall not be wanting for your Grace's health and prosperity, and for the blessing of God on the union so soon to crown your Grace's happiness.'

Llewelyn replied, with Easter only a few days away:

'Since Harry has satisfied you, as I well knew he could if he had a mind to it, he has surely earned a holiday. Let him come home for the feast, and he'll work with a better heart when we send him back to you. My lord de Breos has forsook the King's court for mine on this occasion, the King being in any case set on proceeding to Portsmouth to embark for France, and his lordship asks particularly after the boy, who is a fixed favourite with him. It is surely a Christian act to

61

content them both, so let him come.'

And Harry came, armed for the journey with Adam's reluctant permission and the Prior's blessing. He had been resigned to spending a frugal Easter with the brothers and watching dutifully through the vigils of Good Friday, but all his devout thoughts took wing wildly, like startled birds, when the Prince's welcome command was cast among them. By the time he was three miles up the valley he had pocketed his cap and was galloping like a child let out of school, and singing as he rode. One holiday now, and soon another for David's wedding, and the budding world so beautiful and diverse!

He had only begun to discover its real subtleties when he began to carve them. To have made a leaf is truly to have seen a leaf for the first time. What manifold delights God must know! And to have made man! Such a piece of work, for instance, as my lord de Breos, so express and wonderful in movement, so admirable in proportion and form. He thought again of the smooth, taut action of the muscles round that handsome mouth as it played its dazzling repertoire of smiles, from the first almost imperceptible quivering to the loud, gay, explosive laughter; and of the slow, beautiful raising of the arched eyelids as they opened on stunned dark eyes, that first dawn in the grass by the Mule. Masterly sculpture, far out of his reach; and yet these could be made again in stone, and even the secondary form would carry a deep satisfaction in it. He was beginning to love stone.

But the ride was long, and by the time he was half-way to Aber his fingers had lost the sense of creation, and he thought no more of stone. There were other ways of looking at that admirable engine of flesh and blood and bone, other ways of delighting in it. Better have it articulated and active and aware of itself than fixed and final, however beautiful. The arms to wrestle and embrace, the hands to hold and direct weapons, the legs to dance and grip a horse. Better just once to see de Breos ride at a gallop than make ten stone copies of his and the horse's action; better but once to hear him shout with laughter than to draw, however perfectly, the mechanics

62

of his mirth.

Harry rode in at the gates of Aber enchanted with being and doing, and content to let others make.

The village outside the maenol was busy and populous, and the sunlight quivered over the fresh greens of the hills, uncurling with new bracken like the prodigious carved fronds that hold up the vaults of churches. Within the courtyard there was bustle and colour and energy everywhere, and about the kitchens frenzy. The stables boiled with horses, and there were new pavilions encrusted along the curtain wall to house the train of knights who had ridden in from Brecon. This time de Breos came with ceremony and impressively attended, and everywhere about the kennels and the mews his livery glittered.

It was Maundy Thursday, and they were just coming from Mass, the two magnificent dark men together; de Breos's hand was familiarly on Llewelyn's shoulder, and the matched dozens of their followings streamed after them. The Princess walked on de Breos's other side, silent and tall and slender in blue and white. She looked like an opening flower, she who had raised five children and weathered twenty-five years of care and intrigue and vigilance. She walked with her eyes fixed ahead, faintly smiling as the velvet of her sleeve brushed the brocade of his, and the dew and glow of the spring was on her like a shaft of sunlight on the hills.

Harry's heart liquefied with love at sight of her. He slid hastily from the saddle and ran to meet them, falling on his knee at the Prince's feet.

'Ah, my little archer!' cried de Breos. 'I missed you at the gate to see me come.'

Llewelyn took him up and kissed him heartily.

'Not so little now. He's grown like a bean in a wet summer, this year and more since you've seen him. Rising fifteen, and a voice on him like a young bull, as you'll find soon enough.'

De Breos marked with a secret, sympathetic convulsion of his own vitals the tension of delight that transfixed the slender young body as Joan embraced it in her turn.

'Your mother will be happy, Harry. We've missed you.

63

Well, my lord, do you find him much changed?'

She held him off by the arm to be admired, a tall, slim fifteen-year-old just beginning to put on the proportions and the form of manhood. Large and deft of foot and hand, but not yet sure of his body, he moved with the darting, tentative, unfinished motions of young animals. The brows above the green eyes were level and black, and straight as his wide, resolute mouth. Eyes and mouth smiled together for pleasure in the April world and his holiday, and the presence of people who contained for him much of the charm of living. He coloured easily, but with excitement and delight, not with shyness.

'A long leap nearer what he was always meant to be,' said de Breos, throwing about the boy's shoulders the arm that had lain so gracefully upon Llewelyn's only a moment ago. 'Not otherwise changed, I thank God! When first I met him he was already too much of a man for me. And what have you been doing, Harry, all this while since last I saw you? Have you brought home prisoner any more crushed adversaries?'

'There have been no wars since Kerry,' said Harry practically.

'What, not even between cantrefs?'

'No, my lord. Gwynedd does no raiding now, you're living in the past.'

'I wish you would tell my steward, he suffers from a strange dream that certain enterprising Welshmen cross the border now and then and prick out a few head of cattle for themselves. And how have you fared with your prize of war? You have the length of leg for him now.'

'Nobly, my lord,' cried Harry, glowing, and drew breath to praise his chestnut horse; but Joan laid her hand on his arm and reminded him gently: 'Your mother's waiting, Harry.'

'Madam, I'll go to her. My lord, with your leave! Will you not come to the stables afterwards, and see for yourself how I have used him? I groom him myself, he stands like stone for me, but he plays the devil with the stable-boys.'

'I'll come, gladly,' said de Breos, laughing to see the boy withdraw with first an eager leap towards his mother, and then a reluctant moment of walking backwards, still with his eyes on them. He turned at last, with a final inclination of his head, and fled at a headlong run towards the Princess's apartments, where at this hour Gilleis was sure to be.

He burst in upon her at her trestle table, busy cutting out the narrow, intricate sleeves of a new gown for the Princess, and flung himself into her arms so impetuously that he all but impaled himself on her long scissors. She held them away from him and let them clatter from her hand upon the table, and hugged him and laughed and wept over him. He took that as no more than his due, and stayed only long enough to pour out for her all the news of himself and Adam before he was off again to the buttery to coax food out of the maids for his perpetual hunger, and then to the stables to see his favourite properly cared for. There de Breos came to him as he had promised, and leaned in the doorway to watch the grooming, careless of his scarlet and gold finery.

'You have him in fine fettle. I see he fell into good hands.' He patted the glossy neck, and stroked with the tips of long, sensitive fingers the white diamond on the dark red brow.

'Harry,' he said, low-voiced, 'I have an errand for you, if you are pleased to be my confidant in a particular secret.'

'Gladly!' said Harry, flattered. 'What is it you want me to do?'

'A small thing and easy for you. I have a design to make a present to the Prince when David marries my girl. I want to give him two good litters of my own hounds, five couple that I bred out of my best deerhound bitches by an Arabian sire Gloucester has from the East. They make the best and swiftest van chasseours that ever I met with. I've known them bring down the hart themselves, and leave no work for the parfy-tours. But I have a childish fancy to keep my gift a secret, and bring the hounds here privily to astonish the Prince when the wedding-day comes. And that's impossible unless I have the Princess's help.'

'She'll give it gladly,' said Harry, straightening up for a moment to wriggle out of his cotte. He emerged ruffled and flushed to ask: 'Does she know what you intend?'

'Not yet. For I never see her but the Prince is with us. I would have you tell her for me, Harry, some time when there's no one else by, for you're privileged. Ask her of her grace to make some occasion when we can speak of this together, and see how it is to be done. If she'll give me the word when the time is right we can whip the hounds into the kennels and have them ready for him, and no one the wiser.'

'I'll speak to her this very evening,' said Harry willingly. 'I never miss going to say good night to her after she leaves the hall.'

'That's my true heart! But mind, not a word to any other. One whisper is enough in such a warren as this, and every kitchen-boy knows it within a day.'

'Trust me! If it reaches any but the three of us until the day comes you may take my Barbarossa back again.'

'That's a pledge indeed! And you'll be her messenger back to me? It will need but half an hour together, and the plot is laid.'

'I'll be her messenger.'

'You shall have a puppy for yourself from the next litter,' said de Breos warmly, and reached an imperious hand over the chestnut's arched neck. 'Give me a cloth, Harry, I can keep my hands from him no longer.'

They finished the grooming together, in strong content with each other, and boy-like dismayed at the powerful scent of the stables that clung to de Breos's brocade by the end of it. 'No matter,' said he, shrugging it off with bravado, 'my wife's not here to scold.'

In the clamour and brilliance of the hall that night de Breos leaned on Llewelyn's arm, and they drank cup for cup, laughing together, as that day they did all things together, every word and gesture an earnest of their new amity.

'I'd give this ring,' said de Breos, 'to have de Burgh walk in at that door now and see us so fond.'

'I doubt the sight would give him no pleasure,' said Llewelyn.

'But his face would afford me entertainment for a month

after. I wish our good justiciar no harm, but one reverse will do him none, and it's not only among the Welsh that this union will be seen as a check to a power that was growing too insolent. It was no part of my designs to fall into your hands and set this arrow flying, my lord, but I'm as willing as you now to see it close its course with a hit. It's the mead, no doubt,' he said, laughing, 'but I begin to be glad your little archer brought me down at the ford of the Mule. Faith, I'm in such spirits I begin to feel I've got the best of the bargain.'

The faint sounds of music from the hall drifted on the darkness, curling past the windows of the tower upon a wandering wind. Joan stood with her back to the room, the cloak of her brown hair about her, listening to the light footsteps moving about the bed.

'You need not wait, Gilleis,' she said without turning her head. 'I'm tired, I shall sleep early. You go to your bed, too.'

'After so many late nights,' owned Gilleis, smiling as she turned down the covers, 'I shan't be sorry to lie longer, and nor will you, madam, I dare say. Though I won't say we're so pleased to lie alone. I miss Adam when he stays so long away. Where will the Prince sleep to-night? He won't remain at Degannwy?'

'No, he'll ride back to Aberconway and spend the night there, he has business with the Prior.'

She was taciturn to-night, her voice cool and distant even when she spoke. It still displeased her when Llewelyn turned in his abrupt way to show some tenderness to his elder son who was none of hers, and no doubt she resented it that he should steal one whole day and night from the feast to visit Griffith in his enforced retirement. Not that the Prince had ever wavered in his fixed determination that David alone should succeed him. No, it was a more irrational fear that made her so implacable against any acknowledgement of the relationship; fear of Welsh law that gave the bastard rights equal to his brother's, and of Welsh perversity that veered obstinately to him because his mother was a lady of Rhos and not the daughter of an English king, and because he had their

67

own impetuous and insubordinate temperament, and such a grievance as they loved.

'You should not mind that he is fond even of this stranger child of his,' said Gilleis in her gay and gentle voice, that could venture so far into territory forbidden to other women. 'It would be shame if he did not cherish his own. And well you know David has no rival with him. Hasn't he made sure and doubly sure David shall be his only heir?'

'He gave Griffith Meirionydd and Ardudwy once,' said Joan.

'And took them back from him fast enough when he found he plundered his own territories like an alien raider. And hasn't he kept him fast under lock and key since his threats against David grew too bold? You know he'll never suffer Gwynedd to fall into any hands but David's.'

Yes, she knew it. No one but David, close kin to the English king and strong in a title legitimate by English law as well as Welsh, could have any chance of holding the principality together and perpetuating what his father had created. Even if the Prince had loved the two half-brothers equally – and the wild, defiant elder, by his very likeness to his sire, alienated love as often as he attracted it – he would have staked the future on David. Wanting any other inducement, thought Gilleis, watching the tall, slender figure with an affectionate smile, he would have laid all his conquests and achievements in David's lap for his mother's sake.

'Don't grudge him a day,' she said, 'now David has Gwynedd and Builth and bride and all.'

'Did I seem to grudge it when he told me he was going?'

'No, bless you, you gave him your good word to take with him.'

And that in itself was remarkable, and Llewelyn had not failed to notice it. Gilleis had seen the quick, piercing look he had cast at his wife. Her only frowns, her only inimical silences, had to do with Griffith.

'Leave me now, Gilleis. But tell Harry to come and say good night to me at once, for I shall be sleeping soon.'

Gilleis kissed her hand and her cheek, and went to look for

Harry in the hall. It was still early, and with the Prince and his immediate train absent, the knights of Brecon, and the Welsh freemen, and the privileged men of the bodyguard had taken possession, and were dancing to pipe and harp and the clapping of hands. Harry came out to his mother flushed and breathless, to listen to her message where she could make her voice heard.

'And why don't you come and sleep the night with me, Hal, afterwards? With David and Owen both gone as far as Aberconway with the Prince, what merit is there in guarding an empty lodging?'

But she knew he would not; he cherished his privileges dearly. She sighed and laughed, and kissed him. 'There, then, run to the Princess.' And she twitched her cloak over her head and ran in her turn, for a soft, clinging rain had begun, hanging on the night air like heavy dew.

Joan was sitting at her mirror when Harry entered the room, as many a time lately he had seen her sit and gaze silently into her own face. It seemed to him that there was a special tenderness in her touch that night, and that speech came to her with difficulty, though when she spoke her voice was low and even as he had always known it.

'Harry, I recall that you asked a few days ago for an audience in private for my lord de Breos. In the matter of these marvellous hounds of his.'

'I've heard they're all he claims', said Harry eagerly, thinking he caught a faint note of irony in the beloved voice. 'I've heard tell of them from others besides my lord himself. It will be a princely gift.'

'I never doubted that,' she said with a shadowy smile. 'Well, it's yet early, and the opportunity offers, my lord de Breos may come to me now, since he's so urgent for secrecy. Let him have his child's pleasure of surprising the Prince, if he wants it so much. Go and bring him to me. But discreetly, remember he's on secret business. Bring him by the passage through the armoury, he will not know that way alone.'

'He's still in hall,' said Harry, springing up willingly. 'I'll go to him at once.'

'Then let him say his good nights, and seem to be going to his bed, so that no one will for look him back or wonder where he's bound. Since the game is his we must play it his way.'

'He makes all things play his way,' said Harry laughing. 'It's raining now, there'll be no one stirring.'

'That's well. And, Harry!'

'My lady?' He swung about, his hand already outstretched to the door.

'Not a word to anyone. We must keep his secret faithfully.'

'On my life!' said the boy fervently, and only half in jest, and ran down the staircase and back through the rain to slip unobserved into the hall.

The weather, the hour, the occasion, all were with him. Some of the elders had already withdrawn, and some of the knights, finding Welsh entertainment tried their endurance too far, had followed the old men's example. The men-at-arms and the servant girls, the brewers and the bakers and the huntsmen and the grooms had taken the music below the fire with them; and they, who had to be up and hard at work by dawn, would never prolong the night too far.

He looked for de Breos, but the lord of Brecon was not at the high table. He had already done his part perfectly in ignorance, and betaken himself to his own room. Harry found him half undressed, lying flat on his belly on his fur-draped bed, his chin on his fists, restlessly awake and fretted by his own company. He welcomed the boy gladly and boisterously, throwing an arm about him and drawing him close.

'My lord, I'm charged with a message to you. From the Princess Joan.'

De Breos was up in a moment, the fur coverlet swirling from his vehement spring. 'God bless you for a good lad, Harry!' His face was vivid in the lamplight, the eyes brilliant and solemn. 'What says the Princess Joan?'

'She says I am to take you to her.'

'Now? Ah, you brought me luck as always you bring it!' He was on his feet, light and quick as a cat, smoothing his black hair before the glass, stamping his feet into his soft leather

70

shoes. 'Give me my cotte, there, Harry! So, you'll make a good squire yet. There, am I presentable?'

He was far more than that, he glowed in the dim light, smiling into the boy's dazzled eyes, that only once, and for how short a time, had seen in him something less than perfection.

'Well, take me! We mustn't keep my lady waiting.'

They let themselves out into the soft, clinging rain, and de Breos surrendered himself to the boy's hands, and followed where he was led, by devious ways beyond the new pavilions to the passage behind the armoury, and so in darkness and blindness in the moonless night to the tower. All night thereafter Harry felt his fingers tingling from the grip of that long, vital hand as his friend trod trustingly on his heels.

They climbed the stairs softly. Joan was sitting in her high-backed chair, and as they entered she rose and came a few paces to meet them. The long braid of her hair hung to her waist, fair against the dark blue of her gown, and her face was pale and bright.

'Madam, here is my lord de Breos.'

'My lord,' she said, hardly louder than the whisper of the rain, 'you asked to see me.'

'Madam, that was my desire.'

'Come in, cousin, and welcome.'

To Harry she said, level and low: 'Go to bed now, child. Good night!' She kissed him. He had never felt in her lips such poignant sweetness, her touch had never been so lingeringly fond.

'Madam, good night! Good night, my lord!'

He slipped away down the stairs, his heart swelling with pride and pleasure, the confidant of his lady, the trusted friend of the lord of Brecon. The hall was still flickering with torchlight, but the music had ceased, and one by one the flames were burning down.

He ran through the rain to his own silent, empty room, but he was too excited and alert to want to go to bed, and with Owen and David absent there was no one to order his going. He threw himself down just as he was, and lay hugging the

71

satisfaction of his secret, so content in his solitary wakefulness that he had no idea of the passing of time or the gradual stilling of every sound about him as the maenol sank to sleep; until at length he, too, slept, wandering over the threshold as lightly and innocently as an infant.

It was the barking of a dog that awakened him; one short, wild burst, and then the sound tailed off, appeased, into silence, but for Harry's quick ears it was enough. He started up in a quiver of concentration, alarmed but unafraid. He had no notion how long he had been asleep, and his senses quested out into the stillness and quietness, challenging the thing he had heard. Why had the hound given tongue? They never spoke at night without a reason. And if someone was stirring, and had roused him, why had he suddenly fallen silent, as though satisfied? Someone had answered him, and someone he knew well.

Harry slid off the bed and crossed to the door, looking out into the dark towards the gate. Somewhere in that direction there was a murmur of voices, subdued and brief, the muted pacing of a horse's hooves on the hardened earth, others following. Who could ride into Aber in the night and hush the dogs with a word?

There could be only one answer, but he went shivering out into the night to be sure, his heart beating vehemently now, and the piercing cold of his sudden awakening shaking him from head to foot. From the corner of the armoury he saw a lantern at the gate, and two men of the guard reaching to the bridles of steaming horses. He saw the foremost rider's cloak billow as he dismounted, and he knew the long, light pace that sprang from the earth resilient as a child's though it belonged to a man already growing old. Two steps were enough for him, even in the dark, and by now there was a faint, lambent light softening the blackness, and the clinging rain had ceased.

Through what uncharacteristic change of plan he could not guess, Llewelyn had foresaken Aberconway after all, and ridden home to his own maenol and his own bed.

Harry found himself running almost before he knew why,

72

confused but determined. The secret had been entrusted to him, and he would see it kept. De Breos might well be already fast asleep in his own quarters, but the time that had passed could not be long. Why should the Prince decide to ride home, unless he had found his business with the Prior completed in time to allow him to cover the miles between and still enjoy a night's rest in his own chamber? Had it been very late he would have stayed, as he had intended. For all Harry knew it was not yet half an hour since he had conducted de Breos to the Princess's presence, and their planning not yet completed.

Roundabout in the dark he wound his way to the royal tower. The Prince must not break in upon them now and spoil all, and it was surely in the direction of his own apartments that he had set off at such a pace from the gate-house. He could go directly, but Harry must go deviously and keep out of sight. If de Breos was long gone, and the Princess already asleep, then nothing worse had happened than the waste of a little energy and a little breath, of both of which commodities Harry had plenty, even at midnight.

He ran confidently out from the passage behind the armoury, and plunged into the deep doorway, and into Llewelyn's arms.

A sharp, faint cry was startled out of him, not of fear, only of astonishment. He flung his arms round the hard, lean body to keep his balance, and panted: 'My lord!' on a gusty breath, nearer to laughter than alarm. If there were two within, and they needed a warning, then this flurry at the door would surely suffice; now he had only to draw the Prince off for a few minutes, and all was well.

'Harry, you here?' said Llewelyn, and tightened his great hands on him and dragged him in at the door. There were others behind him, three or four as yet unrecognisable in the darkness, but not David, not Owen. Why had he left them behind when he himself rode for home? 'What are you doing abroad at this hour?'

For the first time he felt a thin, terrifying doubt rise in him like nausea. The big hands had never held him like this, they hurt his arms and sent sharp cramps tingling down into his fingers. And the full, fiery voice that had often roared at him without frightening him was tight and low now, and chilled his senses, but he would not believe in fear.

He lied valiantly: 'My lord, I heard you come, I heard the dogs. Will you not come to the kennels just for a minute? I went to look at Marared, and I'm anxious about her. It's her first litter – and she's restless and whining. I'm feared all's not well with her. If you'd come and look –'

A torch came glowing in at the door, carried by someone he was too agitated to identify. And why were they all so silent? Llewelyn plucked him round to face the light, and now he could see, dark against the brightness and yet sufficiently defined, the loved and revered hawk-face. It stared at him terribly from under drawn brows, the far-sighted eyes piercing him redly, the long mouth a stony line. He hardly recognised it. His heart failed in him. He groped with numbed fingers for a hold on the Prince's sleeves, understanding nothing, only afraid.

'Is that what you were doing, up and dressed in the night? Why lie to me? What end can lying serve now?'

'Why should I lie? She's fevered – if only you'd come to her, you know what's best to do.'

The hands that held him jerked him round and drove him towards the staircase. 'My lord!' he implored, his voice breaking in a child's whimper. 'What is it? What have I done?'

'Ay, what have you done? Come, and let's see!'

He was thrust mercilessly up the stairs, stumbling and panting but silent now like them, astray in such a wilderness of fear that he hardly knew what was happening to him. The Prince stretched a hand forward over the boy's shoulder and hurled open the door of the bedchamber.

In the great bed there was a sudden convulsion of movement that broke in two with a cry, and the naked lovers started upright and apart, staring into the torchlight with dilated eyes of horror.

The breath went out of Harry's body in a gusty, voiceless cry, as though a mailed fist had driven a violent blow into him below the heart. The pain was physical and terrifying, darkening his vision and softening his bones. His knees gave under him, and he fell in a heap of shocked flesh, retching over fists doubled hard into his middle. He was wailing out of his agony: 'No! No! No!' over and over in a frenzy of protest, but there was no breath in him to give voice to his cries.

'*This* is what you have done. Look at it! Look well!'

Llewelyn took him by the hair and jerked up his head, dragging him forward until he leaned upon the end of the bed. He could not avert his face, he could not turn aside; but there was nothing there he had not seen already in that first instantaneous revelation, and it was in his eyes now open or closed, it would be in them even when he slept and make his dreams hideous. He crouched helpless under the prisoning hand, feeling the great dull anguish within him grow hot and expand to fill him to the finger-tips, to the end of every hair.

He had adored her, picked his way by her as by a fixed star; and here he saw only a loose woman taken in the act, a poor naked woman stricken and shamed, holding up the covers to hide pallid, weary breasts that drooped with the burden of forty years. Her face was tired and lined. He saw for the first time the grained lines round her mouth, the softness of the pale flesh at her throat, the dry, colourless tint of dust dimming the long hair. An old face, a soiled face, that might have belonged to a dead woman but for the fixed and dreadful stare of the grey eyes. Beside her the man crouched, tensed like a handsome beast hunted to exhaustion, and a long tress of her hair lay over his shoulder and hung down upon his naked breast. His black eyes, stretched wide with desperate bravery, glared back at Llewelyn, but Harry saw his fear as naked as his too admirable body. The print of them both went into him and stamped itself on his vision for ever.

Joan said, and from first to last they were the only words she spoke that night: 'Let the boy go.' Her voice was unbelievably heavy and slow, as though the words were stones she could hardly lift. 'He's blameless, he knew no wrong. Can

75

you not see it? Let him go!'

Harry felt the clutch of the hard fingers in his hair relax, and in a moment relinquish him. He fell against the skirts of the bed, and dragging himself to his feet with crippled, clumsy movements ran dementedly out of the room, blundering past the silent men who stood aside to give him passage. They heard his broken running on the stairs, growing faster and wilder as it faded, and then he was gone into the darkness and quietness of the night outside, and they forgot him; or if any remembered it was the woman, still and mute among the shards of her shattered world.

De Breos stretched a hand out almost stealthily and reached for his cotte.

'No,' said Llewelyn harshly, 'let it lie. Get up, my lord, let me see what manner of delights you offered her that you got the tree to bow.'

Scarlet stained the fine cheek-bones in the pale face. Slowly de Breos put back the covers and rose from the bed. He stood erect and stared straight, refusing acknowledgement to shame, as the Prince looked him over from head to foot and back again to the face.

'I did not think there was the man anywhere on earth, my lord, could do what you have done. Take it for your comfort. Not every baron of England achieves an unparalleled deed before he dies. Well, cover yourself. It cannot be repeated. You do not dazzle me.'

De Breos wrapped his cotte about him with hands that were trembling with recovering fear, live fear that would not accept an ending. The first death was over, he mustered to his support all that he was, Brecon and Builth and Hay and all the manifold complexities of his honour. He should have felt a host at his back, but they seemed to him a world away, even the handful who snored in Llewelyn's new pavilions at this moment.

He tried to look at Joan, but he could not bear the sight for long. She had not moved. The great eyes, grey and void as glass, stared at Llewelyn without change or expression, but somewhere within them there was a deep, disquieting spark

76

coming to birth, and something warned de Breos that he would do well to turn his own eyes away, never to see it, at all costs to avoid understanding it.

Llewelyn wrenched his head aside, and they saw his mouth contorted by one awful convulsion of grief.

'In the name of God,' he said in a suffocating voice, 'cover yourself, madam!'

She crept from the bed as though infinitely tired, and drew on her gown with blind movements of hands that were past trembling. She was not afraid; fear would have been irrelevant now, when she had already pulled down the roof over her own head. She stood silent still, watching Llewelyn, and the consciousness behind her blank eyes had drawn nearer to the surface; a little while, and it would show through.

'So it was truth they told me,' said Llewelyn, uncovering the fierce dark face that would not betray him again. 'I laughed at it first. Then I was angry that they should think me fool enough to credit so clumsy an attempt to damage the strength we had between us. I made the assay to prove they lied. And all I have done is prove it true. Well, speak! Have you nothing to say in your own excuse?'

Her lips moved, saying: 'Nothing!' but there was no sound.

'Call the guard,' said Llewelyn without turning his head. 'Have them take into ward all the knights of Brecon who came here with this felon and thief, and see them made fast in irons. Then bid them come for these.'

'My lord, my men have no part in this, the crime is mine only.' De Breos moistened his dry lips with a tongue that rasped like leather. Two of the men who stood silent behind Llewelyn turned and went from the room.

'My lord, your men pay for being a traitor's fellows, as you for being a traitor, a spoiler of the house where you were a guest.'

The pale and desperate face could grow no paler, nor could anything now call back the blood to his cheeks. 'I deny nothing of my fault. I take the guilt upon me for what I have done, and beg you to hold her to be as deeply wronged as you. The thing was my doing, I planned it, I got my way of her. Of

77

your grace, let me stand to it with the sword.'

'I would not ask the meanest among my bodyguard to meet you in arms, You have put yourself outside the grace of honourable men. Stand to it with the law, like other felons.'

'So be it!' said de Breos, stiffening his back. 'But let me tell you this, my lord, I do not repent me of what I've done. No, whatever it cost me! It was worth all I have to have had your lady's love, as she has mine. Dispose of me how you will, yet I did and do love her, and shall until the day I die.'

It was said for her, and she did not hear and would not see him. The only last comfort he could have had in this nadir of his fortunes, and she did not grant it. It seemed to him that she did not know he was there. She watched Lleweyln, and counted over the wreckage she had made, and the light behind her eyes had burned into such unimaginable purity of anguish that it illuminated for him his own eternal loss no less than hers. By that light they saw coldly and clearly at last. All the evidence was assembled, everything fell into proportion. There had never been one moment in their association when she would not have sacrificed him and all he meant to her to smooth one line out of Llewelyn's forehead.

She had not always known it, but she knew it now, as she assessed and told over within her husband's face all that she had forfeited, all that she had brought into danger, all that she had broken and destroyed. She would have torn out her own heart and her lover's to restore it.

Heavy feet trod uneasily on the stairs below. A dozen armed men came into the room, muffling their weapons and moving softly for awe of the unbelievable disaster that was fallen upon Aber. They laid hands with implacable gentleness upon de Breos, and looked at Llewelyn for orders, hesitating to touch Joan. She had been flesh of that princely, outraged flesh so long, to ravish her was to assault the sovereignty of Gwynedd, almost to blaspheme against order and God.

'Take them away,' said Llewelyn.

De Breos made no resistance when they led him to the door. He passed close to Joan, looking with longing into her fixed countenance, and she moved her head without a glance at him, so that he should not for more than a second blot out for her Llewelyn's face.

'My lord,' said de Breos with a crooked smile, 'if you but knew it your debt to me is already paid.'

Harry lay all night long curled under the covers of his solitary bed, tensed and aching with wakefulness, contorted with complex pains that would not let him lie quiet for a moment. Even there it was not dark enough for him, and even there he found no safety, for with the dawn he would have to emerge and face the light that waited to assault him. He knotted his fists into his eyes, but he could not rub out what he had seen, and the memory of it ate into his brain like some fearful corrosion that could never again be slaked away. He sobbed into his pillow without the alleviation of a single tear, coiled about the burden of his love and hate and shame and rage like a wild beast about its death-wound.

They had betrayed him vilely, taken his worship and trust and turned it to their own hateful uses. Worse, they had caused him to betray his prince and foster-father. Who would ever believe he had acted in innocence? And even if they believed him, how was he helped? To have been such a blind, gullible tool was almost worse than being a traitor. How could she have done it? How could she have destroyed his image of her, that immaculate image of which he had had no doubts at all? Distrust the Princess? Question whatever she chose to do? It would have been like doubting the integrity of God Himself! In all that lifetime of majesty when had she ever failed of being whole and incorruptible?

Deeper than the injury to his pride, though that cut to the heart, deeper than the loss of his honour and the shock to his faith lay the wound to his love for her, not more than half-understood, but felt with every fibre of his flesh and spirit.

That was at the beginning of the interminable night. But by the end of it, when the light began to penetrate within the folds of his bedding and prick his raging sensitivity like knives, his dishonour had taken pride of place in the catalogue of his martyrdoms. At all costs he must clear himself in the Prince's eyes, justify his actions, however foolish, however childishly confiding, and be received back into his old position of trust. It was not that he wanted to avoid blame; he blamed himself. Or punishment, if he was held to have merited punishment more than he already suffered. But he could not bear to be contemned as a mean traitor, the affront to his self-respect was unendurable.

He dragged himself shivering out of the bed, made himself presentable, and went to beg an audience of Llewelyn, steeled to such a pitch of resolution that he had thrust his way past the guards at the foot of the private staircase and was half-way through the knot of agitated officials in the ante-room before the chamberlain noticed him and haled him back by the arm.

'Let me in to him,' said Harry fiercely. 'I have always free access to him, you can't keep me out.'

'Not to-day. And if you're wise you'll not wish for it. Be off and let my lord alone, this is no place for you,' said the harassed chamberlain, and thrust him out at the door.

He slipped back again less boldly when no one was watching, and crept along the wall into the darkest corner, with ears stretched for the fearful whispers that were being passed from man to man through the room. David and Owen, it seemed, had been left behind at Aberconway, and knew nothing yet of any disaster. That had been done of design, clearly, to preserve David from the horror of his mother's disgrace and have his good brother at his side to bear him company if the news flew too fast to meet him. Harry's ears burned indignantly, hearing his own name pass. His part was known, though how judged he could not tell from the snatch of words he caught. They were talking of the politics of catastrophe, of David's imperilled match, of King Henry's shadow like a shield over his great tenant's head, of possible war, of the news flying hot-foot through Wales, and the ancient enemies of the de Breos clan taking joyfully to horse and heading for Aber. It would cost William a deal more than one castle, they were saying, to get safe out of this coil.

Harry wormed his way to the inner door, and was making

himself small in the shadow behind it when Ednyfed Fychan came out, grim-faced, to despatch a messenger. The boy was in Llewelyn's presence before anyone could reach a hand to halt him, and had slipped round the court judge's slow bulk and flung himself on his knees at Llewelyn's feet.

'My lord, be just to me! Let me speak! Visit it on me as you will, only don't believe me traitor.'

The Prince looked down at him with hollow-rimmed eyes burning in a gaunt face drawn by anger and grief to a semblance of starvation. He was expressly handsome and elegantly-appointed that morning, the short silken beard that encircled his lips and outlined the strong bones of his jaw glossily combed, his dark, curling hair carefully groomed. Even the movement of his hand towards Ednyfed as the seneschal re-entered the room was measured and controlled, and apparently without passion, yet they all felt the titanic tremors of the covered fire, and stepped with wincing care, holding back from the limit of its blaze.

'Put him out,' said Llewelyn.

'You should not be here, boy,' said Ednyfed shortly, vexed but not unkind. 'You heard his Grace. Out!'

There were three of them beside Ednyfed, the chaplain-secretary, the judge and the captain of the bodyguard, the highest inner council of Llewelyn's court. All of them looked down at the wild-eyed boy and frowned him away, but he would not take the warning. When Ednyfed with fraying patience took him by the arm, he leaned forward desperately and laid hold on Llewelyn's knees.

'My lord, give me justice! I swear I didn't betray you, I'm not the wretch you think me. I didn't know –'

The Prince's chair screamed upon the boards of the floor as he thrust it back, withdrawing his person abruptly out of reach.

'I bade you go. Have I to give orders twice? Now go!'

The captain of the guard rose and took hold of the boy by the other arm, but Harry fought him off passionately and followed Llewelyn on his knees, sobbing with vehemence.

'My lord, believe me or kill me! I won't be thought traitor.

81

I won't rise from my knees until you hear me. I didn't know that they – that she – They both lied to me!'

Fire blazed at him for one instant from the deep eyes hollowed with the memory of the long night. Llewelyn clenched his fist and drew back his arm, saw the quivering frantic face jerk with apprehension and palely maintain its ground, waiting for the blow. He sprang out of his chair and away to the draped wall beside the narrow window, gripping the tapestry until the murderous lust had left his hands.

And all for this child's little, fledgling honour, that hurt him no more than a toothache, while the world others had spent a lifetime constructing fell to pieces round them and the tendons of their hearts were severed one by one. Some day there would be a time for appeasing him with the justice he wanted, a time for comforting him, but not yet; he was too sharp a reminder of intolerable pain and loss, it was impossible to look at him or speak to him without revulsion.

'Take him away,' said Llewelyn hoarsely, without turning his head, 'before I forget whose son he is and do him an injury. God's blood, he shames his father's memory!'

The fist could never have dealt him such a killing blow. For a second time he recoiled stunned into his darkened vision and nerveless flesh, feeling the heavy anguish of despair gather ponderous and hot inside him like molten lead. They put him out, not roughly, and shut the door against him, and he could neither resist nor speak. But in any case there was nothing more to be done, nothing more to be asked. He knew the worst of it now.

When he could make his numbed legs serve him again he took refuge in the remotest corner of the kennels, and hid in the straw there to fight out for himself the implications of his utter rejection.

He was disbelieved and dishonoured, cast out of the Prince's favour for ever. Even in his own eyes his status was lost. He shamed his father's memory! That rankled and festered until all his Talvace blood rose to accuse him. He might never be able to restore himself in the Prince's regard, but he must, if he was to live with himself at all, do something prodigious to redeem himself in his own estimation, and wipe out that affront. There was only one way in which he could demonstrate before all the world how he respected his father's memory, and how worthy he was to maintain it.

To stay here longer was impossible; Aber had cast him out. But after all, he was a man now; his father had been just the same age when he fled from home to deliver his foster-brother. It was time for him to take up his father's quarrel, that had been waiting and beckoning and reproaching him so long. They should see if he shamed his memory!

The pain and desperation had turned all to a fury of energy that would not let him be still for a moment. It drove him back to his own deserted room for his cloak, and the few pence he had of his own, and then to the stables, where he saddled Barbarossa with hasty, trembling hands. If he ceased for an instant his feverish activity he would break into helpless tears, but if he continued to drive himself into motion he would keep his dignity yet, and launch himself on the road to atonement and restitution. No good-byes to anyone. Best not think of his little, pretty, loving mother, or Owen, or David.

But to think of David, riding from Aberconway in happy ignorance of the calamity that waited for him, was in any case unbearable, and he turned in extremity to any minor annoyance, the straps of the harness stiff under his hands, a broken buckle, a tangle in the red mane, to ease the burden of his rage and grief.

He had only a dagger by way of arms, but that would have to suffice. He could not take his sword; it was Llewelyn's sword, he could touch nothing belonging to the Prince who had condemned him and cast him out. He sank his face for a moment into Barbarossa's glossy neck and sobbed aloud. The horse at least was his own, fairly won; he need not be left behind.

They did not halt him at the gate. He had always had liberty to go and come as he pleased, and they had more urgent things to do in Aber that day than shepherd him back into the maenol if he strayed.

Gilleis was with Joan in her sealed prison, the only attendant allowed in to her. How could she leave that silent, stunned presence to mind the comings and goings of her own child, until she had got at least a word or a tear or a sound out of her mistress and friend, something to show there was still a live mind in her? Moreover, Gilleis did not know the half of the story of that night until she was let out of the guarded room at noon and walked into Owen's anxious arms on the steps of the great hall.

He had left David alone with his father not ten minutes earlier, and he knew the whole of it. He held Gilleis in his arms as though she had been his own mother, and: 'Where's Harry?' he demanded urgently. There were enough minds in Aber breaking their wits on the problems of state; one man at least had time to think of the boy.

'I don't know. I've been with the Princess all the morning. God help us all, Owen, I hardly know what I'm doing or what to believe. If only she'd *speak*!' She saw the special trouble and tenderness in his face, and knew they were for her. 'What is it? What is it about Harry? What has he to do with this?'

He told her what he knew of it, and it was enough.

'Dear God!' she said, aghast. 'I carried her message to him myself last night. What has happened to her that she could do him such a bitter wrong? And how could they believe it of him?'

'Hush, now, there's not a soul believes Harry knew what he did, not even the Prince himself. And our lady'll never let him be blamed unjustly, no, nor de Breos, come to that. Let him be what he will, he's not so base as to let the boy suffer.'

'But even to have been the instrument!' she said, in agony. 'Dear lord, he'll break his heart. We must send to Adam and fetch him home.'

'We'll do that,' said Owen. 'But first we'll find Harry. I shan't be easy about him till we do.'

They looked for him in the kennels, in the mews, in every corner of the maenol, but they did not find him. The gate-keeper's boy owned to having seen him ride out during the morning, but judged confidently that he had not gone far. Owen, less sure, took horse and combed every haunt of the boys of Aber, the smithy low by the water, the mill and the banks of the leat, the steep tracks that led to the upland rides; but there was no sign of Harry's dark-red horse anywhere on the soft, pale spring green of the hills. He'd come home with the evening, he told Gilleis with better heart than he felt, hunger and darkness would bring him back to forgive and be forgiven. But the night came down on the salt marshes and the flat fields of Aber, and still Harry did not come.

CHAPTER FOUR

Aber: *May* 1230

The two huts lay in a fold of ground beside a spring, several miles beyond the highest sheep-fold that penned Llewelyn's flocks. On every side the grey-green uplands of coarse grass extended, broken by out-crop rock and deep, peat-brown patches of bog; but their small dimple in this empty world was sheltered from the winds and open to the sun.

Saint Clydog's cell was a plain beehive of wattle and daub and turf, with a lancet doorway facing east to the Holy Land; but Madonna Benedetta's was a squarely-built box of good cut stone, with two windows looking south, and carving on the lintel of the door, for Adam Boteler had built it for her when she chose to retire into the anchorite life, and kept it in repair. It had an inner and an outer room, and John the Fletcher, who was growing old in her service, slept across Benedetta's threshold at night, and fished and carried and cooked for her during the day.

She had tried to send him away many times, saying that he was, and in her employ had always been, a free man, and it was unfitting for an anchoress to have a servant waiting upon her. But he would not go, and called Saint Clydog to his support, as he always did whenever there was a point on which she must lose the debate. Saint Clydog was cantankerous by nature, and would always take the opposite side to a woman in any argument, and he had settled it once for all that a hermit must of necessity have a boy to run his errands, since he may not leave his cell himself, and since his especial blessedness gives him a clairvoyance which may at any moment need to send warnings and exhortations to other people, often at a distance.

Once he had had a boy of his own for the purpose, but the poor fellow had been subjected to so much running about on his master's supernatural business that he had finally tired of the life and continued running, to what new employment Saint Clydog's clear sight had never yet succeeded in revealing to him. Since then he had claimed a minor share in John the Fletcher, tempering his demands on him to defer to Benedetta's prior claim. On the whole he was more comfortable so; it would have taken him the rest of his dwindling life to get used to a new face.

They were sitting outside on the sun-warmed turf of the hillside, in the bright afternoon of the first of May, Saint Clydog facing east with his beads fumbled beneath linked hands in the lap of his gown, and Benedetta unashamedly facing the sun as she embroidered at an altar cloth for the church of the community at Beddgelert. Often they sat the whole afternoon and said no word, but they had known each other for a long time, and silence was no bar to their communion.

'You've been watching the track from Aber for the past ten days,' said the Saint abruptly, 'and I know why.'

'That I can well believe,' agreed Benedetta, threading her needle. She had to narrow her eyes against the sun, but she would not turn her face away. The sun was her fellow-countryman, who visited her all too rarely in this misty northern climate, and its warmth was like an Italian voice saluting her, in an alien land where the swart, wild herdsmen who brought her milk and bread had intractable names it had taken her years to learn to say, and avoided the necessity for attempting hers by calling her simply 'the holy woman'.

'After a week of your company I remember I said there's no one so knowing as a saint, and I say it still. And no one so inquisitive, either.'

'I must always be about God's business,' said Saint Clydog smugly, 'even on your behalf. You are anxious because your son has not been to pay you his Easter visit.'

'He is not my son,' she said quite calmly.

'In the spirit he is the son of many parents, but not least

87

of you. You are afraid there is some reason why he cannot come.'

She said nothing to that, but sat steadily stitching. She had sewn nearly fifteen years of her life into such lengths of linen as this, she who had hardly put a stitch into a dress before, and would not willingly have done so even now if it had not been the fair price of the life she had chosen. Along with the tranquillity and safety of her calling she had accepted with good grace the immobility and monotony, and the obligation to perfect this dreary skill. You cannot make a one-sided compact with God.

'I have been wondering,' went on the Saint, casting a sharp sidelong glance at her beneath his bushy white brows, 'how many more days than ten it will take to make you pack up and go down to seek for news of him, if he continues absent.'

'I have taken my place here. I have no other. Have I seemed to you so restless since I took this life upon me?'

'You have taken no vows. And I've always known that you will not live out your life here – you with your saint's face and your devil's hair.'

'What do you know of my devil's hair?' She always kept it covered from sight now under her white wimple, and even when she loosed it about her shoulders in her own inner room its crimson was dusty now with silver, and its texture a little dry and harsh, as though the sap in her had reached autumn almost before the summer was over.

'Devil's hair, Judas-hair on as true a head as ever took thought for another,' said the old man angrily. 'The ways of God are inscrutable.'

'I always knew you had seen through me,' she said serenely. 'And did you blame me for striking a bargain with God?'

'I found no fault in you. Man and woman alike must do the best they can with circumstances. And as for the validity of your holiness, that's for God to judge, not for me. As He will, when the time comes.'

'Then why are you concerned with the constancy of my vocation here?'

He said, suddenly with the simplicity of a child, disarming and confounding: 'May I not grieve at the thought of losing you?' And before she could draw breath he added in his usual crusty tones: 'Look at the track now. How is it you have no sense of time and events after all these years with me?'

She looked, and there were two riders winding their way at a canter along the stone-grey ribbon from Aber. She put down her work in her lap and sat tensed, watching them; and while they were still hardly more than coloured, moving dots in the monotone she said with certainty: 'Not Harry.'

'There are other men in the world.'

She watched unwaveringly until the two riders had drawn close enough to be recognised. The one in front, big and burly and fair, was Adam Boteler, the one behind, dark and young, was Owen ap Ivor. When they were nearer still, she saw how grave they looked and how urgently they rode, and rose to meet them, letting the linen fall from her hands.

'Adam, what brings you this way? I looked to see Harry here before this. He's not ill?'

Adam checked in the act of dismounting. The question he had been ready to toss into her lap from the saddle was already answered.

'So he's not been here? Not since Easter?' He doffed his cap in a reverence to Saint Clydog, and bent to kiss Benedetta's hand. He had known her even before she had met with the boy's father and set her heart on him lifelong, and once he had had her favours, though now it seemed to them both that that must have happened to two other people, lòng since dead.

'We hoped to get word of him from you, but that's one more hope turned out hollow. I doubt, then, you've not heard what's shattered the festival at Aber. God knows they've had no time for visiting.'

'I've heard nothing. No one's been near us till you. What's happened?' Alarm made her voice quieter and her body wonderfully still. She stood looking up at him straightly from those wide-set eyes that still had their full, pure colouring, a grey as rich and positive as the iris-purple to which it darkened in shadow. Her face with its breadth of bone and its resolute, adventurous, challenging mouth still seemed made for courts and camps rather than the cells of a hermitage, though the old man had called it a saint's face. But who could be sure what Saint Clydog understood by a saint?

'It's a sorry tale enough, in all conscience. Owen here is the better man to tell you, he was closer to the storm than I.'

'Not close enough to be of any use,' said Owen ruefully as he dismounted and made his salutations. 'Neither to the Prince nor to Harry. Why, the short of it all is that the Princess has been surprised with William de Breos in her bed. And through no fault of his own Harry's tangled sadly in the bad business, and came out of it with some blame and a deal of grief, and he's taken himself off somewhere with his hurts and can't be found.'

'Child, what are you saying?' Benedetta gaped at him aghast, labouring some way behind this galloping conclusion. 'I'm too old for such shocks.'

'I doubt it did come a thought too roughly,' said Owen, abashed, 'but Adam and I have done everything in such haste these past days, looking for him, I'm out of the skill of going more softly.'

'But the Princess and de Breos! Here, sit down and tell me the whole of it, it will be time saved in the end.' And she drew him down with her into the tussocky grass, and he poured out the miserable story gratefully, easing his mind of details that had been festering unexpressed for days. Adam lay down wearily beside him and added here and there a glum word of his own. Saint Clydog, motionless with his hands halted on his beads and his eyes on the eastern sky, listened and was silent.

'God or the devil only knows what alchemy he used to win her. If it had not come out as it did I would not have believed it from any man living. And God alone knows how the Prince got wind of it, though there's some malice in this somewhere. There are those that had good reason to want to break this alliance with Brecon at all costs, de Burgh in England and for that matter Griffith in Degannwy, if he'd had any way of getting hold of so apt a weapon. And as for blaming Harry for trusting them, that's fool's talk, in cold blood nobody blames him. Nobody can, for we should every one of us have taken her word without a tremor, and done her bidding without question. You might as well suspect the Prince's own right hand of designs on his life because it reaches for a sword.'

'But the thing happened,' said Adam bleakly. 'The Princess is in close ward, David's torn in two, and Harry's gone. I wish to God I'd kept him safe in Nanhwynain with me, but what could I do when the Prince sent for him?'

'And here's Adam has spent his every waking minute hunting for him ever since, and I've given the chase every hour I could snatch from the Prince's business or David's company and never a word of him anywhere. And where could he go? All his friends are here.'

'Perhaps it was not his friends he wanted,' said Benedetta half to herself, and sat for a while thoughtfully frowning with her chin in her palms.

'Indeed they've cost him enough of pain to set him running,' owned Adam, 'though I doubt if even de Breos wished him any.'

'I meant more than that,' she said. 'At Harry's age, and with his high temper, think what a load he has to heave off his heart now. Is it to his friends he'd take it? If I know the boy, he'd rather have someone to fight than someone to comfort him. Oh, he'd have brought you his sorrow, Adam, or run to his mother with it, but he wouldn't come to you with his disgrace. That he'd visit on someone who could be made to pay dear for it first and wipe it out of the record afterwards. The Prince would not listen to him, you said?'

'Think how he was pressed,' pleaded Owen, flushing for his foster-father. 'The wound was new, and God knows no man ever took a worse thrust, or one less deserved. And into the bargain he had Gwynedd on his heart, David's inheritance, everything he's spent his life serving. Could you have seen Harry's trouble clear, past such a trouble of your own? And indeed that's not the whole nor the best of his excuse, for the real reason he ordered him out was for Harry's own sake. Innocent or not, the boy's been the instrument of all this fearful coil, and he could not so soon look at him or speak to him fairly, and did not wish to be unjust. I pledge you my word, in the evening when he had put by the first and worst of it he sent for Harry to come to him, and was as moved as any of us when he heard he was lost. He's given me men and leave to hunt for him since, and he'd do more, but the balance of peace or war's still hanging over him. And our Welsh princes running to Aber like hounds on a blood-scent, they aimed only to strengthen his hand but, by God, they've forced it. Even if he had the will to draw back, even if he thought it wise, I doubt he could not do it now, not even he.'

'I never thought of blaming him,' said Benedetta mildly. 'With a world toppling on his shoulders small wonder if he couldn't see the boy's injury. But Harry would not be able to see any other, not yet, not till his smarts cool a little. I doubt the affront to his honour would hit him hardest, and be most in need of soothing. And the devil lent the Prince words better left unsaid, if a man had time to look them over before he uttered them. That mention of his father – you did well to get the words so exactly from Ednyfed, for I fear they matter more than Llewelyn ever meant or knew. "He shames his father's memory." That was more than enough to sting him into action.'

Adam sat up sharply in the grass.

'You think he took it as a reproach to him for failing in his duty as a son? What, has he gone to salve his pride on Isambard? I never thought of it; this bitter business here at home put it clean out of my mind, but he was harping on his vengeance again last autumn, and took it very hard that we wouldn't let him go to court with David at Michaelmas, to take the measure of the Lord of Parfois. You could very well be right!'

'That's where his father's memory draws him. That's the challenge that's always been waiting for him. If he wanted a deed to hurl in the teeth of all who doubt him, that's where he'd turn for it. He'll show you all whether he shames his parentage.'

Adam came up from the ground with a spring. 'I'll down

tools and ride for Severnside to-morrow. If you're right, then he'll surely make first for Strata Marcella, and we may overtake him in time.'

He did not add: 'His father's buried there,' but she knew that was what was in his mind. The dedication of Harry's misery and rage belonged to no other altar than his father's grave. It was there he would go first.

'I'd come with you, gladly,' said Owen wistfully, rising after him, 'but I can't go so far from Aber yet. The Prince might bid me go, but David – he can ill spare me, the case he's in. But I hate to see you go alone.'

'Take John the Fletcher with you,' said Benedetta. 'He'll be fain to go, and he's not afraid to leave me now. Wait, I'll call him out and we'll ask him.'

She ran to the doorway and called him forth from laying the fire on the hearth-stone against the evening chill. He came ambling out with his slightly bowed stride, a massy, ageing countryman, knotty and solid as an oak, wiping his hands on his short homespun cotte. He listened with sharp eyes, darting from face to face as Benedetta told him of the journey Adam had in mind. It wanted only the mention of Parfois or of Isambard, and the old fierce gleam kindled in his glance; he had an ancient score still outstanding against the Lord of Parfois on his own account, and a longer and more deadly one on Benedetta's.

'Master, if you want a companion on that road, I'm your man. She's no great need of me for a while, she's safe and holy here, she can spare me.'

'Then come,' said Adam, 'and more than welcome. If the boy's there, we'll find him. Come down to Aber this evening, and we'll have all ready to leave at dawn.'

When the two of them rode away, in better heart for having found at least another credible place in which to search, Benedetta stood for a long time watching them, and her face was quickened and restless, like a lake troubled by a wind from the sea. She took up her embroidery and sat down with it close to the silent Saint, but the light was already declining, and she could not see to work the infinitesimal stitches. She

93

laid it down again and sat very still, with a rare irresolution in her quietness.

'I marvel,' said Saint Clydog, pausing in his unwontedly earnest and concentrated prayers, 'that you don't follow your heart and ride with them. How if the boy should really have run his head into the lion's mouth? Will you be content then to sit here and pray for him?'

'Who spoke of content?' she said, in a voice as roused and tempted as her face. 'I pay my debts, I keep my bargains. What is it to you whether I am content?'

'You might ask the same of God,' said Saint Clydog shortly. 'Or do you think He does not care, either?'

In the night she left her door open to the starry darkness, to have at least the feeling of the Saint's nearness filling her loneliness in John's place; and she heard on the stillness the low, monotonous cadences of the old man's voice, praying aloud before the crucifix under its little penthouse roof.

'It's late, friend,' she said from the doorway. 'Are you not going to bed?'

'Not to-night,' said Saint Clydog, easing his weight from knee to ancient knee in the darkness. 'I must keep vigil to-night with a dying man.'

They brought de Breos out from his prison in the height of the morning, in broadest daylight and publicly, that the statement of the power and audacity of the Prince of Aberffraw and Lord of Snowdon might be more emphatic, and the challenge to all dissenting authorities more deliberate. Nothing was done secretly, nothing in haste. The court of the maenol had convicted him. More than eight hundred people witnessed his end, among them his own captive knights whose imprisonment was to terminate with their attendance at this spectacle, that they might carry a true account back with them.

Llewelyn had set his course straight ahead, where his anger and his injury led him. To turn aside from absolute justice would have left him exposed to the suspicion of weakness and timidity, encouraged the encroachments of the English and confounded and dismayed his own princes, who had gathered to Aber like ravens out of Snowdon, eager for a death. By the time he had peace of mind enough to consider mercy it was in any case too late to consider it; nor did he contemplate it for long. Only to a superficial view was it even expedient. Better by far, and at all costs, to stand firm upon his human and sovereign rights and demonstrate them once for all in the eyes of the world and in the teeth of England, even though they were rights no one else would have dared to assert.

And this was the end of it, this melancholy morning of the second of May in the field above the salt marshes, with the gulls crying along the tide, and a troubled wind ruffling the strait and tumbling the broken clouds above the gallows. It rained in fitful scuds, light and vicious between the watery gleams of sunlight. The ladder glistened, and all the trampled grass was trodden into slimy mud outside the ring of armed men.

The free Welshmen who had travelled many miles to watch him die sighed with fulfilment when he came riding down the track from Aber between his guards, the hated scion of a hated stock, whom they would never in their hearts have seen as an ally. He was bare-headed, and not even his hands bound, but one of the guards led his horse in case even at this late hour he should make a hopeless bid for his liberty. He was carefully and elegantly dressed, and calm with a remote, almost absent calmness. He had known for several days that he was going to die, and lived with the thought of it so closely that he had grown numbly used to it without growing resigned. He did not know how to achieve resignation, but he had managed exhaustion. He was in his thirtieth year, and even at this pass, deathly pale and fallen away as he was, good to look upon. There were not wanting a few women who pitied him.

From the foot of the ladder he looked back towards Aber, and saw the clouds rolling over Moel Wnion, and the long dark line of the curtain wall receding into the cleft of the river valley beneath. He saw the hunched shape of the royal tower peering over the wall, but the place of his brief triumph and his everlasting fall meant nothing to him now because she was not in it. Somewhere in the narrow huddle of prisons hidden from sight, she was walled in with her memories that were not of him.

There was no gain for anyone, nothing but incurable and unbearable loss; and for him the ignominious death of a thief and a traitorous guest taken in the act.

He climbed the ladder wearily but unfalteringly, because there was no other way left for him to go. If they had but known, those irrepressible tribesmen down there muttering and howling for his blood, all his debts were already paid. What they were taking from him now was not so much, he was stripped to the bone already. Who would think a game so lightly begun could have such an appalling ending?

He tilted his head compliantly to the touch of the hangman's hands without fully realising what he did, still straining with all his senses towards the place where Joan was; and mercifully, his eyes being full of tears, he had no warning of the moment when they jerked the ladder away.

'Why him?' said Joan. 'Why him, and not me? Was I less to blame? Am I to be grateful for my life when it's left to me with the stain of his death upon it?'

It was almost dark in the barred room where she was confined; she would still have it so. The two thin candles were all she could bear, and even by their pallid gleam she would not look now at her own face. But at least she spoke at last, sometimes ironically, sometimes practically, sometimes as now with the words of bitterness and passion, but always calmly. The first time she had broken her silence it had been to assert Harry's utter innocence of complicity in her crime, and to dictate the full story of the use that had been made of him. That was something Gilleis would never forget. All the rankling bitterness she had been harbouring against her mistress, even as she pitied her, bled away into the ink that vindicated the boy. If he was lost, he was not dishonoured.

'We were like two who vowed to die together,' said the

Princess, 'and one crept out of the bargain and survived, and now has the other on her conscience lifelong. And worse than that, Gilleis, worse than that is to be glad of life on such terms, and to look back and see how small and faint a thing it was we staked our lives upon. That's the cruellest offence of all.'

'Then why?' said Gilleis, the comb stilled in her hand. 'Oh, many a time I've wanted to ask you, why did you do it? What was there in him, comely as he was, to bring you to stoop to him? All this waste for everybody – *why*?'

'Do I know why? The thing happened of itself, like a gale, an act of God. He came when the time was ripe for him, and I had no way of standing him off. I could do no other. Do I know why?'

She was past forty years old, at the turning point where the season begins its long decline, and he had appeared at her shoulder, ten years her junior, handsome and gay, like a magical perpetuation of the spring that was leaving her for ever. A year later and he would have meant nothing, she would have set her feet already on the downward path and been absorbed in the harvest. A year earlier and she would not have felt any need of him, or fallen into the anguished error that there was virtue in beauty and youth beyond their temporary and borrowed grace. But he had come prompt to his hour, filling the moment of desperation and uncertainty with the blinding charm of his laughter. And he was dead for it.

'Only when I no longer had a choice,' she said, 'only then did I understand that there had been a choice, and that I had made it wrongly. For all of us. That was the inmost sin, and it was mine, not his. What do they say of me now? What do they say of Llewelyn's justice? That he dared reach as far as King Henry's vassal but stopped short of King Henry's sister?'

'No,' said Gilleis. 'No one says he dared not. Not even the English.'

'Then what? How do they account for me?'

'They feel no need to account for you.' Was it better to say it or leave it unsaid? Either way there was nothing but pain, a piercing pain or a dull pain. 'They know all through this land,' she said, 'how well he loves you.'

'Loved,' said Joan, accepting the sharper agony without a tremor. From first to last she had done no lamenting for herself; the ruin that had overtaken her was her own work. 'I know what I have lost, and of how much I have robbed him. It's late to grieve for that, but at least I would not have him lose more than he need. You must be my eyes and ears, Gilleis, if you will, now that I'm deaf and in darkness.'

She had asked no questions until then, but there were things she had to know. She knew, none better, in what a quicksand she had left Llewelyn stranded. She gathered herself erect, the faint, sunken spark of the old alert fire flickering in her eyes for the first time since her fall.

'Did my brother sail for France?'

'Yes, my lady. The fleet left Portsmouth the first of May.'

'Did he know what had happened here before he sailed?'

'They say the news reached him ten days before. At least he gave orders for the care of my lord de Breos's estates before the end of April.'

'But he did not question the charge against him.'

She did not say: 'Or against me!' but her lips contracted in the mournfullest of smiles. She knew her brother; it was not his concern for her she had feared might drive him into action against Llewelyn. And after all, perhaps it had been foolish to suppose that he would postpone yet again his long-delayed dream of invading France and sweeping triumphantly through Poitou and Anjou like a warrior-emperor, merely to remonstrate on behalf of a compromised half-sister and a rash border-baron. Henry was not troubled with loyalties; all his affections were capricious.

No doubt he had raved and reviled the long-suffering officials who surrounded him for a matter of hours, though more out of jealous pride for his own dignity and the sanctity of all things that were his than out of any regard for William's freedom or William's life; and then he had pushed the affair into someone else's hands, most probably Ralph Neville's since de Burgh was reluctantly bound for Brittany with him, and had turned back to his glittering toys of ships and engines and men, and his swollen dreams of reconquest.

The faint spark burned more steadily, from somewhere deep within her.

'And what has happened since? Have there been letters passing on behalf of the crown?'

'The Prince wrote to the Chancellor, and there came a letter in reply. I don't know what he wrote, but it seemed to me that Ednyfed was very content with it. And they've made no move. They're being very discreet. You see it's five days since, and still all's quiet.'

Five days since the poor, spoiled body had been taken down from the gallows above the marsh and buried without honours. All that energy and arrogance and gaiety smirched and broken, and the world surely the poorer even for that. There had never been malice in him, the mischief that spilled out from his finger-ends was a natural gift, for good or evil. But it seemed that no one was prepared to venture on avenging him. Henry in Brittany could not yet know that his vassal was dead, but Chancellor Neville knew it, and had replied to the blunt notification in apparently cautious and urbane terms; that was a fair indication of the way the scale was declining.

The facts, it seemed, were too clear to dispute. The boldness of the Prince's justice might have startled and alarmed the whole realm of England, but no one could deny that it was justice. Then they would not move for her, either. If they let his death go by without protest they could scarcely charge Llewelyn with any ill-usage of her.

She breathed more easily for that, and the stony coldness within her softened with the first meagre spark of warmth. If anyone could win such a gamble against the power of England it was Llewelyn, with his iron front and his approaches direct as arrows, and the recent daunting memory of Kerry reverberating like an echo to his every word. The warmth burned into a slow, bitter ache within her heart, because he did not need her, he could play the game no less well without her. Yet she embraced the reawakening pain, and was grateful for it.

'Has he sent word to the widow?'

A death was a death, but a marriage was a marriage, and sound business could not wait on personal grudges.

'Yes,' said Gilleis heavily, thinking of the four little girls who were left fatherless, 'and to her brother, the Earl Marshall, too, for the children and the estates will surely come into his ward.'

'What has he said to them? Do you know?'

'I know what's being said about the court. They say the Prince has told them that this offence and this penalty were between none but my lord de Breos and himself, and are settled, that he bears no ill-will against the house of Breos, and still desires for his part that David's marriage shall take place according to the contract.'

It rang true. It was what she would have had him do, whether the poor woman in Brecon, doubly bereaved of her husband and of his faithfulness, accepted or refused his offer. The more tremendous the stake and the more dangerous the bid you make for it, the more inflexibly and doggedly you must stand to your throw. Not a step back, not a glance aside.

'And I've heard that he means to send an envoy to the Chancellor and make a formal claim for Builth, as the girl's marriage portion.'

Joan smiled; it was a pale, brief thing, but it was a smile. His instinct was always true. Not one item nor one scruple must be abated from the due he exacted, and nothing wanting from the due he paid. And he had paid, he was paying yet, a longer score than the short and horrible agony on the gallows.

'They've made no answer yet?'

'There's been no time, my lady.'

'They'll compound with him,' said Joan with conviction. 'He'll win his game.' She hesitated for a moment, longing and fearing to ask, and at last she said in a low and constrained voice: 'How does he look? Is it well with him?'

At the naked sound of the words she felt her own incurable mutilation, and shrank, sick with the certainty of his. And all Gilleis could do was turn her face away, and fumble in vain for a lie.

'No, let it be!' said Joan. 'God help me, I know!'

She drew the gown closer round her shoulders, shivering, putting the unbearable regrets from her. It could not be undone. There was no going back.

'You've had no word yet from Adam?'

'Not yet,' said Gilleis, very low, and her lips quivered. 'It's only six days since they set off for the march, it's early yet.'

'I marvel,' said Joan, 'that you can keep from hating me. And still you are so gentle.'

Suddenly her face was wrung by a convulsion of uncontrollable pain, and she bent her head and hid between her thin, pale hands.

'Oh, Gilleis,' she whispered behind the rigid fingers, 'if only I could put right this one wrong! Of all the treasons I committed against my will I most repent the offence against Harry. Oh, Gilleis, to betray a child – and one that loved and trusted me –'

Gilleis opened her arms and took the fair, bowed head to her breast, protesting through tears that Harry would come back, that Adam and John between them would find and bring him home.

'He'll come, and he'll not hold it against you for ever. Things pass, even this will pass.' What better was there to promise her? She could not lie to her. 'Ah, don't grieve, don't grieve! When King Henry comes home he'll surely intercede for you, and see you delivered out of this sad place.'

'Delivered?' said Joan, breaking strongly out of the circling arms, and raising a face fixed in wonder, derision and despair. 'What do I want with deliverance? In his palace or in his prison, where Llewelyn is is the only home I have.'

CHAPTER FIVE

Parfois: *May* 1230

He rode in at the gates of Strata Marcella in the dusk, tired out and ready for his bed. Mist was rising over the level water-meadows that fringed Severn, and there was a vaporous moon afloat over the black ridge of the Long Mountain, on the English side of the river. He would have to wait until morning to see more of the place than that dark lizard-back against the sky, and the drifting bluish mist between.

Here he was not known, and did not intend to make use of his real name, which would mark him out almost anywhere in North Wales as the fosterling of the Prince of Aberffraw.

He lighted down modestly at the gate-house and doffed his cap to the brother who came out to him, inquiring with appropriate humility for a night's lodging; and being directed to the stables, took care of his horse like any other roving journeyman before he looked for his own entertainment. In the light of a hanging lantern in the stable-yard, busy grooming their mounts and whistling over the work, were two servants in the familiar livery of Earl Ranulf of Chester.

Harry withdrew himself into the deepest shadows, his heart thumping. Old Ranulf had known him from infancy, and often on his visits to Aber brought him small gifts, a fluffy speckled eyas from his own mews, or some finely worked jesses. If once he caught sight of Llewelyn's fledgling roaming here alone so far from home, he was very likely to probe deeper into the matter, and end by leading him back to Aber by the ear.

But it was too late to withdraw now. There could be no

surer way of drawing attention to himself than by riding out hurriedly again at this hour of the night. He went gingerly about the business of seeing Barbarossa fed and bedded, averting his face from the lights; and only when he was drawing breath to nerve himself to enter the hall of the commonalty did he remember that he was wasting the worst of his fears. Earl Ranulf could not possibly be here in Strata Marcella; he was away with the King's host, somewhere in Brittany or Poitou.

There were, of course, many among the Earl's household who would also know Llewelyn's foster-son well, but the danger of being haled back like a runaway child was less grave from any of them. On the other hand, they might very well carry word back to Chester, and so in time to Aber. He would still do well to keep out of sight, and spare to let his voice be heard.

He slipped into the hall unobtrusively, and took his place among the lowest, where the packmen and pedlars and the poor journeymen sat. Earl Ranulf's grooms were at the highest table, well away from him, and three more men in the same livery had joined them, but by good fortune Harry knew none of the five, and was certain he could not be known to them.

Voices were rising at the main table. Suddenly he heard the name of the Princess Joan pass, and his heart turned in him with a sharp, vindictive stab of recollection.

'The Princess of Gwynedd?' said a lean Welsh pilgrim hotly. 'Ah, get off with you, man! This world's full of gossips who'd take the name of the Blessed Virgin herself in vain if it served their purpose, but is that any call for you to abet them? The Princess is known here in Wales, let me tell you. Whoever bred that tale about her may swallow it himself, he'll find no one else here to do it for him.'

He had raised his voice in his partisan indignation, and now every ear was stretched, the whole room listening.

'Spare your anger, friend,' said the oldest of the men from Chester. 'I'd have said the same myself, on all counts, a

103

month ago, and I'd be saying it yet if I didn't know different, more's the pity. The tale's all over England and Wales already. Where've you been that you haven't heard it?'

'I did better than you when it first came into Chester,' added his fellow ruefully, 'for I laughed.'

'So did the Prince when someone first whispered it in his ear. But he's laughing on the other side of his face now.'

Harry drew away from the trestle table very softly, and curled into his cloak in the dimmest corner. The pain he had ridden off into the freakish May wind and the sweet, active aches of his body was back again in full measure, gripping his throat so that it was hard to breathe. The image engraved upon his inward vision blazed into unbearable clarity again.

The pilgrim said slowly and solemnly: 'This is no deceit?'

'No deceit, but a certainty.'

'God have mercy on us all!' said the Welshman. 'And what's become of her?'

'She's in prison there at Aber, and he'll neither see her nor hear her name spoken.'

'And the lord of Brecon?'

The youngest groom twirled an imaginary noose round his own throat, and choked in it in horrible mimicry of the gallows-agony.

'*Hanged?*' said one of the journeymen hoarsely. 'What, William de Breos? Hang the biggest baron in the march? By God, he'd never dare! Not even Llewelyn!'

Dead! Harry had never thought of death. Imprisonment, reparations, long legal battles back and forth across the border, bishops running hither and thither, the King's envoys galloping to appease and pacify, he had foreseen all these, but never this ultimate simplicity, this direct and resolute despatch. He shrank into his corner, sick and stunned.

'By God, he did dare. The thing's done. Yesterday morning, and we heard it in Chester before night. De Breos is dead and buried, let the King's officers do what they will.'

'But to hang him out of hand! A great lord like him! Like a

104

sneak thief or a murderer!'

Harry had seen men hanged once, two outlaws who had preyed on pilgrims using the hill roads to Beddgelert, and killed and robbed three or four times before they were taken. He had been sick and shaken at the sight of their contorted dance on air, and the struggle they put up for their last breaths. Everyone had reassured him that the felons had only their deserts, and he had owned that they were right; but still he had not been comforted.

'God have mercy on his soul!' said the pilgrim, generously enough for a Welshman who felt himself affronted in the person of his prince; and there was a half-grudging and half-awed growl of: 'Amen!'

Dead and buried, the handsome, athletic body that stepped so vigorously and rode so well; the laughter strangled in the round, brown throat, the blue-veined lids lowered once for all over the gay and arrogant eyes. He had only his deserts, that was certain. He had stooped to the meanest and most damaging of thefts, violated the laws of hospitality, betrayed friendship. And yet how could they bear to do it to him? How could they bring themselves to spoil a creature so alive and beautiful?

'You're very quiet, young sir,' said one of the packmen, edging closer to him along the bench by the wall, and leaning to peer at him with narrow, shrewd eyes that missed nothing of his unwillingness to be seen. Harry had thought himself plain and ordinary enough to pass muster anywhere, but suddenly he was uneasily aware of the silver chasing on the hilt of his dagger, the modest gold clasp that fastened his cloak, and even the good homespun cloth and court cut of his cotte and chausses. The insinuating voice asked civilly: 'Are you looking for work in these parts? I know most of the masters in Pool that can do with likely lads. Maybe I can speak a word for you.'

'I thought of trying further south,' said Harry, feeling cautiously for his purse against his thigh, under cover of the folds of his cloak. It was an effort to keep his voice firm, or his wits alive to his own situation. 'Maybe as far as Hereford.

Unless there's some patron hereabouts who needs a prentice stonemason.'

'They'd want to know how you left your old master,' said the packman, showing broken teeth in an ingratiating grin as he edged still closer. He was on the side away from the purse, but Harry kept his hand on his money none the less. The group at the main table had broken up now, its members were making ready for bed, and most of the torches were out.

'I was apprenticed to a good master the past three years, but he died a month ago, and there was no one to carry on his business. There'll be nothing for me to learn in Pool. In Hereford I might get taken on for the works of the cathedral. But I'd as lief have a lay patron if one offers. I've heard this Lord of Parfois, over the Severn, keeps his own masons. Would there be any use in my going there?'

His head was aching with weariness and strain, but he might as well get his information from a willing source, however little truth or trust he was prepared to give in return.

'Ah, you don't want such as my lord Isambard for a patron, lad, God forbid, he's a cruel hard master. You'd far better come with me into Pool to-morrow, and I'll see you well placed with a good mason who knows his trade and treats his men well.'

If I went with you, thought Harry, not too exhausted or too wrung to preen himself a little on his knowingness, I should be picked up somewhere in the ditch penniless, with a broken head, and nothing on me but my shirt and chausses – if you left me those.

'Thank you for your offer, sir,' he said, 'I'm sure you mean it kindly. But I think I'll try there at Parfois before I move on.'

'It would be no use now, lad, he's away from England with all his knights. Even his master-mason's not there, for I know he's building down at the manor of Erington.'

It was said too confidently to be anything but true, and moreover Harry should have realised the probability for himself. The King had summoned all the knight-service of the country to his muster for France, where else would the Lord of Parfois be? Nevertheless he found himself startled and shocked to be brought up thus against the absence of his enemy, a check he had never foreseen.

Now what was to become of his bid to re-establish himself? There was no guessing how long the army would remain in France. Campaigning was an expensive business, so he had heard Llewelyn complain, and the rapid assaults and resolute marches of the clansmen of Gwynedd were cheap by comparison with the kind of triumphal progress the King had fitted out for France. Could he even afford to winter there? And would the French Queen-mother and her advisers let him? No, surely he would bring his fleet home for the winter with whatever advantages they could gain by then. But even so it meant Harry must keep his courage and resolution screwed to the point of action for months, and provide for himself meantime into the bargain, unless he was prepared to creep home to Aber with his tail between his legs.

It was too much for him. He felt the tears stinging his eyes, and in pure rage with himself made short and effective work of his informant.

'Then I'll head for Hereford,' he said, and stood up, giving a suggestive flick forward to the dagger at his belt, so that the sharp eyes that were studying its hilt so lovingly should be left in no doubt that it had a blade, too, and was for use rather than ornament. 'Alone!' said Harry, all the more aggressively because his voice was none too steady.

'As you please, young sir, as you please,' said the packman hurriedly, and withdrew with a lingering look that ran down the boy's side like chilly water and settled in his groin where the thin little purse was hidden.

The last of the torches went out. Harry lay down, wrapping his cloak about him in the dark, and under its shelter made fast his purse, knotting it into his shirt under the belt of his chausses, so that even with a knife it should be impossible to get it away from him without awakening him. Then, feeling the irresistible tears growing too great to be contained, he drew a fold of cloth over his face and clenched his teeth in it to muffle and suppress the tremors that shook him.

Everything was ill-done, everything! Everything betrayed him, time, chance and men, even the best and most beloved; and now events had conspired to make a fool of him and snatch his enemy away out of his reach, leaving him caught by the heels still in the swamp of his disgrace. But he would not go back. He was a man, with a man's craft, and he would show Adam he could live by his hands as surely as he would show Llewelyn his honour was to be reckoned with on equal terms with his father's. He could very well do what he had pretended he was bent on doing, look for a master and work for his living until Isambard came back to Parfois. Never on any conditions would he go back to Aber until his vengeance was accomplished.

He lay with his muffled face buried in his arms in the piled rushes of the corner of the hall, and wept out of him helplessly the too complicated tensions of his grief; until gradually the complexities fell away and left him abandoned to the sole thought of de Breos dead, the admirable engine broken, the audacious spirit silenced. Then he felt himself in some incomprehensible fashion reconciled with this chief of his betrayers, and quit of all grievance against him; and the tears came more freely for being recognised for what they were, the earnest of his desperate grief for a man he had loved and admired, who was now pitifully and irrecoverably lost.

He awoke from the absolute sleep of the young at first light, refreshed and calmed, and picked his way very quietly out of the close warmth of the hall into the sweet, chill air of the morning. Beneath the flank of the east end of the church there was a grave he must visit.

He had never been to Strata Marcella before, but he knew exactly where to find it, close under the wall. There was no mitre on it, though it lay among the tombs of the abbots; there was no lettering to identify it. There was nothing but a single leaf carved in the edge of the flat stone, one small leaf uncurling strongly as if to hold up an invisible abacus. He traced it with his finger-tip, kneeling in the grass; unless you knew where to look you could easily pass by and never know there was a leaf there. Adam had carved it, long ago. The hollows were outlined delicately in yellowish moss now, as though he had inlaid his work with gold.

Harry said his prayers more solemnly and attentively than he had ever yet said them in his life. When they were done he did not rise, but remained kneeling, staring over his clasped hands at the little symbol in the stone. Nothing was ever put into words, no vow ever made, but when he rose from his knees he had promised that young mysterious, Protean father of his that he would not rest until he had confronted Ralf Isambard and exacted from him a full repayment for untimely death.

The sense of having committed himself filled him with purpose and peace. He looked up from the wide water-meadows, eastwards across the silvery pools the Severn had left in every dimple after the spring floods, across the broad main stream of the river with its faint, drifting wreaths of mist, to the black hog-back of the Long Mountain, indented in half a dozen places along its vast, forested flank by the seamed valleys where brooks flowed down to join the Severn. Behind the ridge the eastern sky was growing pale and clear as primroses, and outlined against that radiance, hard and black among the feathery fringing of trees along the distant crest, showed the towering shape of the castle of Parfois on its rocky outcrop, staring out over Wales.

As he watched, the first rays of the still hidden sun fingered their way out of the east and launched themselves, quivering like a flight of iridescent birds, across the highest point of the crest. The castle remained dark, but close to it a sudden tapering shaft of gold sprang into sight, embracing and refracting the vibrating light, prolonging itself in a splendid, aspiring tension towards the sky.

For the first time in his life he was looking at the tower of Master Harry's church of Parfois. To him, in the astonishment of that apparition, it seemed that for the first time he had caught a glimpse of his father, not through the eyes of

109

Llewelyn, or Owen, or Gilleis, or Benedetta, or Adam, though all of them had loved and honoured him, but in his own fallible and vulnerable flesh and hot and hapless blood, the same he had conferred, for better or worse, upon his only son.

The woods were thick below Parfois, and crowded him down to the riverside, where a narrow path threaded the undergrowth. All the way from Buttington, where he had forded the Severn, the trees had shrouded his movements and covered him from sight, until now, by his reckoning, he was close to the outlet of the stream that came down from the crevices of the castle rock, and somewhere on his left hand, far above him, the ramparts of Isambard's curtain-wall fretted the noon sky.

The river had left the tide-mark of its spring spate on the sodden bushes and flattened grass, and under-cut here and there a crumbling section of the bank, leaving a perpetual swirl of frothy brown water. He was skirting one of these pools when he caught the rustle of shaken bushes, and knew that he was not alone. He did not make the mistake of halting; that would have been to betray his awareness. He went on slowly leading Barbarossa along the twisting path; and in a moment the tremor of leaves had moved alongside him.

Not an otter, then; an otter, and for that matter any other beast, would have removed itself from him, not kept watchful pace with him. These borders were notorious for the number of their forest outlaws, since the river provided an effective means of retreat if pursued, and the wanted Englishman was apt to be a welcome ally on the fringe of Wales. Harry loosened his dagger warily in its sheath, and paced on with ears stretched for the small sounds that accompanied him.

He waited until his emergence upon a clear view of the river gave him opportunity to halt in apparent innocence and look across the sunlit water, which here moved unimpeded along a cleaner shore, though still overhung with trees. Carefully he fixed the clump of bushes that trembled faintly before it stilled; and dropping Barbarossa's bridle he flung himself into the thicket, plunging low to take the watcher about the knees and bring him down.

He touched smooth naked flesh that slipped through his startled fingers like a fish, and a light body fled from him through the threshing branches. The next moment he heard the neat plash of a dive as the watcher took to the water.

Harry picked himself up scratched but dogged, and plunged after. Near the edge of the bank, tucked under a low bush, he stumbled over a tight little roll of brown homespun and coarse linen, laid neatly in the grass between a pair of shoes of roughly sewn leather. He stooped and snatched up the roll with a muted shout of triumph, and kicked the shoes out into the open; they were so small that he laughed with relief at the sight of them. So he had made all that needless effort to frighten a mere child, an inquisitive boy!

He looked out into the river, still laughing. Ten yards out from the bank a sleek, small head surfaced warily, trailing streaming hair.

'Come in with you,' he called reassuringly. 'I'll not touch you.'

The head hovered, apparently untroubled by the current; he knew from the movement of the surface how the boy turned into the stream with a stroke just strong enough to maintain his ground; by the ease with which he moved in it he must spend half his young life in the water.

'I took you for a masterless man, not a child, and I've got a good horse to lose. Ah, come away in! Do I look as if I mean you any harm?'

The sleek head and a naked shoulder dipped against the stream, the boy ventured nearer but still held off dubiously from the shore. Harry could see the honey-coloured flesh gleaming through the soiled water, and the large bright eyes in the wary face watching his every move. The floating hair was the muted brown of the little leather shoes; when it was dry it would probably be a dark corn-yellow. He looked about

111

eleven or twelve years old, and as wild as a hare. When Harry made an incautiously abrupt movement of his hand the head ducked out of sight instantly, leaving only a quivering ring upon the water, and broke surface again a dozen yards away.

'You'll have to come in the end,' said Harry reasonably, grinning at him. 'I've got your clothes.'

'Put them down,' said the head sullenly, 'and go away and leave me come in in peace.'

'You might run away from me. And I want to talk to you.' A creature who so clearly lived on familiar terms with these woods and this river was the very ally he needed, and none the worse for being only a boy.

'I won't run away,' said the swimmer, but with an intonation which inspired no great confidence, any more than it indicated any in him.

'By your leave, we'll make sure of that. Here are your clothes, come and take them.'

'I can't!' shouted the child in exasperation. 'Fool, why don't you look what you've got there?'

Even then he didn't understand. He let the edge of the bundle slip out of his hand, and it unrolled to his feet a rough brown gown and a linen shift instead of the chausses and tunic and shirt he had expected. He let the hems fall as though he had been burned, and withdrew hurriedly and a little indignantly into the bushes; but before he reached the path again he looked back once over his shoulder, very quickly. It was only a broken glimpse between the lattice of the branches, but he saw her heave herself out of the water shimmering, and shake her hair like whips round her head, and before he hastily averted his eyes he saw that she was laughing.

And that was strange, for when she stepped out on to the path five minutes later she was grave enough. She had wrung out her wet hair and coiled it in a knot on top of her head so that it should not hang down on the shoulder of her gown. The drab homespun had a tear or two in it here and there, and the skirt was kilted nearly to her knees, but she came out of the bushes like a queen emerging from her robing-room. She had her shoes in her hand, and the small bare feet, where they were not still muddy between the toes from the river, were honey-coloured like her arms, and the slender long neck, and the shoulder that had glistened momentarily out of the water. She looked thoughtfully at him, and more thoughtfully still at Barbarossa, and her bright blue glance came back to him again, to look him over shrewdly from head to foot, and make unfathomable guessses about his origin, his estate and his business there in the forest. She had not missed even his heightened colour and somewhat excessive dignity; and she was older than he had supposed, probably within a year of his own age.

'Why were you following me?' she said accusingly, as though she had set out to prove in one utterance her uncompromising femaleness.

'I following you? *You* were following *me.*'

'I was only trying to get back to my clothes. And then you attacked me.' She eyed him warily still, but she was not really afraid of him; the measurements she had taken had roused her curiosity but allayed any fears she might have been harbouring.

'What were you doing?' he asked, himself no less curious. 'It's cold yet for swimming.'

'I was putting down eel-traps. They began to run three weeks ago. What are *you* doing here?'

'Do you live here in the forest?' he asked, ignoring her question.

'Yes. A little way up-river yet, and then a little way inland. With my father,' she added with emphasis, to warn him that she was not unprotected, and revolved between sharp white teeth the tender end of a long grass she had pulled from its sheath. Her eyes, he saw, were as blue as the zenith, and fringed with long, dark-gold lashes, and when her hair was dry it would be only a shade darker than the smooth forehead beneath it. She examined him steadily, missing nothing. Not even the hopeful packman at Strata Marcella had made so rapid and shrewd an inventory of his dress and

113

person.

'My name is Aelis,' she said. 'Tell me yours.'

'Harry,' he said, and choked just in time upon the rest of it. Why make it easier for anyone who came inquiring for him? He did not think they would follow him here into the wilds, but it would be foolish to be too complacent.

He expected her to pounce upon his too obvious change of heart, and demand another name, but she smiled as though he had told her more than he knew.

'Where do you come from, Harry?'

'From Chester,' he lied, and felt the need to spread out for her the whole story he had prepared, of his dead master and his broken apprenticeship. He might as well perfect it upon her before trying it upon others of a more sceptical turn of mind. But it seemed he was still underrating her. The bright, deliberate eyes lingered expressively upon his horse and too princely harness, flashed from the texture of his sleeve to the chased hilt of his dagger, then looked him challengingly in the eye. She laughed. It seemed he would have to change his clothes and part with Barbarossa before he could hope to pass muster in his chosen part.

'And what are you seeking here in the forest?' she asked, drawing still nearer to him.

If lies were of no use to her he'd try her with at least a morsel of truth. 'A place to hide in,' he said. 'Only for a little while, a week, two weeks maybe.' That would be long enough to explore and map the approaches of Parfois, but after that he must go into Pool and find work, for he could not pay his way much longer on what he had in his purse. He had even thought of going as far as Shrewsbury, which was a charter town, and used to taking in fugitives and asking no questions; but it was too far from this fortress on which his whole heart was now set. Pool would have to find him a living, he did not greatly care what he did to earn it.

This time she did not laugh, nor did she ask for any more from him than he had volunteered of his own will. She gave him a sudden warm smile and said indulgently: 'Why didn't you say you were a runaway? When I first caught sight of you not ten yards from me I got such a fright, I thought you were from the castle. I'd never have run from you if I'd known you were an outlaw.'

Bright with curiosity, the blue eyes searched him through and through, but she would not question him further; all those who were running from justice, from villeinage, from debt, from their families, were natural allies to her. She and her father had always lived precariously half within and half without the law, scratching a meagre crop legally out of a couple of fields enclosed in an unprofitable assart years ago, and poaching fish from the river and conies and hares from the woods, even an occasional hart when it could be done without too great a risk.

'Have I said I was an outlaw?' he protested, uneasy in so unfamiliar a role.

'Ah, you can trust me,' she said disdainfully. 'You're not the first that's gone to earth with us, and you wouldn't be the first we've put across the river by night, if that's what you want. You've no need to be wary with me, I'm not anxious to be in your secrets. The less we know the less we can let slip. You keep your counsel. There's a boat at the mill, if you daren't show yourself at the ferry or the fords.'

It dawned upon him then, for the first time, that she had taken it for granted he was English, and it astonished him out of all measure. It was as though he had been brought up suddenly against his image in a mirror, and seen himself as a stranger. How did she know? He did not even feel himself to be English, for all his name and his blood, for all his father's Latin education at the comfortable Benedictine abbey of Shrewsbury, and his mother's good mercantile stock from London. He knew the facts of his parentage, but they did not affect his vision of himself as a young Welsh clansman bound by fostering as closely as by kinship to the royal house of Gwynedd. And here this wild girl looked him over, Welsh cloth and all, and knew him for English. It seemed he was owning another attachment now, whether he would or no, being bound into new patterns of loyalty by ties he had never yet recognised as realities. More and more with every step now he belonged to his father. The very soil this side of Severn knew him.

'All I want is a place to lie hidden,' he said. 'I can pay.'

'Ah, pay!' said Aelis good-humouredly. 'What will you cost us? You'll help me with my snares, and we'll be quits. Come away, then, and I'll bring you to my father. Nobody bothers us. We're well away from the track to the mill, and a good mile off the road up to Parfois, and these woods are poor hunting, the other side the Mountain gives better sport. Nobody'll look for you here.'

She coiled up again the slipping knot of her hair, that was beginning to glisten at the edges with drying strands of gold, and began to lead the way barefoot along the narrow path. He followed her, leading Barbarossa by the bridle, and it seemed to him suddenly that everything had become strange and new to him, and held a kind of unexpected and tremulous promise. For the first time in his life he had no idea what was to become of him, what unpredictable and daunting creatures were to cross his path. He was frightened and happy. Not for the world, not even the old, familiar and delightful world, would he have turned back now.

The knot of heavy hair slipped from its coils again, and hung loose about her shoulders. For one instant he was transfixed by the memory his mind had been struggling in vain to excise, the bright, coiling gold dried into limp, fair tresses drawn across blue-veined breasts, and the sword-thrust of hate and anger and love split his heart again. Then the balance swung back and held him poised, shaken but resolute, and the pale, unforgettable disfigurement of the immaculate image was dazzled out of his mind's eyes by his stolen glimpse of Aelis, aloof and self-reliant in her young, fresh, virginal nakedness.

'This is the place,' said John the Fletcher, throwing a satisfied glance over the narrow, fenced field and the low roof of the hut receding into the twilight of the trees. 'Only two false casts, after fifteen years, is not bad remembering. And there's the man, thanks be to God for him, the same that helped me carry the pair of them up from the river, him dead and her with the life just in her. I had the fear in me all this while he might be dead and gone himself before now; it's a long while to leave a man and expect to find him again not much changed.'

They had crossed the Severn at Pool and ridden downstream, without over-much hope in them but resolute to try every chance that offered. At Strata Marcella the gatekeeper had remembered the chestnut horse, or they might never have known whether they were on the right trail or no; and when they had combed every village on the Welsh bank, and every street in Pool, John had set his face for the assart where Master Harry had been brought ashore after his death. It had been a fated place for them once, it might be so again.

There lay the hut before them now, the low undercroft and the one small room above, the starved clearing fields, the corner of poor grazing. The man who slipped his rabbit snares so deftly out of sight within the undercroft as they appeared was perhaps forty years old, old enough to be the same taciturn young woodsman of fifteen years ago; but the girl who sat milking the lean cow in the home corner of the pasture was no more than fourteen or fifteen.

'And there's the horse we're looking for,' said Adam in a vast sigh, nodding towards the dark recesses of the undercroft, where a lofty red head nuzzled contentedly in the hayrack. 'Who says we've not been guided? He's here!'

The man of the house came towards them with a wary face, his eyes expressionless. The short, crisp beard had two curved streaks of grey in its brown now, but he was not greatly changed.

'Good even, masters,' he said flatly. 'Are you out of your way? This path leads nowhere past here, you'll do better to keep to the riverside.'

'Good even, Robert,' said John the Fletcher. 'We're not out of our way, by God's grace we've found our way well enough.'

'You know me?' said the man, withdrawing a step and

117

casting a glance aside at his daughter, who picked up her milking pail and approached them with a blithe and innocent face, but sharp and watchful eyes.

'Time was when I did, for a passing while, and you knew me, too, but it's fifteen years since, and I doubt I'm changed more than you.' He stripped off the capuchon from his head and leaned nearer, but the man looked up at him sturdily and shook his head. 'Ah, well, the light's going. But you'll remember the time when I tell you. Do you mind a day about this time of year – but the floods were later that spring, I recall – when you and I took two queer fish out of the Severn?'

He saw the broad shoulders stiffen and the bearded head come up with a start to stare at him again.

'Ay, you remember. A man and a woman tied naked in each other's arms, the man dead and the woman barely living. Thrown in to rot together, from the stage where Isambard unloaded his stone – ' He never spoke of it, but the memory of that day was in him intact still, not one molten detail dimmed or cooled. He had been waiting all these years to repay the debt, and he had but to let the words form in his mouth and he was shaken and aflame with the old unassuaged fury.

'For God's sake leave that name alone,' said Robert softly. 'I know who it was did it, and so do you. That's enough. So it's you, is it, after all these years? I never thought to see you again. How is it with the lady? Is she still living?'

'She is, and well. I've left her but two weeks ago, safe in Wales. And your good wife?'

'Dead these seven years. The autumn fever took her. But here's my girl Aelis helps me in her mother's stead, and a good lass she is.'

'I'm sorry for your loss,' said John. 'She was the gentlest soul, I mind how she nursed my lady all those hours we thought we'd never get the breath back into her. The girl's like her, if I'm remembering well. She had the same yellow hair.'

'She had. Well, how it all comes back to me, and I've not thought of it for ten years, I dare say. It was the year before Aelis here was born. Come in with you both, if you'll not mind a poor man's hearth and poor folks' fare.'

'We were glad enough of it then,' said John, dismounting. 'And this is Master Adam Boteler, who was foster-brother to that same Master Harry we brought in here dead that day, and has taken his wife and son for his own ever since. And Robert, it seems you're always to be our salvation, for this time we've lost the boy, and by the look of things you've found him for us.'

Robert froze into stillness with Adam's stirrup in his hand. 'Boy? What would make you think I know anything of any boy?'

'His horse,' said Adam. 'That red beast with the white diamond yonder in your undercroft. There's no mistaking him. If you doubt we're honest we can tell you the whole history of that horse, up to the time he galloped out of Aber with Harry on his back. We've been looking high and low for him ever since.'

Aelis drew nearer to her father's side, and her fingers sought his sleeve. Robert hesitated, looking narrowly from face to face.

'You're father to him now, you tell me? Then what ailed him to run from you? What's he done amiss?'

'Nothing amiss. He ran because of a grief not of our making, and no shame to him,' said Adam. 'Nobody's set against him, and there's only a good welcome waiting for him when we take him home. Boys take things hard at his age, you know it yourself. Man, do you think we'd mean him anything but good? He's Talvace's son. For God's sake don't keep us on thorns, but if you've got him here, tell us.'

Robert had made up his mind. 'He's here,' he said. 'He's been with us the past fifteen days.' He shook off the insistent hand that pulled at his sleeve. 'Leave worrying, girl, can't you, you see these are his friends. Well, sirs, that's the truth of it. Ever since he came I've been plaguing my memory to know where I'd seen that face before, and never could get to

119

the bottom of it, It's plain enough, now you tell me whose son he is. Well, come in, come in! Turn your horses into the paddock there. He's off somewhere in the forest now – where was it he was bound, Aelis?'

She would know; she was in all his planning and all his preparations, though she still did not know to what ambitious end all this strange reconnaissance was dedicated. She said in a small and wary voice: 'He was going to try to climb the castle rock on the blind side. I told him it couldn't be climbed, but he laughed at me. He said he learned his business on Snowdon, and he'd write his name on the stones of the Lady's Tower before night.'

Adam and John exchanged a long, disquieted glance. 'Is that what he's been doing all this time he's been here with you?' asked Adam, eyeing the girl anxiously. 'Climbing and scheming about Parfois?'

She nodded, beginning to be afraid, though of what she did not understand. She pushed back the tress that fell over her forehead, and stared back at Adam with great solemn blue eyes. 'He's there every day. Sometimes in the gully between the castle and the church, sometimes climbing on the sheer face. And he draws things, scratches them on the rocks and sits and frets over them for hours.' She had caught the infection of their uneasiness, and was trembling. 'What is he trying to do? What is it he wants?'

Robert looked from Adam to John, and shook his head. 'Only too well I see what he wants! If I'd known what was in his mind I'd have made shift to get out of him where he came from, and sent word to you somehow, but hereabout we never ask questions of them that don't want to share their secrets. I never asked the boy so much as his name. Come into the house, then, and wait for him. By the shape of it,' he said grimly, leading the way, 'you've come just in time.'

Harry came down the sandstone cliff below Parfois in the last of the light, in high content with his own performance but no nearer to achieving his main purpose. It seemed to him

120

that the place was impregnable. The one formal way of approach, the long traverse which had been shored up into a ramp when the fortress was built, was guarded half-way up by two watch-towers, and from that point on had a broken sandstone cliff on either side. He could climb it without great difficulty, but even if he did he would have achieved little, for he would merely emerge upon the level plateau on which the church was built, and between that and the wards of the castle there was a forty-foot-deep gully, crossed only by the drawbridge at the gate-towers. The outcrop on which Parfois stood was an island in the air, sheer on all sides, the curtain-wall with its six great towers rose out of the solid rock.

The most precipitous face of rock, beneath the Lady's Tower, was also the blind face, the only side not overlooked from any turrets, short of leaning out from Isambard's insolent lancet windows and looking vertically down the cliff. But when Harry had taken advantage of these factors and mastered the climb on that side, there remained twenty feet of well-built stone wall above him to the nearest loopholes, and not even the clansmen who had nursed him up the crags of Eryri had yet found a way of walking up a smooth wall.

He had scratched his initials on the lowest courses of the masonry, just as he had promised Aelis he would do, and that was achievement enough for one day. The problem of overleaping the wall would need more thought. Yet he was in good heart as he dropped through the rough scrub-land into the forest, and made for his supper and his bed; and it was a stunning shock to reach the edge of the clearing and see the two strange horses in the paddock. The roan was almost invisible in the deepening dusk until he moved and called softly; the grey was pale and almost lambent, a horse sketched in subdued light. He recognised them both.

He stopped on the instant, drawing back into the trees. The most frightening thing was that now they had found him, a part of him, hitherto in subjection, rose in thankfulness and wanted to run to meet them; but the part of him where his pride resided was more potent, and soon stamped down the relieved and craven child. He was not going back. That was certainty.

He was Harry Talvace, and he had every right to be here about his father's business. It ought to be possible for him to walk in upon them and say so, and firmly hold to it. He ought to be capable of asserting himself and sending them home without him, or even commanding their allegiance in what he was setting out to do. The trouble was that he was not sure of his authority. To be over-ridden and dragged back home unwillingly to Aber would be humiliating enough in any circumstances, unendurable with Aelis looking on.

He stood irresolute, scuffing his feet against the terraced fungus round the bole of a tree. It was manifestly unfair to think of Adam as an oppressive father, Adam who had never in his life lost his patience with son or apprentice, and preserved in himself enough of the boy to feel tenderly for other boys. But the fact remained that whenever he had come into head-on collision with Adam over any issue, whenever they had stared each other out eye to eye in a test of wills, Adam had always won.

No, he couldn't risk facing him. He had everything to lose now, it was no longer merely a question of his honour, no longer a gesture of defiance made in the face of all who doubted him; some part of his own heritage, even of his own identity, lay within the walls of Parfois, and until he possessed himself of it he could not be complete.

Yet it was not so easy to turn and go away through the forest, and leave them there waiting for him. There was Robert to be thought of, and Aelis. They had taken him in like a son, accepting him without question because they thought him hunted and in need of shelter. He owed them what he had no means of repaying, unless they would accept the gold clasp he had unpicked from his cloak to make him less conspicuous; and if they took that, would it be safe for them to try to sell it, even in Shrewsbury? People had been suspected of theft and banditry on less evidence. But they could sell the good, plain clothes he had exchanged for these old patched weeds of Robert's, at least those were not so rich as to provoke suspicion. If only Aelis would come out from the hut!

And come she did, when he had almost given up hope of her, and was withdrawing with many backward glances into the woods. She appeared suddenly against the lighted doorway, and went round to the back of the hut to shut up the pen on her few scrawny fowls; he heard them muttering sleepily on their perch at her step. He dared not whistle to her at that distance, the men in the hut would hear, and he was desperately afraid that she would go in again and close the door against him. But instead of turning back she came quickly along the edge of the open ride and into the trees, at every few paces checking and listening, and he knew that she was straining her ears for sign or sound of him. She had understood him very well; she knew he would not come in.

He waited until she was within a dozen yards of him, and then called to her softly and urgently between the trees.

'Aelis!'

His own voice sounded discomfortingly plaintive and small to him, and alarmingly irresolute, but it reached her. She turned gladly and flew to meet him, and he caught her by the shoulders and held her close to him there in the dark.

'Harry, they're here! They came for you. We wouldn't have told, but they knew Barbarossa.'

'I know,' he said feverishly. 'I know their horses as they know mine. Aelis, I'm not coming in. I can't go back with them.'

'But they mean you no wrong, they only want you home. There's nothing to be feared of –'

'I'm not feared,' he said, affronted. 'But I have things I must do. I can't go home till they're done, I won't.'

'Come in,' she urged, closing her cool fingers strongly on his arm. 'Come and talk to them at least. They've been in dread for you, you can't leave them without a word.'

'I must. If I came in they'd get me home, and I can't go home yet. Tell them nothing. You haven't seen me, you don't know where I've gone. Some day, when they've given me up, I'll come back to see you again. And, Aelis – my cloak buckle – it's for you, if you know of a way of turning it to use. And my clothes –'

'I could bring them to you,' she said eagerly. 'You can't go anywhere in those tatters you've been roaming the woods in. And I could loose Barbarossa to you –'

'No, I'm better without him. I must go into Pool and find work to do there, and what would a prentice mason be doing with a beast like him? And the clothes, too – I'll do better in these. And, Aelis, I'll come back, I promise I will –'

She heard the tremor of tears not far below the level of his voice, and knew how terribly he was tempted. 'They'll be main sad for you,' she protested, herself in tears.

'I know! I'll make all right one day, but now there's no way for me but to go. Take care of Barbarossa for me till I come again.'

'How if they take him away with them?' she said, wiping her eyes on her sleeve.

'Then let them, for he'll be as well with them. But maybe they'll leave him in the hope that I'll come back for him. They'll want you to send a message if I do, but Aelis, you won't do it, you mustn't do it, not unless I bid you –'

'I'll do what I please,' she said sullenly, muffling a sob against her forearm. 'Someone has to think for you, if you're such a great fool, and don't know your friends. And there's your mother waiting at home for you, and you'd let her go on grieving –'

'Let my mother be!' he flashed, shivering and raging, and pushed her from him roughly in a convulsion of nervous distress, only to snatch her back to him the next moment in a quick, remorseful embrace. 'Oh, Aelis – oh, Aelis, I can't help it! I'll send word to her when I can, I will, but not this way. I can't stop now, I must go on. I've no choice –'

The lighted doorway across the clearing darkened with the shape of a man. Robert's voice called: 'Aelis!' placidly into the night.

'Good-bye!' breathed Harry, and was gone, slipping away

124

through the trees in shivering haste.

'What are you doing there, girl? What is it?'

'A fox,' said Aelis loudly and viciously, 'skulking round the pen in the dark, the creature, and off like an arrow when you come out to him. You'd need a trap to take the likes of him.'

She hoped her voice would carry to Harry's ears and set them burning. She hoped he'd find no one to employ him, and have to come creeping back here, and he'd see if she'd do as he bade her or as she pleased. Serve him right if they hauled him back home with a flea in his ear instead of treating him like a man and an equal.

All the same, she kept a blank face and a silent tongue, at some cost to herself, when she went back into the house. And in the darkness of her own bed, while they sat out the night with waning hope, she made her pillow damp and comfortless with tears.

CHAPTER SIX

Parfois: *November to December* 1230

It was half a year before she saw him again.

She was kneading bread, her arms flour to the wrists, when the doorway behind her was darkened, and she knew even before she whirled to face him that this was not her father coming home from his snares. He had not entered the room, but stood warily outside it, looking in at her, and before he would step inside he asked: 'He's not home, then? You're alone?'

'Dear God!' she said, easily recalling her indignation even after six months. 'Is that any way to walk in on a girl, when you haven't shown your face nor sent a word all this time? You should come with your cap in your hand and ask leave before you step in here. I'm not sure if I'll have you over the door-sill.' She had him by the hand by then, and was drawing him in to the hearth, for the early November mist was on his shoulders, and his face looked thin and cold.

'You'll not try to keep me?' he said warningly, looking her in the eyes without a smile.

'I'll never try to keep any man who doesn't want to stay, don't think yourself so sorely missed. We've done without you all these months, we can do without you still.' She pushed him into a seat on the stone beside the fire, and brushed the moisture from his hair, taking care not to be too gentle about it; and when he made no move to stop her she unfastened his damp cloak and hung it to dry. 'Are you hungry? Though why I should care, when you left us like you did, is more than I know.'

Once, if addressed in such a tone, he would have denied his hunger stiffly, even while it stared nakedly out of his eyes;

but now it seemed he had learned sense enough not to climb on his high horse quite so easily and unprofitably.

'I am,' he said almost meekly, 'but I'd just as soon not eat you out of home, when I've brought nothing in. I can't stay but a little while. I didn't want your father to know I was back, for fear he'd want to hold me.'

'You're your own master,' said Aelis tossing her head, and brought him the end of a loaf, and cheese, and milk to drink, and watched him sidelong, not without satisfaction, as he devoured his meal. 'By the looks of it,' she said, 'they haven't been feeding you any too well, where you've been. Did you find that work you were looking for?'

'Yes,' said Harry indistinctly round a mouthful of bread. He had found it and endured it, but it had opened his eyes to what apprenticeship meant under another master than Adam. He'd learned from it, too; not, perhaps, very much about masonry, but a great deal about keeping his temper and holding his tongue, even under injustice. It had been a choice between bearing what he had or running back to Aber where he was privileged and protected, and for Harry that had been no choice at all. If he wanted to reach his goal he must come to terms with the stages of the journey, however comfortless.

'Did you bind yourself?'

'No,' he said shortly. How could he bind himself, when he did not know the day or the hour when Isambard might come home? It was unthinkable to pledge his word to stay for a fixed term when he might not be able to keep it.

'Then they'd never take you on as better than a labourer.' She knew what that could mean, when the labourer was as young and inexperienced as he, and she looked him over again carefully for the signs of his servitude, ignoring the forbidding stare that warned her off from probing.

He was still wearing her father's patched chausses and cotte, the short, rusty brown one she had mended for him; it needed more mending now. He was taller by a good inch than when she had last seen him, or he looked so for being noticeably thinner. His cheeks were hollow, and his hands

127

scarred and soiled.

'I see he starves his boys,' she said, 'as well as working them hard.' Her measuring glance moved to the corner of his mouth, where the line of his lips was prolonged in a short red scar, and then to his cheek-bone, which bore a suggestive blue stain. 'And beats them,' she said.

'What's that to you?' said Harry haughtily, turning the bruised side of his face away from her. 'You said you know no reason why you should care.'

'Oh, Harry!' she said suddenly in a child's wail of reproach, and fell on her knees by him, flinging her arms round him. The hunk of bread was knocked out of his hand and dropped on the edge of the hearth-stone. Aelis snatched it back and blew the ashes from it for him, blinking back tears.

'Oh, now, it's not been as bad as that,' he said, shamefaced, and laid his arm awkwardly round her shoulders and drew her close to him. 'The worst was keeping my hands from my dagger and my mouth shut. The youngest gets the kicks from all the rest, that's nothing new. One of the journeymen was a good fellow, and taught me what he knew, and stood by me all he could. But I missed having you to talk to when I had an hour to myself.'

If the tone was a little condescending she did not complain; it was startling enough that he had brought himself to say it at all, and so he must have felt, for he coloured to the brows. He had wanted to give her something to remember him by; the feel of her warm and strange in his arm had surprised the clumsy offering out of him before he knew. Almost he repented it, it seemed to him so inadequate, not to her deserving, but to his weight and worth. But when she looked up at him astonished and unguarded in her pleasure his heart swelled, and he was glad he'd spoken.

'You're not going back there?' she said, fearful and jealous for him.

He shook his head.

'Where, then, if you won't stay here with us? Harry, what is it you're about?'

'There's a thing I must do,' he said. If there had ever been

128

a time when it had been a whim and not an obligation, that time was gone now; the thing was there waiting for him, blocking his path, and there was no way round it to his manhood.

'Will you come back here again when it's done?'

'Yes,' he said, 'when it's done I will. And when it's done I'll tell you.'

'I wish you'd take me with you,' said Aelis from under the shadow of her tangled golden hair, in a tone he had never heard from her before.

'That I can't do. But I'll come back. And look, I want you to have this. It's very little, all I've managed to save, but it's for you to use until I come back. Did they take Barbarossa away with them?' A new constraint came into his tone when he spoke of 'them'; it cost him a giant effort now, as well as a convulsion of remembering pain, to look back towards Aber.

'No, he's below in the undercroft. They left him here for you.'

He looked down into the fire, his lashes low on his cheeks. 'Did they wait long for me?'

'A week or more. They inquired for you everywhere. In the end they had to go, there was no sense staying. They said you'd come back for your horse, and my father promised to send them word.'

'And you?' he said with a pale smile.

'I didn't promise anything.' And she was promising nothing to him, either; he knew that was what she meant, but he did not ask for anything. She must judge, too; he thought she would trust him and let him have his way.

'You could put on your own clothes again,' said Aelis practically, pleased when she saw his eyes brighten. Yes, where he was going now he could at least appear as himself; the face was avowal enough, his dress should match the face. She went and fetched out the folded garments for him, and went about her business at the clay oven outside while he stripped and dressed himself again in the good Welsh clothes that had been made for him. The sleeves of the cotte

129

were grown a little short on him, but that was no great damage.

'They're dry and clean,' said Aelis over her shoulder. 'You'll take no hurt from them. And don't forget your good cloak. I'll hide these rags away; father'll never know you've been here.'

She turned, hearing the stillness that followed the rustling of his movements, and he was standing in the doorway, looking at her with a strange, soft look of mingled reluctance and resolution.

'I suppose you're off now, now you've got everything out of me you wanted.'

'Aelis –,' he said.

'Go on with you, then, and see you keep your word and come back afterwards.'

He hesitated before her a moment, and then he took her hands and bent his head, and gave her the solemn kiss of kinship; and before she could draw breath and touch her astonished fingers to her lips, he was out of the paddock and away across the clearing into the trees.

All through the hours of dusk he crouched beneath an overhang of bushes under the broken edge of the plateau on which the church stood, and listened to the comings and goings above his head, where the garrison of Parfois boiled with agitated preparations for its lord's home-coming.

The company had moved fast since landing at Portsmouth with King Henry late in October. Word of their approach had hardly reached Pool before they themselves were in Ludlow. To-night, according to the rumours that were running round the streets of Pool, they would camp at Montgomery, and cover the last short stage to Parfois in the morning. In every village round the Long Mountain at this moment the news was blowing like a cold and killing wind. The jackal de Guichet, they said, was bad enough, but there were limits to his powers; but the old lion acknowledged no restrictions within his own honour, his rule was as absolute as plague. Word of his home-coming sent the very wild beasts

130

quaking to their holes.

The climb had been no trouble to Harry, bred as he had been among the crags of Snowdon. This wedge-shaped promontory that led up to the isolated rock on which the castle itself stood was nowhere quite sheer, and stunted trees rooting precariously in its crevices afforded cover for one solitary boy, though they would not have hidden an approach in numbers. But there remained the problem which had been gnawing at his mind for months as he waited for his enemy to come home: how was he to get into the castle itself? There was only one way in, by the drawbridge and the gate-towers; he had racked his brains for an alternative, but there was none, short of procuring an ally within the walls, and that idea he did not entertain for a moment. No, since there was but one way in, by that way he must go.

At an ordinary time it would have been almost impossible to enter undetected, but tomorrow morning, when the Lord of Parfois brought home from France his forty knights and their followings, and the entire population of the castle came out to meet them and bring them in, then one more insignificant boy might very well slip unnoticed into the throng and get by the guard at the gate unchallenged. Once in he could lose himself among the excited household, and never be in one place long enough to be an object of suspicion, until he could find a means of encountering Ralf Isambard alone. Beyond that he did not look. There might be nothing beyond. Yet he could not stop short of that moment, and that was enough for him to know.

The sounds of Parfois were becoming familiar to him. He heard the hollow thudding of hooves and the duller sound of feet constantly tramping the timbers of the drawbridge. He heard many voices as people passed on the pathway from the bridge to the ramp. He heard vespers sung in the deep dusk from his father's church, and his heart stilled and quietened in him with wonder, as though at last he felt himself to be drawing near to the heart of a mystery.

Cramped and cold in his hide, he listened as the sounds of the day fell from him into silence one by one, until he could

131

hear the measured pacing of the watch on the walk between the gate-towers. Then, closing all, the chains of the bridge rattled evenly through their pulleys, and Parfois withdrew for the night into its impregnable walls. He crouched still for a time after that, for there was no haste, and now that it was time he found himself afraid; there might be something to lose there, as well as something to find.

When the silence had been undisturbed for a long, chilly while he crept out of his nest and drew himself gently up the last few yards of broken rock into the long grass and bushes at the edge of the plateau. There were stars but no moon, and the sky had cleared into a frosty blackness. He could distinguish, when he emerged from the fringe of trees, the toothed edge of the curtain wall, its merlons jagged against the stars; but between him and them, breaking the serpent-line that coiled round the entire rock, the dark shape of the church loomed.

When he looked up, the tapering masses drawing his eyes aloft even in the dark, he could see the tall tower prolonging its leaping tension towards the stars. By daylight it had been a sculptured shaft fluted with runnels of light and darkness, withdrawing stage by stage in charmed proportion, shedding weight and gaining impetus as it soared. Now it was a pillar of darkness covering him from the eyes of the watch as he stepped out from the trees and walked steadily across the open space of grass.

There was a small wicket set in the great west door. He laid both hands to the ring and turned it, and it gave to his cautious thrust and let him in.

In the cold darkness within he groped his way to the narrow stair that wound upwards into the triforium, and climbed it, clinging with nervous hands to the stone. Many a time Adam had drawn him plans and elevations of this nave; he knew its proportions and could find his way about it even in the night. It was not only because of its convenient position and its many sheltering solitudes that he had chosen to watch out the night here. In the dawn, before the host came home, he would surely be presented at last with one window into his father's spirit, and add to the many aspects of Master Harry he had borrowed from other people one at least which was his own.

He felt his way along the narrow walk of the triforium to the distant end, close to the east window that showed a shapely pattern of starry lancets against the blackness; and there he wrapped his cloak about him and huddled into the corner with his back against the wall. It was hard lying, but so much the better, he would be in no danger of falling asleep.

There were times during the long hours of dark when he did drop into an uneasy doze, but never for more than a few minutes together. He was cold to the bone, and with the first faint grey of pre-dawn he got up and began to walk the passageway, stamping his chilled feet with an infinitely small, puny sound against the flags of the flooring.

The light came slowly. About him the walls grew out of the dark in gradations of grey, paling and solidifying, put on bulk and proportion and form. Details unfolded like flowers, the carved heads on the corbels along his walk grew features and hair, and smiled and grimaced as he passed; the procession of the capitals of the nave burst into ebullient growth, leaf unfolding from leaf in the vigour of life itself. Colour came later, even in the glass of the great east window; first there was only the shape of comparative light, then gradually the lattice-work of the lead cames, a filigree of shapes that had no meaning until the warmth of approaching dawn conjured into them cloudy reds and blues and greens, and with every minute breathed into them a purer brightness and a sharper clarity. Then almost abruptly there was colour in the stone, too, a warmth of sleeping gold gleaming through the grey. Shadowy and mysterious, the inverted keel above his head floated, half-defined.

His hands, which were apprenticed to the same mystery, arched and spread their fingers before him in air, involuntarily reproducing the tension and precision of the vaulting. They thrust and tensed with delight in their own intricate machinery of bones and sinews, as the ribs that sprang

133

from the piers of the nave seemed to quiver with joy in their own energy. Then the drifting cloud that had massed before the rising sun parted, and a single shaft of direct light leaped through the east window, setting the rose tracery ablaze with glowing colours, and flew like a lance from end to end of the church, calling out of shadow the strong, slender ribs that patterned the vault with great starry flowers, turning the roof-rib to gold, and glittering in the curls of all the singing cherubim on the painted bosses.

He stood quivering to the gradations of light that sang in the roof, and did not know what it was that moved him so, the hour, or the true beauty of the proportions and spaces about him, or the marvellous and frightening sense of having drawn so close to the spring of his own being. He stared and was satisfied. So much of him was drawn into his eyes that he never heard the drumming of hooves cross the plateau from the ramp, or the rattle of the chains as the draw-bridge was lowered in haste. Only when the hollow reverberations of the horses' feet on the timber rolled along the rock fissures below did he start out of his trance to the realisation that a company of mounted men was riding into Parfois.

Already? No, it was impossible, they would not march out of Montgomery much before this. Where was the haste? He stood tensed, straining his ears. The cavernous rumblings did not continue long; perhaps a score of riders, no more. Then quietness again. Some advance party with orders in preparation for Isambard's reception. His part was to lie hidden here until the main body arrived, and all the household poured out to meet them. A score of men, and mounted at that, were no use to him; he needed hundreds.

The wicket in the west door opened silently; he did not mark it until its weight carried it gently right back to knock against the wall. The sound, in itself small, was magnified by the lofty roof, and startled him painfully, and he drew back with a bounding heart into the shadows of the triforium as a man stepped into the church.

He was tall and lean, a long dark shape in a sombre cotte of

134

dark brown or black, cut short below the knee for riding. Harry saw the jut of a sword-hilt at his hip, and watched him strip from his hands gauntlets that flashed sullen gleams of light from the iron rings banded into their backs. One of Isambard's advance party, and by the cut of him a man of importance. His dress was austere enough, but rich and ample, and worn with an authority that comes only by birth, and his movements had the unmistakable quality of nobility, the absolute conviction of one who has never had to hesitate or use caution and humility in order to placate his betters. They were also startling in their fierce, fluent grace. He walked forward into the middle of the nave, and stood looking straight before him at some point above the high altar. His face was in shadow, and Harry, fascinated and fearful, ventured to lean out a little from his eyrie to watch what he was at.

The man below could not have seen the movement, but he felt some shifting of the air above him, or heard, perhaps, if he had a wild beast's hearing as he had its gait, the mere rustle of a sleeve against the stone.

'What's that? Who's there?' he cried sharply, and reared his head instantly to stare into the trefoil opening.

Clinging close in the shelter of the stone, Harry looked down into a face suddenly vivid in the quickening light. Short, crisp hair, iron grey and still thick, lay close as a helmet on a head magnificently and subtly shaped, and was cut squarely across a great fleshless forehead. A clean-shaven Norman face, with a long, straight nose and an arrogant jaw, and eyes burning darkly in great hollow sockets. Why, he was old! The hard brown flesh was grown leathery and dried. And yet he was beautiful. The essential beauty showed through everywhere, and gave him a kind of timelessness that matched his movements. Through the stretched yellowish skin of the great forehead every moulding of the bone transmitted its permanent grace; through the thick, clinging hair the skull imposed its noble shape. Out of this splendid, imperishable lantern the deep eyes glared as though a stranger and a savage inhabited the dwelling an angel had abandoned.

Then he knew that he was looking at Ralf Isambard, lord of Mormesnil, Erington, Fleace and Parfois.

The moment had come upon him too soon; he felt his knees soften, and clung with rigid fingers to the pillar behind which he sheltered.

'What, are you there?' said the voice below, full and clear but very low. 'In the old place, at the old time? Will you come down to me, or shall I come up to you? Who calls the measure now?'

Harry felt his way backwards to the wall, out of range of the searching eyes, and leaned there a moment to breathe more easily.

'Very well,' said Isambard equably, 'I'll come to you, since you will not come to me.'

The sound his long-toed riding-shoes made on the flags was not clumsy, and yet curiously halting, like the pace of a lame man whose lameness shows only when he forgets to brace himself. The steps approached without haste the bottom of the staircase, and began to climb. On those narrow treads he must go carefully in such gear. Harry withdrew inch by inch along the dim passageway to the end, where he could have the wall on two sides of him, and flattened himself into the last shallow embrasure, beneath the last curved corbel. He hitched his belt round to have the hilt of his dagger readier to his hand, and loosened the blade in the sheath.

His inside was molten but his hands were steady. As well now as after days of hiding and waiting. Better. His bones bore him up again. His heart rose in his breast, not with hope or dread, only with awareness and acceptance. It was here; he had not to wait for it, and he was glad.

The measured step on the stairs had ceased; somewhere below there out of sight Isambard had stopped. Why?

The answer to that was made plain to him with a stab of dread when he ventured to peer out of his embrasure, for the tall figure was already at the top of the staircase and advancing silently and at leisure along the stone corridor. He had stopped to put off his shoes, that was all. The long feet in their well-fitted brown chausses made no sound. He was smiling, if that could be called a smile that drew his long mouth out of line, plucking the left corner obliquely upwards.

He said in the same low, intent voice: 'Is this what you expected of me, Harry? Should I rather have brought with me the cross from the altar?'

Harry's heart had begun to beat thunderously. The man had a devil. How else could he know everything, the name, the intent, all? How near should he let him come before stepping out to confront him? He wanted space to move, some yards between them when he closed. He was young and quick, he had surely the advantage provided he kept room to recoil out of range. This man was old, old, by Adam's reckoning five and sixty years.

Now, he thought, stiffening his sinews. He drew breath hard, and stepped out from his shallow niche and stood in the centre of the walk. The last of the stone heads his father had carved looked over his shoulder. He had paid it no attention, for the light still reached it only by reflected glimpses; but Isambard had lived with it on close terms for fifteen years, and knew it line for line and feature for feature. He saw the stone face and the living face unbelievably alike, and checked in his steady advance, himself for a moment still as stone. Then the two faces which had seemed identical showed him as suddenly all their diversities. The likeness was there, Master Harry's divination had been marvellously guided; but he had carved a man, and this, after all, was no more than a boy, not yet grown. The stone face, lively and young as it was, had a certainty about it the boy could not claim as yet. The one was made, the other still making. He knew now who it was who stood before him.

'Well, well!' he said softly. 'You are welcome. I've waited a long time for this.'

Said Harry: '*So have I!*'

He set a hand to his belt, and drew the hilt of his dagger forward with a gesture there was no mistaking. Braced with feet apart, his eyes steady upon his enemy, he waited for

Isambard to draw. The devilish smile, oblique and sharp as a scar, had come back to the gaunt face. When at length Isambard moved his hands to his belt it was not to the hilt of his sword, but to the buckles from which it hung. He unfastened them without haste, still smiling, tossed sword and sheath out from him through the trefoil opening, and let them fall into the presbytery. The clash they made on the stones below jarred Harry from head to heels, and for a moment shook the intensity of his concentration. He touched his hilt significantly.

'We're matched, my lord.'

Isambard followed the gesture and laughed, moving his hand slowly towards his own dagger. The crooked smile was fixed and deliberate. Harry waited no longer. All the years of waiting and longing and wondering poured together into his braced hands and poised, quivering feet. He plucked out his dagger and hurled himself with all the weight and skill he had upon his enemy.

The shock of the assault carried them both a yard or two back along the passageway. The blade tore Isambard's cotte not an inch below his heart, but he had caught the lunging wrist in his left hand and jerked it outwards and downwards, and the thrust sliced through cotte and shirt down his ribs, and left only a harmless surface graze behind. He had not attempted to draw; Harry was aware of that even in the heat of his attack, and it enraged him past measure and gave him strength beyond normal. A long right arm as hard as steel took him about the body, prisoning his left arm above the elbow, and the grazed breast leaned violently over him and broke his balance. Feeling himself falling backwards, he drove his heel hard into Isambard's instep, and brought him down with him, heaving and struggling on the stones.

The fall broke their hold on each other, and Harry tore his wrist free and stabbed again, but again his forearm was caught and held, and this time he did not draw blood. Isambard let his weight lie over him and held him down, and deliberately lifted the boy's right arm and dashed his elbow hard against the paving.

Pain flashed like fire from shoulder to finger-tips, and all his shrieking muscles tingled into helplessness. He fought to make his fingers remain closed on the dagger, but they would not obey him. He tried to reach across with his left hand and snatch the blade away, but his hands were held apart, and he was pinned down struggling and sobbing until the dagger slid slowly out of his fingers and clattered on the flags. Then, still smiling, Isambard forced the boy's wrists together, enclosed and held them mercilessly in one lean, muscular hand, and with the other picked up the dagger and tossed it after his own sword.

'Well, have you done?'

He held him down one-handed, smiling at his heavings and pantings as he struggled to break free; but as soon as he tossed the straining wrists away from him and sat back on his heel to rise, Harry made a furious lunge for the hilt of the dagger Isambard himself had disdained to draw. He had it half out of its sheath when a hard knee came down on his forearm and smashed him to the flagstones again.

'What, have I to strip myself before you'll cry enough?' said the deliberate, amused voice, not even blown after all this tussling. And he an old man!

Harry lay still, gathering his breath and tasting his chagrin, and the hatred he had never truly felt until then congealed about his heart like heavy fire. To struggle was only to weaken himself; he could not displace the weight or break the grip that held him down. They were still only man to man, and there was still quietness as soon as they were quiet. He drew long, soft, angry breaths, waiting mute and dangerous inside his helplessness like a beast in its lair. Sooner or later Isambard would have to loose his hold of him. He had promised nothing, asked for no quarter, made no submission. It was not yet over.

'So, that's better!' said Isambard grimly, and drew off from him and rose to his feet in one quick movement; but he kept his hand on his dagger this time, and swung that hip away from the boy.

Harry, heaving all his angry energy into action, caught one

dazzling glimpse of the lean, clear profile black against the sunlit air, framed between the cusps of the trefoil, with a drop of thirty feet at least behind him, and the stone flags of the chancel below. The boy rolled over and came on to one knee in a single lunge, and hurling himself at the man, caught him round the thighs with both arms, and swept him with him through the opening.

For one moment Isambard was caught off-guard, but he had lived in and trained and trusted that hard old body of his for sixty years, and in emergencies his very muscles thought for him. His long right arm went round the pillar at his shoulder, his unshod feet stiffened into the stone of the floor to resist the thrust, and gripped it immovably. Harry's weight swung him round but did not tear him from his hold, and it was the boy and not the man who hung for a long, palpitating moment suspended on the edge of the drop. Even then he did not fight to recover his own hold on safety, but strained at his slipping grip on the man, dragging him outwards.

Isambard braced his weight back and held fast. He thrust his free left hand into the back of Harry's collar, took a fistful of him, cotte and shirt and all, and twisted until the boy's cheeks purpled and his eyes began to swim. Choking, he shifted one hand from his enemy to claw at his own throat, and instantly the fist that was strangling him heaved him roughly back from the edge and flung him down in safety at the foot of the wall. This time he was not released. The pressure on his throat ceased at once, but the hand had only transferred its hold to his arm.

'No more of that!' said Isambard grimly, clapping the bruised wrists together again and pinning them fast. He stooped over the gasping boy, and with deliberation and without apparent anger struck him three light, stinging blows on the cheek with his open right hand. Not even hard blows a man could take with dignity, only the manner of measured punishment he might have dealt out to a misbehaving child with whom he had not lost patience.

'That's for despising your own life, fool,' he said calmly,

'Learn to kill like a reasoning man when you must, not like a woman crazed with spite.'

The boy crouched, glaring up at him fiercely, still panting, his suffused face marked now by the lean white stains of the blows, just beginning to flood with angry red. He set his teeth and said nothing, but his eyes were eloquent.

'I see he bred a good hater,' said Isambard, looking him over at leisure as he held him, and smiling at what he found. 'Well, well, this is a memorable home-coming! For you, as for me, boy, there'll be a warm welcome in Parfois. Let's go and savour it.'

He jerked him to his feet, and separating the thin wrists he held, twisted them together again behind the boy's back, and so thrust him painfully before him along the passageway to the staircase. As they went they heard the clatter of feet in the porch of the church, and voices that spoke in reverent under-tones, but not from awe of the holy place.

'De Guichet!' called Isambard, in a tone of high content. 'Here am I, and with a guest for you. Call the guard, let them take good care of him, he's a desperate firebrand.'

Three or four knights had come hastening in at the sound of their lord's voice.

'Do you know this face?' said Isambard, turning Harry about in his hands to display him to them all, and taking him by the chin to jerk up his face to the light when he turned it haughtily aside. The brief martial exercise, however un-orthodox, had put the lord of Parfois in the best of humours. 'Well? His temper should name him, if his face is something marred.'

One of them, a thickset, bearded knight who by his manner might well be the seneschal de Guichet, said after a long, astonished stare: 'This is Talvace's kin, surely.'

'Talvace's kin, surely! It seems it was a son they carried off into Gwynedd. He's too like, the signs are too many on him to be son to any other man. We know, do we not, how to entertain a Talvace in Parfois? Here, take him! See him safely lodged in the Warden's Tower. And feed him,' said Isambard carelessly, after a searching look into the bruised, defiant face. 'Never let him say we starve our visitors, expected or unexpected. He'll be better sport, fed. He's puny enough now.'

They received him readily, and haled him away across the moist grass just touched in the hollows with rime. And thus, not anonymous among hundreds but the centre and focus of a tight little group of a dozen guards, Harry crossed the drawbridge and made his entry into Parfois.

'And which of them,' asked Isambard lazily, stretching out his long legs before him across the bare floor of the stone cell, 'sent you to kill me, Harry? That fiery little mother of yours? Or Llewelyn? We used to be good enemies, that great prince and I, but somehow the enmity's grown cool of late. He's had his hands full with other matters, and so have I. No, I doubt it was not Llewelyn. I dare say he's bred you true to a Welshman's bounden duty, and taught you the sacredness of a blood debt, but I think it was not he who sent you here alone on such an errand. Well? Have you nothing to say?'

Nothing. The boy had not spoken since they thrust him into this sandstone cell under the ground and left him with his single candle and his narrow bed. He was neither too sullen nor too frightened to talk; when he had something to say he would speak up loudly enough. The trouble with him was that he was utterly astray here. There was nothing about him he could understand, nothing of which he could be sure.

What did they mean to do with him? Isambard would make little ado about hanging a marauding boy who had attempted his life, especially one who was no business of the county justices or the crown, and had no one in England to take his part. But if they meant to kill him, why delay? Why lodge him here thus roughly but not in any great discomfort? And above all, why should Isambard come down here in person to visit him after supper, splendid and ceremonious in his brown and gold brocade, attended by servants bringing in a gilded chair for him, and a page carrying wine? And why send all the hangers-on out of the cell? If he was merely bent on amusing himself with his prisoner, did it matter who heard?

'Or was it Benedetta?' asked Isambard.

No answer. Harry stared back at him with wild, wary eyes, the lids drooping a little with weariness.

'I see you know that name, Harry. Am I right in calling you Harry? It seemed to me you could have no other name. Come, you can tell me so much without giving away any other man's secrets.'

'Harry is my name,' said the boy grudgingly, in a voice that creaked a little with distrust and disuse.

'Good, I see you still have your tongue. I began to think you had bitten it out. So you are acquainted with Madonna Benedetta. Then she's still living?' No answer, but perhaps he found something in the watchful face that was not quite mute, for he smiled, and deep within the hollow eyes a spark kindled. 'And was it she sent you on your mission to pay me my due? She had a score to settle, I grant her that. But time was when she could have commanded a grown man to do her errands and pay her debts.'

Harry's lips tightened angrily at that slur, but he remained silent.

'And Adam Boteler, is he yet living? And that fellow of Benedetta's who helped her away to Shrewsbury when the Welsh took the town? Fifteen years, Harry, and you see I forget nothing. They soon withdrew from it, it was too hot to hold long. Shrewsbury will never be Welsh again for more than a matter of days, and Llewelyn has the wit to recognise it. It's exposed, but it's English to the bone now, nothing can change it back. Just as Poitou and Anjou and Normandy and Gascony, and all those pleasant counties where we've spent so many foolish months and so much good money are French, do what we will, and will continue French from this on. We may hold them again at a price a hundred times their worth to us, for a few months, a few years at a pinch, but French they will still be, and in the end we must leave go of them. Even Brittany, for all Peter de Mauclerc's homage to our lord the King. Let him call it an English fief if he will, it makes no difference to the truth, it's but a word. And that's all we brought back from this expensive jaunt of ours, boy. Thanks be to God, and to our expert shepherding, for failure may have cost us enough, but success would have cost us and our heirs dearer far. Henry's had his royal progress, since have it he would, now perhaps those of us who do the work here at home may find our hands a thought freer.'

He looked up over his wine and caught the stunned green eyes, hopelessly puzzled and disquieted, and laughed. 'How you stare, Harry! Am I not to think aloud in your presence? Your father grew used to it. Does it confuse you that I should do the talking and you the listening? Talk, then, and I'll be silent.'

He waited, the crooked smile twisting his mouth, but Harry had nothing to say.

'So I'm to credit them all with this attempt on me, am I? I have a long reach, remember, and a long memory.'

'I came of my own will,' said Harry abruptly. 'No one sent me. They've been looking for me to take me back.'

'Ah!' Isambard leaned back in his chair, smiling. 'You can speak to the purpose when you choose. Well, I see they've instructed you in the story of your birth, since you had so thriving a grudge against me. And what else have they taught you about your father? There was more to him than the dying. Have you a grain of his art in you? I've seen you have his curst temper.'

It seemed to Harry that there was nothing he could usefully say to this bewildering and terrifying man, and indeed that he was not required to speak. Whatever was to happen to him would happen without any provocation on his part, and nothing he did in conciliation could ward it off. Better to be silent. He was very tired. All he wanted, all he hoped for now was to be left alone to come to terms with his plight. And he had so nearly succeeded! An inch higher and a thought quicker, and he could have climbed back down the rocks vindicated and free, with all his debts paid.

'True,' said Isambard, grinning at him, 'it's a pity to think

144

I might have been dead by this, and you ten miles away on your road home. But these reverses visit a man now and then in his life, you'll find. No doubt God had his reasons. Come, let's see if you can be made to speak again. How did you pass the lower guard? Have I to hang all the garrison for letting you slip through?'

'I never passed through the guard,' said Harry perforce. 'I climbed the rocks.'

'Well, well, you encourage me. Ten whole words out of you at a stretch! One more question, then.' He spread his long, lean hands on the arms of his chair, and the rubies in his two rings took the candle-light and burned into crimson. Deep in his cavernous eyes the same red glowed steadily. 'When they took Master Harry out of the river below here, where did they bury him?'

Harry held his breath, catching at that as at the first land-mark by which he might hope to get his bearings. The tone had hardly changed, yet he felt at once that this was different; to this Isambard meant to have an answer.

So his enmity followed even the dead. After fifteen years he was still pursuing his feud against his master-mason, un-willing to let even his bones rest. Suddenly Harry felt the narrow cell so filled and overfilled with his own dread and hatred that he could hardly breathe.

'What do you want with my father's burial-place?' he said thickly through the gall that scalded his mouth. 'You pro-vided him his death, others have provided him a grave. You let him be.'

'To do strict justice,' said Isambard equably, 'John the Fletcher provided him his death, and Benedetta procured him to do it. But I don't quarrel with your version. Harry, Truth is more than the naked facts. I killed him. Now answer my question. Where does he lie?'

'Where you'll never trouble him, my lord. As safe from you as you are safe now from his vengeance –'

'Ah, that may well be,' agreed Isambard with a hollow, dark smile.

' – but not from mine, my lord! While you leave me alive, I

shall be waiting to get a weapon into my hand again, and you within my reach.' He was trembling now with the intensity of his detestation, his voice precarious with passion. 'I always heard tell of you that you were a wolf, but never that you were come so low as to prey on dead men. As you would hunt him to the end, God helping me I'll hunt you, and see you into your grave before ever you lay hand on his.'

'Gently, gently!' protested Isambard with galling mildness. 'You're wasting your heroics, there's no one to hear. Better leave showing me all the good reasons for hanging you out of hand. I might be tempted to do it, and no one would be less pleased than you if I did. Never use words as gambling counters, Harry, unless you're prepared to pay the score in good coin afterwards. It's well for you I have other uses for you. There's this one thing you have to tell me before you hang. When that's settled, we'll see. Come, now, I mean to have an answer.'

'You'll never get one,' said Harry, setting his jaw.

'Oh, but I will, Harry, and from you and none other. Never doubt that.'

The voice was silk, but it chilled Harry's blood none the less. There was a stony determination there that set him examining his own resolution in a panic, in case there should be weaknesses in it he never suspected. How did he know how far his virgin courage could be stretched? It had never yet been tested. He moistened his dry lips, and held his tongue, his eyes enormous and apprehensive upon Isambard's face.

'We have infinite resources,' said the lord of Parfois delicately, 'and all the time in the world. We can afford to go gently about our negotiations. These limited comforts we've provided you here, Harry – in what order can you best spare them? We'll take, say, food from you to-morrow. The next day, drink. Then warmth, perhaps, and last of all, light.' He saw the long lashes drop for an instant and the lips contract fearfully, and laughed. Had he known it, he had merely started the echo of another man's voice in Harry's over-

146

burdened mind, saying bitterly: 'Light is the last thing a man should willingly surrender. Except breath!'

'A week wanting all these, and who can tell what tune you'll be singing? No need to take to cruder means until we must. You'll not change your mind, and tell me what I want to know to-night?'

He had risen from his chair, taking the refusal for granted.

'Not to-night nor any other night,' said Harry doggedly.

'Ah, well, sleep on it. Your spirits may be a little duller and your wits a little brighter to-morrow,' said Isambard tolerantly, and left him to his uneasy solitude.

'No!' said Harry.

He had been saying it nightly now for three nights. If his voice was less steady this time it was because he was cold, not because he was afraid. They had ceased to bring him food at the end of the first day, taken away his carefully hoarded drop of water at the end of the second, and the third refusal had cost him his coarse blankets and the thin straw palliasse on his plank bed. It was added cruelty that Isambard never asked twice. The boy's contemptuous: 'No!' was always accepted without comment, and with no attempt at persuasion; but each night a soft, sidelong, tormenting smile recognised the growing reluctance and diminishing arrogance with which he spat the refusal at his questioner.

'Very well!' sighed Isambard, and reached a hand to take up the candle in its iron holder from the rocky ledge of the wall. The boy sat hunched on the edge of his bed, his slight shoulders rigid; the green eyes followed with an uneasy glitter the deliberate progress of his captor's elegant, muscular hand through a meagre yard of air, and lived through a wilderness of reluctance and temptation during its passage. His folded forearms hugged his cramped belly. Three days without food is a starvation-while to a boy of fifteen. But he minded the passing of the light more. His eyes lingered wistfully on the flame, followed it through air as Isambard lifted it. Shadows quivered in his fallen cheeks. He shrank a little more compactly into himself.

147

'In three days,' said Isambard, 'I'll ask you again. Three days this time – not one.'

No answer, but the pinched face reflected clearly enough how the boy's heart sank within him. Above the guttering candle-flame Isambard's crooked smile offered him sympathy; voice and face had a devilish gentleness when he pleased.

'Think once more, Harry, before I go. Only a few words, and you can be taken out of this cell, fed, warmed, lodged in a better place,' he tempted softly. 'No need to condemn yourself to darkness.' The light from below conjured into sharp gold and black every subtlety of the great forehead, and made the cajoling mouth piercingly beautiful and kind, but the demon still inhabited the gaunt pits of his eyes. 'Tell me, and spare yourself.'

Harry swallowed the soft strangulation of tears and clung with desperate hands to the obstinacy that must do duty for his flagging courage. 'No!' he said, so relieved when it was out that the recoil made him faint and set him shaking.

The face, the hand and the candle withdrew backwards, still smiling at him, for the smile seemed to embrace all three, as though the withdrawing brightness emanated from the man rather than the flame. The door closed on them slowly; they thinned into a long, faint strand of light and vanished, and everything was dark, dark for three days; except that now there was no way of distinguishing night from day, and time, like hope and pleasure and companionship and all the human things it measured, had stopped.

A hand took him by the shoulder and shook him awake, and he started up with a cry, for a moment not knowing where he was or what was happening to him. There were torches and men in his cell. He clung shivering to the comfortless bed that seemed now the only tenuous security he had, but he was plucked away from it and hustled through the doorway, still bemused with cold and sleep. It could not be three days since he had been left in the dark; was it even three hours?

They thrust him stumbling up a winding stairway cut in the rock, and along another passage into a large, smoky room, blackened and bare but for certain engines and implements that stood against the walls, and a low brazier in the centre. He saw Isambard standing impassive beside the flame, de Guichet at his shoulder. Hazily through his sense of nightmare and unreality Harry knew the long shape of the rack with its ropes and pulleys, and the blackened irons laid by the brazier, and the whips dropped into sconces on the wall. He had always known this would come next. It seemed Isambard could not wait three days.

Now there was nothing left to him but the conflicting passions of his terror and his furious pride, knotted together in inextricable warfare in his bowels. He would not speak, not if they started every joint in his body, not if they beat or burned the flesh off him. Not even for his father's sake or his honour's sake now, only because he would rather die than give Isambard best. He might endure to be forsworn and dishonoured, but he would not endure to be defeated.

'You know, I imagine,' said Isambard briskly, 'the purpose of these instruments? Look at them, look well! You understand their use?'

Harry said: 'Yes.' But the croak that came out of his parched throat was hardly recognisable. He understood; his shrinking flesh understood, and had no hope of being spared anything.

'I want certain information from you, and I shall get it. Will you give in now, or later and at greater cost?'

He dragged out of himself somehow a better voice, loud and passably firm from sheer despair, that said: 'I'll never give in.'

Isambard made a motion of his hand to the men who held the boy pinned by the arms, and he was half-dragged, half-carried between them to the rack. He let go then of every dignity but the dignity of defiance, and fought like a wild-cat, lashing and struggling and biting, wearing himself out uselessly in an effort that could gain him nothing. But in fact he did get something out of it, a confused, exhausted numbness

149

that almost comforted his aching muscles, and robbed even his overwrought mind of its sharpest awareness as they over-powered him. He was stretched helplessly on his back, the smoky ceiling leaned to his face; he felt the straps drawn tight round his wrists and ankles.

'For the last time, Harry!'

'No!' he said in a hoarse scream; and even then he was still able to feel that it must be by the grace of God that what felt like the terror of an animal in extremity should produce a cry of respectable human rage.

He heaved and strained in his thongs, gasping for breath, trying to brace himself, creating the agony before it came.

But it did not come. There was a long, strange, dream-like while without motion or sound, and then Isambard's voice, controlled and cool still, saying: 'Let him up!'

Now he was hopelessly confused and lost, and the fear he had extended himself to contain shook him from head to foot as they unstrapped him and stood him on his feet again. He could hardly stand, he had to cling to one of the arms that helped him up. He looked at Isambard with great bruised eyes in which tears of bewilderment were helplessly gather-ing.

'You should have taken it further, my lord,' said de Guichet, eyeing the trembling boy with a hard, measuring state. 'A little real pain would get more out of him than all the threatening.'

'You under-estimate the little fool's curst nature. You might cut him to pieces and he would not speak,' said Isam-bard, thoughtfully frowning.

'You could put it to the test in a very few minutes, my lord.' De Guichet had one of the whips from the wall in his hand; he drew his arm back quickly, and slashed Harry across the face.

The boy gave a faint, startled cry, and fell back a pace, putting up his hands to his bleeding cheek. What happened then he never saw, it remained always a confusion and a blank to him, but certainly there was another cry, louder and more astonished than his, and a sudden sharp impact like a blow, and the clatter of the whip falling. When Harry smeared away the blood from his face and opened his eyes again it was to see Isambard standing with one foot flattening the whip to the floor, and the bronze lantern of his face blazing with such an intensity of dangerous, silent fury that even Harry, who was no longer threatened, shrank with sympathetic dread. De Guichet confronted his lord with a pale face and fixed, fearful eyes.

'My lord, I thought to get you what you wanted, and what you'll never get by patience,' he protested defensively, but with resentment thick in his voice.

'You thought! Did I bid you lay hands on the boy?'

'No, my lord, but –'

'Then keep your hands from him until I do so bid you.'

The flame died down abruptly, the bronze head cooled into quietness. He turned on the guards who held Harry between them, and looked at his prisoner for a few minutes in silence. Then he said quite calmly, drawing his gown more closely about him as though the scene was finished: 'Take him back to his cell.'

The boy was led away staring dazedly. The large eyes, dilated with exhaustion, had the lost look of a child frightened among strangers.

'And leave him a light,' said Isambard.

In pure reaction from terror he broke down and wept himself into a deep, swooning sleep as soon as he was alone with his blessed candle; but when he awoke strangely refreshed and heartened he had his wits again, and could reason about his escape. If there was one thing sure about it, it was that Isambard had abated nothing of his purpose, and if he had halted his experiment in terrorisation short of the act, it was not from any impulse of pity, but the result of a calculated probability that these methods would not get him what he wanted. It was not compunction that restrained him, but an inherent sense of economy that objected to seeing time and effort and pain squandered uselessly.

This reflection went far to set up Harry again in his own

esteem, for it meant that Isambard had been sure of his victim's obstinate silence even under torture; more sure of it, if the truth were told, than Harry himself had been at the worst moment. It also made a pattern of sense out of the minor ordeals through which he had passed, and put him on his mettle for the future. For if he was right, then this lull foreboded some new and less direct assault upon him, and it behoved him to be ready for it.

Nonetheless he was almost gay that morning. He had his light back, and his blankets, they brought him food, and in every movement he was acutely aware of his still resilient sinews, and the smooth round joints that turned and bent in such a beautiful and ingenious fashion. Suddenly every finger was a marvel and a joy to him. All kinds of pleasures became apparent now that they showed as points of brightness in such an overwhelming dark. He trusted nobody and hoped for nothing, but the little delights that fell into his lap by the way had their due in appreciation at last.

He waited with roused senses for what would come next; and what came was so transparent that he had hard work not to laugh, and set out without more ado to take every advantage of a stratagem that would not have fooled a child in arms. Two of the youngest and pleasantest of his guards began to spend their time in his cell with him day and night, watch and watch about. Isambard was taking it for granted, it seemed, that a boy of fifteen could easily be seduced into giving his confidence, or at least some incautious fringes of it, to companions not so far from his own age and under orders to ingratiate themselves with him. Even if he did not allow himself to betray his secret directly he might let slip something that would provide a clue. But he never would! What, when he was already forewarned?

He welcomed them with open arms, talked freely, played draughts with the younger and learned tables from the elder. He revelled in their company, but he told them nothing. When Isambard came down in the evening with his question, delivered with a dry, impersonal smile as though the brief upheaval in the night had never happened, Harry gave his answer with only the slightest convulsion of fear at the pit of his stomach. It was accepted without comment. The lord of Parfois turned and went away.

It was the same the next day, and the next, and still nothing happened. He was uneasy in the face of this unnatural quietness, but he watched his tongue and waited. And in the afternoon of the fourth day his guards suddenly trooped into his cell and ordered him up and out with them.

'Where are you taking me? asked Harry, feeling the familiar knot contract in his vitals. It seemed the present experiment was being abandoned as ineffective. What came next?

'Up to fresh quarters, lad,' they told him, grinning at his suspicious face. 'Fine lying, fresh air and the whole place to yourself. You'll think you're in a palace.'

His heart sank, perversely convinced that he was to be transferred to some damp hole where he would be able neither to stand upright nor lie at full length, and chained there in darkness. But when they brought him up into the higher reaches of the Warden's Tower and shut him into his new prison he was stupefied to find it all they had claimed. There was a good bed along one side of the small, square room, a bench and a heavy table, even a brazier; and most wonderful of all, there was a high window, narrow and barred and unshuttered, but if it let in the wind, it let in the light and the sun, too. Many a time he had slept in worst quarters when he had attended David on his seasonal progresses in Gwynedd.

He stood in the middle of the room and stared mistrustfully round him, wondering why he should be so favoured. Was Isambard bent on winning him by kindness now? His strategy changed with bewildering suddenness, but everything he did was devoted to the same end, that was certain. When he came in the evening – it was by this time unthinkable that there should be an evening when he did not come – he might let slip something that would make sense of this new move.

It was later than usual when the lord of Parfois came. His

153

face was serene; Harry had never seen him so content. He looked all round the room, checking its appointments with satisfaction.

'Well, Harry, are you comfortable here? Is there anything you need?'

'I need my freedom,' said Harry.

'An error, child. You want your freedom, it isn't a necessity. You came here of your own will, I fear you must stay at mine. But at least you may be comfortable in your captivity.' He turned from the window, which was on a level with his face, and came to where Harry stood. 'Turn to the light. So!' He raised his hand, and with brusque, impersonal fingers which nevertheless had a surprising lightness of touch he felt the edges of the cut de Guichet's whip had left on the smooth cheek. 'Closing well. You have clean-healing flesh, there'll be no scar.'

'You're concerned for my face,' said Harry, curling his lip.

'I'm concerned that no one shall mar it but myself. You're my meat, Harry, no one else's. De Guichet is zealous, but he overdoes things. Proportion is all, as you should have learned in your craft, and excess, as in this case, is so often unnecessary.' He smiled, moving away without haste. 'Well, if you have any needs you may ask. I'll leave you to your rest. Good night, Harry!'

It was impossible, but it was happening. He was at the door, he was going away without having asked the question. Harry could not bear it.

'My lord – !'

Isambard turned, his brows raised inquiringly. The contentment in his eyes engendered at its heart a faint, malicious spark of amusement. 'Well?'

'What is this game you are pleased to play with me? You bury me underground, you threaten me with starvation and torture, you ask and ask always one thing of me, and then suddenly this ease. And no reason for it! And after all this questioning to one end, now you have nothing to ask!'

'Ah, that!' said Isambard, smiling. 'That need not trouble you any longer, you'll not be pestered again.'

'Not – ?' Harry gaped at him, brought up short. 'My lord, if you have repented of this pursuit – '

'I never repent, Harry. No need to trouble you farther, I know what I wanted to know.'

'You *know*?' It was a trick, it must be a trick. And yet he had that smoothness of satiety about him, in his voice, in his smile, even in the touch of his hands. 'I don't believe it!' said Harry violently. 'You can't know. Who else could tell you? And well I know you never got it from me.'

Isambard laughed, gently, tantalisingly. 'Are you so sure?'

'Do you think I've let my tongue slip once with those creatures of yours marking my every word? No, my lord, you'll not fool me. I know what I've said and what I've not said. I'm sure as death.'

'Very well, then you're sure. It's well to have so rock-like a certainty. I envy you. Good night, Harry!'

He could not go like that. Harry ran and caught him by the arm, clenching his fingers desperately into the folds of the wide velvet sleeve.

'You're lying! You must be lying. You *can't* know. I've never said a word to betray it. Every waking moment I've been on the watch – '

'And sleeping?' said Isambard, grinning. 'None of us knows what he betrays in his sleep, Harry. Did you ever think of that?'

He wanted to cry out scornfully that it was a lie, but the dreadful truth knocked the voice out of him. How could he, how could anyone, be sure of his silence while he slept? With this one issue so heavy on his mind, might he not have muttered some confused reference to it in his dreams? His mind fought off the idea furiously, and yet it came back to fret his certainty again. How could he be sure?

'Did I not say, Harry, that I'd get it from you, and no other?' said Isambard, still laughing at his stricken face. He plucked his sleeve gently out of the boy's hand, and turned unhurriedly and walked out of the room.

The door which had opened hastily to let him through was just swinging heavily to when Harry roused himself out of his daze of doubt and consternation, and flung himself after in a burst of despairing rage.

'Devil! Devil! Damned carrion crow!' He clawed at the edge of the closing door, but the butt of a lance shoved hard under his ribs heaved him back gasping into the room, and the door closed on his convulsed face. They heard him battering furiously at the panels and shouting hoarsely: 'What do you want with him? If you affront him, I'll kill you. Do you hear, Isambard? I'll kill you! Leave him alone, you devil! Leave him alone!'

Isambard had halted and turned in the passage, frowning a little, in two minds whether to go back to him, but in the end he did not; he merely waited for a little while, listening until the torrent of defiance had grown strangely shaken and softened with moments of entreaty. He smiled, recognising conviction. The muffled voice behind the door sank at last into hopeless silence.

CHAPTER SEVEN

Parfois: *December* 1230 *to January* 1231

The boy who brought him food in the morning was a young fellow he had never seen before, and not one of the men-at-arms, but by the look of him one who belonged behind Isambard's chair in his great hall, or about his wardrobe to help him to dress. He was fair and pertly pretty, and not above seventeen, and his manner towards the guards in the ante-room indicated that he was a privileged person in the household. Some page from a knightly family, most likely, thought Harry, eyeing him distantly out of the obscuring mist of his own preoccupations. The youngster addressed him with condescending friendliness, and got a morose answer.

'You could be civil,' said he, injured. 'I'm sure *I*'ve done you no wrong.'

'No, I know it. I ask your pardon,' said Harry, stirring himself out of his lethargy of despair. He had been wakeful all night, gnawing over and over the tangle of his doubts and fears, and unable to worry his way through them to any certain hope. He would have given anything to believe that Isambard was lying. But why should he lie? Only to torment? There could be no other reason, and yet that did not accord with the placidity of his face and his voice, nor did it match with the image Harry was beginning to form of him. Everything he did had method and purpose. And if he was telling the truth, what terrible damage had been done unwittingly, and what incomprehensible and cruel outrage was to come of it? He was a prisoner here, helpless to act, and already frayed and fretted with too much and too bitter thinking. He stared out of his constricting net of anxieties and fears at this clean, smooth, well-intentioned boy, and wondered why he should

157

be expected to make the effort to answer him at all.

The page came and sat on the bench beside him and spread his arms confidentially across the table, leaning close. The heavy door of the room was fast shut, but he sank his voice to a mere whisper as he said: 'And I could do you right, if you had the wit to listen to me. Unless you want to rot here. It's nothing to me, if you don't choose to speak me fair.'

Harry's mistrustful face turned to him slowly. The youth grinned at the dubious stare he got, but not unkindly.

'What do you mean?' The voice was grudging, and slow to have any truck with hope after so many bewilderments and frustrations.

'Here, you'd best be eating. It gives me a reason for staying. And you'll need it before to-morrow if you show sense.'

It did not sound like a threat; there was even something of a promise about it. Harry pulled the wooden platter towards him, and broke the bread. 'You're his man,' he said ungraciously.

'Don't listen, then, if you're so curst. I'm my own man. I'm as free as he is, and my father's Gloucester's knight, not his, if you want to know. You're a fool as well as surly,' said the boy, and stuck his neat, short nose in the air and bounced up from the table in dudgeon, but Harry caught him by the sleeve.

'No, don't take offence! I'm so low I can't help doubting every man who comes near me. What did you mean? God knows I don't want to rot here if I knew of a way out, surely that's plain.'

The page sat down again, readily appeased. The face he leaned so confidentially close to Harry's was glimmering with triumph and self-importance. 'He's given me the task of looking after your wants and bearing you company. And you're to be allowed the freedom of the outer ward, to take air and exercise with me sometimes. But don't think you'd ever get past the gate-towers. No one ever has. There's no way out for you there.' His voice sank to the finest whispering thread of sound. 'But *I* know of a way.'

Harry held his breath and reined in his heart from hoping.

'A way out of Parfois? For me?' He had begun to tremble at the very thought.

The fair boy brought his closed hand out of the breast of his cotte and opened it proudly under the edge of the table. 'Do you know what that is?' It was a small bronze seal, deeply cut. 'That's his little personal seal, the one he sometimes uses to give authority to his special messengers. He gave it to me so that I could come in and out to you as I like. Whoever has that,' he whispered impressively, 'can go where he pleases and give what orders he pleases inside Parfois, and he won't be questioned.'

'You'd be questioned fast enough at the gate-house, seal or no seal,' said Harry gloomily, 'if you had me with you.'

'I know that, but we're not going near the gate-house. I know a way out of Parfois that hasn't been used for years, but it's still open if you know where to find it. There's a sally port under the rock. And old Ralf doesn't know I know how to get to it.' He leaned back, glittering with triumph. 'Well, what do you say to that?'

'You'd let me out?' whispered Harry, dry-mouthed. 'Why should you? Why are you doing this? And how can you? As soon as they find I'm gone, what will your life be worth?' It was a trick, it must be a trick. Yet if there was the slightest chance of the offer being genuine, how he would leap at it!

'Ah, but I shall be gone, too. I shan't be here to be either questioned or blamed. Whether you choose to come with me or not, I'm leaving Parfois to-night. It was through you I got this chance, why shouldn't I share the benefits with you? But if you're too suspicious to trust me, stay and be damned. What do I care?'

'No, don't be so quick to offence,' entreated Harry hastily. 'Would you trust easily, in my shoes? Why are you going? How have they misused *you* here?' His eyes flickered involuntarily over the rich dress and pampered appearance of his visitor. The boy laughed, not at all displeased.

'Nobody's misused me. But I don't like it here, and I've good reason for going. I'll tell you if you like. My father is Sir

Humphrey Blount, a knight of Earl Gilbert of Gloucester, who died last month. There's a girl my elder brother wants to marry, and my family want it, too, but she likes me better, and I like her, and her parents won't force her. So when my father had to leave in the summer he thought fit to send me here to my lord Isambard, to keep me from under my brother's feet until Isabel's safely wed. Old Ralf likes me, and I've made myself very serviceable to him, and behaved myself circumspectly here. They think I'm reconciled, but I've only been biding my time for a chance like this one you've brought me now. I've not been allowed out of the wards, except under escort, that I owe to my father, I know. And to get to the passage I know of isn't easy, but with this little key I can open the doors now. I'm for home to-night, whatever you choose to do.'

'But your father'll only send you back again,' said Harry, still dubious. 'Where's the use of it? Either that, or he'll see you moved somewhere else out of your brother's room.'

'He won't, then, for he took the cross in the summer, after he'd placed me here, and went off to join the Bishop of Winchester in the Holy Land,' said young Blount delightedly. 'And my mother's on my side, and will talk my uncle round to her way of thinking, and in no time I shall be betrothed to Isabel. Her parents would as lief have me as Humphrey, and she'd a good deal rather.'

The picture was so circumstantial that it began to be convincing, and Harry's heart hammered in his breast with hope and dread. He gripped the slender hand that dandled Isambard's seal. 'You mean it? You'll take me out with you?'

'Why not? I owe old Ralf nothing. If he's trusted me I've never asked him to, and I've never promised him fealty. I can't help you once we're out, though. I'm for Shrewsbury, I know where I can get a horse there –'

'I'll need no help, once I'm out,' breathed Harry, thinking with feverish urgency of the grave under the lee of the church at Strata Marcella, and the little curling leaf on the threatened stone. If Isambard was not lying it might be already late. 'Get me past the walls and the rest is for me to do, and

I'll be grateful to you lifelong.'

'Mind,' said the page warningly, 'it's rough going down the rocks even from the gully. It has to be at night or we'd be seen. The way down on the eastern side, where I'm bound, is not so steep, but on the other it's a hard climb and a risky one. Which way are you bound? Back into Wales?'

'Yes, but I know the climb, I've done it already. Only let me past the walls and I ask no more.' He was trembling now, he hated the thought of the long hours of the day dividing him from his hope. 'When can we go?'

'After supper, but soon after, or they'd wonder too much at my coming for you. I'll have orders to bring you to old Ralf, they'll believe that. But hush, now, we're getting too loud, and I'm here too long.'

He rose, flashing down at Harry the easy, sidelong smile of a born conspirator. 'I'll come again at noon, then we'll have all settled. On my life,' he said in a quick, light whisper, 'I'm glad you've given up thinking I mean to trick you. I'm not used to being so mistrusted. If I don't put you safely on the outer side of Parfois, may I never see Isabel again. There! Could I give you a better pledge?'

At the last moment, when the barred window was already darkened, and the echoes from the outer ward grown scattered and few, Harry suffered an agony of fear that after all this would be like other nights, that Isambard would come with his taunting smile and his small, shrewd ironies that stabbed like knives; but instead came young Thomas Blount, true to his word, with his tilted nose and his provocative swagger, and flung open the door of the room with a flourish. He stood on the threshold dangling two keys in his hand, and did not bother to step within.

'You're to come to my lord Isambard in his own chamber. You may walk with me like a civilised man if you care to, but I warn you there'll be an archer behind to keep us in view, so I wouldn't advise you to try any tricks, they'd do you no good.'

He waved the men-at-arms in the ante-room imperiously

out of his path, and led the way out without even turning his head to make sure that Harry was following.

'Look blacker, fool,' he said out of the corner of his mouth as they stepped into the cold darkness of the outer ward, 'and drag your feet. You're not going to your wedding. There's no archer, don't be afraid. That was a flourish for them.'

There were still a great many people about in the outer ward, but once they had passed through the archway to the inner ward the night world about them was quiet, troubled by only a few echoing footsteps. Harry had never been here before. He saw it now as a crowding darkness of giant shapes against the merlons of the curtain wall, dominated by the eyeletted walls of the tall hexagonal keep. Spears of light from loopholes stabbed outwards into the night and charmed up in sharp black and white disconnected passages of masonry.

'Where are we going?' whispered Harry, quivering at his guide's shoulder.

'To old Ralf's tower, just as I told you. Ah, leave fretting, man!' he said impatiently, feeling the fingers that clutched at his sleeve tighten in suspicious anger. 'We're not going near him, he won't bother us. We're going there because the door we want is there. There's another in the keep would have done just as well, but seal or no seal, they'd have wanted a better tale than I could think of before they'd have given me the keys of the keep. This one unlocks his private wine-cellars under the tower, and this one is of the inner cellar, where the best wines are. I said he wanted some of his favourite French wine – there's an envoy from the Chancellor in with him to-night, so it rang true enough, even though he's never sent me to bring it before.'

'That's a mort of doors between the garrison and the postern, if they were pressed,' muttered Harry.

'Parfois never has been pressed. They've never yet had to use it. But his lordship's grandfather was a cautious man, and provided himself with a secret way out at need. Hush, here's Langholme coming from my lord. Keep close and look sullen.'

He twirled his keys airily for all to see, gave Isambard's

body-squire an amiable good night, and giggled like a girl as soon as they were past.

'In here, now, and quickly to the right, where it's dark.'

They slipped like shadows through the great doorway of the Lady's Tower, and along a dark stone passage to a low oak door set in the inner wall. Thomas unlocked it with the larger of his two keys, and taking from its sconce the last of the torches that burned along the passage, led the way through to a narrow spiral stairway, and began to descend without hesitation into the depths.

'Are you not going to lock the door again? Suppose some-one tried it? They might really want wine from below.'

'No. Wait until I let you through into the last cellar, and then I must take the keys back to the steward. He'd be sus-picious if I kept them long. It means I must leave the doors unlocked, but that's less risk than having him come looking for me within the quarter-hour, as he surely would.'

'And your things? Where are they? You're not leaving Parfois empty-handed?'

'On my soul,' sighed Thomas, injured but patient, 'I never did see any fellow could find all the devil's arguments like you. When you're away down the mountain you'll still be sure I've laid a trap for you somewhere. If you must know, I dropped my bundle off the wall four hours ago, down into the copse under the eastern end of the gully. How could I come and fetch you away with my belongings under my arm? I know exactly where to lay my hands on them. Here, through here!'

The second key let them into a vaulted stone cellar, and groping torch in hand along the far wall behind the piled casks of wine, Thomas brushed the cobwebs from a low, insig-nificant door.

'There!' He drew back the groaning bolts and turned the rusty iron ring, and the door opened inwards with a protesting creak. Beyond there was the reddish darkness of sandstone and a breath of earthy coldness. 'Now will you wait for me here in the dark till I take back the keys, and not imagine I've locked you in to starve? There's your warranty of a way out.

And here, keep my purse if you like, till I come back. You can be sure I'll not leave that.'

'I need no pledges,' said Harry, shamed. 'I'll wait.'

He did not have long to wait, though it seemed an age to him. Within a quarter of an hour Thomas was back, hugging himself with pleasure in his own cunning, and they passed together through the little door, and drew it to again after them. From that moment they drew breath more easily, not afraid to talk above a whisper, and undismayed by the echoing sound of their own footsteps. Already Parfois seemed to lie behind them, and Harry had almost lost that tense expectation that at every step someone would reach out and take him by the shoulder to haul him back into captivity.

There were hanging cobwebs at first, but the torch swept a clean way through for them. The passage continued narrow, clearly cut and low-roofed, a safe and secret way out of the castle by which the garrison could retreat towards Shrewsbury, if too hard pressed, and by which it could receive stores and reinforcements in time of siege, or emerge to raid and counter-attack by night.

'It comes out in the gully, well to the eastward end. You'll have to pass under the gate-towers to get down to the west. But you'd do better to come down with me and make the long trip round.'

'No,' said Harry, already in his mind scrambling down the rocks in the dark to Severnside. Should he make for Robert's assart? No, he would lose time rather than gain it, and a horse would be little help to him, for he'd have to go down-stream to the ford. No, to-morrow was time enough to re-claim Barbarossa and see his friends again. To-night he must make the shortest time of it he could to Strata Marcella, re-assure himself that his father's grave had not been desecrated, and warn the prior of Isambard's malignant interest in it. There was a boat at the mill, and the current would help him down-river in the crossing and bring him quickly to the water-meadows by the abbey. Or if by any chance the boat was not there, or too securely chained, he could swim across at a pinch. The level would be reasonably low now, for the autumn had been dry; and the cold he could bear in such a cause.

'As you please,' said Thomas airily. 'I'd rather you risk your neck than me, but if it's a question of time you're justified; it would take you two good hours and more to work your way about.'

The passage in which they walked had changed its nature gradually, and Harry had not noticed it until he stumbled in the broken formations of the flooring where all had been smoothly levelled before. He looked up, and the flickering torchlight showed him a vaulted cavern-roof innocent of tooling by men. They were in a deep crevice of the rock, and the faint lightening of the darkness before them was the mouth of a narrow cave opening upon the December night.

'We'd better douse the torch here,' said Thomas. 'Someone might look over from the gate-towers and catch the gleam of it. And from here on keep your voice down. When we come out in the gully, go to the right and keep close in under the rocks, and you'll be safe enough, for there's a good overhang.'

Harry was shaking with relief and joy. To the last moment he had feared a trap, but this was the fresh air before him, the dim air of the ravine he knew, hemmed in with rock on both sides between the church and the castle. He felt for Thomas's hand and wrung it in the momentary blindness after the torch was quenched against the rock.

'What you've done for me I'll never forget. God speed to you, and I hope you get your Isabel.'

They emerged into the sharp, clean cold of the open air, and overhead hung a crumpled ribbon of stars. There in the channel of rock they parted, Thomas going to the left, Harry to the right towards Wales. They embraced at the last, but did not speak for fear of the clarity with which even a whisper might carry here. Thomas was quaking with giggles like a girl, but Harry would never again be so easily taken in by that, after this experience.

Their hands parted, they were away into the night.

Harry went slowly and cautiously through the gully, feeling his way at every step until his eyes had accustomed themselves to the darkness, and could judge distances and distinguish the shapes of the weathered planes of rock that leaned over him. He knew when he was beneath the gate-towers because he could see how the machicolations projected against the sky rounded shapes of darkness void of stars; but he heard not a sound, not even the tread of the watch on the walk between the towers. He was alone, the whole of the night was his.

The ravine widened and opened upon the sky, the curtain-wall with its vast bulk of darkness curved away from him to the right, and left him. He was on the rocky slope he knew already from more than one climb, and somewhere here on these smoother protected faces of rock were the plans he had scratched and pondered over so many months ago. He began to descend, and in confidence that he was now too far from Parfois to be heard he abandoned his caution and swung his way down the cliff with frantic haste. Several times he tore his hands and barked his shins, and once he missed his footing and came crashing several yards down the slope before he got a desperate grip with fingers and toes and knees, and clung sweating till he recovered his breath.

He could not go fast enough now to satisfy him. Hope and foreboding struggled in him and drove him, and there would be no peace for him until he saw his father's grave immaculate and at peace still, and knew quite certainly that Isambard had lied. And even then he must warn the brothers to be on their guard. The lord of Parfois was a law to himself; if he ever did discover where Master Harry lay buried, the Severn would not stop him from pursuing the dead with his living and virulent hatred, the Welsh border would be no bar to him, even the sanctity of the church would not restrain him.

The rocks gave place to tufted waste grass and bushes; he was down, and with nothing but a graze or two to show for it. He knew these sheep-slopes, he knew the woods below. He made good speed down to the river, and then there was a path to aid him as far as the mill. The boat was there, tied up and rocking gently to the swirl of the dark water inshore. It was not chained; he untied it thankfully, and thrust softly out into the current.

He was in midstream when the clouds that had covered the moon parted and drifted away, and before him on the distant bank he saw the gracious, massive shapes of Strata Marcella pastured like sheep in their silver meadows. He pulled strongly across into the inshore current, and let it carry him down abreast of the church before he grounded the boat and climbed ashore.

Here in the open grass he broke into a headlong run, lurching and recovering as the tussocks turned under him. He homed to the nameless grave like a pigeon, and fell on his knees beside it with a great sob of thankfulness. The ground about it was undisturbed, the stone unviolated. Isambard had lied. He was absolved, neither waking nor sleeping had he betrayed his trust.

All the tension went out of him. He leaned his forehead against the stone, and was suddenly so weary and so content that it seemed to him there was nothing left to be desired in life, and nothing more he need strive for. He had meant to say a prayer of thanks for his escape and for his mercy, but all he did was to spread his arm protectively across the stone, and lie there breathing deeply, embracing his father, and as gratefully at rest as though he had flung himself into Master Harry's living arms.

Behind him the grasses stirred almost silently, but he heard, and raised his head sharply. Cloud was advancing steadily again over the moon's face, and its shadow rolled across the mitred stones of the abbots, and covered the dark inward movement of the men who had followed him up from the water. Six of them, ringing him round, closing in on him from all sides.

He opened his mouth to shout a warning to the brothers in their distant dortoir; if it was not yet much after Lauds they might be waking, and hear him. But a hand was over his lips before he could utter a sound, and an arm took him round shoulders and breast from behind, and pinned him helplessly against a broad chest. They wound him in a cloak to pinion him from struggling, and twisted folds of the cloth hard round his mouth.

Isambard stepped into the dwindling lance of moonlight without haste, and walked the bright shaft of it until he stood face to face with the swaddled and muted figure of the boy. The stretched, polished skin over the lofty cheek-bones and the finely moulded forehead gleamed golden, the pits of the eyes were black but bright. He was smiling like a happy demon, almost tenderly.

'Well done, Harry!' he said softly. 'Did I not say I'd get my answer from you, and none other?'

He smiled for a long moment into the raging eyes that would have struck him dead if they could. He looked from the waiting ring of his retainers to the blank and nameless stone, and in the last pale ray of moonlight his eyes caught the small, obscure shape of the carved leaf. He bent to trace its lines with a finger-tip, and lingered over it long.

'Take him back,' he said over his shoulder, without turning his head. 'He's told me what I wanted to know.'

Aelis was out before dawn, in the frosty end of the starlight and the faint gilding of the still unrisen sun, making the rounds of her rabbit snares high on the hillside. She saw the little procession of horsemen climbing the ramp towards Parfois, and crept up through the trees to see more closely, for it seemed to her that the middle figure of the five was bound, and one of those who rode beside him led his horse by the bridle. They passed close to her, where she crouched still in the bushes. Four men in Isambard's livery, and one, slender and smaller than they, wound tightly in a dark cloak, the lower part of his face swathed, and his feet roped together under the horse's belly.

They might muffle his body and cover his face as they would, but they could not hide Harry Talvace from Aelis. She would have known him anywhere by the very set of his head, the mere shape of him, even so cramped and disabled. She slipped through the bushes alongside the sorry procession

168

until they passed in through the lower guard of the castle, and disappeared up the tree-shrouded ramp. Then she turned and snatched up her rabbits, and ran for home with her bad news.

Where had he been all this time, that she should see him now being led prisoner into Parfois? What had he done, where had he slept, who had fed him? This was the first and only certainty, that he had fallen foul of Isambard, and was now in captivity. And even if the Prince of Gwynedd should send an army to set him free, how were they to get him out of that impregnable hold? She remembered his scratched plans and his frowning concentration, and for the first time fully understood that all that persistence had been devoted to the cause of breaking into Parfois. But now what miracle of ingenuity would be needed to get him out?

She should have slammed and barred the door on him while he was changing his clothes that day in November, and kept him there until her father came. She should never have let him slip away silently to Pool in the first place, but clung fast to him there among the trees and called out the men to overpower him. Better that she should suffer his anger and displeasure than that he should fall into the clutches of the lord of Parfois.

For no good reason she suddenly thought of the bruise on his cheek, the slight blue stain he had tried to hide from her, and burst into angry tears as she ran.

Within the hour Robert set out up-river to the ford by Pool, to carry the news across the river to the castellan at Castell Coch; and before the morning was out, a rider was despatched on the long ride to Llewelyn's court at Aber.

Harry lay all day long on his bed without a word to anyone who came in to him, and would not touch food or drink. In the evening Isambard himself opened the door of the room, and even in his small closed hell of hate and despair and self-disgust, Harry knew who had entered, and drew himself erect before him. He would not even have turned his head for anyone else, but in the presence of his enemy, now truly and irrevocably his, no longer merely the legacy of his father's wrongs, he stiffened his back and reared his head.

'What's this I hear of you?' said Isambard in the formidably courteous voice in which he habitually gave his orders. 'Refusing food and turning your back on the world? No man should do that unless he's ashamed of his dealings with it. Are you shamed? I know no reason why you should be.'

'And you, my lord?' said Harry through his teeth.

'It's well known of me that I am not subject to shame. But why should you condemn yourself because you were taken in by an elaborate trick and an accomplished liar? Thomas lies as naturally as other men breathe, if he told truth he would be untrue to himself. It may not be a virtue, but there are times when it's an asset. He and I should be hiding our heads perhaps, but not you.'

'What do you mean to do,' demanded Harry, looking fiercely up at him from under drawn brows, 'now that you've tricked me into this betrayal? If you disturb him, if you dishonour him, I swear to God I'll never rest until I've killed you. There's no name vile enough, my lord, for creatures like you who vent their spite even on the dead. Did he so outdo you, living, that you have not the generosity in you to let him rest even now?'

'He so outdid me, living,' said Isambard with a dark and hollow smile, 'that even now neither one of us can let the other rest. But just now we are concerned with you. You are another matter. If you think I shall allow you to sink into this silly shame of yours and eat out your own heart until you die of despair, you are in a great mistake, boy. Now you will get up and make yourself presentable – I'll see to it that the wardrobe shall provide you with clothes that will fit tolerably – and you will come to supper at my table and take your place among your peers, and behave yourself like a man and a Talvace, instead of a sick and thwarted girl.'

'No!' said Harry, startled and stung into what was almost a cry of pain.

'But I say yes. You'll come, boy, because if you do not I shall have you dragged there. And you'll eat, because, by

170

God, if you refuse I'll have food forced into your mouth and stroked down your throat, like medicining a hound. You'll carry your humiliation – since nothing can stop you seeing it so – in quietness and with a good grace, as other men have had to learn to do before you. Yes, and you'll brush sleeves with young Thomas, liar as he is, and restrain yourself from flying at his throat. He's no match for you, and I won't have him abused for being so good at the one thing he does well. You hear me?'

He put out an imperious hand and tapped Harry smartly on the cheek to turn the boy's face to him. Their eyes met in a long, arching stare. Isambard smiled.

'Leave the small game go free, Harry. Save all that fine, lusty hatred for me. I am the only enemy here worth your steel.'

171

CHAPTER EIGHT

Aber, Parfois: *January to April* 1231

'God witness,' said Llewelyn, drumming his long fingers on the arms of his chair in a hard-driven rhythm that was always a key to the stresses of his mind, 'it could not have come at a worse time. Well, we must do what can be done. My obligation to Harry is sacred for his father's sake, even if I did not love him like my own. As God knows I do.'

'My lord,' said Gilleis in a low voice, 'I well know you do.'

Yes, she knew, and she had never blamed him. Yet he had been to blame. He had never willed to injure or dismay the boy, but the thing was done and could not be undone. He looked out through the open shutters at the grey January sky over the strait, where the islands had vanished in frosty mist. The sea moaned and cried uneasily across the salt flats between, the incoming tide hissed beneath the field where the tragedy had ended. How many thing had been done last spring that could not be undone? The boy's fate was the last and the least reverberation of that disastrous thunder, but not the least pitiful.

'Soon or late he would have gone,' said Gilleis. 'A little thing could have set him on his way any time these past three years, and it would have had the same ending.'

She did not say a word of blame. How could she accuse the traditional education he had received at Welsh hands, when she herself was not entirely innocent? She had wanted him safe and sheltered, but she had wanted vengeance, too. Now she would have given up every lingering resentment, every long and bitter hatred, to have the boy back at Adam's banker, humbly cutting stone.

'The place is impregnable,' said David sombrely. 'There's

172

no way of bringing up siege engines to the walls.'

'If it were not, I cannot assay it. I'm in no case now to make war on any marcher lord. Wales has the first claim on me, and there's grave enough danger threatening Wales now; God forbid I should do anything to add to it. De Burgh is speaking us very fairly and friendly, but both his hands are gathering up the borders round us. He has an appetite for land and castles I would not willingly see in the King himself, but he's a more dangerous man than the King.'

'But no soldier,' said Owen with a brief grin, remembering Kerry.

Llewelyn's blazing smile showed abstractedly for an instant and was gone. 'That's to make our own prowess less. I grant you we put a check on him once, and could again, but never think you saw the true measure of de Burgh in Kerry, there's more to him than that. It isn't the soldier we have to fear. He gets his conquests without fighting for them, and every one moves in upon us more closely. He has his new marcher holding of Cardigan and Carmarthen now, if the grant's confirmed – and confirmed it will be. And only a month ago he won two successes without a blow struck. You know them as well as I. John de Breos in Gower is no longer a tenant of the crown, but of de Burgh's new fief. And since Gilbert de Clare died in Brittany on his way home from this French campaign, the earldom of Gloucester and all its lands go to a child, and boy and barony are handed over to de Burgh. That makes him the master of Glamorgan. What Marshall leaves Welsh in the south, Hubert devours. It's only a matter of time before he begins to move north, and I have an itch in my sword arm says the time's running short.'

'It might be well to strike first, before it runs out,' said David. 'It's coming to that in the end.'

'So it might, but not westwards at Parfois. And the time's not ripe yet. When the hour does come I shall need a good, clear cause, every man I have and all the speed I can muster. I cannot touch Parfois. If I sent my army against a border lord on a private quarrel I should be throwing Wales into

Hubert's hands. At best it would provide him with the opportunity to strike elsewhere while my back was turned, and at worst – and he'd see it plain enough – with an excuse to raise the whole royal power against me. What Hubert orders, Henry does.'

'It's true,' said Owen. Not even for young Harry could Llewelyn be asked to throw away Wales, which was David's birthright. And who would be more bitterly indignant if he risked it than young Harry himself, whose pride in his prince and jealousy of his rights had no match even among David's own blood-kin? 'But the border's alive with irregulars. If a few more join them, these next few days, who's to blame you for that? Let me go, and if I run my head into a hornet's nest you may disown me.'

'And do you think a dozen or so irregulars are going to break a way into Parfois? Nobody's ever done it with arblasts and trebuchets, let alone bows.'

'Not by force,' admitted Owen. 'But there may be other ways in, or ways of bringing the quarry out.'

'If he gave his parole he might be let out of the walls,' said David with no great conviction.

'He'll never give his parole.'

No one said no to that; they knew their Harry.

'Well,' said Llewelyn heavily, 'we'll manage as best we can. I can do one thing in the light, and that's send and treat for him in open negotiation. It may be that Isambard will let him go for a price. He's an older man and maybe an easier since he had me galloping the best of my horses lame over you, Owen. But even if he refuses, we have something to gain. We can at least bring the case to the light, and make it dangerous for him to harm the boy privily. We stand to England in a different relationship since John's day, and no prisoner for whom I have offered ransom can vanish now without an account being demanded. If he won't deal, we'll send formal notice to King Henry, and see that the law has at least knowledge of the matter.'

Adam said unhappily: 'But I doubt Harry went there to kill, and his standing at law may not be all we could wish.

174

And the King's writ hardly runs in the march, to take a felon out of the hold of such as Isambard.'

'That may be true, but it has vigour enough to ensure that he shall not be hanged out of hand.' He saw Gilleis shrink in Adam's arm, and turned his face away into the shadow of his hand, wishing the words back.

Wales was a different matter. The march might be a girdle of lawless palatines, only elusively within reach of the King's justice, but the shadow of royal displeasure was at least a curb there; but Gwynedd, though it formerly owned Henry as suzerain, was a free principality, and could harbour runaways and make short work of captured felons with impunity. That was his achievement. The final and absolute statement of his sovereignty had been the hanging of a felon out of hand.

All our acts, he thought, come back upon us sooner or later. But Henry was not involved with my prisoner; he sailed for France and abandoned him without a tremor. Isambard has there under his hand a piece of my heart, and draws me by it with cords of custom, and indebtedness, and love, and guilt. And still I deny to answer. Like Henry, for a dream of empire; but his dream was a pageant in the sun through a conquered land, over soil alien to him, among people speaking a language he knows, perhaps, but not his own; and mine is of a country preserved and perpetuated, peopled with my own blood, speaking my native tongue, and the work is to be mine, and the fruit for David and for Wales, after I'm gone. Oh, God, does that justify me?

'And one thing I can do in the dark,' he said, 'behind my own back while I keep the peace. Take your party, Owen, and go to the march. I'll send Philip ap Ivor to Parfois to treat for Harry's release. Whatever the answer, Philip will meet you at Strata Marcella when he comes from Isambard, and if the man will not come to terms, then it's for you to act as you think fit.'

'How many men may I have?' asked Owen, brightening into eagerness. It was only just, as well as practical, that the task should be his. He had once been a prisoner in Parfois himself, he knew the castle and the country round it, and owed his escape from it alive to Master Harry and none other.

'You'll do well to keep your numbers within bounds. Take a dozen men, and if more can serve you, send for them.'

'Will you take me for one?' asked Adam.

'There's no man I'd rather have. Come and welcome!'

'Send Philip here to me, Owen, as you go down. We'll put him on his way to-day, and you shall follow at first light. Gilleis!' Llewelyn caught her by the hand as she rose, with one of those warm, moving gestures of his that came so suddenly out of the very centre of his royalty, to join him by the heart with the simplest of those who moved about him. Touches like that had bound men to him for life, and their sons after them.

'Girl, never doubt but he'll come back to you whole and hungry, as he always used to from the butts or the wrestling when you were fretting over his lateness.'

She said: 'God grant it!' and clung for a moment to the great, warm, vital hand that could put heart into her even now. Adam drew her arm through his and led her away, for she was half-blinded with tears. She had lost too much already in Parfois to believe easily that anything of hers could come unmarked out of it.

When father and son were alone David stood warming his hands at the brazier, and looking down with a clouded face into the red glow. 'Philip is a good man,' he said slowly, 'and carries weight. He's dealt with the King too often to want influence, even with Isambard. But –'

'Well?' said Llewelyn, dark-faced, knowing what was in his mind.

'There's one who carries more, and could do this office to better effect.' His brows were drawn together in a frown, his face still; the reflected light from the brazier made his fairness ruddy that was usually so pale and clear, but even so the likeness was extreme. It caught and twisted at the heart, and there was no armour against it. 'If you would but use her,' said David, and turned his back and went to stare from the window at the frosty strand and the shifting, misty sea.

'I have full confidence in Philip ap Ivor,' said Llewelyn, his voice harsh and dry. He felt for the words that should follow, the first step that was as hard as a death, or more truly, as hard as being born again. And yet it could have been said so simply. The hour may come within weeks, within days, to-morrow; and then, before I take the field with the fate of Wales in my hands, I have a need of her and a use for her here; and then I shall be loosed from this dumbness that binds my tongue, and I shall be able to say to her what needs to be said, and what as yet I cannot say.

He opened his lips, struggling to put off the pride and bitterness that held him mute; but the slight rustle of the tapestry at the door spoke first, and eloquently, and when he looked up David was gone, leaving still silent on the air between them the name that was not to be spoken.

Isambard was in his bath, washing off the sweat of the hunt, when they brought him word that there was a groom at the lower guard in Llewelyn's livery, asking safe-conduct for an envoy from Aber. He threw his head back and laughed like a young and boisterous man, till the drops flashed from the clustering wet tendrils of his iron-grey hair.

'The gods have no imagination,' he said, stepping out of the tub on to the towels spread on the rugs before his glass, and turning himself about beneath Langholme's ministering hands. 'They're for ever repeating themselves.' He was known for a devout man, the lord of Parfois, a patron of pilgrims and collector of relics, and long ago he had taken the cross; when he wanted to blaspheme he turned to his classical education and its multiple gods, and loosed his barbs at them.

'So the news has leaked out already, has it?' said he. 'Now I wonder how did they get word so soon? I'll swear the boy was alone, he told me himself the enterprise was his own. Llewelyn's well served in these parts, it seems. Well, fetch de Guichet here. I'll have him send an escort down to the riverside to fetch in our guest with ceremony. And tell the chamberlains to have an apartment made ready for him in the King's Tower, the best they can offer. Leave me now, Walter, I'll dress myself, there's other work for you. Take young Harry somewhere out of sight – the armoury, if you will, he's spoiling for exercise, he'll make no difficulties. Provide him with playmates enough to keep him busy until supper, and see no one tells him we have a visitor from Aber. And Walter!'

Langholme turned again in the doorway. 'My lord?'

'Let him be late in coming to the table. See to it! We'll have them both off-guard.'

They ran in all directions to do his bidding. He stood flexing the body he had preserved to himself by hard exercise and the austere living that wore so deceptive a cloak of luxury. There would not be a man at his table that night who did not eat more and drink deeper than he. He examined himself from head to foot, assessing without vanity the beauty that had once given him an honest pleasure, and he marked without fear the changes that moved in upon him now daily. He had seen to it that his spare flesh should not go soft with time. or lose its springy vigour; but the years had revenged themselves as best they could. The slender loins and wide shoulders kept their elegance of shape and movement, the skin was clear of wrinkles except for the lines of experience that had graved themselves into his face; but the flesh was drying and withering now, hardening between weathered skin and shapely bone. The straight, tall thighs grew lean and leathery, the arched rib-cage broke through the shrinking flesh and etched its pattern in glossy light on the taut skin. The magnificent engine was strong and skilful still, but the suppleness and the sap were drying up in the long sinews, the head was already a death's-head. He smiled; he had been on intimate terms with death for a long while, it had no terrors for him.

'They might well send a priest to you,' he said to his own image, and reached for the clean shirt Langholme had laid ready for him.

Philip ap Ivor rode into Parfois somewhat before the early dusk of the second of February. In all his discreet and circuitous years as one of the most trusted of Llewelyn's clerical envoys, he had seldom had such a royal reception. He wondered, as he dismounted in the outer ward, precisely what it foreboded. Not, he thought, an easy success. No one goes to the trouble to dress up compliance so elaborately. He ran a shrewd brown eye over the formidable ramifications of Isambard's favourite castle, and speculated on which of the stony holes under it held young Harry.

There was not a word said of business until they came to table in Isambard's great hall, where the envoy found himself in the place of honour at his host's right hand. On his own right there was an empty place, no doubt to be filled by some trusted official of the household. Isambard, like Philip, would be concerned with the discreet placing of witnesses to what was said; the contredanse had begun.

Philip looked round the high table in the blaze of torches and candles, and was encouraged. There were knights there not of Isambard's following, there were two English clerics of rank whom he did not know, and a burly young man whom he recognised as a nephew of Hubert de Burgh. The justiciar, he knew, was on excellent terms with Isambard. It would be well, if the opportunity offered, to precipitate the coming encounter there in public, before all these independent witnesses. They might not avail to get Harry out of his prison, but they would make it extremely awkward for Isambard to remove him quietly from the world afterwards.

They were very civil together, and very punctilious. The old wolf had lost neither his looks nor his sparkle.

'And what is troubling my lord the Prince of Aberffraw and Lord of Snowdon?' He managed to turn Llewelyn's imposing new title, compounded of the old sacred name for a reassurance to the Welsh, and the added flourish for English ears that had scarcely heard of Aberffraw, into a satirical comment, but he did it with great delicacy. 'In what particular can I be of comfort to Prince Llewelyn?'

He, too, it seemed, wanted the encounter to be public. He

had raised his voice so that it carried through the babel of the many conversations at the high table, and even reached the nearest of the lesser knights below.

'In the matter of his foster-son, who is missing from court since last spring. It has come to the Prince's ears, my lord, that the boy was seen some days ago entering Parfois, escorted by four of your men. I come to you to know if it is true that you hold him here in your charge.'

'His Grace has, I believe, more than one foster-son,' said Isambard, spreading his brocaded elbows comfortably. 'Without, of course, numbering the one he himself holds in charge at Degannwy. With which one are we now concerned?'

'With Harry Talvace, my lord.'

So he would have names named, would he? There was far more in this than met the eye.

'Yes,' said Isambard readily, 'Harry Talvace is here.'

'As your prisoner, my lord?'

'As my prisoner.'

'Taken in trespass on the hither side of Severn?'

'Taken in trespass on the hither side of my own guard, your reverence, if the whole truth be told.'

'Ah!' said Philip ap Ivor. 'That was not how we heard it at Aber. As the tale came to us, my lord, the boy was seen bound and muffled, being led up the slopes from Severn into Parfois. But not then within your gates.'

'Very like. But you are speaking of an occasion some days ago, when we recovered him after an attempt at escape. The boy has been in my custody since November. As for how he first came into my hands, you shall ask him that for yourself.'

'Then I may see him?' said Philip, promptly securing at least this concession.

'Very simply, your reverence. You have only to look down the hall at this moment.'

Harry had come into the lower doorway at the right time, and was moving up between the tables to take his normal place among the young fellows of knightly family, his peers.

Langholme had done nobly. The boy was flushed and gleaming with exercise and haste, his eyes bright, his cheeks freshly scrubbed, his dress a suit in rich Flemish cloth, long ago outgrown by Isambard's younger son, and re-fashioned now for the involuntary guest. If Philip had been looking for a pale, sickly, ragged and possibly fettered prisoner, Harry would be a considerable shock to him.

They saw each other at the same moment. Harry halted sharply at sight of the slender, elderly priest, austere and grey beside Isambard's splendour. The face meant home to him. He paled, and flushed as richly again, and his composure was shaken for a moment; but the small, testing smile in Isambard's eyes straightened his shoulders and stiffened his back. He left his place and came round the high table to kiss Philip's hand, and was himself embraced and kissed. Philip made use of the moment to compose the countenance which he was afraid had almost betrayed his surprise and consternation, and to revise all his ideas about his errand.

Nothing was as it seemed here. The boy was so far from being ill-used or closely confined that he apparently lived a normal life, at least within the walls, going and coming much as he pleased, and eating in hall like a member of the household. Princes enjoyed such easy captivity, but seldom commoners. Did Isambard intend to let him go gracefully, after all? Was he, for some reason, anxious to have good relations with Gwynedd, and using Harry's well-being as an elaborate move in the game?

'For to-night, Harry,' said Isambard, 'your place is there beside his reverence. You will want to talk to him about home, and he has things to ask you. He would like to know from you how you came to fall into my hands. Tell him.'

Philip's thumbs pricked; in the sudden certainty that any further public avowal was designed to serve Isambard's purpose and not his, he made haste to speak before the boy could open his mouth.

'My lord, we should perhaps postpone this discussion until after supper. I had no intention of turning your table into a

181

business conference.'

'I could not discuss in Harry's absence what closely concerns him,' said Isambard, 'and I trust we can all be relied upon to continue our exchanges like civilised men. Speak out, Harry! Where was it I took you, within my own domain or outside it?'

Harry had lost the high, blooming colour he had got from two hours of strenuous play with blunted swords, and was pale now with a bright, wary, aggressive pallor. And it was surely not merely over-confidence of his good usage here that gave his eyes that insolent green blaze, and his voice the sharp, clear edge of defiance.

'Within it,' he said firmly. 'In the church, where I had climbed and hidden overnight.'

'For some lawful purpose, no doubt, Harry?' prompted Isambard, the small, devilish smile growing warmer and fonder.

Harry's palms were slippery with a sudden, chilly sweat. He understood very well how he was being tempted, and for what purpose. Whatever he did would play into the hands of Isambard, whose traps were always dual, and could not be evaded. If he boldly avowed his real purpose thus publicly, he put himself in the wrong, and his cause past any help from the law, which would tamper here in the march only on unassailable grounds. Isambard did not mean to let him go for money, and was ensuring that the crown should not intervene to take him out of his hands perforce. The temptation to evade the truth was suddenly almost more than Harry could bear, so achingly did he want to go home. The first glimpse of Father Philip had made his heart turn and contract in him with the pain of the memories that tugged him back towards Aber, older memories than the bitterness and anger that had driven him away.

But if he lied, saying that he came to Parfois with no felonious intent, and attacked only when he was surprised and frightened, Isambard would have won a better victory. He would not find fault with the falsehood. Harry felt in his blood with what calming delight and fulfilment his enemy would embrace the lie that made him the victor. That was what he wanted. It would even be worth surrendering his prey, to have brought him down to the ignominy of lying to excuse himself. Everything that terrible man laid in the way between them was a test or a trap, and all his will was bent to break the son as he could not break the father.

'According to such law as I know,' said Harry loudly and clearly, 'it was lawful. By our Welsh code it's legal to kill in repayment of a blood-debt. No, it's an obligation! I came to kill you, my lord, for the killing of my father.'

The brief silence seemed to stretch down the long room and hold fast by the pillars of the door, and every eye in the hall fixed greedily on the three at the high table. Isambard broke stillness and tension together, saying with careful serenity, and to the hall in general: 'Lucky for us both that intent and act are sometimes so far apart. As you cannot choose but see, he did not kill me.'

Even the oblique implication that he had feared to put his purpose into effect seemed to Harry a new pitfall for his integrity of hatred.

'I did my best, my lord,' he flashed fiercely. 'How many times in your life have you been nearer dying?'

The cavernous eyes, guarding in their depths those distant red flames of intelligence and appraisal, looked back at him laughing. The lord of Parfois pondered for a moment. 'Perhaps three,' he said mildly at last, as if he were answering the simplest and most natural of questions.

'Then do me justice, my lord!'

'Be quiet, child,' said Philip, laying a hand restrainin :ly on Harry's arm, though he would have preferred to lay it about his ears if he could have had him to himself for a moment. Who could make a success of any embassage with such a turbulent brat at his elbow, over-ready with all the wrong answers?

'I ask your pardon, Father,' said Harry, quivering to the touch. 'But I was asked, and I must answer truly. I know no reason to be ashamed of it. I did what it was laid on me to do. But not well enough!'

'You are making things difficult for his reverence, Harry. He is here to inquire into your case and treat for your release, and I am prepared to listen. But I fear your position at law is more vulnerable than you suppose. The pity is that your Welsh code does not run here in England, where the offence was committed. But I grant your sense of obligation, and I am willing to overlook your trespass.'

'My lord,' said Philip warmly, 'this is generous in you.'

'On conditions, of course,' said Isambard. 'I will entertain your offer for his ransom, if he will publicly close his blood-feud against me, and pledge himself to think of it no more.'

'I will not,' said Harry loudly and quickly, before the temptation could lay hold too treacherously on his heart again.

'My lord, the boy is overwrought, he's saying what he does not mean. Can we not talk the matter over later in private? He'll be reasoned with, give him time and quietness.'

'No,' said Harry. 'This is the time, and I am saying what I mean with all my heart. My debt is not discharged, and I cannot and will not forgo it until it is paid. God grant me another chance, and I'll make better use of it!' He could not help it, for an instant the restraint he was arduously imposing on himself slipped like a mask from his face, and the bitter blaze of his hatred flared from dilated eyes, burning ferociously upon Isambard's calmly smiling countenance.

'That could hardly be called a conciliatory speech,' said Isambard delicately. 'You'll understand that I'm loath to set him at liberty without some guarantee. I have the reasonable man's preference for continuing alive.'

There was no sense in expecting any help from the boy, the only thing to be done was to exclude him as an irresponsible minor from the consideration of his own fate. 'My lord,' said Philip, 'you shall have from the Prince the pledge you cannot get from Harry. Let us discuss what his ransom should be, since you are so generous as to entertain the possibility, and I will get for you full assurance that he shall be restrained from ever infringing your territory or your person

184

again. If necessary the Prince will keep him in close ward until he sees reason. You know him, you know he'll hold to his bond.'

'I know Harry, too,' said Isambard, laughing. 'He's no less a man of his word.'

'The Prince has an authority over him he'll not deny. I am empowered to offer you five hundred marks as his price, and he may be held until you have the guarantees you want from Prince Llewelyn.'

'No. Unless he will forswear this feud of his own will I cannot release him.' He said it thoughtfully, as though he might reconsider, but Philip knew then that he had no intention of changing.

However, he tried. 'A thousand marks would come nearer the worth of his release, in my own view, considering the circumstances. I will go so far.'

'I regret, your reverence, that I cannot come to meet you.'

'My lord, you have been forbearing with him, and I dare make an appeal to you to have pity on this headstrong youth, and trust his future good behaviour to us.'

'Why, if he would ask me for pity, I believe he might gain it.'

Harry believed it, too, and pity from Isambard was something he could not and would not bear; the mere thought of giving his enemy that satisfaction made his jaws set desperately to prevent the emergence of even one word or sound that might be mistaken for an appeal. Philip cast one glance at him, observed the signs, and thought better of making any demands on him.

'I am concerned to find him like this,' he said, sliding away from the immovable barrier. 'This is not the mood, these are not the spirits, in which I've known him at home. I fear he is not in such sound health as you may think, my lord. I trust he is allowed air and exercise? Perhaps if he might ride – under escort, of course!'

Isambard smiled. 'I've lost fledgeling birds like that before,' he said, 'even under escort.'

'You said he was a man of his word. Will you not accept his parole?'

'I would if it should ever be offered. Try him, your reverence.'

They were always back to Harry, do what Philip would. On whose side was the young mule supposed to be? He set his teeth against every concession that might have got him his liberty, bent on doing Isambard's work for him, as Isambard had all along intended he should. He had put it on record firmly that he had attempted a sacrilegious felony, and was justly restrained in consequence. He refused to plead his youth or excuse his act or promise amendment. The Welshman in Philip understood and warmed to him, but the thwarted diplomat would willingly have beaten him.

He saved his last throw for the end of the meal, when the wine was flowing freely. Turning again abruptly to Isambard he said: 'My lord, to return to the matter of the ransom. You have refused my offers. I ask you now to name your own price, and the guarantees you shall have also.'

Isambard's deep eyes flashed to Harry's face and lingered there, untroubled by the naked hate and defiance that stared back at him. He smiled mockingly into the bitter green glare. 'How can I put a price on a Talvace?' he said.

Owen and Adam came running to meet the little priest as soon as he rode through the gate and paced wearily into the stable-yard.

'We'd all but given you up, Father,' said Owen eagerly, holding his stirrup for him while Adam took the bridle. 'We've been looking for you these five days, and never a sign. Have you any good word for us?'

'Good, yes,' said Philip ap Ivor sturdily. 'The first and best word we could ask, and we must be grateful for it. The boy's alive and well, and in no hardship.'

It was indeed the first and most urgent measure of good, and they breathed the more easily for it; but they read in the tone no less the failure of his mission.

186

'But he won't let him go,' said Adam flatly.

'He would on terms, that's the rub. But on terms he knows the boy won't accept himself or let us accept for him. He plays him like a harp. He'll overlook the trespass on his lands and the assault on his person – oh, yes, there was an assault, and by all the signs a bitter one, too – if Harry will renounce his feud henceforward, but Harry will die first. He'll show mercy on him, if he'll plead for it, but Harry'll cut his tongue out rather. He'll give him a greater measure of liberty even so, if Harry'll give his parole, but Harry'll give him nothing short of a dagger. I can get no sense into him nor out of him, though I've been at him without relenting for days.'

'You've seen him and talked to him, then? And Isambard let you speak freely?' asked Owen, marvelling.

'Let me? The man's so sure of himself he pressed me, would have me reason it out with the boy until I was satisfied. The only concession I could not get was leave to see him alone, but it's plain I should have got nowhere with him even so. It's been time and breath wasted. And yet,' said Philip, shivering as the bleak little wind from Severn ruffled his grey tonsure, 'I swear he has received very tolerable usage there, better than I dared expect, and why he keeps such a particular hatred against the lord Isambard is something I cannot fathom. There's some personal thing and deep between them. The father's quarrel was enough to move him to act, but it's some new offence against himself has sharpened his enmity to this extreme. He says no word of what's been done to him, he shows no mark, but the thing is there, and I cannot account for it.'

They looked at each other across his furrowed forehead, and saw each his own thought staring back at him.

'But we can, Father,' said Owen grimly, 'or so I think. Come and see the thing that met us when we rode in here six days ago.'

They led him through the great court and round the cloister to the flank of the east end of the church, where the mitred graves of the abbots lay. Close under the grey buttresses

187

of the wall one of the long stones was propped on its side, the grave beside it laid open to the frosty sky.

Open and empty. Nothing remained of Master Harry but the faint dark staining of the stone where he had lain, a slender shadow outlined in rime at the bottom of the coffin.

Philip ap Ivor stood staring down into the blank cavity for a long moment with drawn brows and tight lips.

'This is profanation,' he said harshly, looking up at last. 'A sacrilegious outrage against a holy place. Men have been excommunicated for less.'

'So they may have, Father, when those responsible could be named. But who's to show who did this? We may know it very well in our hearts, but what is there to prove the offence on him?' Owen's voice gathered anger from his own helplessness. 'Look here, where they've chipped the stone when they raised it. Those marks are no more than a few weeks old, that's certain, but within that time no one knows when they were made. If it had not been for Adam's quick eyes we might never have seen anything amiss. He came running back from the grave the day we reached here, saying someone had been tampering, and we could scarcely believe it. But we looked, and there were flakes of stone in the grass below, and these fresh marks. And when we prevailed on the prior to let us raise the stone, this is what we found.'

'I know every inch of that stone,' said Adam jealously, leaning to finger the carved leaf with a gesture of ungovernable tenderness. 'You couldn't so much as bruise the mosses on it but I'd know. And I know the scores of an iron crow on stone too well not to know how these frets were made. We've lost him,' he said, grieving. 'Even his poor bones we couldn't keep safe.'

'None of the brothers ever heard any disturbance in the night,' said Owen sombrely, 'but in the night it must have been done, between Lauds and Prime. That's time enough for the wicked work, if they knew where to find him, and it seems they did. And if they did, they knew it from Harry. Where else could they have got it? Only a handful of us ever knew.'

'He never would have told them,' said Adam stoutly. 'I know Harry, he'd die rather.'

'Dying's a hard enough thought for old men, and terrible past bearing, maybe, for a boy. But God knows I don't say Harry told them wittingly, for I know him, too, and know him as stubborn in holding fast as any grown man among us. I say they must have got the knowledge from him somehow, by what manner of deception I know no more than you. And if I'm right, what better reason could he have for being so implacable against Isambard?'

'But if he'd known of this outrage,' said Philip, looking from one to the other of them with searching eyes, 'the boy would have told me in Isambard's presence. In open hall, I tell you, he spat out his detestation of that man for every page and scullion to hear. He is too full of hate even to be afraid, he would have accused him to his face.'

'Isambard would hardly make him privy to what he's done, if this is indeed his work, as I swear I believe with all my soul it is,' said Owen. 'But Harry may know only too well that through him the secret of this grave's no secret. That's an issue he'd surely hold close between the two of them as long as he thought no absolute harm had come of it. He'll be clinging to the hope that we'll keep his father's bones safe for our part – and Isambard he wants for his own.'

'And this is how we've done our share,' said Adam bitterly.

Philip considered, gnawing his lip and frowning. 'You've found no witnesses? No one heard men abroad at night or saw the river crossed?'

'None on this side Severn. Beyond that we haven't ventured.'

'And what has been done in the matter?'

'Nothing as yet. We were loath to prejudice your dealings there, or do anything to rouse tempers until we had Harry back with us. And then, the prior's reluctant to make any accusations against Isambard but on good, solid evidence. Would not you be? The brothers have to live here, and it's but a perilously little way across the river.'

'True, we must not put them in more danger than is needful. But this is a matter for the bishop, so sacrilegious an act as it is. We must make the facts known to him, but make no open accusation. Let the proper authorities do that, and in due form of law. I must talk to the prior.' He looked round questioningly towards the river. 'Was there never sign of a boat having put over from Parfois by night? No trampling of the grass? Nothing?'

'If there was, it escaped notice,' said Owen, 'and no one was looking for such signs, well it might pass them by. We know he's thorough, and puts such fear into those who serve him that they do his work as he will have it done. And I doubt the night in question was well past before ever Adam called attention to the sacrilege, and what signs there were to be read were long gone.'

'Well, now that I am here and can have the tale formally, direct from the prior, it's for me to join him in sending word to the bishop. And you, where have you lodged your men? Not here? If you're to do any service to Harry, you must not appear in this.'

'They're in Castell Coch, Father. I thought better not to burden the prior with such dangerous guests. If it should come to their being used, we could be the cause of burning his roof over him. But come in out of the cold,' he said, seeing how the little priest hunched himself like a ruffled bird inside his gown. 'Let's hear all you have to tell us.'

They looked back at the corner of the church, for Adam was not with them. He had wandered away along the narrow trodden path through the grass while they were talking, to the small hollow cove where boats came in to the abbey meadows. He was standing at the edge of the water, looking into the turgid grey-brown eddies that poured down towards Breidden with such force and in so absolute a silence. His face was as bleak as the frost. They called to him twice before he heard, and then he started and came after them at a rapid walk, like a man driven by some urgent pain he could not slough off. Seeing the set of his countenance, Philip

190

looked down the river where he had looked, and paled with apprehensive anger.

'You think he took that way? What, cast the poor remains into the Severn when he took them from the grave?'

'What else?' said Adam, low-voiced. 'He threw him in there newly dead, and Benedetta with him living, to sink or swim together. John the Fletcher took them out of the water and out of his power for a while, but do you think a man like Isambard would ever forget or forgive the crossing of his decree? What would he do with Harry's body when he found it at last, but toss it back again to go downstream as he willed it to go, and leave its poor slender bones scattered all along the banks of Severn without a name or a resting-place? And if ever he got his hands upon Benedetta again, he'd send her after. That's the man he is,' said Adam abruptly, and strode before them at a furious pace towards the guest-house, pursued by the pain he could not outdistance.

They forgathered again at Castell Coch near Pool, on a day in March, Owen and his twelve picked men. Three of them had kin along this border, and had spent the patient weeks just past in picking the brains of their cousins regarding the habits of the household of Parfois. Two more, with Adam, had been across the river in the villages beneath the Long Mountain, in Leighton and Forden overlooking the river, and even into the hamlets that lay inland, in the high valley of the brook beyond.

There were men and women there who looked narrowly at Adam when they clapped eyes on him, and being alone with him in quiet places called him tentatively by name. They brought him in after dark to their hearths, and answered his questions as well as they could; and soon they spoke of Master Harry Talvace, drawing up the image of him slowly out of the well of memory. They had not thought of him often in the years between, but he had never been very far from the borders of their hard and wary lives. He came back readily when his name was spoken; they saw him not tools-in-hand in his lodge under the church, nor frowning thoughtfully over his tracing tables, but naked to the waist and brown in the harvest-fields, swinging a sickle instead of a mallet, a slender young fellow with grass seeds in his tangle of dark hair, who might have come out of any cottage in the hamlet. That was what they remembered of him best. It was long since Adam had thought of him so, and he gathered the warmth of their recollection to him as gratefully as if he had salved one bleached and solitary bone of the beloved right hand out of the Severn, and laid it back in holy ground.

So Adam at least came back with a grain of comfort, though for the dead Harry, not the living. For the rest, there was little to report. They recounted all that they had learned in their careful reconnaissance, clustered in a corner of the great hall with the dogs round their feet in the rushes.

'So he's kept close within,' said Owen at the end of it, 'and that's no more than we expected. Never a glimpse of him since that good little lass saw them dragging him back into the wards. And the place is a nut we're hardly likely to crack with an army, let alone this handful of us. Harry won't be let out of it, we can't go in to him. So we must set about it a more roundabout way. If Harry never goes out and in, there are others who do. And hostages can be exchanged.'

'Those who go in and out of Parfois,' said Adam, 'seldom go in ones and twos. This is border country, and Isambard never had any illusions about the love the country people have for his household. I've seen it again these last days. They ride out by companies, whether it's hunting or hawking there are always enough of them to make for safety. Do him justice, he looks after his own, or at least he sees to it no one but himself shall flay them or hang them. Then there's the matter of the hostage. If we took de Guichet himself – I saw him pass the other day, twice as thick as when I knew him, and the beard changes a man, but I knew that thwarted, ambitious face of his – if we took de Guichet himself, would Isambard give us Harry for him? Not for love! He despises him, and always did. For the sake of his usefulness he might, or for his own honour he might, but if I were de Guichet I'd never feel sure of it. Small use threatening a man with harm to someone who matters not a rap to him. And who does matter to Isambard?'

Once, he thought, there had been someone who had mattered all too much, but by the grace of God and Llewelyn she was safe out of his reach now, calm in her sanctuary above Aber; a refuge as sacrosanct as the grave and almost as narrow. But for one other person, perhaps, Isambard had cared in his time, before affection changed to anger and hate; and not even the last and holiest stone cell of all had kept Master Harry safe from his insatiable enmity.

'We'll not make do with de Guichet,' said Owen. 'We can do better than that.'

His dark eyes were shining hotly in the torchlight. He was remembering, too; the air thus near to Parfois was full of memories. He remembered a homespun breast rough under his sleepy cheek, and an arm that cradled him, and the steady rocking of the horse under them on the long ride into the fringes of Wales that day; and suddenly at parting the terrible knowledge in him that, if he let go of Master Harry now, he would never get him back again. He remembered clinging frantically to the stirrup-leather, and being lifted back to the saddle-bow and comforted. Comforted but not deceived. And then Adam holding and reassuring him in his turn, himself utterly without comfort.

'There's one at least,' said Owen, 'who rides out from Parfois almost unattended when he pleases. I've been following every move he's made outside the walls these last ten days. He and his falconer go out perhaps once in a week along the ridge towards the Roman road from Shrewsbury. There's good sport over that high pasture, I remember it well from my time there as a boy. And there's a copse I know of, the end of a tongue of woodland that gives good cover for a retreat to the river with a prisoner. He passes through it every time he rides to the old earth fort on the crest. That's the place where we'll pick off our man. We could climb to the church rock, as Harry did, but getting a prisoner down the slope again with us might be too dangerous and too slow. No, we'll wait for the opportunity outside, if we wait here a month and more. And we'll take no seneschal or steward, either. We'll have someone whose liberty others will be glad to buy with Harry's, if he himself will not – we'll have the old wolf himself, Ralf Isambard and no other.'

It was on the fifteenth of April that they waylaid the lord of Parfois on his own ground, in the thick copse of scrub-oak and brushwood threaded by the narrow path that linked the main approach of the castle with the highway to Shrewsbury. They had lived wild in the forests below for nearly three weeks, waiting for their chance; and three sorry weeks they had been, saturated with spiteful April rains that had discouraged even Isambard from his usual activities. Twice Iorwerth's warning signal had fetched them hastily to their pre-arranged places; but on the first occasion Isambard had shunned the dripping copse and ridden away down the softer slopes eastward of Parfois, with his attendants strung out after him like beads on the string of darker green he left in the wet grass; and on the second it had been a full-scale hunt with a dozen or more guests and very nearly fifty retainers, and Owen had held his hand, unwilling to venture against such odds.

They had waited long and patiently for this third call. It came in mid-morning, and brought them all slipping through the branches and the coarse grass to lie hidden on either side the narrowing of the path with their bows strung and their shafts fitted, listening for the soft thudding of hooves that came as a reverberation along the ground rather than a sound.

This time it did not turn aside. This time it wanted the confused, drum-like fullness of great numbers. From the edge of the trees Iorwerth's green woodpecker laughed again.

'Good!' breathed Owen soundlessly into Cynan's ear, in the bushes close to the path. The leaves were not yet full, but they served for cover, and the undergrowth was thick here. 'Put an arrow into the ground in front of him when I give the sign – far enough ahead to be seen in good time.'

Iorwerth had three bowmen with him in the rear, to ensure that once the party entered the wood they should not turn and leave it again. Adam was ahead with two more, to halt any who managed to break through. They would do no killing unless they must. They wanted nothing but the person of Isambard, and a sufficient start on their withdrawal to the river.

Ralf Isambard came into sight along the pathway, splendid in black, riding at a gentle trot. His dress was too rich for his usual strenuous hunting, nor were there hounds abroad, or Iorwerth would have known and signalled it long ago. He had no hawk on his wrist and no falconer at his elbow, only a handful of decorous gentlemen of his household, riding as though to welcome guests on the road and bring them courteously homewards. He wore a sword, but it had the light, ceremonious quality of a court decoration rather than a weapon for use in earnest. Owen counted nine riders at his back, three of his squires and six who might be knightly, officials or soldiers of the household, but peacefully disposed, it seemed, this morning of April. It was hard to believe in such luck. Ten swords to be reckoned with, but never an archer among them, and the soft, constant rain dulling all sound.

Owen dropped his hand upon Cynan's shoulder when Isambard was still some twenty yards short of them. The arrow left the string lightly, almost lazily, and struck and quivered in the centre of the path, some yards before the horse's feet.

The hand that held the rein tightened without even a start, the head that had been inclined easily forward in thought came up smoothly and instantly, every muscle in formidable control. Either he was smiling, or the gaunt hollows of his face gave him the daunting appearance of a smile. He was still, tensed and alert on the sidling, startled horse; but he had not been startled.

'Halt there, my lord!' cried Owen from his deep cover. 'There are archers all round you. Make a move and we drop you.'

Isambard lifted a hand without turning his head, and snapped his fingers at the shifting, uneasy murmur at his back. 'Do as he says. Be still!' The arrow in the path still vibrated faintly and rapidly, humming like a bee. 'Well?' said Isambard. 'What do you want with me?'

One of the young men at the rear of the little procession tugged at his rein and made to wheel and ride out of the wood. Iorwerth dropped a shaft across his path, and he thought better of it, jostling back nervously into his companions. Isambard had not so much as looked round.

'Walk your horse forward till I bid you halt,' ordered Owen. 'You only, my lord.'

He had half-expected that the response would be a thrust of the long spurs and a head-down gallop for the open, and those ahead had orders to bring down the horse if Isambard tried it; but instead he stirred gently in the saddle and brought his mount edging forward in obedience to the order, dancing restively past the quivering arrow, and almost abreast of Owen's hiding-place.

'Enough! And now dismount.'

Very slowly and deliberately Isambard slipped his feet clear of the stirrups and leaned forward as if to swing himself out of the saddle, but in the act he jabbed home hard into the beast's side with his right spur, and drove him not forward, but flinching sidelong into the bushes in a wild leap; and leaning both hands on the pommel of his saddle he vaulted out of it and dropped crashing into the bushes almost on top of Owen. Old he might be, but he sprang to meet whatever situation he encountered with the alacrity of a boy. He fell on his feet, coiled hard into a ball, and used all the weight of his body and the power of his long legs to project him forward again after the enemy who recoiled from his reaching arms. Owen eluded the embrace, but Isambard flung one arm round Cynan, bow and all, before he could either spring back or draw.

The broken twigs flew crackling from the fall they took together. They rolled with the bow whining and humming between them, and the fitted shaft snapped off against the

196

stony ground. The head lay harmlessly flattened into the grass, but the broken shaft pierced through Cynan's tunic and shirt and stabbed and splintered against his ribs. He flung his weight sidewise and rolled away from the stab, and finding firm ground beneath his knees, heaved himself up with all his power and broke the hold on him. He was on his feet in an instant, and leaping back out of range. The string of the bow, snapping at the notch, coiled with a fierce whine about Isambard's arm, like a spring released.

But for that he would have got his sword out of its scabbard, and the fight they could not afford would have been on in earnest. But the momentary paralysis and the matter of seconds it took him to unwind and cast off the incubus cost him his chance. Owen had closed in behind him and flung a cloak over his head and shoulders, and twisted the skirts of it tight round his body and arms. Cynan flew to pin the struggling legs, and Meurig slid sidelong through the trees to help him.

It was all but over, and they had him. Owen drew breath and plunged back to the little group, still hemmed into a few yards of the pathway. There had been some disturbance there, too, when their master launched his attack. Three of the foremost had tried to ride to his aid, and one of them lay now propped against a tree with an arrow through the fleshy part of his right upper arm, clutching it tightly with his left to slow the bleeding. The other two had taken the warning, and reined in in time. Somewhere behind them one of the younger squires had been pulled from his mount, and was sitting dizzily on the grass nursing a shocked head in his hands, too stunned to give any further trouble.

The rest had taken the lesson. They crowded the path, uneasy on their uneasy mounts, looking from tree to tree in search of their assailants; but they kept their hands from their swords.

Owen reached through the branches to the bridle of Isambard's horse, that stood tossing his head and nervously trampling the path. He parted the bushes and drew the beast in to them, and left Cynan and Meurig to hoist the lord of

Parfois across his own saddle and hale him away hastily among the trees towards the river. Owen was swinging back to order the rest of the party to dismount in their turn when he heard a voice raised suddenly at a little distance in a long, challenging hail.

All the tensed heads came up hopefully, all the too quiescent bodies braced, all the wary eyes gleamed. The young squire who crouched clutching his head suddenly slid like a snake for the cover of the bushes and lifted his voice in a great shout of: ' *Á moi! Á moi*, Isambard!'

Iorwerth reached out of the leaves for him and choked him mute, but the damage was done. Not for nothing had this little procession presented the air of a party setting out to receive guests. Suddenly the earth was drumming and quivering with the beat of hooves, coming at a fast gallop along the grassy verges of the Roman road from Shrewsbury.

There was no time left for anything but withdrawal. Owen bellowed orders, and the bushes threshed as the Welsh circled their enemies and took to the thickest of the woodland on their way to the river valley. No time to stampede the horses and leave the riders unfurnished, and no sense in it, either, for there were other horsemen coming fast and in numbers, and they could not hope to stand off all of them. The only course was to plunge into the close-set thickets where riders could not follow, and run for the Severn.

But it was late even for that. The Welshmen, crouching low and running like hares, overtook the two who led the laden horse only a matter of minutes before they were themselves overtaken. Isambard's men were mad to establish their zeal now, and the woodland rides were not yet too steep and overgrown to give them passage. Crashing merrily on their heels came the newcomers, horseman after horseman, knights and squires and grooms, flashing the red and green mascles of the Earl of Kent's livery.

Owen waved Cynan furiously onward, and turned to stand off the assault. The bowmen slipped backwards from tree to tree, fitting and shooting as they could, the lancers aimed for the men rather than the horses, and brought down three in the first onslaught. Then the riders crashed among them as they hugged their covering trees, and it was a chaos of hand to hand fighting and opportunist running, without shape or direction. Some way ahead in the bushes a horse bellowed, and Cynan's angry voice roared defiance. They had reached the muffled prisoner and overrun his guards.

So it had all been for nothing! They could not hold him now, they could only hope to come off with their lives and unidentified. Outlaws from the forests to the south, grown over-bold; let them be taken for that, and they might yet make another and a better attempt.

But to be so near, and then to fail!

Adam ran crashing downhill in a narrow dark ride, almost into the arms of a man who came striding suddenly out of the bushes, sword in hand. The sword was dabbled at the point, and the man was laughing. The short, iron-grey hair, ruffled from his unceremonious usage, stood in tangled locks on the magnificent head Master Harry had loved to copy in stone. The clear, imperious voice, lately gagged by the folds of an archer's cloak, was singing gently to itself, and did not fall silent even when he instinctively took one dancing step back from the collision, and then as readily translated the movement into a forward lunge that almost passed Adam's startled guard. Only then, as they swung in a half-circle with a hiss of blades between them, changing places on the slope like a pair of dancers with only a foot of air separating their faces, did Isambard know his mason again.

They flung each other off and stared for an instant, each of them aware that he was known, each conscious that this recognition made many things plain. Then Adam closed in again furiously, pressing his opponent with a flurry of strokes, and for a moment Isambard gave ground. He parried almost mechanically, his eyes leaving Adam's face only by swift, flickering glances; and suddenly he leaned hard forward and caught Adam's blade on his own, and with a fierce turn of wrist and elbow wrenched the weapon half out of a shocked and bruised hand. Adam recovered it strongly, but there was an instant when Isambard could have killed him, and they both knew it. Instead he lowered his blade and drew back a rapid pace or two, nostrils wide and long lips smiling savagely, and suddenly turning away, vanished into the bushes.

Adam ran on towards the river confounded and astray, to blurt out his concern and incomprehension into Owen's anxious ears. They drew off as best they might to lie in hiding until nightfall and lick their wounds; and in the dark they crossed the river by the ford at Buttington and went to earth with their defeat and their chagrin in the forest under the ridge of Gungrog Fawr.

Owen had a badly gashed forearm, Cynan some splinters of his own shaft lodged deep under his ribs, and all of them minor cuts and bruises; but they had left behind them on the crest several of their enemies wounded by lances and arrows, some probably dead. They had come off lightly. But they were known now, Parfois was alerted, and the thing was to do again, and against infinitely greater odds.

And why, thought Adam, sleepless and sore in his damp cloak under the trees, why am I here to fret at it still? Why did he withhold his hand and leave me yet alive?

CHAPTER NINE

Parfois: *April to May* 1231

'Ah, they'll show their hand again,' said Isambard, shrugging off his escape lightly. 'I'm warned now, I know what to look for. They're over the river by this time, and so should I have been if you had not come so prompt to your hour. It hardly suits me to challenge their comings and goings formally. Let them stew, and they'll soon betray themselves. And when they do I shall be ready to move.'

His thirst was deeper than usual that night, his colour higher and his eyes brighter. That brief brush had done him good, body and spirit. He had withdrawn early with his guests, for they were bent on leaving next morning, and their business with him was not for the openness of the hall.

'Well, so the Earl Marshall's gone. And half of south Wales to be disposed of in consequence. His brother gets Pembroke, no help for that. But this wardship of his over the de Breos lands, that's a plum indeed, and one the King won't willingly confide to Richard along with his earldom. I don't wonder my lord of Kent is holding out his hands for it. But it seems it's already fallen into other hands.' He smiled, watching the smooth, impenetrable diplomatic faces that maintained their benign reasonableness even for him.

That poor rash fool de Breos, who had run his neck into Llewelyn's noose a year ago at this same season, had left a fine bone of contention behind him with his wide lands and his four little daughters. Now that their good uncle of Pembroke and natural guardian was gone there would be more than one pair of noble and greedy eyes turned on their fat marcher holdings. But it was not the earl's death that had sent these influential couriers of de Burgh riding hard across country to Parfois, it was the fall of the coveted prize into the hands of Richard of Cornwall. How had Hubert let Elfael and Brycheiniog slip through his fingers in the first place?

'Hardly the best hands,' said Warrenne carefully. 'His Grace the Earl of Cornwall is an excellent young man, but very inexperienced to be put in charge of so grave a trust.'

'True,' agreed Isambard, obliquely smiling. 'He has certain claims, of course.'

There was no need to labour that, de Burgh knew well enough how delicately the business of displacing him would have to be undertaken. Richard was the King's brother; according to Henry's mood and caprice that might make the young man either indispensable or unthinkable, but even for de Burgh it made it difficult to disparage his stewardship openly. Moreover, he was recently married to Earl William's sister, which gave him a family claim to an interest in the children and their estates. 'His marriage is but two weeks old,' said Isambard thoughtfully. 'He may be somewhat off his guard where other matters are concerned.'

They kept their admirable calm at that, permitting no shadow of a smile to answer the wicked look he gave them.

'The justiciar is chiefly concerned,' said Warrenne, 'that Brecon and Radnor should be in the hands of someone who understands their importance to England. You of all men, my lord, know that at this moment the issue between Wales and England trembles on the verge of war, and that Brecon and Radnor may be vital to us. No one can present that point to the King so well as you. You have kept this march inviolate from the encroachments of the Prince of Gwynedd, and you have seen his inroads on those less wary and less able than yourself. Moreover you think, as does the justiciar himself, in terms of England, and like him you see no advantage in clinging to old and now artificial connections with territories on the mainland of France. The future of England is here in these islands. If this nation is to grow great in establishment it must grow here, my lord. Westwards into Wales.'

'And northwards into Scotland,' said Isambard softly.

'My lord, no one has ever proposed any threat to the

202

sovereignty of King Alexander – '

'Not yet,' said Isambard. 'That's still to come. Not in my time, and not in Hubert's, maybe, but come it will.' He rose abruptly, and began to walk the wide chamber with his wine cup dangled lightly between his fingers, a habit of his when he was thoughtful. 'I am with the Earl of Kent in this, as he well knows. I divested myself of all my own French honours and laid them in my elder son's lap on condition he should be content to be French, as I had discovered I was English. A man cannot be both. And I see, as Hubert does, that the sea must be our frontier, but within that frontier we can and must be a unity. Nevertheless, I should advise him to tread gently as yet in the march. If he gains this custodianship from the Earl of Cornwall, he will be master of a third part of Wales. He should beware of presuming too far on the patience of the Prince of Gwynedd.'

'The justiciar has no territorial ambitions for himself,' said Piercey quickly. 'He is thinking for England.'

'He is thinking for England,' said Isambard bluntly, 'and for Hubert, too. I have no quarrel with that, provided he sets them in that order. But if Hubert provokes Llewelyn into action, it's England that will take the blame and the blow, and let him remember it.'

Nevertheless he would hold with Hubert, that he knew. It was this very vision that drew him to a man with whom he had so little in common besides. The rest, even Ranulf of Chester, still saw only their own palatines, and built at them and fought off encroachments on them feverishly, looking no farther. But this low-born de Burgh, this double man despite himself, even while he leaned back greedily, hankering after lands with the ambition of the landless, even while he envied the de Blundevilles and the Marshalls and composed about himself a synthetic replica of their hereditary splendour, yet saw England by glimpses as Isambard saw it, an empire not decomposing and falling to insecure tatters like the Emperor's sprawling hold, but compact as a clenched fist, solvent as a Jew's treasury and self-sufficient as a well-run manor, a power not hemmed in but completed and transmitted by

203

the sea. For the sake of the veritable man of state Isambard, born to dominion, forgave the collector of castles and amasser of manors. Moreover he was perversely drawn to a man so apt to be hated.

'None the less,' he said, turning again to face them with a calm and decided countenance, 'I think it indeed needful that this march should come into the justiciar's hands rather than Earl Richard's. He shall have my support in seeking to have it transferred to his care. You may tell him I'll do what he wishes.'

'And you'll come yourself to the King, my lord? The court is now at Windsor, but with these Welsh raids already infringing the territory of Brecon who knows how long his Majesty will be left in peace there?'

'I'll come,' said Isambard, 'as soon as I have dealt with these Welsh raids of my own. If my agent can pick up their traces clear of the garrison at Castell Coch I'll have my friends from Gwynedd running for Aber within a week. And if the King leaves Windsor in the meantime, the justiciar may send me word, and I'll come to him at Gloucester or wherever he may be.'

'My lord,' said Warrenne warmly, 'he knew well he could rely on you. Your counsel on all matters concerning the march carries such weight that the King cannot fail to listen to you.'

'It will be no hindrance, either,' said Isambard dryly, 'that as at this time there is, as I hear, a certain animosity between the King and his brother. Between my arguments for him and young Richard's against, I doubt not that Hubert will get his way.'

It was fifteen days before Isambard's inconspicuous agents in Pool and about the hospitable courtyard of Strata Marcella picked up traces of the Welsh marauders. Looking for them was in effect looking for Adam Boteler, who alone had been marked and recognised; and Adam had orders to remain out of sight in Castell Coch until the second attempt was ready to be launched. It was no part of Owen's plan to let his whole company lurk there, now that they were compromised; in case of close inquiry that would have been all too clear an indication of Llewelyn's unofficial complicity in the enterprise, and however little doubt Isambard himself might have on that head, it would not do to let it be established and admitted. They were and they must remain irregulars, to be disowned at need.

So Adam sat chafing in Castell Coch while Owen and his men camped in the forest beyond Gungrog Fawr, and waited until they should find a chance to cross the river again. Owen was for trying to get word through to Harry in his prison; there were men in Leighton who had kin within the castle, and for the sake of Master Harry whom they remembered well might be willing to risk the carrying of a message. But April ended, and their daily reconnaissance confirmed that still the fords and the ferry were watched, and the river shore on the English side patrolled day and night. They waited; he would not keep this up for ever, he was not so wary of his life and liberty.

If Adam had not issued from his hiding-place early in May they would not have been discovered; but the messages which had come from Llewelyn were grave enough to warrant a risk which by then appeared so slight. The disturbances on the borders of Brecon, whether officially encouraged or not, had grown to such proportions that the King had despatched his brother the Earl of Cornwall to the march in haste to try and suppress them, and was himself in the act of setting out from Windsor to join him there. A breath on the flames, and there would be fire from end to end of the march; and the Prince was in urgent but still friendly correspondence with King Henry in the effort to settle the dissensions peacefully and without affront to either Welsh or English honour. So wrote Llewelyn from Aber; and between the lines they read plainly that though he might still be arguing for peace he had ceased to believe in it or greatly to desire it. It was only a question of the hour.

So Adam slipped out of Castell Coch at dusk, and himself carried the word to Owen in his camp in the woods overlooking Cegidfa; and a beggar who had hung about the gates for some days and been fed from the kitchens went after him every step of the way. By the next dawn Isambard had the news for which he had been waiting; and the following night he put two parties across the Severn, one upstream from them and one down, and converged upon their hiding-place from either end of the ridge.

The alarm came at about three in the morning, a barn-owl's screech out of the night from Meurig on top of the ridge to Iorwerth waking and on guard at the camp. They had damped their fire till there was no red, and yet the attackers came fast and unerringly for them, from the north and from the south. Iorwerth shook Owen awake and they stood to their arms rapidly and in silence, but silence and darkness did not cover them.

'Glad am I,' said Adam in a hurried whisper into Owen's ear as they deployed among the trees, 'that I never went back, to leave you a man short.'

The assault from the north came with a flurry of tinder among the trees, and a crackle of sparks on a driving breeze. The full foliage of May did not burn, but the mould of dry, dead leaves and brushwood on the ground caught fiercely, and flared down upon them so fast that they were forced to turn and run, having no time to take the harder way up to the crest. Southwards the long arms of Isambard himself were stretched to receive them; the fire died on their heels after that brief flare, and left them on the points of English swords.

The archers loosed blind in the darkness, but could do so only once without imperilling their friends, for after the shock of meeting it was stark hand to hand work without any daylight art about it, first a hacking and swinging ahead at any flesh that moved, then body to body fumbling where everyone panted out words in his own tongue to be safe from his comrades, and even swords were of little use. They clutched and wrestled, feeling their way to one another's throat with the dagger or the naked hands. They shortened swords and used them like daggers at armpits and neck. Then the wind rose, fanning the few sparks left alive in the brushwood; the fire flared into life again and gave them light to see by, and they broke apart from their terrible embraces and sprang off to blade-length and lance-length.

The capricious blaze, devouring the easiest fuel, hissed between them and drove them apart, and Isambard came leaping through it, grinning like a demon and bringing with him a shower of sparks and the smoky, scorching odour of hell. For a moment he launched himself upon them alone, and Owen closed with him gladly against the glare, though dazzled by the flickering gleams and blinking shadows. Then the fire died down and Isambard's more timorous followers came hurtling after him, and by sheer weight swept their opponents before them down the hillside.

The fire burned out behind them. Darkling they drew off as best they could, dragging their wounded with them, carrying them when they dropped. Three times their number drove them unrelentingly a mile and more through the broken copses and across the brook south of Cegidfa. They fought, and ran, and stood to fight again, tiring, separated, driven now like hunted hares, until Isambard called his men back at the brook and let them rest at last.

Owen had then Adam and three others still marshalled at his back, not one of them whole, though these at least could stand and go. Searching back wearily and wretchedly through what was left of the night they found Iorwerth dragging himself painfully along the grass like a trampled snail in a slime of blood, and two more who crawled and swooned by turns in the fringes of the wood. Three bodies they brought down hacked and clawed from their camping-place, and Meurig, last of all, they found in the dawn on the crest of the hill, pinned to the ground by his own lance. By the time they had brought the dead down into Cegidfa, Iorwerth was also dying, with the priest from the church kneeling by him; and before noon one of the other two worst wounded followed him.

Owen laboured over the living, mending them as best he could, and over the dead, making them ready for burial, until he fell and lay like dead beside the last of them, but still conscious and aware, and Adam and some of those who had come with the priest to their aid carried him away and bedded him in quietness in one of the cottages. When he had strength enough he turned his face into his arms and hid from the light. He had lost half his command, and failed of winning back Harry for whom he had come. He did not know that Isambard, unsure of the numbers with which he had to deal, and always thorough, had brought forty men to sustain the assault against his dozen; and even if he had known it would have brought him no comfort.

Every one of the dead men ached in him like an amputation. Iorwerth had taught him to ride, Morgan had been his idol in boyhood by reason of his prowess at wrestling, Meurig, unfree but irrepressible, could never be kept out of any fight though his only real duties with the army were as a baggage-servant. Owen fingered them over with his exhausted and beaten mind, and bled and burned without tears. Even when Adam lay down beside him, groaning with the stiffening of his grazes and flesh wounds, Owen did not stir. Even when he laid his hand on him gently, he did not uncover his face.

Harry was so intent on his work that he did not hear the door open. He had moved the table under the direct light from the window, and was bending over the tough, cross-grained wood and the awkward knife with knit brows, breathing heavily. Isambard, putting the door to very softly behind him, was stabbed by yet another of the recollections that fronted him every way where Harry was. If the boy had growled over his shoulder: 'Stand out of my light!' the illusion would have been complete. I see, thought Isambard, that all human life moves in inescapable circles, and brings us back to moment after moment we thought past. Why? Is there yet something that can be changed? An imbalance that can be adjusted?

He came silently almost to Harry's shoulder, and still the boy was not aware of him, so perfectly was every sense concentrated on the block of wood before him. He must have picked it up from among the sawn logs in store for fuel. But where did he get the knife?

'I see you *are* his son,' said Isambard.

The boy's head came up sharply, the green eyes flashed their invariable challenge, and flew back jealously to the shape of the opening flower that was heaving itself painfully out of the wood. With a violent movement he clenched his fingers hard on the knife and pared the flower cruelly out of the block like a blemish from an apple. The grain was too complex and cross for him, the blade stuck, and in the same instant Isambard stretched both arms over the boy's shoulders and seized his hands, forcing them apart and wringing them until he twisted with pain and let go both the knife and the wood. Isambard caught up both, and stood for a moment staring down with a formidable frown at Harry, who nursed his bruised wrists and glared back, expecting a blow and tensing every muscle to receive it without a tremor.

It did not come. Isambard's quickened breathing stilled again. He looked at the torn flower, his eyes hooded.

'Was it worth so great a violation to do me such a little hurt?'

The boy was silent, his mouth set.

'Who gave you this knife?' It was pitiful, the broken blade of a dagger that he had bound with strips of rag to give him a handle, and sharpened as best he could on the edge of the stone under the window; the worn hollow, paler in colour, was there to be seen. If he had been asked where he got it, that obstinate jaw of his would have remained clenched, but Isambard knew how to ask his questions now. He had only to say, with that threat of punishment in his voice: 'Who gave you – ?'

'No one gave it to me. I found it in the armoury and hid it. It was thrown away for waste.'

The poor make-shift clattered on the table under his startled eyes. Why had it never occurred to him to use it for more than carving? And why, if his enemy had the same thought in mind, should he toss it back to him so carelessly?

'Why have you not asked me for tools, instead of breaking your finger-nails and your heart on firewood and trash?'

209

'It shall go very hard, my lord, before I ask you for anything.'

'God's life, you arrogant imp,' cried Isambard between laughter and exasperation, 'do you presume to be prouder than your father? Or are you simply afraid to show openly what you can do where he's been before you?'

'My lord, I know better than any that I am not his match,' said Harry, stung and colouring vividly. 'I never meant to challenge him, I was carving only to pass my time – ' His voice faded out wretchedly on the disclaimer, for that, too, was spoiled and finished now that Isambard had stripped it bare.

'Not his match! And have you not the heart in you to be anything but best? How many are his match? How many in this world do you think stand in the front rank? Are all the rest of us to give up and sit on our hands rather than serve humbly where we deserve?' He held the mutilated carving close before Harry's face and made him look at it. 'There! Dare to tell me that you see nothing there of him, that you have no feeling for the strokes of your hands, that you have no will in you to venture after him! Say it, if it's true, and I've done with you, you may rust unprovoked for me. Only to pass your time! Faith, that's the first lie I ever heard from you!'

Harry sat mute, his lashes lowered, his cheeks burning resentfully. But when he looked up again fleetingly at the spoiled flower he could not keep all the compunction and fondness out of his eyes.

'Get up!' said Isambard abruptly. 'Come with me. It's time you looked at your inheritance.'

Harry jerked up his head distrustfully, eyes flaring wide. His inheritance? What kind of talk was that from this man? If there was anything here that came to him from his father, it could be nowhere but in the church, and he had never yet been allowed past the gate-towers, and could not believe in any such concession now. Nevertheless his eyes had begun to gleam with an excitement that was unwilling to be lured into hope.

'Ah, no!' said Isambard, discerning his flight and plucking him back to earth. 'Not that, not without your pledge. But come and see!'

Hard fingers encircled his arm and haled him out of the room, and he went like one in a dream, unable to resist but ready for some treacherous pitfall to open under his feet at every step. There had always been a trap waiting for him somewhere along the way when Isambard loosed the reins a little, and it would be the same now. But they went together down the narrow stone stairway, and still he was not jerked back again. They crossed the outer ward, followed by covert glances and whispered wonderings that halted for a moment the bustle and business of the day.

'Here, in here!'

The lean hand gripping his arm thrust him in at a door in the long encrustation of buildings that clung to the curtain wall on the sunny side, where the best light fell and the day lingered longest. A large, bare room with big trestle tables in the centre and benches along the walls. There were several chests and one great press, and on the tables were laid out some unfinished drawings and a litter of instruments. There was no one in the room at this moment but themselves. Isambard pushed Harry gently forward and closed the door behind them.

The boy stood looking round him with a wary face and large, intent eyes. Isambard's hand on his shoulder brought him to the bench at the end of the room, where a film of stone-dust coated the floor, and several fragments of carvings and half-cut blocks of stone lay pushed together against the wall, as though discarded long ago. There were drawings, too, rolled aside out of the way, and ranged along the bench a great array of tools, mallets, chisels and punches, from the coarsest to the needle-fine, all their handles polished and worn with use.

He looked round at Isambard; the green eyes questioned frantically.

'Yes,' said Isambard, 'this was his tracing-house. Those are his tools.'

211

He watched the quivering face that was averted haughtily from his too close perusal. 'Twenty-four years old he was when I found him in the provost's prison in Paris, and paid his fine to get him for my own, him and that foster-brother of his whom you know well.'

Was he living or dead this day, that same Adam? Last night's lesson had been taught blind, there was no way of knowing how many had survived to get it by heart.

'A part of your father's gift I think you have, if you can learn not to deface it for spite because I am in the same world with you.'

Harry drew breath to deny the slur, and then said nothing after all, seeing in his heart that it was true enough. He put out his hands almost against his will, took up one of the mallets and swung it testingly to get the feel of its balance, picked up a punch at random and applied its point, none too deftly because his hands were tremulous, to a half-defined fold of drapery in the nearest block of stone. The mallet tapped with a sweet, small, occupied sound. The boy smiled faintly, and then bit hard on his lips and gnawed the smile away. He looked at the handle of the punch he held, fitting his fingers wonderingly into the shape another hand had worn in it; a good hand, muscular and slender, shaped very much like his own.

'His tools,' said Isambard softly. 'Your tools, if you want them.'

He heard and would not hear. In his extremity he put down the punch he could not hold steadily, and began to handle the half-shaped blocks of stone, dragging them forward and turning them to the light. One of them, small and dusty and obscure in its corner, took the sunlight as he drew it towards him, and showed him the vigorous sketch of a face he knew well, a face he had seen long ago in the triforium, when he had crouched against the wall in the last embrasure of the walk, listening to the approaching footsteps of his enemy. He had not marked it then, but he remembered it now.

'A study for the last head he ever made,' said Isambard,

212

watchful and patient at his shoulder.

'His signature at the end,' said Harry in a whisper.

'So I used to think, too. When you stepped out of hiding and fronted me, this same face looked over your shoulder. Then I knew better. Look again! This is no signature at the end, Harry, but a prophecy at the beginning. Do you not know yourself?'

Harry stared, and was slow to see his own face, and yet he could not but believe. Love reaching out to him took him by the heart and wrung him. He shut his eyes upon a rush of tears, and painfully contained them, but the springs of fondness in the middle of his being were weeping inconsolably for the stilling of the quick hands and the creative mind. He felt older than his lost father, and desperate with protective love. He wanted to hold him safe from every profaning touch, and fend off every malignant thought from him. He wanted above all to know that he still lay safe and quiet in his nameless grave; he was heavy and burning at heart with his longing to ask, but he would not. It was fear that locked his tongue, but mercifully he mistook it for pride, so its bitterness did not poison him.

He stood there silent beside the bench for a long time, fondling with a wondering hand the unknown contours of his own young head in the stone, thinking himself strangely wonderful suddenly, and a terrible responsibility.

'Your tools, if you want them. Tools can be used as weapons, Harry, but if you'll promise these shall never be put to any purposes but those for which they were intended, you may work here whenever you wish. This bench shall be yours. My mason shall provide you with materials, and if you choose to work under him and learn from him, he shall find you enough to do. The tasks he'd give to any apprentice, until you prove yourself. You'll not be privileged. Well?'

The silence continued long, while Harry picked up and laid down tool after tool, smoothed a finger-nail along the chisels, hefted the mallets, turning and twisting like a caged animal with the fury of his longing and the rigidity of his pride.

'Unless, of course, you're afraid to venture where you dread you'll prove less than excellent?'

'I pledge you my word,' said Harry with a tearing gasp, 'I'll not misuse them.'

'That came out of you like drawing a tooth,' said Isambard critically, 'but the first time's the hardest. Come, let's try you once more. To-morrow I must leave Parfois for a matter of some days. Give me your parole until I return, and you shall be free to go where you choose about Parfois, and free to use this tracing-house. Otherwise I fear you must wait in closer confinement till I come back, for I'll trust no one but myself to keep you safe for me. And you – if it please you to give me your word?'

It did not please him; almost he wished the first pledge back again, so naked did he feel now without his armour of obstinacy. But the giving had begun, and now it was harder than ever to draw back. The feel of Master Harry's mallet in his hand, the way the heel of it swung in his palm, filled him with a fever of ambition and impatience, and he could not wait the threatened few days for the assay. Trembling, he hugged the most worn and shortened of the punches to his heart, thumbing its point, and wrestled with the words of compliance that rose all too readily.

'Well? Will you give me your pledge?'

'Yes!' he said, the word jerked out of him furiously, and twisted away to hide from the malicious smile he dreaded. Such a despair seized him at the sound of his own acceptance that he made a half-hearted attempt even then to deliver himself. 'Only until you return! After that I promise nothing – '

But only silence answered him, and when he looked round he was alone in the room. Isambard had accepted his bond on the instant without a word of triumph or mockery, and left him alone to exult and grieve over his father's belated legacy. Suddenly he took the visionary image of his own manhood into his arms, his ruffled hair against the stone curls, and burst into a storm of silent weeping.

CHAPTER TEN

Aber: *May to early June* 1231

It was late before the members of the council left Llewelyn's chamber. Owen could not bear the emptiness of the ante-room and the abrupt murmurs of the low voices behind the inner door. He went out and sat on the top step of the stair-case like a banished child waiting to be admitted. He was still sick and light-headed with the fever that had kept them so long immobilised at Cegidfa, and made the ride home such long-drawn discomfort to him; but the sorry account he had to make of his stewardship weighed more heavily on his spirit than his wounds did on his body. At least two of the five he had brought back with him were in worse case than he; and Adam, who had perhaps come off lightest in actual injuries, was by no means to be envied for that, for the same story Owen had to tell to the Prince, Adam was at this moment tell-ing to Gilleis. Owen thought wretchedly that his own was the lighter task of the two.

The door of the inner room opened. He roused himself wearily to exchange greetings with the elders as they passed him, and went in to his foster-father.

Llewelyn had been in council for several hours, and was no less weary; nevertheless, he saw the labour and pain with which Owen bent his knee to him, and reached to take him up before he could complete his reverence. His kiss was brusque but warm, and his hands transmitted a vital vigour of which no one else had the secret.

'No, no ceremony, boy, we're alone here. There, sit, and take your time. No one will disturb us now. I ask your pardon for leaving you waiting at the door, but I'm pressed, Owen, the days crowd me, and there are things I must set forward

215

while I may. I had your despatch from Meifod.' It was his way of saying at once that he knew the worst of what was to come, and had only the details to learn.

'I've lost you six good men,' said Owen, 'and gained you nothing. I took the best I could, and this is how I've made use of them.'

'Did they reproach you?' asked Llewelyn sharply and dryly. He poured wine and brought it across the room to Owen's chair, pressing him back brusquely when he would have risen to receive the cup.

'They had no time,' said Owen bitterly.

'They had no will, and well you know it. The like is waiting for us all, when God so designs. Tell me the whole of it, and if you have done ill, you shall hear of it.'

Owen eased his stiffened shoulder wound against the cushion, and began the story of his failure. He was not sparing with himself, and yet the tale ran more readily than he had supposed possible, so completely did he trust the listener. From Llewelyn he would get his deserts, and be grateful for them. He had never rested with such absolute confidence in the judgement of any other, excepting once for that brief while in his childhood, when he had been in the care of Master Harry.

'How he found us I still don't know. Adam fears it was through his coming to us from Castell Coch, and indeed it may be so. Yet I cannot feel that Adam was to blame. How could he know the man had his creatures planted even there to watch for him? I should have allowed for it that he was no ordinary man, and could move like a thunderstorm when he willed. He knew straitly where we lay, and all our dispositions. He could not plan for the way of the wind, that was luck, but for the rest he had everything at his finger-ends. And he fights like ten men still, as old as he is. I cannot feel that we had been negligent, had we been dealing with another man. But we were dealing with Isambard, and what I did was not enough.'

'Twice luck was with him,' said Llewelyn. 'Once with a favouring wind, and once with reinforcements when he most

216

needed them. For neither of which favours can you be blamed. The devil has looked well after his own.'

'And once we all but had him safe,' said Owen, groaning into his hands, for he was very tired. 'I ask myself every hour now if we might not have held him and still drawn off well enough if I had but kept a better watch on the road to Shrewsbury. I meant to try again and better, either to get at him, or to find a messenger who would carry word to Harry inside Parfois. For you know he has a measure of liberty – ?'

'I know. I have it all from Philip ap Ivor. I know what that man owes to Harry, and what to me, and I have kept the account, and in good time I shall take what is due. A measure of freedom to the son, and the last indignity to the father's bones – what manner of dealing is that?' said Llewelyn, smouldering.

'And I fear him,' said Owen feverishly, 'truly, sir, I fear him. This forbearance with Harry is too capricious and cruel for me. If he so mortally hated the father, living and dead, how can we trust his indulgence with the boy? If Harry should come to worse harm through me –'

'You take too much to yourself. It is not your blame, and I will not spare to you what is mine.'

The Prince's voice was hard and hot. How often in his life had he admitted guilt before anyone but God?

'It was I sent the boy out after his act of vindication. These six lives are all of my spending, and if I were free I would go with any army and take them back with usury. But I am not free. It is no part of my duty now to give any thought to the making of my own soul or the righting of what I have done wrong. God deals as He will, I as I can. I am the servant of the cause I have at heart, and you and I, and Harry if need be, are coin to be spent for it.'

'Did they get so bad a reception at Worcester?' asked Owen, dismayed by the tone rather than the content of this speech. The Prince's envoys had returned to Aber from the latest of the long-drawn conferences with the King's representatives, two days ahead of the battered remnant from Parfois.

'No, not ill at all. There were civil looks and fair speeches, and there's another meeting called three days hence, at Shrewsbury. But it means little now, for the mountain is in motion, and slide it must. Two ideas over-large for reconciliation are fronting each other now, and there'll be no peace until there's been – no,' he checked himself, 'I won't say a settlement, but at least a temporary losing and winning that shall silence us both until we get our breath for the next bout. Sometimes I have a fear in me that this is but the first of many engagements in a struggle which is new, in scope if not in kind.'

He crossed to the window to set wide the shutter on the last night of May, and heave the smokiness of his long closeted hours out of him in great, assuaging breaths. 'You know the crown still holds back from acknowledging our title to Builth? The act of denying matters little. So my constable continues to hold the castle, let the King garrison the title as strongly as he will. Yet the sign is there to be read. They deny their own law, denying my right, and the precedent is there to stead them in the next encroachment. They are ready, as they think, to devour me. But by God, they shall find me stick in their gullets and rip their bellies open.'

'De Burgh is the mover,' said Owen, propping up his drooping eyelids. 'My heart misgave me when I saw his livery at Parfois, for Isambard is close and confidential with him, and sure they had some business between them that bodes us no good here in Wales.'

'They had indeed! Have you not heard it yet? They brought me the news back from Worcester. Isambard joined the King at Hereford early in May. He must have left Parfois no more than two days after his raid across Severn. King Henry respects my lord's views on all that pertains to the march. And the upshot of it is that he has taken the custody of the de Breos lands from the Earl of Cornwall, and bestowed it upon his beloved justiciar. De Burgh hems me in on every side but where the sea is, save only Chester, where I thank God for Earl Ranulf. The cause is complete now, I need no more to show me the time is on me. Now there wants only the occasion,

218

which, God willing, shall be of my choosing.'

'I thought at least to have taken Harry off your mind,' said Owen wretchedly, 'so that you might give all your heart to this. And I've done nothing but lose you six good men.'

'All my heart is given to this. Harry, poor lad, must wait his turn. The keeping of my vows, the honouring of my obligations, all give way to this. If I live, I will redeem all my pledges, and if I die, I will answer for their going unredeemed in the judgement.'

He leaned his great bronzed forehead on his hand, turning his face gratefully to the cool of the night air, and went on talking in the soft, absorbed voice of one alone with his own spirit.

'I tell you, boy, we are engaged with more even than I knew. While I have been busy compounding a kingdom here for my son, I have borrowed from the English as I thought fit. There is no way of standing them off in the old fashion. I have paid for my court and my campaigns by means they showed me, by taxation, and rents, and fees levied on settlers in my townships. I have given lands and privileges to get knight service, and kept my army in the field by contracts my forefathers never countenanced. I have settled the succession by English law and not by Welsh, to make it hold the firmer, and stop their mouths from questioning it. So, while I stood off their changes and challenges with the right hand, I let them in with the left. And I see that by the left or the right, by compact or by conquest, come they will. There is no way of preventing. All we can do is shape the means by which they approach us and the terms on which they will live with us in the time to come, that we may keep our honour and our identity, and be their free neighbours and allies, not their villeins. And I know this, that if we are to gain such a bargain with them we must first know ourselves who and what we are, and set a true value on our blood and our tongue. Not we only of Gwynedd, not the men of Powis, not the gnawed remnant of Deheubarth. But we Welsh. And this is more than the ambition with which I began, and more than my son's inheritance. If I die for it, if David must die for it in his turn, no matter, so the spring survive and the unity grow. And if Harry dies for it, his death be on my head, and I will answer for it to God and to him when my time comes.'

When his voice had ceased there was silence in the room. He stirred himself at last and looked round, to find one even more worn out with weariness than himself. Owen had dropped asleep in his chair. The heavy brown head lolled a flushed cheek on the red cushion that supported his bandaged shoulder.

Llewelyn crossed to him, smiling, and gently shook him awake. He started up in alarm, staring dazedly, and then, realising his lapse, paled with mortification.

'My lord, give me your pardon! I've ridden far to-day – and then the wine – '

His long fever had peeled the flesh from his bones and left him half his proper bulk, and the brown of his cheeks was yellow and drawn. When he started to his feet he had to lean hard on the arm of the chair while a moment of dizziness passed.

'Go to bed, boy,' said Llewelyn, holding him reassuringly between his hands. 'You can, with a quiet mind. What you attempted was not blessed, more's the pity, but none the less it was well done, few could have done better. I find no fault with you. There, go and sleep! Who knows if I may not have need of you by to-morrow?'

In the late afternoon of the second of June a courier rode into Aber on a reeking horse, the last of a chain of messengers who had carried urgent news from Cydewain. Llewelyn was close in his chamber with his chaplain-secretary and Ednyfed Fychan over the dictation of letters, and his seal was already on the credentials of the envoys who were to represent him in Shrewsbury; but David, when he heard what the messenger had to report, on his own authority brought him in to the conference and shattered it.

'What is it?' Llewelyn looked round from the table with a formidable scowl. 'Did I not say I was not to be disturbed?'

'My lord and father, blame me for this interruption, not the courier. But this cannot wait.'

Llewelyn looked from his son to the rider, who was dusty and streaked with sweat from his gallop. He pushed the papers from him as though he knew already he had done with them.

'Speak out, then. What is it?'

'My lord, I bring word from the march by Montgomery. A week ago the garrison there made a sally against us and surrounded and took a company of our men.' The man came up from his knees coughing the dust out of his lungs with the words. 'The number I do not know. But they took them into the castle at Montgomery, prisoners.'

'This I know,' said Llewelyn, his face dark. 'Come to the news.'

'My lord, yesterday the Earl of Kent came to Montgomery, and himself saw the prisoners. He ordered them out to execution on the instant, and it was done. Beheaded, every man!'

'*Beheaded?*'

Llewelyn came to his feet with a leap that shook the chair jarring back across the floor-boards, and tumbled the scattered rolls of parchment to the rugs.

'Has he dared? In my face! He spits this in my face!' He whirled away from them to stalk the floor for a few raging paces, and as abruptly rounded on them again. 'Is there more?'

'My lord,' said the messenger hoarsely, 'they are saying the heads are sent to the King of England.'

'Two days before the King's envoys were to meet mine!'

'This he could not do in folly, fool though the man can be,' said David, white to the lips as he watched his father's face. 'This is deliberate.'

'It is deliberate. He conceives that he is ready.' Llewelyn plucked the pen from his secretary's hand, and swept the remaining letters from before him. 'Leave these, they'll not be needed. There'll be no meeting in Shrewsbury. Hubert shall see where to-morrow will find me, and I'll be there before he looks for me. Ednyfed, the writs go out within the hour. See to it!'

'They've been ready this week past,' said Ednyfed Fychan, and swung to the door with alacrity.

'And send my captain here, and Rhys with him. It is time,' said Llewelyn, drawing a great breath. 'He'll choose it for me, will he? So be it! We shall see who'll come best out of it. But was it necessary to kill my men in cold blood? Was there no other gage he could have flung in my teeth? By God, he shall rue it! I'll make him pay dear for every head.' He swung on the messenger again, his hawk-face sharp as a sword. 'Is the earl still at Montgomery?'

'As I heard it, my lord, he's already gone back to Hereford.'

'So much the worse, I would have wished him to see his township burn. But he'll keep. What I owe him shall be paid in full, and I'll make him count the coin over in his ruin. David, see this good fellow fed and housed, and come back to us here. We have yet some planning to do. Before dawn we march.'

They ran every one, ablaze at his fire, to do his bidding. The columns for support and supply had been alerted long ago, the clansmen waited only for the signal, and his great seal on the writs his messengers carried would bring them out to join him like bees from a hive disturbed. He had only to call and they would come, eager and hungry.

'I have dealt moderately,' said Llewelyn through his teeth, flexing his great, shapely, sinewy hands before his face to take hold on the challenge and the promise in the air. 'I have held my hand time and again, and even when they drove me to act I have abated my askings to keep the balance true and save Wales from worse enmity. But now we cannot be so saved. They think their hour is come to close on me, and to deal moderately now would be a thing in their littleness they could not but mistake. Now they shall see that I can do extremes, and by God they shall learn to keep their hands from Gwynedd while I am yet alive.'

Owen, when he heard the news, came limping in great haste through the furious bustle of the maenol to claim his rights, afraid in his heart of being rejected.

'I am fit,' he persisted, holding Llewelyn fast by the sleeve, for he was apt to flash away from armoury to store and stable to council chamber disconcertingly upon his universal errand of supervision. 'David is my prince, and well I know this is not border play this time. Where David goes I must go. You would not leave me behind?'

Llewelyn turned from the harness that was being checked out of the armoury, and looked at his foster-son for a moment from so far away and by so dazzling a light that he seemed hardly to know him. Recognition came with a sudden warm and brilliant smile out of his preoccupied frenzy.

'Ah, you! Leave you I would, if I did not know you'd fret your heart out worse than I'll let you fret your body in the field. Yes, you shall come, if you'll be ruled and do as I bid you. I would not let you from David's side willingly, no more than I'd send him into the battle without a shield.'

He saw Owen redden with pleasure, and laughed, flinging an arm about his shoulders so forgetfully that it was a worthy as well as a willing sacrifice Owen made for him, containing the pain of the embrace. 'And, Owen, I have yet a use for you here and now. Find Gilleis and Adam for me, and bring them to the chapel. I would have you all three witness a certain vow I have to make before we march.'

Owen brought them within a quarter of an hour, grave-faced both, and heavy-eyed from nights broken with too much thinking of Harry. It seemed to Llewelyn, watching Gilleis approach, that she had lost flesh sadly in the year of lacking her son, and her rose and white had faded into the pallor of prisoners. Half at least of her day she spent in the closed and sealed place of her lady's captivity, half of her night imprisoned with the boy. And yet she neither pleaded nor complained. Her great dark eyes questioned and hoped, but without reproach. And even now, he thought, all I have to offer will seem so little to a woman.

It was dark in the wooden chapel even in the early evening; the candles on the plain, linen-covered altar guttered faintly in the draught before the door was closed, and after its closing there was an astonishing silence, all the sounds of the activity without banished to infinite distance.

Llewelyn kneeled and prayed. Even when he raised his face open-eyed to the altar the silence still continued for a while.

'Bear with me,' he said. 'I am not adept with words without my elders by me, and this is matter for care. A man never thinks, when he undertakes one journey, that he may not return from it to contemplate another. And yet I think my time is not yet, and God wills well to hear me.'

He set both hands before him on the crucifix. His touch could be wonderfully gentle, but it was never tentative; he laid hands on holy things with the same direct and innocent fearlessness he used towards men and women.

'So be my witness,' he said, 'that before the face of God and in your presence I swear this: that when God's good time serves me to do it without injury to my foremost obligations to Him and to my country, I will take and destroy the castle of Parfois for the wrongs of Harry Talvace dead and Harry Talvace living. If my foster-son be still held there, by the grace of heaven I will take him out of his captivity. And if not, yet I will not spare of what I have sworn touching Parfois. So help me God I will not forget nor fail of making good my word on my enemy and Harry's.'

Owen said: 'Amen!' gladly, but his was the only voice to answer. Adam would have echoed it, but he was intent on his wife's face, and in his anxiety he let the words go by him. She was regarding the Prince with the faintest and saddest of smiles, in which he thought he could read affection and indulgence, and surely also a soft, secret gleam of derision. Llewelyn turned from the altar in time to catch that disconcerting look, but it neither puzzled nor disturbed him. When he was roused to such a peak of experience, confronting the issues of life and death for thousands besides himself, all things became simple to him. Things which had bewildered him were clear as crystal, problems which had daunted and defied him gave like locks opening to the right key. The power of words which he had disclaimed sprang golden in his mouth.

'Well I know it, girl,' he said, 'this fills neither your arms nor your heart. Yet it is all I have, and, if it does not loose you, yet it binds me. Take it for a pledge of my faith that God will hold Harry safe for us, howsoever we miss him now.'

'My lord,' she said, 'I do believe it.'

'So trust, then, as you have spoken, and, if God will, you shall yet stand by the altar of the church of Parfois, when the day comes for me to fulfil my oath, and see Master Harry's bones honourably buried there.'

He saw her blanch and veil her eyes, and said no more of that for kindness. He was moved and promising miracles, the recovery of things lost, the wholeness and holiness of things profaned; but the faith she had professed was perhaps no more than a conviction that the star of the Prince of Aberffraw would not fail him, and that God would humour him and not cheat him of the fulfilment of his vow. Yet Llewelyn felt the forces of heaven moving him, and aligned himself with them boldly, going without hesitation where they carried him.

The thing which had seemed so hard was simple now, the gulf that had appeared unbridgable shrank to a child's leap, and vanished as he stepped over it.

'Gilleis, one more thing I must lift from my heart before this hour breaks over me.'

She raised her eyes to him quickly, wondering and doubting.

'Go to your lady, and ask her if she will receive me.'

She was sitting beneath the narrow, barred window when he entered the room, and the first thing he saw was the light lying ashen in her fair hair; there was more grey than gold in it now. She had grown heavier in her enforced stillness, her body was ripe and full that had been so slender, and moved with something less than the old negligent grace. But her face was not full but fallen, the pale skin stretched over slight bones, the eyes grown enormous and calm like grey glass. They looked upon him and gave no sign. Her hands were spread upon the arms of the chair, as she used to sit beside him on occasions of state, erect and observant, quick to anticipate, deft in manipulation. She was richly dressed. He saw and understood that she had prepared herself for him. She was a king's daughter and the wife of a prince, whether in his palace or his prison.

For a year he had neither seen her nor permitted her name to be spoken in his hearing. He had thought that he must come back to her now as a stranger, learning afresh the shape of her wide forehead and tapering face, and the way she had of opening her eyes wide to take in entire the person to whom she spoke. He had expected to have to batter his way laboriously through the months that had separated them, as through the stockade of a castle into which he must break by force of arms. But at the first sound of her voice even this changed woman became familiar to him, and the veil of estrangement between them broke and drifted like gossamer.

'You are welcome, my lord,' she said. 'There was no need to ask permission, your prisons are always open to you.'

Gilleis had gone, and closed the door quietly behind her. He stood just within the room, looking steadily at the Princess, and went headlong where his genius pointed him. Constraint and ceremony could have nothing to say to her that would not be wearisome to hear as it was costly to say. There was no time. He had always been at his best when he was pressed hardest.

'Joan,' he said, 'I need you.'

In spite of herself she stirred so sharply that he felt her astonishment recoil upon his own flesh and set him trembling. If he had spoken of forgiving, or pitying, or even loving, she would have been ready for him, but to be needed was something she had not looked for.

'That cannot be true,' she said. 'You have done without me well enough for a year, and so you can now.' She said it very mildly, without reproach or complaint, only uttering what she felt to be true. He saw now where Gilleis had learned her patience and endurance.

'I have done without you, but not well. Without you nothing is well. I need you. I am going into the field to-morrow against King Henry's army and against the Earl of Kent in

226

particular, and God knows what the outcome will be. It is a long tale.'

'You need not tell it,' she said, 'I know it already. Do you think I have not been following all that you have done and all that has been done to you all these months?'

'If you know it, you know the need I have of you. Always before when I ran my head, and my country, and my son's inheritance into danger, and stood to it in arms, always I had you by my side, heart in heart with me. I am well served as princes go, and I have wit to know it. But when I go from hence to this testing I must leave affairs here in one pair of hands, the closest and dearest to me. There is no other I can trust,' said Llewelyn, 'as I trust you.'

At that word she raised her head and looked at him again, and long, and behind the clear disillusionment of her eyes a burning darkness had gathered and hung, glowing from deep within her. The pale mask of her face fended him off, incredulous, but the bright creature within, so long coffined and mute, knew that she had heard aright.

He came nearer, and the light of the June evening turned the tanned planes of his hawk-face and the ridge of the bold, importunate nose to copper, and picked out the russet reds in the short, dark beard, scoring deeper the deeply graved lines of audacity and laughter. The laughter had been absent for a while, but it had not withdrawn far from him, the marks of its permanent habitation were still there.

'Don't think this is merely habit,' he said, 'though habit it has been for twenty-five years. Without you I do well enough? Ay, so I do, for a man lamed and distracted in mind. Self-maimed and a sinner against the truth, such I am without you, Joan.'

'And I,' she said, very low, 'what am I?'

'You are that part of me that I cut off, and I never have been and never shall be whole without you.'

She turned her head a little and put up her hand to shield her face. 'The diseased part,' she said.

'No, but wounded. And I who should have healed it severed it.'

227

'Dear God!' she said in a shaken whisper. 'Be careful what you do with it now. Do you think you can restore it and it will knit again without festering?'

'By the grace of God, yes,' he said, and leaned and took her gently by the wrist, but did not force her hand away. 'Do you not feel the two halves closing? Flesh of my flesh, blood of my blood, I want you though you poison me, but well I know you never will. Come back with me to the place that was and is yours, be to me as you were before. Complete me. Make me a whole man before I go out to take the field with Wales in my hands. With one hand only, how shall I carry it safely? The heritage of your son and mine!'

'Have you forgotten,' she said harshly, starting and quivering at his touch, 'my offence against you?'

'Have you forgotten mine? Even in the right a man can offend past any forgiveness. The measure of my outrage and anger was the measure of my love for you. God witness, at the worst I never ceased to worship you.'

He had used another word of power. She looked up, and the prisoned creature within her was bright and burning close within her eyes, frantic for freedom.

'Nor I you,' she said, amazed, and let her hand slip into his and be held fast. 'God witness!' she said after him. 'At the worst, even when I was bound and blind and mad, I swear it never touched you or anything that was yours. If you could take my love in your hands, you would not find one mark upon it, not one. Never a break nor a blemish!' She leaned her head against his sleeve and drew deep breath. 'I am in the dark still. It will always be a mystery, a thing that happened to me like the seasons, like floods and lightnings, without question or escape. And yet I would not lay it all on him —'

She broke off there. It was the first time they had mentioned the third who was there in the room with them, though they had both felt his presence, and she, indeed, had lived with it close and uncomforted for a year.

'Yes, speak of him,' said Llewelyn, looking down at the heavy ashen head that lay so still upon his arm. 'It's meet we should. It's time we should.'

'He was blown in the storm as I was, however the thing began. Your rival he never was. You never had a rival.' The beautiful voice bled words in short, hard sighs into his arm. 'When he came he was weak and in pain. And so young! He needed all those things in me for which you had no use, pity, indulgence, even forgiveness. By his youth he showed me how late it was, and by his admiration that it was not yet too late. He made me know that I was growing old, and that everything he was was slipping out of my hands. And I closed my hands and grasped it while I could. And then I could not loose.'

She was silent for a moment. She turned her head a little, and he saw that the calm had come back to her face, but now there was light and colour in it, as if the blood curbed and slowed to solitude and stillness had begun to flow again.

'You it never touched,' she said. 'Your place it never threatened. The world would not see it so, but I tell you, this is truth. And yet it all but shattered your life and mine and all our work, and killed an unfortunate, rash young man no worse than the most of men, and hardly deserving of death. Night and day, I never can forget him.'

'You need not,' said Llewelyn, 'as I have not forgotten him. Wherever we go, he will go with us, that I know. But he will not go always between us.'

He took her by both hands, and drew her up to stand breast to breast with him. His arms he folded round her, and so held her for a moment passive; then with a sudden sharp sigh she embraced him again, quivering, and lifted her mouth to him ravenously.

There was the taste of death in the kiss, but she accepted the price with the prize, and clung to the bitterness and the bliss alike, knowing them for ever inseparable now. Llewelyn felt the chill shudder through her before it died in his heart. He held her face cupped and cradled in his great hand, hard against his cheek, and the beat of his blood passed into her veins and drew her own blood into the same passionate measure.

'Death is waiting for me no less,' he said low and gently into

229

her ear,'and for you. When the time comes that we must face William de Breos, we'll face him. What's in store for us then is not for us to ordain. God be thanked! And let God dispose.'

She could not speak, but her lips shaped against the pulse in his throat: 'Amen!'

After a long while of silence he unlocked his arms from her. He was smiling. His long-sighted eyes reflected gold back to the sunset, and the brightness did not fade as the sun went down. She saw the pale flame she had lit in him burn tall and steady, a miracle of faithfulness out of unfaithfulness. He would be a lantern to his clansmen, and lightning striking at his enemies. And she had thought herself quite spent!

'Put on your robes and your crown, my lady,' he said, 'and come with me to the hall.'

In the court a little groom was crossing from the stables, in haste for his supper. He saw them and halted, standing at gaze for a moment open-mouthed and great-eyed, and then he whooped like a huntsman hot after game, and turned and ran like a hare for the hall, bounding as he ran. The word was before them, the fire ran through the brushwood. Heads came bursting from every doorway to see them pass, and the warm hum of excitement and eagerness span after them in a golden thread, the voice of the brightness that flashed like sparks from face to face. The old formidable unity, that had seemed lost and broken irrecoverably, blazed torch-like through Aber to confound its enemies.

David was coming from his own lodging, pale and grave and preoccupied, with his child-wife by the hand. He smiled as he looked down at her and answered her quick, light speech with conscientious gentleness. Some distance behind them her ladies walked; they were kind, but they oppressed her with their insistence on her royalty, and it was hard to live up to them. She had never fully understood why her life should have changed so suddenly and drastically, though she knew by rote the duties and privileges of married ladies, and did her best to play her part decorously. So suddenly fatherless, and so abruptly given to a husband, translated from the familiar

230

company of her sisters at Brecon to this barbarous foreign court where she was the last and loneliest of the children, Isabella had looked round her forlornly for an anchorage to which she might ride in safety. And she had found it. She held to it confidingly, at rest in David's hand.

He was more than usually serious and thoughtful tonight, he went with his eyes on the ground and his brows drawn, and smiled only fleetingly when she poked fun at Ednyfed's wife to amuse him and get his attention. He had his eyes downcast when they came to the corner of the great hall, and he did not see the Prince approaching, leading by the hand an unknown lady. A tall lady in dark blue velvet, with a string of agates round her neck and a golden diadem in her hair; a lady Isabella had never seen before in her year at the court of Gwynedd. Child and woman looked at each other with the same wonder and wariness, attracted and afraid.

Joan saw a little girl of eight or nine years, eyeing her alertly and clinging to David's hand. The child wore a soft yellow woollen cotte and a brocaded surcoat stiff with gilt thread, and smoothed at her finery with her free hand as she approached, aware of the need to look her best before this unknown lady. The soft, rounded face had a fresh, high colour, and was framed between two short braids of wavy black hair. Innocent and anxious, her father's long-lashed dark eyes looked up bright as swords.

She tugged furtively at the hand she held, drawing close against David's hip. He looked sidelong at her with a quick smile, and she frowned and nodded his attention quickly towards the stranger. David raised his head, and saw the two who walked towards him hand in hand.

He checked and stood amazed, half afraid to believe, and the colour of incredulous joy flushed through his fairness and made him bright as a rose. The child, watching him hopefully but without understanding, shone with reflected eagerness. For a long moment there was silence as they converged upon the steps of the hall, until David got his voice again.

'Why, here's my mother home at last,' he said, and came smiling to meet her, putting forth the child by the hand to her, a little clumsily because he could not see well for the tears in his eyes.

'Madam, here is one I beg you to love and cherish as your own child. Here is Isabella, my wife and your daughter. She has been waiting a long time for your kiss.'

Joan drew near and took the dead man's child by the hands, and kissed her. The soft, shy fingers quivered in her palms, the half-formed flower of a mouth tasted of the spring and the sun. The great black eyes were clear without a shadow as Isabella, recognising the bright aspect of love and unaware of its dark face, looked up and smiled.

CHAPTER ELEVEN

Parfois, Aber: *June* 1231

The first cluster of strong, uncurling leaves in imitation of Master Harry's capitals in the nave came flawed out of the stone, a little pretentiously conceived from too much ambition and a little clumsily executed from too little practice. But the second, which was more truly his own, fell within his range, and he had the feel of his tools by then, and went at it easily and gently, bullying neither himself nor his material. Once he almost marred it in sheer nervousness when Master Edmund came to his shoulder and watched him for a while; but the old man scolded him first and praised him after, both tersely enough, and he mastered his dislike of being observed at work, and stood to his strokes sturdily from then on, whoever approached him.

He heard the door of the tracing-house open towards evening, when he was alone there and lost in his unfolding leaves, and taking the newcomer to be Master Edmund again, schooled himself to continue steadily. The strokes of the mallet came neat and light and even, an engrossed and happy sound. The hand that poised the punch moved with delicate care, still a little hesitant but gaining confidence. Not until he paused to choose a finer punch did the presence a yard from his elbow speak to him.

'And you did not even know who I was,' said Isambard's provokingly amiable and considerate voice. 'A month ago your blood would have curdled when I entered the same room with you.'

Harry tried too late to suppress the start which had betrayed him, and made his selection from among his father's tools with fierce concentration. Other things also, it seemed,

233

were changing. A month ago he would not have made any reply to the hated voice; but now it seemed to him that his own dignity called for one. He looked round with the fine punch in his hand. Isambard was still in half-harness; he could only just have ridden into Parfois, and in his own apartments in the Lady's Tower no doubt Langholme was waiting to disarm him.

'Welcome back, my lord,' said Harry, vexed at the lame, false sound it had when it was out.

'Am I indeed welcome? And to you?' Isambard swept aside some of the dusty drawings that lay on the end of the bench against the wall, sat himself sidewise there and made himself comfortable with his back against the stone sill of the window that gave the sculptor light. He laughed again to see how the boy scowled to find this added shadow cramping his vision. There was a reference there of which Harry knew nothing. 'That's very civil of you, child, considering my return shuts the gate on you again and pens you within the wards. Unless, of course, you're willing to extend your parole indefinitely? Are you?'

'No, my lord.' And then, setting his jaw, he said the words for which Isambard was waiting and listening: 'If you'll be so good as to move aside from the window, my lord, I'll go on with my work.'

The note of the soft, remembering laugh that answered him was something he could not understand, and it daunted him. He looked sidelong at the man who sat with wide shoulders spread against the light, and folded arms quiet on his breast, lounging at ease.

'No, Harry. This time no. Move for you I would, but the light's too far gone already, and I won't have you spoil your eyes or your work by pushing too hard. Let it lie till the morning. Not at my orders,' he said patiently, seeing the mutinous tightening of Harry's lips, 'but because your own good sense tells you to. It's a poor craftsman who'll ruin his own work even to spite his worst enemy.'

He watched with a slight smile as Harry turned an abrupt shoulder on him, and with deliberation set his left hand once more to the fine edge of the leaf. The mallet hesitated in air. The light was indeed too far gone, and the smooth curve pleased his eye and dared him to mar it. He wanted finer detail yet, but he knew the evening would not serve for it. After a brief struggle with his own obstinacy he turned back to the bench and quietly laid down his tools, and began to roll down the sleeves of his cotte.

'Well done!' said Isambard. 'We shall make a reasonable man of you yet, if we keep you long enough. You still say no to holding by your parole, do you?'

'My lord, I gave it only until your return, and you are returned.'

'Returned and made welcome. That was more than I hoped for.' He reached to pick up one of the row of chisels, testing its edge against his thumb. 'And do you know what news I've brought back with me from Hereford, Harry?'

'No, my lord.' He stood frowning down at his work, but the frown was one of concentration and pleasure. He turned the block of stone between his hands to observe in its deeply cut faces the play of what remained of the light.

'Wales is at war,' said Isambard carelessly. 'Llewelyn burned the town of New Montgomery to the ground three days ago.'

He had his satisfaction this time, and in full measure. The caressing hands quitted the stone as though it had burned them, the sullen face came round to him glittering with the green of startled, ardent eyes. 'At war?' said Harry's lips, framing the words silently.

'Two days before the date fixed for one more tedious parley at Shrewsbury, our noble justiciar chose to sting him into action by executing certain prisoners at Montgomery. His calculations may have been accurate,' said Isambard with a sardonic grin, 'but between you and me, Harry, I doubt it. Howbeit, he did it, and your great Prince of Aberffraw and Lord of Snowdon took fire like a pitch-flare, and is busy now setting light to the borders. While my lord King Henry debates and hesitates, and leans on his bishops to bring the fire to heel with a little holy water.'

'And Montgomery's burned?' said Harry, himself as bright and fierce as a torch.

'Houses, shops, tofts and all, and the church into the bargain, Harry. And certain unlucky clerics and ladies inside the church, so I've heard, though I doubt if the fire inquired who was within before it caught. They builded close-set under that rock.'

'And the castle?'

'Harry, Harry, you're too ambitious! Did you ever see New Montgomery castle? As well begin throwing stones at Parfois. But he's after Radnor, now, castle and all, and the mere climb up a mound won't stop him. Llewelyn's blood is up, he means to scorch his way through de Burgh's lordships and wardships from Powis to Gwent, and for all I can see he'll do it. Did you speak, Harry?'

'No, my lord.'

No, he had not spoken, he had only drawn breath deeply into him like a cry of protest. He turned aside to the bench again, but this time his averted eyes hardly saw the pleasant thing he had created. The hand he put out to touch it moved blindly, only to give him an excuse for steadying his fingers against stone. He could not keep still. He walked a few paces furiously, trying to contain his rage and desire. The Prince was in arms, the border was ablaze, and he was penned up here, chipping stone! And they had been so near, as near as Montgomery, and he had known nothing!

'Yes,' said Isambard softly, smiling at his hunched back, 'your prince is in the field, and you, his faithful foster-brother, not by his side. What a disgrace to a young man bred in the time-honoured ways! You'll never venture to show your face again in Wales, Harry, after such a defection.'

'It ill becomes you, my lord,' flared Harry, quivering and glaring, 'to taunt me with it.'

'Ah! I see I've touched a sore spot. And your David, your prince-brother, will he hold you excused?'

He saw the braced shoulders flinch, and the lips caught in and bitten hard. An unbearably sore spot! He fingered it again, gently, experimentally: 'How if I should let you go to your bounden duty, Harry? On your parole to return here to captivity as soon as peace is restored between England and Wales? How then? Would you give me your word? And keep it?'

Harry wrung his hands in a sudden convulsive rage of grief, and flung round and stalked to the door with rapid, angry strides, to put himself out of reach of this ignoble baiting. The dignity of his withdrawal was jarred a little by the sharp collision of his hip with the corner of Master Edmund's tracing-table; he had been too angry to look very straitly where he was going.

'We must find a way of bridling that temper of yours,' said Isambard critically after the boy's rigid back. 'It affects your judgement.' This he had uttered in the same mild tone, but he raised his voice to a sudden peremptory crack like a whip-lash as Harry reached the door. 'Come back!'

Come or be dragged, thought Harry, reading the tone, and for a moment was inclined to make them drag him; but as soon as he had the door open he heard too many loud, young, boisterous voices raised in the outer ward, and remembered that Isambard's train of attendants had just ridden in from Hereford. To be marched back before so many hardly older than himself was more than he was willing to contemplate. He closed the door again slowly, and turned to look back at Isambard, who sat playing with the chisel and watching him with his crooked smile.

'Come here!'

And when Harry with a grim face had marched himself back obediently to the bench, and stood staring him out eye to eye: 'It is neither civil nor gracious to turn your back and walk out when you are asked a straightforward question. If you had been my page instead of my prisoner, that would have cost you a whipping.'

'And is it civil and gracious, my lord,' burst out Harry furiously, 'to taunt me with a default I cannot help, and mock me with offers you never mean to fulfil? Is it not enough that I am mewed up here, without your holding out such promises to torment me?' He was quivering with passion; the

237

hands that had swung the mallet and steadied the punch would have made botched work of it if he had put them to the test now, but they might have cooled capably enough if he could have got them on a sword.

'How do you know I am mocking you? Put it to the test, and see. Answer my question! What if I should let you go to your prince and your duty, on your parole to return here as soon as peace is made again? Would you give me your word? And keep it?'

He held off still, distrustful and in an agony of bewilderment. 'My lord, you know this is no real offer. You're tormenting me for your sport. It's unworthy!' he said, twisting.

Isambard tapped the head of the chisel gently against the bench, held him steadily in his eye and smiled. 'Well, Harry? Would you swear?'

The boy held his breath for a moment, struggling, and heaved out of him at last in a monstrous gasp: 'Yes, surely I would!'

'And keep it faithfully?'

'Yes, and keep it faithfully.' He wrenched his head aside, frantic to contain the sudden threat of tears welling in his eyes. Answer and have it over, and be loosed the sooner from this cruel teasing. And answer truthfully, because in the end there's no other way.

'Go, then,' said Isambard, laying down the chisel so softly that the metal made no sound as it touched the bench. 'I take your word.'

'Go?' Knocked clean out of words but for that faint echo, Harry stood helplessly eyeing him through the glitter of his distress.

'Yes. Go to your foster-brother, I accept your word.'

It could not be honest, of course, there was some devilish contrivance in it to take him in a worse snare, something that would not merely make him prisoner, but undo him utterly. And yet he could not but seize the offer with both hands, trick though it must be, and fight his way through the complex treacheries as they came. His eyes began to glitter with a very different light, burning away the sheen of tears.

'You mean this, my lord? I may go? I shall be passed through the gates?'

'Put it to the test, Harry. To-night if you will.' The oblique smile jerked at the corner of Isambard's mouth. 'More, you shall have money for the journey home, if you need it.'

'I thank you, my lord, but I need nothing from you but this grace.'

'And for nothing but this grace do you intend to have to thank me! Not even a horse, Harry?'

'Nothing, my lord.'

The shadows of the deep smile tugged at both hollow cheeks. Isambard's fine chain-mail rang softly as he slid from the bench and stretched his long arms. 'Go, then, Harry, you'll find the way will be open. I shall look to see you again when your prince and my king make their peace.'

There had never been a plainer dismissal. Harry turned dazedly, so lost in the wild bewilderment of joy and disbelief that he had to grope his way for a few paces before his feet grew wings.

The voice behind him said: 'And, Harry – !'

He caught himself back from the delirium of flight with difficulty, and looked back. Isambard was tilting the unfinished block of stone between his hands, and examining with grave attention the springing leaves. 'I shall see that this is left untouched for you. You can finish it when you return.'

Harry came down from his prison pale and tense, washed, tidied and trim for his journey, though still he did not believe in it. He had begged back his own old clothes, only to find that he could barely get into them, and perforce he was still wearing the suit which had once belonged to William Isambard, the old wolf's second son, the man of affairs, the courtier, who somewhere in comparative obscurity in the royal household awaited his long-delayed inheritance. If he was really allowed to leave the castle, then this enforced endowment should some day return with him. But he did not believe, he did not believe, he told himself so all the way across the outer ward, desperate with the fear he had of believing and being

239

disappointed.

No one paid more attention to him than on other occasions, no one halted him. His passage to the gate-house had the abnormal normality of a dream, where all things, no matter how fantastic, are taken for granted. He stepped into the shadowy passage, where the chill of night fell first, and his heart rose into his throat protesting, daring him to believe that he would ever reach the other end of the tunnel. The guards stood back and watched him pass. He stepped on to the bridge. This could be the crux of the whole cruel joke, to let him on to it and then begin to raise it and bring him scrambling back. He trod stiffly, his ears strained for the first grinding engagement of the chains. Nothing. He could hear the desultory clash of arms shifting on the gate-towers, and the trees stirring with the rising breeze that came with the cool of the evening.

He stepped on to the trampled grass. The plateau was almost deserted at this time; a few falconers and huntsmen were coming back into the wards, and Isambard's old chaplain ambled in on his mule. After that Harry was alone, walking the long diagonal path from the bridge to the ramp, with the church on his right hand. He watched it to the last moment before he entered the trees. The colour of the stone by this soft light was like the feathers of doves, bluish-grey with a living lustre, the gold of the day lingering still on the upper stages of the tower. Chin on shoulder, he gazed until the trees took it from him; and that, from one whose whole heart was away on a wild ride to Aber, was the greatest of tributes.

And now he knew in his soul that he did believe, and only his cautious, earthly, suspicious common sense was nagging at him that he did not and must not. If they turned him back at the lower guard, the remnants of his distrust would not be enough to save his heart from breaking. But he clutched jealously at the shreds of scepticism, and went on with a bold front and a pale and frightened face, afraid even to hurry to the testing point in case too noticeable an eagerness should tip the balance against him.

He came to the narrow passage between the towers, half-way down the ramp. Here it would happen. The guards would let him come abreast of them as though they had orders to let him through, and then pluck him back. Half of him believed, half disbelieved. Torn in two, counterpoised against himself, hardly breathing, he came and passed. They eyed him and waved him through.

He was on the outer side of the defences of Parfois. He was walking away down the ramp, stunned to find himself there at all, free and alone and on his way home.

So, if this was a trick, it was a deeper and more subtle one than he had supposed. He fretted at it all the way down to the riverside, and by the time he had turned instinctively towards the forest and Robert's assart he had fumbled his way through the cloud of bewilderment and was beginning to understand. He was to be allowed to go free, having given his word to return voluntarily into captivity; a promise so easy to make now, so hard to keep in cold blood later, when the time came to make it good. He was being tempted to break faith, let out on a long, long line in the deliberate hope that he would gnaw through it and never come back.

So he's sure, thought Harry, his mind suddenly clear and dark with hatred, that I shall fail him, that he can get from me what he never could get from my father. Then he would have triumphed over my father's blood at last. That's what he wants, that's what he's always wanted of me. But I'll not fail him!

He turned back from the assart to the ford, after all, and waded the Severn in his shirt with his cotte and chausses under his arm, and went a good half of the way to Castell Coch before he dared take to the woods and lie waiting for full darkness; for it had burst on his too eager mind that once already he had been loosed out of Parfois to provide information by his movements, and he could not take the risk of doing as much again. Maybe they suspected that he had friends in the district, maybe his refusing a horse had only served to confirm their speculations, and they were relying on him to lead them, like the simpleton he'd proved himself on the first occasion, straight to Robert and Aelis.

This time they would be disappointed. He lay up in the woods until it was dark, and then with infinite care and many halts to confirm that he had the silence to himself, he worked his way roundabout back to the ford. Naked he waded across in the warm June night, and naked he slipped through the woods until he was dry, and put on his clothes again among the bushes near the silver-gleaming river. With Barbarossa under him he would not need to strip again.

· Aelis had shut up the fowls, and was sitting on the bottom step of the wooden ladder that led up into the hut, listening to the night. She heard among its soft, stealthy sounds the small, crisp snap of a dead twig under an unwary foot, and froze into stillness, listening. Her quick senses followed a man's step round the rim of the clearing by the paddock fence. Suddenly and softly Barbarossa in the undercroft began to stir and stamp and whinny. Trembling, Aelis slid from her step and advanced into the open, turning slowly after the invisible visitor.

'Harry?' she said in a whispered call that hardly disturbed the silence.

He was wildly moved by the tone, so tentative and yet so bold, afraid to believe and yet fending off disappointment with so much resolution. It set him quaking with an excitement for which he was not prepared, and he came bursting out of the thickets in haste to satisfy her.

'Aelis! Here I am!'

She spun on her toes and ran, and flung herself into his arms.

'Harry, it *is* you! How did you come here? How did you escape? Are they following you?' The rapid questions fluttered in his face like blown feathers, like the stroking caresses of hands. She embraced him with all her strength, and he felt by the tingling of his body the change in hers. She had been a little, wild, hard, boy-like creature, and suddenly in his absence she had become a woman. Small, high breasts pricked his heart, bringing the blood flooding up through his

242

throat to his cheeks. He held her stiffly, frightened by the translation of so simple a companionship into something so unfamiliar and daunting, while she stroked him still with questions and entreaties.

'Will you stay now? At least over-night! Is it safe for you here? Have they hurt you in that dreadful place?'

'I'm well enough, Aelis, I'm very well. But I can't stay. I must get back over the river. At dawn I should be on my way home. Come in to your father, and I'll tell you everything.'

But would he? Everything? Would she understand if he did? Or think him mad for letting his sworn word stand between him and his certain and permanent freedom?

As she drew down her arms from his neck, her fingers brushed his chin, and she felt the fluff of downy beard that told her suddenly he was sixteen and almost a man. She drew back from him a little, from breast to knee shrinking warily into herself, but not so softly that he did not feel the recoil. His risen blood stung in his face. The arms that held her so gingerly tightened instinctively at the threat of withdrawal, jealous of their privileges.

'Now you'll ride home,' said Aelis, startled and glad and sad and afraid all in one convulsion of feeling, 'and we shan't see you again. Now you're free you'll never come back here.'

He drew her with him towards the house, reaching his hand into the undercroft to the warm silken touch of Barbarossa's stretched muzzle.

'Yes,' he said, in the voice which had deepened and filled and gained formidably in authority since last she had heard it, 'I shall come back.'

Did he mean only because of his sworn word to Isambard? He had thought so when he spoke, but once the words were out he heard them in a different sense. And Aelis arched herself away from him like a drawn bow in his arm, and laughed softly and derisively with joy, mocking him and herself as she said: 'And even this time you know well you've only come for Barbarossa.'

So he himself would have avowed, honestly enough, only an hour ago. Now he knew better. The feel of her body braced

243

against the pull of his arm excited and roused him; he took both arms to her and dragged her back to him, pleased with his own strength and stirred and challenged by hers. She doubled her fists into his chest and fought him off vigorously, and down they came together in the long grass at the edge of the paddock.

Her small, firm breasts heaved under him. He cupped his hands round them, lying over her, and the delight of their shape shuddered through him with as wild a triumph as if he had created them. Her mane of hair lay spread under his cheek, cool and heady as meadow-sweet. He fumbled inexpertly but ardently after her lips, and she turned her head aside from him defiantly so that he encountered only her ear; but when he persisted, laughing and panting, she turned towards him again with a sharp sigh of astonishment and pleasure, and met him mouth to mouth.

'You shan't go back,' said Gilleis, straining him to her heart, dusty and tousled and travel-stained as he was. 'You shan't! You shan't! No one has the right to extort such a promise, God will absolve you from it.'

'He won't, Mother. And if any of his bishops takes so much upon him, I won't listen. I gave my word, and I'll abide by it.' He was on his knees at her feet, his arms round her waist, hugging her littleness to him boisterously. She clung round his neck, laughing and crying, holding him off to marvel at his growth and mannishness, snatching him back to rock him like a small child on her breast. It mattered nothing how foolishly she behaved, there was no one else to see.

'The Prince will never let you,' she said, all the more fiercely because she did not believe it.

'The Prince will understand that I must. He'd thunder if I tried to slip out of the obligation. But I shan't. And you – you're a fine one to talk! If my father's son broke his word – why, you'd beat me first and turn me out afterwards.'

'I wouldn't. I'd claim you got your good sense from the Otleys, and commend you for it.'

She stroked back the tangled dark hair from his forehead

that was brown and broad and formed like a man's, with the salients and valleys of thought and reason proudly marked. Who would have thought a single year could make such a transformation? He was grown so big she could hardly embrace him, and so masterful she could not imagine ever again boxing his ears, however well he might deserve it. 'And now you're going to rush away again after the army,' she said, exasperated. 'Stay here awhile with me. Why shouldn't you, when I've lost a whole year of you?'

'Mother, Mother, I was set free to go to my duty. I made it my excuse to come here that I must get the latest news to know where best to report myself, but well you know it was to see you I really came. But I must go to David as quickly as I can. It would be cheating to stay here. To-morrow I must go.'

'The day after to-morrow!'

He crushed her little fist in his big one, and mumbled it against his lips and cheek. 'To-morrow!' She shook him, and he buried his face in her shoulder and held fast, so that they shook together.

'Unfilial boy, you ought to obey your mother.'

'Froward woman, I'm a man now by Welsh law, and you ought to defer to me. And if you weren't the prettiest mother in Aber, you wouldn't get your way with me so easily.'

'Then the day after to-morrow?'

He kissed her heartily, but he said with finality: 'To-morrow!'

She let him think her persuaded, or at least resigned. Time would weaken the urgency of his vow, and events might yet dispose all. The Prince might forbid him to return, Isambard might die, either with the King's host in the field or of sheer old age at home, Parfois might come within Llewelyn's fiery orbit and be stormed and taken. Or even a wound, a small, mild wound or a light fever, might commit this madcap to his bed and to her eager care. She clung to the comfort and the anxiety of the moment. Only let him go safely and safely return in this war she feared.

'And, Harry – !'

He raised a flushed, merry face. 'Yes?'

'You should go and pay your respects as soon as you've made yourself presentable.'

'To Ednyfed?' he said carelessly. 'Supper's time enough, I shall see him in hall.'

'To the Princess,' said Gilleis.

His face sharpened into instant gravity. She saw the old trouble gather very distantly, like a passing cloud-shadow on a bright hill. He rose to his feet, still holding her hands in his. He was already bigger than his father had ever been, and surely he had a year or two of growing to do yet.

'May I go in to her?' he said in a low voice.

'No need. She has come out to us, Harry. You'll find her in her proper place, in the Prince's chamber.'

When he heard her voice call him in he felt himself tremble, and his hand upon the latch of the door was stiff and cold. He went in bitter still with wounded pride and the memory of betrayed love. It was hard even to step over the door-sill.

She was sitting at the table over a despatch brought in only ten minutes previously, alone in Llewelyn's room, in Llewelyn's chair, with the circlet of gold in her piled grey hair, that had still certain rich strands of pale brown in it. She turned her head and saw him enter. Very gently and carefully she laid down the pen, and turned her chair away from the table to meet him. Her face was pale and grave as he remembered it, the eyes wide and plaintive and calm, without a shadow; and her brows were drawn a little with thought and care, both princely. She had to make her way through the cloudy mazes of policy and state back to him.

'Harry!' she said. 'You are welcome home.'

He saw the colour flood her pallor and fade again while she looked at him. The year of his life she had lost was bound up for ever with a lost year of her own. Once, how long ago now, he had said to her: 'Do you know, do I know, what it is to be a prisoner?'

'My lady!' he said, and went quickly forward and fell on his knee to her.

The hand she laid in his wore Llewelyn's ring. Harry bent

246

his head and kissed the cool fingers close to the stone. There was a faint scent afloat above her brocaded lap, and close before his eyes he saw the slow, even heave and fall of her breath through the ageing body. He kept her hand long, lost out of time and beset with the rending memories of the end of his childhood. With resignation and humility she watched the struggles that convulsed his averted face, fighting out between pride and resentment and love and grief the prolonged battlefield of his heart. She waited for what he would say, willing to receive it whatever it might be; and she had long minutes to wait.

She had abused and betrayed him, and yet now that he touched her hand and let his own hands rest upon her knees he felt no change in her, nothing wanting in the affection that could still warm him through to the spirit. Had disillusionment itself been no more than an illusion? He was the one who was changed. Something had happened to his eyes and ears. They saw and heard all the events of a year ago from some new place to which he had never aspired or attained, somewhere above the battle but not out of reach of the pain. He remembered the dead man in his living brightness and in his frightened nakedness, and no longer saw them as separate. He heard Joan's voice pleading with sudden terrible urgency: 'Think of him kindly. Think kindly of all poor sinners. If you think yourself wounded, what must their sufferings be?'

He was filled with something he did not know how to name, for he had never yet had to identify compassion. Reverence he knew, and that also he felt towards her, but this other and more desperate engagement flooded his whole being, brimming over at his heart, and he was possessed without understanding.

He had writhed and agonised over the offence against himself, seen nothing beyond it, challenged the Prince and importuned God with it, banished himself and abandoned her on the strength and spleen of it. And yet if he had thought himself wounded, what must her sufferings have been?

'Forgive me!' he gasped, quivering, his lashes low on his

cheeks. 'Forgive me!'

And he had meant in his magnanimity to forgive her! He did not understand, but neither did he question. When the words were out he knew they were the right words, and laid his head on her knee and repeated them again and again in a passion of joy and gratitude.

Joan uttered a brief, sharp sigh, and leaned to him and lifted his head between her hands. His face came up to her wide-eyed and solemn; he held up his mouth for her kiss like the child Harry, but when she had given it gladly and drawn back from him to look into his eyes she saw that the Harry who had come home was far on the way to his manhood.

CHAPTER TWELVE

Brecon, Cardigan, the Wye Valley: *July to December* 1231

The garrison of Brecon castle made a sally as soon as all the fires were embers, and the smoke of the burning town had begun to settle in a sooty pall over their walls and roofs. They were reasonably certain that their defences would hold against anything short of a prolonged siege, and by the rapidity of the Welsh advance it was clear that Llewelyn was not bent on starving out one de Breos castle, but doing as vast and as widespread damage to the justiciar's holdings as he possibly could before his own impetus was spent or King Henry got his slow-moving host into the field; but they were being forced to feed a great press of refugees, their stores were none too plentiful, and if there was anything eatable still to be looted within the borough they wanted to do the looting themselves rather than leave it to the Welsh. Moreover, they were anxious to discover whether Llewelyn was yet withdrawing and by what road, and to be sure that their way to the bridge was clear at need.

Llewelyn was encamped east of the town, on high ground overlooking the valley of the Usk. He had battered the gates of the castle for sport, and made a few feints at the walls, to keep the garrison on tenterhooks, but he had no intention of wasting time and energy on Brecon. The borough was so much charcoal and ash, and little left in the rubble worth the taking. The prior and his six shivering brothers of the Benedictines were on their knees in Saint John's church, praying for a safe deliverance, mourning the still smouldering timbers of their fine choir roof, and thanking God for their good stone walls. And David and Owen were patrolling the castle hill, and standing off hopefully in case the garrison should raise the courage to come out to them.

It was David who saw them issue from the lower port and sweep down the steep banks of the Honddu into the town. He held off out of sight beyond the priory walls until the quarry was well clear, and then loosed his men joyfully after them down the hill, took them in the rear before they were aware of him in the foul twilight of smoke, and swept them before him as far as the bridge. They turned then and fought, and David, who had outridden his men, found himself suddenly islanded among his enemies, and engaging four or five at once. His impetus had carried him well out over the river, where they could pin him on both sides, while half a dozen of them sealed the end of the bridge after him. And how often had Owen abused him and his father warned him for his too light and impetuous valour!

Owen had been caught on the north side of the castle when the pursuit began, and even when the clamour reached him he had a long ride round with his company to the fight. David wheeled his horse in a frenzied circle to beat his enemies to arm's-length, and for a few confused minutes held them off; but one wrenched at his bridle while another was crossing swords with him, and two more closed in flank to flank and dragged him out of the saddle. He kicked his feet from the stirrups and fell clear, and among the stamping of the horses braced his sword under the armpit of the first man who swung his arm back to strike at him, prised for the cloth where the banded mail was strained apart, and drove home with all the force he could from one knee.

He brought down over himself a gush of blood and the weight of a heavily armed body, and was flattened to the ground beneath the burden, and half-stunned. Vaguely in the distance he heard the clash and shouting of Owen's men as they drove down the hill at the guarded bridge, and somewhere from the further side a closer echo rang back in answer. From the west, where no one kept the narrows, hooves thudded from the solid ground to the hollow-ringing span of the bridge, and suddenly the whole mêlée was swept back towards Brecon by the impact of four horsemen coming at a headlong gallop.

David, heaving at the dead weight that lay over him, saw his own horse rear and recoil before the shock, saw his mounted foemen suddenly closing at disadvantage with the newcomers and being carried with them, locked in a confused mass, back into Owen's arms. He recovered the sword that had been wrenched out of his hand, and hauled himself dizzily to his knees; and someone came plunging down from the saddle with a shout of rage and grief to catch him about the body and hold him in one arm, while the other ringed him with a briskly-circling sword.

'My lord! My lord!'

He got his eyes clear of blood that was not his own, wishing he had had the sense to quit his Welsh habits and helm properly, and blinked unbelievingly at a furious, anxious face that devoured him with blazing greenish eyes and entreated him to be whole and unwounded.

'Harry!' he cried, and came lurching to his feet, crowing with astonishment and delight.

'My lord! David!' Harry felt at him with a frantic hand, seeking the source of the blood. The fight had left them behind by a few meagre yards only, they shouted and still could hardly make themselves heard.

'Not mine!' David embraced him for an instant, gasping and laughing, and would have plunged back afoot into the chaos at the bridgehead, but Harry caught jealously at the stirrup of his own horse and held it for his prince, with so absolute a pride in his privileges that David had not the heart to refuse him. He swung back into the fight on Barbarossa, with Harry clinging by the left hand to his stirrup-leather as they charged. Their weight drove the knot of struggling men swaying to the end of the bridge. By the time the survivors from the foray realised how the scales were tipped against them, and turned once more to take on five men rather than fifteen, they had left it too late. The bridge was littered with their casualties by the end of it, and only a handful clawed their way through by luck to take the tale back to the castle.

David dropped to the grassy bank of Usk to wipe his sword,

and came bounding back to catch Harry into his arms. He hugged and was hugged again. They were both panting with excitement and pleasure.

'But how do you come to be here? Man, but I was glad to see you! But for you I'd have been hard put to it before Owen could get through. Where did you come from so happily?'

'We crossed Eppynt by the old upland track,' said Harry, breathless. 'They told us at Builth we'd find you hereabouts. We had to go out of our way to avoid an English party at the end, and forded the river upstream. Glad I am we did! The fright you gave me, with such gouts of blood on you!'

'And not a drop of it mine.' He held the boy off to look him over from glowing face streaked with smoke and sweat to dusty stirrup-shoes. 'God save you, boy, but you're grown! Such an arm on you, and such a grip! But how did you break out of hold to come to us?'

But he got no answer then, for Owen came plumping down from the saddle beside them and snatched the boy away from him to shake him delightedly between his hands. The hug he got in return made him wince and gasp, and fetched a wail of remorse out of Harry.

'Ah, pardon, Owen, I forgot! They told me at Aber what befell you. Sooth, I'm sorry to have been the cause of it all.'

'I'm well enough, Harry, but it's thanks only to God and you if this madhead here can say the same. Keep your best horse-play for a week or two yet before you loose it on me, that's all I ask. God's blood!' he said, eyeing the boy's sturdy shoulders and long, lissom body admiringly, 'I wouldn't give much for my chances at a fall with you in a year or so.' He patted him happily, still bent on touching to prove him real. 'That was a bonny little charge you made there on the bridge, Harry. Wait till we bring you to the Prince and tell him, you'll be a head taller.'

'And I shorter by an inch off my nose,' said David, grinning as he wiped his grimy face. He looked at Harry's suddenly grave and anxious countenance and leaned impulsively to do the same service for him, guessing at a part of the reason. 'Ah, never worry, you've more than made your welcome even if it had needed making, but it never did. He's been waiting for you as hungrily as your own mother. Come and see!'

They drew off in close order, leaving the field to the dead, and to the parties that would steal out of the castle to salvage the living when dusk and quietness came to cover them. They brought Harry between them, sobered and quiet now, up through the black and reeking town and out to the clean hills, to the level grassy plains where the Prince's army was encamped. When they reached it he had still told but half his tale, and that in brief and difficult answers to their eager questioning. Not until he had seen the Prince's face would the words come freely, and then they might all share the flood.

Llewelyn heard the loud, excited voices, and knowing two of them so well, jumped by the tone of their exchanges to the identity of the third, though it had deepened and achieved a new fullness and firmness since he had last heard it shrilling at him for justice. He tensed to listen, sure that his heart was wilfully deceiving him. But when he came striding out of the tent he saw that it was indeed Harry his two brothers were bringing between them, Harry on the chestnut horse he had won from de Breos at the ford of the Mule.

He would have sprung to meet him, if he had not concentrated so much of his affection and understanding into the bright, measuring stare he fixed upon the boy. He would have taken him between his hands and hoisted him bodily out of the saddle, and held him a moment wriggling in mid-air like a small child before he plumped him down on his feet, but for the tender and strange consciousness he had of past failures, and the way the young shoulders squared and the straight back stiffened to approach him with dignity, shy with the same painful recollection of mutual wounds. Instead, he stood before the entrance to his tent, his falcon's face burned dark copper-coloured by long days in the June sun, and let them come to him.

'We've brought you another son, sir,' said David, smiling. 'He came in time to help us with a company of English down at the bridge of Usk, and well for me he did. No brother ever did better by his brother than he has today by me.'

253

Harry dismounted, cap in hand, with exact and solemn respect and a high colour, and went on his knee before Llewelyn. The great brown hand to which he laid his lips felt the fervour they gave to their kiss as a ceremonious amend for something past; but if they began matching consciences which of them would be off his knees?

'My dear lord,' began Harry, and had to wait a moment to be sure his voice would serve him. 'My dear lord,' he tried again sturdily, 'I have been much at fault. I am set free to join you so long as this war lasts – if you are pleased to forgive me my defection – and to take me back to my place.'

Llewelyn took him by the hands and raised him, and only then, with restraint, drew him into his arms and kissed him. A man can be treated like a child without damage where there's love, but a youngster hesitant and awkward between childhood and manhood needs to be handled like a royal envoy on a mission of moment. Llewelyn did well by him, muting even the brilliance of his smile to a reverent gravity.

'Pleased I am indeed, Harry, and you're dearly welcome. There could not be a more grateful sight to me than you here before me alive and well. Your place is yours always, and well I know you'll fill it like a man.'

'I've given my word and I shall keep it,' said Harry, when all the tale was told. 'Whatever he willed by it, he's made good his part of the bargain, which is more than ever I had the right to expect. And I'll make good mine.'

He looked up appealingly into Llewelyn's eyes, longing to be approved. The Prince was smiling at him, not indulgently as to a valiant child, but thoughtfully and calmly, as he might have smiled at Ednyfed to seal in silence a point of policy over which they were at one.

'So you will,' he said, 'no question. But we have a long way to go before that debt will fall due, and, by God, we'll enjoy you while we have you. Take no thought yet for what follows. A little while now, and King Henry's army of the west will be marshalled there on the borders to meet us. And Ralf Isambard with them. Bear that in mind, and keep your quarrel bright, and the account may be settled before ever you see Parfois again.'

He saw the fierce brightness of hope blaze up in the boy's face, kindling his eyes almost to gold. He had never thought of that; Llewelyn had made him a gift on which he closed his hands greedily. He looked round them all with an imperious lift of his head.

'If we ever meet with him in arms, my lord, remember the man is mine.'

'Yours he shall be,' said Llewelyn, strongly suppressing the gust of loving laughter that filled him like wine. 'You have the prior right to him, Harry Talvace, and no one shall rob you.'

Down the Usk from Brecon the fire ran blazing into Gwent, and burned and battered Caerleon to the ground; and thence, leaving a minor force to pen the garrison of Newport castle within their walls, Llewelyn swung westwards over the mountains. The princes of Glamorgan rose gleefully to join him, and reinforced his host with the musters of Senghenydd and Miskin and Neath. By the end of June they had taken and razed the castle of Neath, that had been a Norman thorn in the good Welsh flesh of Morgan ap Morgan ap Caradoc and his ancestors for a hundred years.

While King Henry was making feverish provisions for relieving the hard-beset garrison at Newport, Llewelyn was riding westwards again across the neck of Gower for Kidwelly; and before the bishops of the province of Canterbury met at Oxford in solemn conclave on July the thirteenth to consider the Welsh Prince's outrages against the church, Llewelyn's constable was in what remained of Kidwelly castle, and the Prince himself with the main body of his army was across Gwendraeth and Towy, and five miles beyond Carmarthen, and his fiery breath not yet spent.

Messengers from the princes of Cardigan came to meet him a few days later, and a courier from Builth, his clearing-house for intelligence from England, overtook him the same day. He feasted them royally at his own table while he listened to

255

the news from the borders.

'Excommunicated, am I?' he said, and threw back his head and shouted with laughter. He was lodged that night in a grange of Whitland abbey, and the wine that danced in his cup and the pasty disembowelled before him on the board had been sent in to him with the prior's own compliments. Moreover, the young man who had ridden from Builth with the word was himself a clerk, and of good repute in his church. 'Well, it's not the first time. And my allies with me, you say?'

'Twelve of the princes, my lord, had the same sentence pronounced against them.' He named them.

'But they hope God had his back turned, I suppose, when de Burgh murdered my men,' growled the Prince contemptuously. 'The sentence is already promulgated, is it?'

'Throughout England, my lord.'

Llewelyn laughed again at that; they had little hope of getting much respect for it in Wales. 'I hope none of the twelve will lose more sleep over it than I shall this night. Well, at least their bishops move faster than their marshals, and are not so tied hand and foot with law and precedent. I wonder if the Archbishop in Italy knows of it? My heart tells me his prayers will be on the side of whoever shortens the Earl of Kent by a head, communicate or excommunicate. And which of the sees of Wales were represented at Oxford?'

'Bishop Anselm of Saint David's was there, my lord, and Bishop Elias of Llandaff.'

'Both Englishmen! But I'll wager they never so much as sent the summons to Martin of Bangor or Abraham of Saint Asaph.'

'No, my lord, they left the Welshmen well alone.'

'You need not tell me. Where is the King now?'

'On his way to Gloucester, my lord. The muster was summoned there and at Hereford, and must surely be due. And we have heard in Builth that a letter has been sent to the justiciar of Ireland, making offer that any knights of Ireland who wish to come venturing for lands in Wales may keep all they can conquer.'

'And so they may,' said Llewelyn with a short bark of laughter. 'But he's very forward to give away what's mine. Let's see if he'll grant the same rights to Welshmen. We'll present him with a test case. Here are messengers from my good friend Maelgwn Fychan in Cardigan. He's levelled the town, now we'll lay our forces together and finish the work between us. There's time yet to snatch castle and all, before I go back to straddle the roads into Powis and let the Earl of Kent break his head against my forehead.'

Harry was down among the bowmen, in one of the loopholed shooting shelters the engineers had thrown up under the walls on the north bank of the river, in the charred and flattened waste Maelgwn and his allies had made of Cardigan town. It was the third day of the onslaught, and he had been crouching all morning at his slit in the timber shed, covering one of the wooden galleries built out from the crest of the curtain wall on the north side of the gate-house.

On his right hand the long, dim, hot shape of the shelter stretched, and beyond the dozen intent bowmen at their slits of light showed a triangle of blackened ground and a charred stump of hawthorn. Beyond, invisible, the ash-smeared rubble climbed the slope to merge at last into the clean wooded uplands. On his left hand, from the open end of the shed, he could see the thinning smoke drifting away and the gulls wheeling and screaming above the tidal waters of Teifi and the bridge under the castle wall.

There along the river bank the fire had burned more fitfully, leaving streaks of green untouched, and living trees. The wooden houses had blazed like tinder, but the stone walls of store-houses and boat-yards along the tide survived, and within their cover, drawn back from arrow-range of the bastions, the princely pavilions were pitched. The nearest broken wall of stone, no more than a foot high, helped to seal the end of the shed, and red valerian flowered in it, and a great clump of ripe barley grass, not even stained by smoke.

There was no work here yet for a swordsman: Harry had reverted to his old weapon gladly. They had no time for a

257

methodical siege, nor was Llewelyn in any mood to construct vallations round the castle of Cardigan and sit down to starve it into submission. Behind them in the march the King's host of the west was mustering. Cardigan had to be settled and done in a few days, and they on their way back to hold the approaches of Wales. The storming of the justiciar's prized fortress was work for the engineers, for the huge siege engines, mangons and arblasts and trebuchets, that hurled darts and charges of stones at the battered walls, and the iron-beaked rams that their crews ran up by night against the bastions and swung and swung on their chain slings to peck holes through the masonry. But there was still work for the archers, picking off any defenders who showed themselves in the merlons or ventured out on to the wooden galleries to drop stones and iron weights on the attackers below. The knights must loiter in the background, waiting for their *coup de main* until there was a large enough breach in the wall, or an opportunity of mounting one of the scaling-towers against it. Harry preferred to let knighthood take care of itself for the moment, and consider himself a bowman.

David came at a crouching run along the timber shed in the heat of the noon, and dangled his leather water-bottle over Harry's shoulder. Intent upon his watch on the gallery slung like a martin's nest against the parapet, Harry had failed to identify the running feet, and reached for the bottle greedily without a word. His eye fell on the familiar slender hand, the topaz ring and the hem of the dark green sleeve, and he turned his head, frowning. Unhelmed, uncovered, in half-armour only, David smiled at him.

'My lord,' said Harry, surprised and disapproving, 'you should not be here.' He was exact in observance when on duty, but it was the anxious foster-brother, not the dutiful subordinate, who shook his head at his prince.

'Should I not? I saw you reach out of your burrow for a sprig of sorrel to moisten your mouth. There, drink! Why do you suppose I went to the trouble to bring it?'

The sun had been on the steep-pitched roof all the morning, and beneath it the air was hot as in an oven. Harry had sweated rivulets of pallor down his smoke-grimed face, and his shirt was glued to his back. He tilted the bottle and drank gratefully until David pulled down hand and bottle together.

'Take it slowly, lad, and taste it! There, let it pass along to your fellows, it's deadly dry work you have in here. Why should I not be here?'

'Because there's an archer up in yonder gallery who's too good a marksman by half, and if he catches a glimpse of you he may guess who you are. Look! There, you see the loophole at the end? Watch, and you'll see his russet-brown against the black of the timbers when he draws.'

Faintly the lighter colour showed, the buff of a leather coat as the archer moved sidelong in search of his aim. A drift of thick smoke from within the wards was ascending steadily into the sky, darkening the upper air. Somewhere among the encrustations of wooden buildings clinging to the curtain wall, the barrels of flaming pitch had found their mark.

'He and I have been shooting it out the past two hours. How near I've come I can't tell, but he's been a deal too close to this slit of mine for my comfort. You mustn't leave cover here, go to the far end, and I'll engage him while you go. If he would but show more than a forearm, just once!' said Harry with bloodthirsty longing, and flattened his cheek against the timbers to squint up at his enemy.

'Take care for yourself,' said David warmly. 'You are no more proof than I am.'

'Never fear, I have too good a respect for this fellow to take risks. Is there no breach yet under the bastions there where they had the rams working all night?'

'There is, and we have three trebuchets battering it wider at this moment. Within the hour we should be able to break through. And faith, we should have reduced the odds by the time we go in, for we've surely thrown half the masonry of Cardigan over the walls. And by the smoke, all that isn't stone within must be afire.'

'You'll call me to you before the attack?' cried Harry, turning a soiled face anxiously, and smearing the running sweat out of his eyes with a bare forearm.

'I'll call you.'

David reslung the empty water-bottle at his hip, shook Harry briefly by a handful of his hair, and wound his way back behind the kneeling bowmen at their slits, to break cover and run for the shelter of the standing walls. Harry took careful aim at the distant loophole in the timber turret, gashed and splintered now by a partial hit from a charge of stones. His shaft struck quivering across the opening, like a bar across the window of a prison. The answer came with a hissing impact that slit the thick boards of the shed, and a steel-shod tip, blunted and dulled, showed through the splintered edges of the wound in the timbers, close to Harry's cheek. He had flinched aside instinctively to flatten himself against the barrier; he recoiled again as hastily, feeling the heat of the steel scorch his ear. That was too close for comfort, but at least David was clear.

Nettled, he turned in earnest to the duel with his unseen opponent. Shot for shot, they matched skills and waited for the grain of luck that would settle the issue between them. Harry forgot heat and thirst in his single desire to have the better of the battle.

It was a chance shot from one of the mangons that gave him his opportunity. The great stone left the cup awry, and struck the wall somewhat below and to the left of the gallery, and there in its impact hollowed the masonry and flung off two or three sharp fragments that flew at random. The largest thudded among the propping timbers of the gallery and snapped one of them, and all the defenders sprang back from the shaken corner and hugged the solid stone wall behind them.

Harry had a shaft fitted and was in the act of drawing when the shock made the gallery quiver; and his quarry, for once forgetful of the danger of showing himself, leaped away from the impact with the rest, and came full into the open loophole. Harry saw his target at last, not a glimpse of a bow arm this time, but the broad russet of a body.

He shot, and saw clearly the convulsion of the two arms that clawed across the riven breast, and the leaping contortion of pain that seemed to lift the man bodily into air. He sagged into the loophole, and there hung for a moment swaying, to slide slowly outwards in a long, revolving fall, like a spider dropping down a thread. He crashed under the wall with a sickening sound that carried through a sudden comparative silence.

The mangon had not been reloaded, the trebuchets stood unmanned, their great arms swinging in an empty balance. Over Cardigan the smoke drifted faintly, trailing out into an attenuated pennant on a rising breeze; and down there to the left, fronting the breached wall and the battered gate-house, a knot of princes gathered from the river bank, and stepped out into the open sunlight. The last reverberations died along the Teifi like receding thunder, ebbing out to sea.

Harry, standing quivering with the bow still humming in his hands, looked round him for a moment without understanding. Then the man beside him caught at his arm and thumped him on the shoulder joyfully, and pointed him to the gate-house. The wicket in the great gate stood open, he saw the figure of a man form in the darkness as in a frame, and a white cloth lifted and fluttering in the breeze.

The archers were coming out of their steaming shelters to stretch themselves erect in the sunlight. Behind Llewelyn's company of princes the captains gathered, stripping off helms and gloves, uncovering their heads to the coolness; and out of Cardigan castle came the justiciar's castellan behind his flag of truce, to stave off at least the further battering and inevitable assault and sack of his crippled fortress.

Harry could not believe it. He blinked at the distant meeting of magnates and shook his head and stared again, until he got it into his dazed brain that it was over. David would not need him at his elbow in the assault, after all. Cardigan had surrendered. De Burgh, the great Earl of Kent, justiciar of England, the King's master, had lost his proudest castle. Llewelyn could leave it safe in the hands of his subsidiary princes, and take his army back in triumph to confront the royal host as it moved in from Hereford.

Harry crept out stiffly to the edge of the ditch, gulping air

261

and feeling the sweat begin to dry on his soiled face. There at the foot of the wall beneath the gallery he looked for the russet-brown leather coat and found it lying among the debris of stones and rubble. The body was grotesquely broken, the head bent aside at a cruel angle, face upturned. Harry saw that his enemy had been a young fellow no more than a year or two older than himself, fair-haired and well-made. The hands that had nursed such an alarming skill lay sprawled empty in the dirt; the face was empty, too, still contorted into the formal shape of agony, but motionless and indifferent.

And he need not have done it! He had loosed the last shot of the siege, loosed it perhaps after the gate had been opened and the flag of truce displayed. Why had he been so set on this killing? The exultation had not lasted more than a moment. He felt nothing now but the sickness of regret and shock, as though he had wantonly broken something beautiful and admirable. And so he had, the wonderful machine that gauged the distance and fitted the shaft and drew the bow.

He was reminded suddenly of another spoiling. He saw again the young groom in Earl Ranulf's livery pantomiming hideously the obscene outrage of death by hanging.

What difference did it make that the body lying under the wall might as easily have been his own, and this broken boy might have been boasting happily of the shot that brought him down? That did not excuse him. He knew the value of making and the violation of breaking, the marvel of the engines of God which sculptors and artists copied so lamely. By so much he was the guiltier of the two.

David was beckoning him. He saw it and was loath to go, but go he did, stiffly and blindly, the poor, disjointed doll still before his eyes.

'What's the matter?' said David, quick to feel discomfiture in him even when there was no apparent reason for it. 'Are you hurt? Did he graze you in the end, after all?' And he laid hold of him anxiously, and handled him with an open concern which Harry felt to be almost an indignity.

'No,' he said, short and hard, putting off the solicitous hands with a gesture over which he would grieve helplessly later in secret. 'I grazed him. He's down there under the wall with the rest of the wreckage.'

At Llandovery a messenger from Builth met them, with word that King Henry's host was on the move westwards from Hereford up the valley of the Wye. From there they made forced marches accordingly, to deploy their forces astride every possible way into the fastnesses of Wales. But they reached the ridgeways of Eppynt without making contact, and David slept two nights peacefully in his own castle of Builth before they got certain news of the King's progress. Scouts came in from the march to report that the English army had left the Wye at Hay and was moving west over the easy upland road towards Painscastle.

'We need not go to them, it seems,' said Owen, roused and serious. 'They intend to come direct to us.'

Builth seemed, indeed, the most likely target for this advance, and with such a force as Henry had collected marching against them they had good reason to provision and garrison the castle for a long and determined siege. But they watched alertly day after day, and their patrols sighted no marching columns on the nearer upland reaches or threading the open, wide valley beyond. Somewhere in the region of Painscastle the English army appeared to have slowed or halted its advance. Llewelyn himself rode out to see why.

From the flanks of the hills he looked down towards the old mound of Painscastle, and the timber fortress another William de Breos, the second of his line, had built there to hold down lower Elfael. Maud's Castle, the English called it, after William's formidable wife, who had held it tooth and nail against the Welsh, and become a monster they used to frighten their naughty children.

'God's life!' said Llewelyn blankly, staring upon the teeming bowl below. 'But this is Kerry over again.'

All the broad green floor of the valley was alive with the colour and motion of men, and patterned with the tents and lines of the royal army. Above these the vast mound, several times added to, heaved its multiple levels of green, and the watchers on the hills saw that the grassy planes had now been enlarged and extended with new, raw erections of earth and rubble that glared in arid whitish greys under the sun.

'There's stone there,' said Harry eagerly, pointing. 'Look where it's stacked. And can you see the lines traced in white there? That's stone, too, they're laying the base of an outer wall.'

They stared, and could hardly believe what their eyes told them. So vast a muster, answering so direct a provocation, had seemed to threaten a determined campaign against the whole of Wales. Why, then, sit down here to build a fortress? Castles are a means of attack when advanced far into enemy territory, but this was no outpost among the clans, but the old Breos link between Brecon and Radnor, one in a chain of marcher castles already familiar and long hated. Turning it from timber into stone would threaten nothing new.

Llewelyn shook his reins and turned his shoulder on the scene. 'I thought we were blocking his way into Wales,' he said. 'It seems King Henry's content with blocking my way into England. Well, if he's chary of moving in for a direct assault, so much the better, we'll keep our own ways open all round him, and pick off his strays as fast as they wander.'

And so they did, all through the hot weather of August, and it was work after the Welshmen's own hearts. They cut off such parties as foraged too far afield, harried the supply routes back through Hay, and raided the English borders as much for devilment as for gain, behind King Henry's pre-occupied back. When they were hot and dusty they even made time to halt and bathe in the Wye and lie in the sun along its banks, while their sentries kept watch from the uplands. Llewelyn prowled mid-Wales from Brecon to Caersws, and took toll from his English neighbours wherever he could, until some among them, like the prior of Leominster, preferred to pay him handsomely for the privilege of being left alone. And all the while the King's engineers and his immobilised army of labourers continued the rebuilding of Painscastle.

'Do him justice,' said Llewelyn, making a passing inspection early in September, 'he builds better than he fights, and past question he makes more speed with it. Surely, Harry, you should rather follow his army than mine, you'd make a career there in your own profession.'

'My profession is arms,' said Harry, so emphatically that he might have been trying to cry down a doubt, couched small and stubborn in a corner of his own mind.

'To understand building may be useful to a soldier also, as you see.'

Said Harry, thoughtfully: 'My lord, *why* have they done so? Why have they let their chance slip? Is it the King's policy? Or the justiciar's? We've done him harm enough in this summer's campaign, and he seemed to mean grim business when he began. Why have they let it all come down to this? Are they afraid of us?'

'Afraid, no. Beware of ever thinking that of your enemy. They're even more wary of me than I thought, that's true enough. Nevertheless,' said Llewelyn, narrowing his eyes upon the distant, feverish activity in the valley, 'surely something happened to change their plans since they began their march. You say truly, this was meant to be an expedition to drive me back into my own mountains, if it could not end me altogether. About the end of July something happened to change things.'

'What was it?' asked Harry, confident of an answer. They were alone on the little headland in the trees; a quarter of a mile back in a bowl among the hills, a company of the Prince's guard was encamped.

'Do I know? You might look and find a dozen things, and any one might be the worm that ate the heart out of their harvest. But I know one at least that fits well enough. At the end of July the Bishop of Winchester came back from his victorious crusade and returned to his see – and to the King's ear. Ever since he heard that news, I think de Burgh has lost his appetite for this war. True, he's suffered enough by me, from Montgomery to Cardigan, but by Peter of Winchester he stands to lose all. And I think he willed to come no farther into Wales, to risk no more time and energy in fighting me, when he has a more deadly battle on his hands, for his very survival.'

'But could he make the King do what he wills? What, curb him here when he thought to go on a triumph?'

'Ay, could he! The King may chafe and complain, but though he has no love for his justiciar, and I think never did have, he'll do what he urges until there's another stronger will at his other elbow to urge the opposite. And that, I think,' said Llewelyn with a sombre smile, 'will not be long.'

'Then if he's so little fain, surely you could close the campaign whenever you please. He'd be glad to come to terms and have us off his hands.'

'Softly, softly, boy! He may sweat a little longer, till I'm sure of my ground. I'm in no hurry to make terms. If I came too lightly they'd suspect I was in haste to cover up a weakness, and be encouraged to take up the quarrel again at a better time for them. No, let Bishop Peter prick de Burgh behind, and the King fret under his thumb a little longer, till they tear each other and let Wales alone. Then I'll let them know, in my own good time, that I'm willing to talk terms.'

Harry rode back into the encampment after him at once elated and sad. The Prince's confidence he prized dearly, and these large and venturesome speculations delighted and enslaved him; but, if they were to give up all thought of a major encounter with the English army, then he had lost the hope of meeting Isambard in arms, and settling his feud in the field. The shadow of his return to Parfois fell like a thundercloud over his spirit. He wished the Prince his triumphant peace, but he longed anxiously to achieve his own deliverance while there was time.

To take to himself every chance that offered, he begged David to send him out with every raiding party that wound its way through the hills to the rear of the English host and crossed the Wye after plunder; and David, not without misgivings, sympathised and let him go.

They had been out on one such party late in September, and were recrossing the river upstream from Hay, and because

266

the summer had been dry and the water was low they did not bother to go down to the ford, but splashed through at a level place that gave them easy passage. The bank to which they climbed was meadow and sallows, and they rode out of the silvery willow-groves head-on into a company of English that outnumbered them three times over. By luck the Welsh were all mounted, for speed was their chief stock-in-trade on such forays; the English had perhaps as many knights and double the number of foot-soldiers. They clashed in equal astonishment, and with the slope of the land rolled back in untidy conflict to the water's edge.

It would have been folly to let this clash become a pitched battle; the English could very well be reinforced, the Welsh could not, and had to circumvent the entire English position in order to get back to their own. Along the bank to their left there was cover in the woods; they drew off in that direction and ran for it, Harry and a handful of the best-mounted keeping the rear and standing off attack to give their fellows time to scatter and run among the trees, where the bowmen among them could deploy and turn to help their rearguard. Nevertheless they left three dead behind them, and lost two more wounded into English hands, before they reached cover.

The foot-soldiers were all left out of reckoning now, and the odds had levelled, and had Harry been in command he would have been tempted to turn and fight it out on those terms; but he was under orders, and he obeyed faithfully and drew off with the rest, running and fighting and running again until the pursuers had dwindled to a handful.

They were still among the trees, scattered but within call of one another, when Barbarossa stepped astray in sandy ground honeycombed with rabbit warrens, and pitched Harry over his head into the grass.

Winded and shaken, Harry rolled head over heels and scrambled up in frantic haste to clutch at the bridle, but he was too late; it slipped through his fingers, and Barbarossa, frightened and indignant, thudded away between the trees. Close and threatening behind came the beat of other hooves.

Harry turned to dive into cover, but a low halloo of pure mischievous pleasure told him he had been seen; and in a moment a horseman came crashing between the branches, and leaped down from the saddle without hesitation to plunge after him into the bushes.

Until then he had seen no faces he could identify among the English party, and few devices, for they had been moving back light-armed and at leisure into Hay, with no expectation of trouble and no parade of their liveries, and the action had been too confused for thought. Now he was presented with the abrupt and awesome apparition of a long, lean, steely body that closed on him with violent, beautiful movements he knew well, and above the light chain-mail of the hauberk he glimpsed at last the ageless bronze head, polished skin gleaming over fine-metal bones. The last to abandon the pursuit, the first to discard the advantage of a horse as once he had discarded the advantage of a sword, and go to earth after his quarry on equal terms, would inevitably be the old wolf of Parfois.

Spoiled and wasted in the long frustration of Painscastle, he burned bright and hard and happy now in his moment of release in action. Harry sprang away from the arm and the sword that probed for him with such disdainful hardihood, and parted the bushes to leap back into the open. The man whirled after him, responsive to the rustle of the drying leaves, and met him blade to blade. The swords hissed and locked for a moment, hilt against hilt. Isambard's deep eyes, quick with reddish flames of pleasure, blazed up into recognition.

'Well met, Harry!' he said, laughing, as they matched bodies and strongly heaved each other off, and came to a swordsman's distance.

Harry said nothing, he was too full of the exultation and the anxiety that stretched his senses to breaking and impeded his breath. He gathered to his aid every last resource of strength and skill he had, and came in like a fury, poised to meet and break the expected parry; and in mid-stroke he faltered and swerved with a gasp of horrified protest, turning his own blade wide at what should have been the moment of impact. Isambard had not lifted his sword to meet him, but deliberately lowered it and lodged the point in the turf, and stood uncovered to him. Harry had barely diverted his stroke in time, his point had sheered down the white surcoat beneath the left breast, and sent a rag of linen fluttering.

Trembling and raging, he heard a voice thick with passion, hardly recognisable for his own, crying hoarsely: 'God damn you, my lord, will you never fight fair? Guard yourself and stand to me! Do me right, and cover yourself, or, by God, I'll kill you uncovered!'

'By God, then, kill me,' said Isambard in soft and smiling invitation. 'There's no one to see.'

Harry heaved up his sword in a fury, and advanced it desperately against the unguarded breast. In his anguish of injury and helplessness and despair he wanted to strike, but when it came to the assay he could not do it. The point wavered and sank; and Isambard laughed, never moving.

'You know well I can't! Not in cold blood – Do me right, my lord! Guard yourself!'

With a long, deliberate movement Isambard sheathed his sword, and reached to the bridle of his grazing horse. Without haste he mounted, and looking back once, flashed a crooked smile at the boy who stood sick and shaking with hatred where he had left him. Then he rode back at a trot by the way he had come, and in a moment Harry heard a voice hailing, and the ringing of harness, and Isambard's voice calling calmly: 'All clean away. You'll see no more of them this side of Builth. Let them go!'

That brought a sweat of honest fear out on Harry to cool the sweat of rage. He turned and blundered after his companions in a daze, swallowing down his detestation and gall as best he might, and in a few minutes was shaken back to reality by a voice calling his name low and urgently through the woods; and there was Morgan ap Einon, wild-eyed and uneasy, leading Barbarossa back towards the river to look for him.

There were no more such meetings. The advance parties of the English host were already moving back upon Hereford; by the end of September the entire army had withdrawn, leaving their hasty new castle garrisoned but unfinished. Early in November the Prince of Aberffraw let it be known, by oblique channels and without suing, that he was willing to discuss terms of peace.

CHAPTER THIRTEEN

Builth, Parfois: *December* 1231

The envoys came back from London early in December, and rode into Builth in the first flurry of the valley snow, though the hills were already white. What they brought was not a permanent peace, but a year of truce, signed and sealed on the last day of November, a year's breathing-space to be employed in negotiations for a firm and final peace to come. Nothing was to be recovered in the meantime, nothing given up. What Llewelyn had taken, Llewelyn kept.

'Ah!' said the Prince, drawing large, pleasurable breath. 'So we go home to Aber to keep Christmas with Cardigan in our baggage, do we? Did I not say if we waited we might have all we wanted? And how did the Earl of Kent stomach the loss of his castle? I warrant he looked sick and sour enough. Or does he think I can be made to give up in a year's time what I made plain I would not restore him now?'

Philip ap Ivor warmed his venerable toes at the fire in the royal chamber, and exchanged a quick glance with his younger fellow.

'My lord, I cannot suppose it gave him any pleasure to part with Cardigan, but I doubt he has other and worse deprivations on his mind. Since September he has lost a liege man from office. His old chaplain Ranulf the Breton is dismissed from his post as treasurer of the chamber, and told to take off himself and his family out of the kingdom. And Peter des Rivaulx holds office in his room.'

'What, Winchester's nephew?' said David, looking up sharply from his stool at Llewelyn's knee.

'Winchester's son,' said Llewelyn bluntly, and laughed as Philip looked severely down his nose, though he made no protest at such plain speaking.

'And it was rumoured before we left London, my lord, that the King will keep Christmas this year as Bishop Peter's guest at Winchester. The bishop already has the King's ear, and by all we could hear he's forgotten none of his old scores against the justiciar. And there's no Langton now to hold the balance true.'

'Small wonder de Burgh's willing to compound with me, even at a price he dislikes paying. He'll have need of all his wits about him if he's to hold his own with Peter des Roches.'

'My lord, that's truer now than ever it was,' said Philip gravely. 'Bishop Peter is come home with honours heavy on him, a crusader fresh from the Holy City, a close friend of the Emperor and deep in Pope Gregory's confidence. And the King's temper is such that he puts a reverent value on such presence as this man has, and such address.'

Llewelyn heard the tale out, and said at the end of it: 'I doubt we've seen the last time that ever de Burgh will come venturing into Wales in arms. God knows I owe him no quarter, as he gave my men none at Montgomery. Yet I'm almost sorry. I never yet bore him so much ill-will as to wish him made a mounting-block for these Poitevins.'

When the two weary clerics had gone yawning to the lodging prepared for them, David came back to his father's presence with a shadowed face.

'My lord, here's Harry asking to speak with you alone. Give me leave to send him in.'

'Ah, Harry!' said Llewelyn with a sharp sigh. He partly guessed what the boy had to say, and would liefer not have heard it. But where was the remedy? 'Well,' he said heavily, 'let him come.'

Harry came in and closed the door after him in purposeful silence. His face was pale and grave, his jaw set in a way there was no mistaking. Llewelyn beckoned him to the stool David had quitted, that still stood close to his knee, but Harry moved it round to front him squarely, so that they could look each other in the eye.

'My lord, I came to ask you for leave to go from here.' He was marshalling his voice and his face as mistrustfully as a general mustering uncertain levies in the field. 'The peace is signed, and my term of freedom is ended.'

'The truce is signed,' corrected Llewelyn gently.

'Within the sense of the promise I made, a truce is peace. I gave my parole to return as soon as peace was restored between England and Wales. It is time for me to make good what I swore.' His lips were tight and pale. Isambard had known only too well how this moment would wring him, how easy his promise had been to make, how hard it would be to keep.

'Thus instantly? Need you be so exact in observance, Harry? There's a certain grace allowable, surely, you need not mount and ride the minute you receive the news. I had thought you would wish to bring your prince safely home again to Aber before you'd consider your term of duty finished.'

He said no word of Gilleis, or Adam, or the Princess, but he knew by the tightening of every muscle of Harry's face and the hurried way he averted his eyes that he saw only too clearly through this deceptive temptation that was being held out to him. The thing he most wanted in the world now was to go back with them to Aber, though it was no less the thing he most dreaded. From Aber return to captivity would be twice as hard, even though he would take back with him the embraces and the prayers of all who were dear to him.

'David is in his own country and his own castle,' said Harry in a low and careful voice, 'and the war is over. There is no danger threatening him. I should be making a pretence if I argued that it was my duty to bring him home. I know you will not ask me to lie to myself. I hope you would keep me from it even if – if – I should be tempted.'

'God forbid,' said Llewelyn, 'that I should ever make it harder for you to keep your word. What you must do, that you must, and you shall be the judge. But in all honesty, I think even Isambard would not grudge you the concession of those few days it would take to ride home.'

Harry turned his head away, and wrestled with himself in silence for a few minutes; and suddenly he slid forward from the stool and was on his knees at Llewelyn's feet.

'I meant to! Oh, I did mean to go home. But now – My lord, I must not! I dare not! If it were to any other man I could, but to him never.' He clung with cold, quivering hands to Llewelyn's knees, and laid his head on them, and poured out everything he carried heavy on his heart, in great gasps that were torn out of him like blood. 'He would not fight me fair! He cheated me of the only chance I had to be free of him. But all the more I must not cheat, not even by a day, to make myself fellow to him –'

This time, when the Prince laid a hand on his head and stroked him like one soothing a child, he did not refuse the comfort or even stiffen under it, but took it thankfully for ease and warmth in the great, discomforting coldness that was closing upon him.

'Not one day less than is due, rather more! Every word, every act of his puts me on test. Among his friends a man can fail a little and not be undone, but before his enemy he may not. And I am the keeper of more than my own honour. He wills to break me, to find the weaknesses in me and prise me apart. And could he do it, he would have ruined more than me. My father had the better of him at all points, him he never could move. Could he bring me to break faith, or to fall short by the least grain of what I owe, I think he would be eased of something that poisons and darkens his life. And I would rather die than give him that satisfaction. Owen told me how he has profaned my father's grave and despoiled his body. But I am the keeper of my father's soul, God alone knows how, and I cannot abate one farthing of my debt, for his sake. Oh, my lord, my father, help me to pay my dues! It is hard enough – truly it is hard –'

'Child, child!' said Llewelyn, grieving, and lifted him into his arms and held him on his knees. They were alone, and no one would ever know. And he was so forlorn, and so in need of help to keep his hold on his duty. He let himself be cradled and comforted, grateful for the respite.

'You shall not fail of any scruple by my contrivance, I promise you,' said Llewelyn in his ear. 'To-morrow you shall ride, with proper provision. No one could ask more than that – one night's sleep on the news, and then the return as due. Never fear, I'll be your advocate at Aber, and hold you excused. You shall not be misunderstood. And shall I not send an escort to bear you company on the way?'

'No! Alone, I must go alone. He'd think I had to be brought back unwilling!'

'As you will, child, as you will. I'll never say the loath word to whatever you need for your own content. There, be easy! This is not for ever, and you shall not be left to carry it alone. Though well I know you'd keep your father's spirit and your own, and come out of it the victor, even had you no friends to be your stay.'

Harry wound his arms round his foster-father's neck and clung to him unashamed. It was like holding fast by a rock, but a living rock that warmed and quickened to his touch. Eased of the solitary weight of his burden, he said in a soft voice: 'You'll not let David take it ill that I have to leave him? If I were free, I would not stir from his side.'

'Lad, he knows it.'

'And Madonna Benedetta – I never visited her – I thought to go when we returned –'

'Have I not said I'll be your advocate? There, never grieve for us who love you, we know you too well to mistake you.'

The boy in his arms heaved a great sigh out of him, like a stone of heaviness. Presently he untwined his arms and made to free himself. The Prince let him go gently, and he stood off with a high colour, but resolutely calm.

'My lord, I would ask something of you.'

'Ask, and you shall have it.'

'I know that for a year you are bound by this truce. But even when the year is over, I would ask that you will never venture for my sake anything that may put David's inheritance into danger. I would rather lie in Parfois till I die than be the means of harming him.'

Llewelyn rose and kissed him with respect and tenderness.

'I will do nothing that shall trespass on your rights and your desires. Now go to David and Owen for a while, and then get your rest. In the morning we shall set you on your way.'

Harry kissed his hand and went, drained and sleepy. When the last light echo of his foot had receded into silence Llewelyn sent for his constable of Builth.

'Find me a reliable man to do an errand for me, one who can get a message by heart and deliver it like an ambassador. And one who knows the roads even in the dark, for I want him to ride to-night. I have somewhat to say to Ralf Isambard before he receives my foster-son back into captivity.'

Rhys ap Tudor rode into Parfois about ten in the morning, when Isambard had just come to table after a morning's riding. There were some dozen noble guests in his company, halted on their way to their own dispersed honours, and the outer ward of the castle was encrusted along the lee wall with the temporary pavilions which had been thrown up to house their retinues. Men-at-arms in nine or ten different exalted liveries gathered in the wards to stare blackly and bitterly at the Welshman who trotted briskly in over the drawbridge, and struck sparks from the frosty cobbles under the gatehouse.

The recent campaign rankled, and the truce terms bit deeper still. Rhys, who was well aware of himself as a living provocation in this place at this moment, was blessed also with the temperament to enjoy his irritant value. He spurred between the silent, scowling ranks with a jaunty gait and an arrogant face, not deigning to notice them, and dismounted in the middle of the courtyard, tossing his bridle to the nearest muttering archer, who perforce held it until a groom came to take it from him.

They could do nothing. The lord of Parfois had decreed that Llewelyn's courier should be admitted, and that word alone guaranteed his safety. For that matter, to give the Welsh direct cause to cry that the terms of the truce were already being infringed might have invited penalties even from the law, if the shadow of Isambard had not been deterrent enough. So they kept what they had to say below their breath, and spat after Rhys's deliberately provocative back only when he was well out of range.

A chamberlain brought him into the hall, and through the scurry of servants to the high table. The babel of the household froze suddenly into silence as he passed, and became a low and guarded rustle of excitement after his passing. Isambard, with a countess on his right hand and a bishop on his left, looked across the loaded board at him and measured him from head to foot with a brief flicker of his hollow eyes. The flame of interest came to life within them. He acknowledged the formal salutation courteously. The man Llewelyn had sent to him had a presence, in his barbaric way, and knew how to do justice to the compliments of princes.

'My lord Isambard, the Lord Llewelyn, Prince of Aberffraw and Lord of Snowdon, sends me to you with a message concerning the future of his foster-son, Harry Talvace.'

'Ah!' said Isambard, faintly smiling. 'Are you Harry's herald, come to assure me of his return?'

'No, my lord. He needs no herald, and of his return you need no assurance. If I am here before him it is because I have ridden through the night, and even so you shall find I am not by many hours ahead of him. He knows nothing of my errand, and it is not the will of the Prince of Aberffraw that he should. I am sent to sue to you yet once more for this boy's ransom. My lord offers you the price of an earl. Two thousand marks for Harry Talvace's freedom.'

The nobility at the high table drew respectful breath and watched with curiosity the face of Isambard, which had not stirred from its contemplative and faintly mocking stillness. The corner of his long mouth drew upwards in the oblique grimace that marked his moments of mild amusement.

'I regret I cannot accept the Prince's most generous offer.'

'Then, my lord, I am bidden to say to you that the Prince of Aberffraw is willing to consider whatever price you choose to put on Harry Talvace's liberty – and not merely in money. Name what you desire of him, and I shall faithfully convey your message to him.'

'I regret exceedingly,' said Isambard, 'that I must disappoint the Prince, but there is no price in money or any other commodity he has at his command that I would take for Harry Talvace. I will name none, and I will consider none he may name, not in land, nor falcons, nor flesh. I am content to keep what I hold.'

Rhys ap Tudor lifted his chin and curled his lip. 'You neither disappoint nor astonish my Prince. He bade me, if you refused to treat, as he said you surely would, to deliver to you another message.'

'Deliver it, then,' said Isambard, tranquilly, 'here, before all these fair witnesses. Let us have in form both the embassage and the reply. Unless you would rather we dealt in privacy?'

'No, faith, this is the place I would have chosen of all places. The Prince bids me say to you in your teeth, my lord, that in due time, when he may do so without offence to his sacred obligations or his plighted word, he purposes to come for Harry Talvace in arms. And he has sworn that when that time comes he will take and destroy Parfois for his sake.'

The hum of consternation and excitement that went down the hall made the green and gilt hangings shake. De Guichet came to Isambard's elbow and whispered angrily in his ear, and some of the young men were on their feet. Smarting already from the ignominy of their long inaction at Painscastle, stung afresh by the agreement that left the Prince of Aberffraw in possession of all his conquests, they would have welcomed the excuse to tear a Welshman piecemeal. But Isambard lifted his head and swept over them one glance of his formidable eyes, lifted his hand and made one controlled and delicate gesture, and they sank back into their places and shut their mouths. It was a fearful thing how daunting a threat he could put into a flick of his fingers.

'I am indebted to the Prince for his message,' said Isambard mildly. 'Before I give you my answer, will you sit down with us and eat and drink? We are no longer at war, you need not scruple to accept my hospitality.'

'I thank you, my lord, but with your pardon I must excuse

myself, not from ill-will, but because I am pledged to be out of Parfois before Harry Talvace enters it, and so far as lies with me, to keep him in ignorance that I have been here. That means I must not meet him by the way. What you do in the matter, my lord, is for you to decide, but as for me, I shall keep to my orders. Give me your answer, and let me be on my way.'

'Then say to the Prince, with my most reverent compliments: Come when you will, fetch him away if you can. Till then I'll hold him safe for you.'

Rhys ap Tudor hitched at his sword-belt and settled his cloak over his shoulder, drawing a cautious breath of satisfaction, for he might very well have got less to take back with him, and of what he now had he would make the most.

'My lord Isambard,' he said, 'I'll gladly bear him that answer. For it is well known of you, my lord, even to your enemies, that you are a man of your word.'

And with that, loudly and emphatically uttered, he made his ceremonious reverences and stalked out of the hall of Parfois, brushing off the dour stares of the young gentlemen-at-arms as a large-minded man brushes off flies.

The worst moment Harry had was when he came to the place where the path forked, and to the left the narrow track wound away into the woods along Severnside. He set his course straight ahead, and rode past it, but in spite of himself his hand fell slack and irresolute on the rein, and Barbarossa lagged, feeling his rider torn two ways.

Not a mile by that track, and he could be at Robert's assart. All the way from Llanfihangel in Kerry he had been struggling to put away from him the thought of Aelis, and constantly she had come slipping back into his senses like a remembered music, or the taste of ripe fruit from a lost summer, now sweeter than ever in life, unearthly sweet on his tongue. He would not think of her; but she would be thought of. So brief a while he had had with her that summer night, and even that while stolen from the duty for which he had been expressly released. It seemed he had not been too

279

scrupulous to borrow a little of the time he owed to David; why, then, should he hesitate to take just one hour from Isambard?

And yet he could not do it. To take from your friends, in the certain knowledge that they would not grudge you that and much more, is well enough, but to your enemy must be rendered the last penny of his dues. Especially when you are the custodian of two souls and two honours, and are going back to the renewal of an ordeal for which even the least indulgence would be a poor preparation.

He held his head straight, he would not turn and look along the dark thread of track between the trees, where the thin snow had been bruised into black ice by a few passing feet, perhaps hers among them. How very little he had ever had of her! A few short weeks of unheeding companionship, wanting the wit to value it, and since then only crumbs of moments bedevilled by secrets and reticences he could not help. Even that one June evening seemed to him now to be marred by his failure to tell her the truth about his conditional liberty. How lightly he had promised her he would come back, explaining nothing, demanding her continued trust, not realising then how grim and exigent his return would be. He should have told her everything. She might have found it hard to understand, she might have tried to dissuade him from keeping his bargain; but at least she would have known that in his own eyes he was bound, and she would have made the effort to accept and bear with his conception of his duty. Now, because he had failed to speak, she would wait for him to come back as he had promised, and who could guess how long before he would be able to keep his word? She would not know; she would grieve, thinking he had forgotten, or never meant to come. And it was such a little way!

The Prince's stout comfort could not help him here. All the fine cords that bound him by the heart to Builth and Aber had been drawn out mile by mile behind him, until they had nearly dragged the heart clean out of him and left him a hollow ache; and yet he had the absolute assurance that all those whom he had left behind there would understand him and be constant with him in love, whatever pains the hard present cost him and them.

But who was going to explain him to Aelis? No one knew the need. No one knew of the unforeseen kiss in the long grass at the edge of the paddock, that had excited them into fever and then frightened them apart and driven them speechless and trembling into the house, to the safety and restraint of Robert's presence. No one knew the beauty that was budding in Aelis, or the worth she had for him. He had not known himself how to value her until now, when he could not, for the integrity of his soul could not, go to her.

And he did not go. He shook the reins on Barbarossa's neck, and kicked his heels into the glossy sides and went on, the newest and most sensitive heart-cord of all beginning to lengthen and tear at him in a gradual, quivering refinement and attenuation of pain. Every pace must be the last it would bear without snapping and leaving him to bleed to death from the wound.

But yard by yard he went on, to the foot of the darkening ramp where the path turned, to the place where the trees crowded in, to the towers of the lower guard; and the thread of anguish did not break, and the pain did not become unbearable. He knew that because still he bore it and still he went on, dimly realising, half in dismay and half in consolation, that ultimately there is nothing that cannot be borne.

The guards challenged him from the towers, and he stood meekly at their order, sensible of the fitted shafts nosing at his breast from the loopholes, and walked Barbarossa obediently forward when they bade him. The tension eased in him then without breaking, and he found a kind of rest, because from this point there was no drawing back, and all the heavy weight of choice was lifted from him.

He had half expected that when they knew him they would put him under close escort to go the rest of the way, but it seemed they had their orders concerning him, for they passed him through without question, and let him go to his surrender alone. He paced up the long ramp between the fringes of trees. On the left hand and the right, just beyond these fringes, the ground fell away. He was ascending to the green peninsula in the air, and the stone island beyond, where no one could reach a hand to him, and now he could not turn aside even if he would.

The trees rustled with a dry, frosty tinkling of leaf and twig, the thin coating of snow crumpled and darkened under Barbarossa's hooves, and the chill wind fingered its way in to him through the folds of his cloak as he climbed higher, and set him shivering; and it was apt that he should be returning in winter, when there was neither flower nor shoot nor harvest nor active seed, but only a sleep out of which, when God turned the glass, something might stir and awaken. He could not believe, he would not believe, that any season could be meant to run utterly to waste.

It was getting dark, the early, leaden December twilight that went before the Christmas feast. The bridge was still lowered when he reached the plateau, and the red, leaping light of pitch-flares from within the gate-house archway corrugated the cross-poles of the span and made of it a ladder into hell. But over against it, still faintly lambent against the wintry sky, the assuaging shape of the church rose and soared. Surely he could borrow a few moments of his captor's time now? He was within the territory of the castle, his parole was almost redeemed; and since he was resolved not to renew it, once he entered the gateway this treasury of his father's spirit and refuge of his own would be out of his reach.

He dismounted, and turned Barbarossa loose on the frosty grass to wait for him. He twisted the great ring of the west door, and crept silently within. The light was almost gone, but surely he could touch and sense even what he could no longer see, and for prayer no man needs his eyes.

The noble, shadowy shape of the nave, almost lost in the closing dusk, preserved still a form the mind reached out eagerly to fill. He went forward and fell on his knees before the high altar, and faltered through a prayer for his mother's comfort; and for a moment such a desolation came on him that he could hardly breathe. Then at the core of his being a little intractable flame of delight quickened; he had opened his eyes and traced in the dimness of the altar frontal before his face the boisterous shape of a small, turbulent but devoted angel, clutching a psalter and bawling out his ebullient heart in praise to God. One of the nine several images of Owen, carved here in heavenly consort. And suddenly the church for all its cold and darkness was full of the laughter and love that Master Harry had put into the making of the stone children, and the same love at its apotheosis touched and comforted the child of his own body.

After all, he was not alone. In Parfois he could never be alone, in Parfois of all places, for it was full of his father. His father's integrity made his footing firm there, and his father's works were all round him, a defiant prophecy of his own works some day to be. They were one force. They opposed their unity to Isambard's solitary and monumental hatred, and while they held fast to each other they could not be moved.

He fumbled through his prayers with half his mind and all his heart lost in an astonishment of grace.

'While you're on your knees, Harry,' said the voice of Isambard softly and dryly from behind him, echoing hollowly under the vault, 'say some prayer for my poor soul. You can hardly do less, seeing the peril I shall be in if you ever win your way with my sinful body.'

Had he come there so silently on the stones that not even the rustle of his clothing or the soft tread of his shoe had betrayed him? Or had he been there all the time in the dimness, quiet and motionless in some retired corner, perhaps himself on his knees? He was a devout man, they said, in his terrible way. His voice had pricked like a sword, the feel of his stillness, there in the dark so close and so silent, had made the hair rise in the nape of Harry's neck. He got to his feet with the conscious dignity of one who knows he is watched and measured. From this moment everything he said or did would be inflected by his awareness of those hollow eyes upon him. The malice that had never been able to let his father alone, living or dead, would now never relinquish him.

'I commend you, Harry,' said the soft voice. 'You come very strictly to your time.' He came out of the dark of the north aisle, tall and shadowy, and silent in movement as a shadow.

'My lord, I've made what haste I could. I left Builth on the morning after our envoys returned from London. Are you content that I have kept to terms, my lord?'

'Very content, Harry – very content.'

'Then I have now fairly redeemed my parole, from the moment when I pass through the gate. I give you to know, my lord, with all respect, that I do not intend to renew it.'

He felt though he could not see the slow, red flames burn up in the bronze lantern of that wonderful head, and the oblique smile tugging at the long lips. The voice of seduction, golden-sweet and rueful, tempted him gently: 'This habitation he left you, these marvels of his making, lie outside the wards. And that spring of comfort you were drinking at just now, that will be out of reach, too.'

'I do not intend to renew it,' said Harry again, himself astonished that he could repeat it so mildly and yet so finally.

'As you will, Harry. Come, then, shall we go in? You must be weary, and supper will be waiting for us.'

He laid his hand upon Harry's shoulder, and so brought him out of the church.

'You'll find your lodging prepared, and your work and your tools as you left them. That at least you may have within the wards. And my company, Harry, my company, in which you take such delight, that you shall have daily.'

Harry released himself with constraint to go and bring Barbarossa by the bridle. Isambard made no move to follow or press him close, but stood and waited for him in quietness.

'I see you've made provision for a long stay,' he said, his eye lingering maliciously on the plump roll strapped behind the saddle. 'That delights my heart, Harry. I half feared Parfois might pall on you now, you're grown such a man of the world.'

'I would not for shame put you to the trouble and expense of providing for me, my lord. It's imposition enough that you must feed me, I would I might spare you that, too.'

'There spoke your father's true son! He would not be beholden even for his life, and neither will you,' said Isambard, amused.

'I'm sorry you think so, my lord,' said Harry, walking beside him with a set face. 'I was about to ask a favour of you, but I should be loath to spoil your image of me.'

'Ask it, Harry, ask it! It's good for the soul to venture something new.'

'I was about to ask you if you would see my horse properly exercised, since I shall not be able to take care of the matter myself.'

'I would have done as much for the poor brute's asking, Harry, you need not strain against your nature. Will you not be as considerate of yourself as of your beast?'

'I thank you, my lord,' said Harry. 'My own needs are simpler. I shall do very well as I am.' The spring of comfort was not out of reach, he felt it quicken in him now at need; just as he was he would do very well.

Side by side they came to the bridge and, treading hollowly over it, reached the outer rim of the torchlight, and there as by consent turned and measured each other. Harry beheld his enemy in splendour of black velvet cotte and surcoat all copper and gold thread, a tall, bright demon coruscating with points of gleaming light. Isambard saw a young, passionate face, a man's face, armed with a glittering green stare that advanced against him as straight and implacable as the sword he had declined to encounter beside the Wye.

'Be pleased to enter Parfois, Harry Talvace. You are welcome home.'

Side by side they stepped from the hollow-ringing timbers of the bridge and into the torchlit tunnel of the gate-house. Behind them the chains engaged, and with a long, grinding rattle the drawbridge rose and sealed them in from the world.

THE HEAVEN TREE TRILOGY: Vol. 1

THE HEAVEN TREE

Edith Pargeter

England in the reign of King John – a time of beauty and squalor, of swift treachery and unswerving loyalty. Against this violent, exciting background the story of Harry Talvace, master mason, unfolds.

Harry and his foster-brother Adam tasted injustice young and together fled to Paris, where Harry's genius for carving drew him into friendship with the enigmatic Ralf Isambard, lord of Parfois, and the incomparably beautiful Madonna Benedetta, a Venetian courtesan. In their company he returned to his native Shropshire to build a church for Isambard beside Parfois Castle. Soaring heavenwards, the tree of stone became an arrow of light: but as it flowered darkening shadows presaged jealous, pitiless revenge – and death.

'If you do not appreciate this superb novel, I despair of you' *Illustrated London News*

'The glamour and adventure of medieval life is there, the colour and squalor, the songs of the students and the groans of the oppressed, but at the centre of the story is this man, the work of whose hands will stand for centuries as a monument to the idealist who could be banished, tortured and destroyed but never defeated . . . Beside this dramatic and intense book almost any other historical novel would appear banal.'
Rosaleen Whately, Liverpool Daily Post

'a rattling good story' *Tribune*

Futura Publications
Fiction
0 7088 3056 0

MONK'S-HOOD
A Medieval Whodunnit

Ellis Peters

At the monastery in Shrewsbury in 1138, the gardens are flourishing under the expert tending of Brother Cadfael. His workshop shelves boast all sorts of medication for every kind of ailment. Then one Gervase Bonel, who had planned to leave his valuable manor to the Abbey in exchange for a house run by the monks where his comfort will be guaranteed for life, is poisoned with Cadfael's own concoction intended for aching joints. As the monk investigates he finds a web of family intrigue, where suspicion has fallen on someone he is certain is innocent.

'Appropriately leisurely pace, meticulous historical detail, nicely human characters' *The Times*

'An ingenious plot . . . the whole narrated with elegant crispness' *TLS*

'altogether irresistible . . . all the classic elements proper to a whodunnit are here, but set in an accurate medieval tapestry' *Oxford Mail*

Futura Publications
Fiction/Crime
0 7088 2553 2

All Futura Books are available at your bookshop or
newsagent, or can be ordered from the following address:
Futura Books,Cash Sales Department,
P.O. Box 11, Falmouth, Cornwall.

Please send cheque or postal order (no currency), and
allow 55p for postage and packing for the first book
plus 22p for the second book and 14p for each additional
book ordered up to a maximum charge of £1.75 in U.K.

Customers in Eire and B.F.P.O. please allow 55p for
the first book, 22p for the second book plus 14p per
copy for the next 7 books, thereafter 8p per book.

Overseas customers please allow £1 for postage and
packing for the first book and 25p per copy for each
additional book.